The Gray Divide

Book Two of the Georgia Gold Series

Denise Weimer

The Gray Divide

Book Two of the Georgia Gold Series

Denise Weimer

Canterbury House Publishing

www.canterburyhousepublishing.com
Vilas, North Carolina

Canterbury House Publishing

www. canterburyhousepublishing. com

Copyright © 2013 Denise Weimer
All rights reserved under International and Pan-American Copyright Conventions.

Book Design by Tracy Arendt
Cover Art by John Kollock

Library of Congress Cataloging-in-Publication Data

Weimer, Denise.
  The gray divide : second novel of the Georgia Gold series / by Denise
Weimer.
    pages cm. — (Georgia gold series ; bk. 2)
  ISBN 978-0-9881897-2-0 (alk. paper)
  1. Families—Georgia—Fiction. 2. Sibling rivalry—Fiction. 3.
Georgia—History—1775-1865—Fiction. I. Title.

  PS3623.E4323G73 2013
  813'.6—dc23

First Edition: September 2013

AUTHOR'S NOTE:
This is a work of fiction. Names characters, places and incidents are either the product of the author's imagination or are used fictitiously, and any resemblance to actual persons living or dead, business establishments, events, or locales is entirely coincidental.

For information about permission to reproduce selections from this book write to:
    Permissions
    Canterbury House Publishing, Ltd.
    225 Ira Harmon Rd.
    Vilas, NC 28692

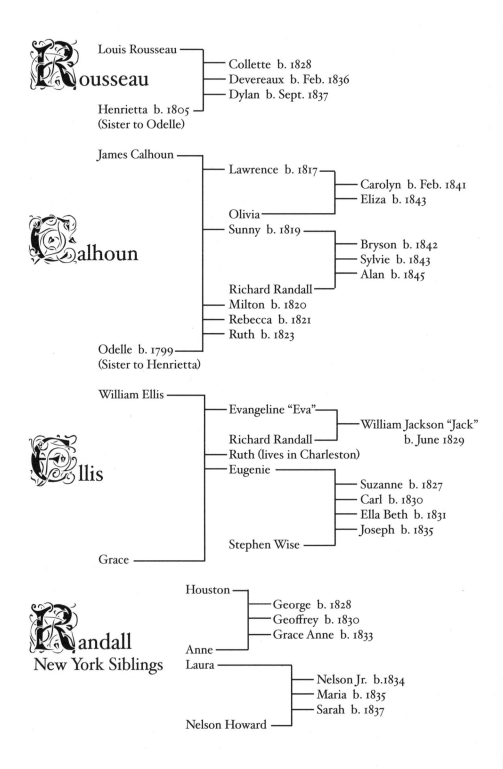

Rousseau

Louis Rousseau —
— Collette b. 1828
— Devereaux b. Feb. 1836
— Dylan b. Sept. 1837
Henrietta b. 1805 —
(Sister to Odelle)

Calhoun

James Calhoun —
— Lawrence b. 1817 —
— Carolyn b. Feb. 1841
— Eliza b. 1843
Olivia —
— Sunny b. 1819 —
— Bryson b. 1842
— Sylvie b. 1843
— Alan b. 1845
Richard Randall —
— Milton b. 1820
— Rebecca b. 1821
— Ruth b. 1823
Odelle b. 1799 —
(Sister to Henrietta)

Ellis

William Ellis —
— Evangeline "Eva" —
— William Jackson "Jack"
— Richard Randall — b. June 1829
— Ruth (lives in Charleston)
— Eugenie —
— Suzanne b. 1827
— Carl b. 1830
— Ella Beth b. 1831
— Joseph b. 1835
Stephen Wise —
Grace —

Randall
New York Siblings

Houston —
— George b. 1828
— Geoffrey b. 1830
— Grace Anne b. 1833
Anne —
Laura —
— Nelson Jr. b.1834
— Maria b. 1835
— Sarah b. 1837
Nelson Howard —

FOREWORD

My personal trip back to Habersham County of the mid-1800s started with a private tour of a summer home of that period, perfectly preserved in every detail, and with the letters and diaries of that family. To the gentleman who offered this glimpse into his ancestors' lives – and who also lent me my initial stack of books and the skill of his historical editing – I owe boundless thanks. Thank you, Mr. John Kollock.

Thanks are also due to Joe Warnke for allowing consultation of his essay, "The Constitutionality of Secession."

Mr. Kollock's cover artwork depicts The The Habersham House Hotel which actually stood on the square of Clarkesville. It looks much like I described The Franklin Hotel in this series.

Most of the places, people and events in *The Gray Divide* actually existed – apart from the main characters, of course. I sought to drop my characters into a very realistic time and place. You met Mahala, Jack, Carolyn, Dev and Dylan in book one, *Sautee Shadows*. I hope you enjoy their journey in The Gray Divide. Next, follow them through the turbulent last days of The War Between the States in Book Three of The Georgia Gold Series, *The Crimson Bloom*!

CHAPTER ONE

May 1856
Sautee Valley, Georgia

he beauty of spring in the Sautee Valley embraced Mahala Franklin as she turned off the red clay lane to pass through her adoptive father's wheat field. The sun warmed her bonneted head, crickets chirped in the underbrush, and Sautee Creek sang its lazy melody nearby. But what the beauty did for her eyes, she only wished it would do for her heart.

She let out a sigh. What was the matter with her? Why did she always want more when she was already given so much? She had a family who loved her, Ben and Nancy Emmitt and their now-grown sons, who had raised her to be strong and unashamed even though some in society disdained her mixed-race heritage. She had her wise Cherokee grandfather, Henry Cornsilk, who worked the farm Mahala's father Michael had left to her in his will. And then there was Martha. Her white grandmother.

Mahala spread her hands over the ripening, golden heads of wheat. As they bent under her touch, she laughed. She'd resented Martha at first, it was true.

But who wouldn't? She asked herself. *After all, she took me away from the Emmitts when I was just a girl. But things have changed so much. She allows me to spend every spring here in the valley, and I enjoy helping her run the inn in Clarkesville. Likely The Franklin Hotel will one day be mine. And she's given me a lady's education so I can run the business by myself if I must.*

The choices she'd soon need to make closed in around her like claws on a bear trap. She was running out of time. And she still didn't know what to do.

One of her two pressing questions was where to live, in the valley or in town.

This was where her true parents, Michael and Kawani Franklin, had wanted her to stay. She thought of her grandfather's face, now lined with years. He would not be able to work her land much longer. As always, her heart ached, thinking of him by himself so much of the time. He could have a room in the cabin to himself and she could take care of him if she found a husband and moved in there.

A husband she could find but not a farmer and a husband. For the only boy she felt any attachment to was bound and determined to make his way to Indian Territory, to where their ancestors had been removed in 1838. And he wanted to take her with him, away from all she held dear. And that was the other question. What to do about Clay Fraser, the Cherokee adopted son of local merchants in Clarkesville. For a long time she had looked on him as a big brother, but his devotion and persistence were wearing down her protests.

Her heart revolted at the idea of leaving, but who else was there for her? She might let him go and wait forever, never finding her soul mate.

Unbidden, as always, the image of Jack Randall rose in her mind. Would he be in town again when she returned to Clarkesville next month, preparing for the summer social season when coastal families vacationed in Habersham County? Like many others, the Randalls had first come to the foothills to escape the threat of dreaded yellow fever, so common on the coast … in fact, the very disease that had claimed Jack's mother's life.

She shouldn't think of him. Jack was wealthy, cultured, and moved in those same social circles of Savannah elite whose status could never be breeched by Mahala's paltry "finishing" at Miss Pettigrew's School for Young Ladies. And he was older than she – by almost ten years.

Yet Jack was the nearest she had come to brushing with his set – the wealthy who could travel anywhere they wanted to, give elegant parties, go off to school, and choose from a list of eligible bachelors or belles whom to wed. Their world seemed so big to Mahala. And there was bound to be more of the outside world coming to Clarkesville soon. In the past couple of years, there had been much talk of a railroad coming through Habersham, even though the idea for an Air Line had stalled out in Atlanta. The latest discussion was of the Clarkesville-Tennessee Railroad that was supposed to run through Clarkesville towards Hightower Gap and on to the Tennessee copper mines. Why, the line was being chartered in the state's general assembly this very year. Clarkesville residents John Stanford, Phillip Martin, George Kollock, William Alley and George D. Phillips were incorporators. And if not now, not this scheme, eventually it would happen. The railroad was bound to come sometime, linking Clarkesville with the rest of the world. A world she did so want to see. A world that would make business at the hotels in town boom. Just as he had predicted from the start, Jack Randall would surely be in high cotton then. For if class and age weren't enough to separate them, two years ago Jack had purchased The Palace Hotel and proceeded to run it with the same genius he exhibited in heading his family's shipping firm, Randall and Ellis. How many times had they gone head to head over customers and business? He was stubborn, self-satisfied and sharp-tongued.

But knowing all this didn't change the way Mahala's heart hammered every time she looked into his green eyes. A reaction she still didn't have to Clay.

If only Randall would leave her alone, she might remember the hopelessness of her unwitting attraction to him. But he seemed to enjoy baiting her. And since the night of the Fourth of July ball last year when he'd showed her his hotel and waltzed with her, she had been unable to forget the sensation of being in his arms. About a month after that, before Jack returned to Savannah for the winter, she'd encountered him while she was out riding. He had actually been nice – normal. They had talked of their families, coming to the realization that their mothers had died the same year. In fact, he'd seemed so interested that he'd led her to tell him all kinds of things about her background, even some of the details surrounding the unsolved murder of her father and his missing gold. Only after they'd sat on their mounts for some time outside the gates of Forests of Green, the Rousseau house where Jack's family was visiting, had Mahala realized she had been doing all the talking. When she had attempted to turn the conversation to him, Jack had politely taken his leave. Why was he so guarded, keeping her always at arm's length?

Because, when it was all said and done, she was not good enough for him.

As she had watched him ride up the long driveway to the white mansion hidden among the trees, a peculiar sense had swept over her. Longing? She had thought herself above emotions like envy, but what would it be like to live in such a style, to be a real lady, to have people like Jack Randall – rather than shutting her out with invisible walls – share the details of their lives? That was something she was sure she could only ever imagine ... to glimpse from her place on the periphery.

Now, Mahala wiped a tear from her blue eyes and then turned the gesture into a wave, spotting Henry walking toward her. She needed to act like an adult. Tomorrow the whole family would be at her eighteenth birthday dinner at the hotel. She could no longer put Clay off. Too many people were awaiting her decisions, and it was past time to make them.

"*Ududu,*" she murmured, using her favored Cherokee word for "grandfather" as he met her on the road between the two farms.

He enfolded her in his sunny embrace and patted her back. "You are sad, my child," he observed.

"I think it's because I can no longer be a child," Mahala replied, pulling back to smile at him.

"You are torn between us and your grandmother," Henry guessed aloud.

Mahala tucked her arm through his and began walking. "You always know me, Grandfather."

"This is not a new problem. You just feel the time has come to decide."

"It has, hasn't it?"

"Only if you know the answer."

A small sob caught in Mahala's throat. "But I don't, *Ududu*. That's the problem. But some things will not wait forever."

"I will, Mahala."

She closed her eyes, pausing and tightening her hold on Henry's arm. "So often I think of you like the land," she said, "never changing. But I know that's not true, much as I wish it otherwise."

"Yes, Mahala, I am growing old, and even the land changes. Only the Creator stays the same. Have you spoken with Him about your troubles, Mahala?"

She paused to look at him. "I'm sure God is too busy with big things like keeping our nation together to bother with my silly problems."

Henry shook his head, the white hairs shining in the sun. "Never. He is our Heavenly Father, Mahala. Go to Him and He will give you guidance."

"I'll remember that." How many times had she drawn on Henry's unshakeable strength? It had been his advice to give her lonely Grandmother Franklin a chance at love that had curbed Mahala's bitterness in the early days with Martha. And that advice had paid dividends.

They walked on, butterflies swooping into their path.

"I wish I could be six again – and life simple," she said impulsively.

"That does not sound like a young woman eager to be a bride," Henry observed.

"It doesn't, does it? And that doesn't seem right," Mahala stated emphatically. "It's not just that Clay wants me to go to Tahlequah with him and I don't want to leave all of you. It's that I think if I loved him enough I would be willing to go – to follow him to the ends of the earth if necessary."

"That seems a logical way of thinking."

"But is it? Or am I just dreaming, longing for something completely unrealistic? After all, many people still have arranged marriages and learn to love one another deeply. And I do feel an attachment to Clay."

Before Henry could answer, Nancy came out of the house, which looked handsome and welcoming. Freshly whitewashed boards now covered the original log structure, and starched curtains hung at the windows. Nancy's many flowers bloomed about the periphery. Nancy hurried forward to warmly embrace Mahala's grandfather. For years she had looked on him as something of a parent herself, their lives were so closely intertwined and her own parents long ago dead and buried. She ushered them into the house, where she had set the table with her Flo Blue and arranged a bouquet of lilies from the garden.

Ben and his youngest son Jacob, the only one still at home, came in, and they all sat down to a meal of ham, peas, carrots and sourdough bread with Nancy's apple butter.

"Well," said Nancy right off, "tomorrow about this time we'll be celebrating in fine style at The Franklin Hotel. Are you excited, Mahala?"

Mahala looked up, hesitating. "I suppose so."

"You suppose so? Why, a girl only turns eighteen once!"

"Thank goodness," Mahala muttered before she could catch herself.

"Do you not want to go back with your grandmother, Mahala?" Nancy quickly inquired. "Because if so you have but to say the word. If you are reluctant to tell her, I will. She has had you long enough." While Nancy had made peace with Martha, she was still jealous over the time the older woman monopolized Mahala.

"That's not it exactly, though I haven't really made up my mind about that, either," Mahala admitted a bit shame-facedly. She sent a pointed glance Henry's way.

"It's the boy," he told the family.

"Oh, of course," Nancy sighed. Mahala was glad the mention of Clay diverted her from examining her hurt feelings over Mahala's indecision about where to live.

"You haven't had enough time to decide about Clay Fraser?" Jacob asked rather grumpily. "He's only been courting you his whole life."

"I know!" Mahala cried, anguished. Jacob had been with her the very first day Mahala and Clay had spied each other from behind the candy jars in Fraser's General Store. He knew the bond between them had been instant, born of their similar heritage. What he didn't understand was how after all this time Mahala still wasn't sure of her feelings for Clay. There was also the fact that Jacob was still smarting from Mary Ellen Smith's rejection of his proposal a couple months back, so she didn't take any offense. But it was hard to be reminded of Clay's great faithfulness.

When Mahala merely bit her tongue, Jacob went on, "Don't keep him hanging any more. It would be cruel."

"I realize that, Jacob. And I will answer him this summer, if he asks."

"I don't think there is any 'if' about it," Nancy said gently, with a tiny smile. She had been privy to the details of the courtship – for, from July through March, that was indeed what it had been. Mahala had consented to spend more time with Clay in an effort to see if her feelings would grow. She had allowed him to twice kiss her cheek and once, in the process, more by accident than design, his lips had brushed hers. While Mahala's ripe figure and striking Cherokee coloring with her surprising blue eyes had drawn the attention of men since she was thirteen, she'd skewed any masculine interest. It had been her first kiss, if kiss she could call it. She had retreated in embarrassment, but she knew the brief moment had greatly encouraged his suit.

"But he has no desire to be a farmer," Mahala reminded them. "Do you all really want me to go west?"

"Of course not," Nancy replied. "But as much as it hurts me to say it, that is not our decision."

"Mahala," Jacob said, sitting up straighter and putting down his fork. Of medium build, he was a serious young man with dark hair and eyes. "I've been thinking. If you should decide to go away with Clay – or if you decide to spend the next year in town, whether you've told Clay 'no' or are preparing for a wedding, either way – I don't want worry about all of us to stop you. You should do whatever is right for you. I am trying to figure out the same thing for myself. I can't see my way clear to move on to any specific thing right now. So I was thinking, if it sits well with Pa and Grandpa Cornsilk, I could stay with your grandfather for a time … help him out some. That way your land will be worked to its full capacity."

"Oh, Jacob," Nancy murmured, as if in pain.

"I can manage, young Jacob," Henry told him. "I would not take you away from your family."

"No – no, I think it's a good idea," Nancy said, though there were tears in her eyes. "Jacob is ready to be out on his own – he just has not known which direction to go since … well … this way at least he'll be close by. It will be a good step for all of us. Don't you agree, Ben? Mahala?"

Both nodded. Mahala reached out to take her brother's hand. "Thank you, Jacob," she said. "That does give me a measure of peace. I will be happy Grandfather will not be alone so much."

"Well then," said Henry. "Let us shake on our new partnership."

As they did, there was laughter all around.

Mahala placed the folded chemise in the wardrobe and gently smoothed it. There. All the unpacking was done. Satisfied, she closed the wardrobe door and the lid to her traveling trunk. She hopped up onto her bed and stretched out her legs, prepared to relax and enjoy the cross breeze traveling between the open window and the cracked-open door of her room at The Franklin Hotel.

She waited to settle back in until the Emmitts and Henry left for Sautee following the noon meal. Every bit of time had been precious. Then, too, there had scarcely been a moment to breathe, they had all been so busy celebrating.

Mahala had been more than surprised when they arrived yesterday to discover her grandmother had closed the hotel dining room to guests. Instead, the tables were all arranged long ways with white table cloths and fresh flowers. Their cook Maddie had prepared a feast, and the father of Patience, Mahala's younger friend who worked at the hotel, had made a beautiful white cake. Family and friends had all been gathered to wish Mahala a happy birthday.

Many of them had brought presents, but far and away the best was the plain box Nancy had produced at the end of the dinner. Curious gazes had turned to her as she made her presentation.

"I've been saving this," she had said, "to give into your keeping, Mahala. I know you already have a Bible – your father Ben and I saw to that long ago – but this Bible is the one I gave to your mother long ago as a Christmas gift. And inside this little strong box is your inheritance – at least, the papers you will want. They are yours to do with as you will."

Mahala had been moved to tears and hardly able to wait to look through the box with her adoptive mother, away from watching eyes. Nancy had explained every item last night before bed, but Mahala found herself wanting to see and touch them again. She lifted the box now from her bedside table and leaned over it, legs crossed. She picked out the deed to the Sautee farm, Michael's last will and testament and a stack of gold receipts given to her father when he had long ago minted coins in Dahlonega from the gold he'd mined from the Sautee lot belonging to his old friend, Rex Clarke. When Michael had wanted to settle down to farming, Rex had refused to sell him the lot. Michael had purchased land nearby instead, but the fight between Rex and Michael shortly before Michael was found by Kawani murdered in Rex's cabin had been witnessed by many. When Ben Emmitt and Henry Cornsilk had found Michael's strong box hidden in the chimney, the receipts did not match the minimal amount of cash enclosed therein. Neither had money or gold been entrusted to Martha's keeping, for at the time, Martha's husband Charles had still been alive. And his disapproval of Michael's marriage to a Cherokee woman had been the cause of the rift in the family. That rift had only been closed by his death. And still the amount of money unaccounted for boggled Mahala's mind. Had someone really made off with more than $5,000?

The most popular suspect had been Rex, of course, but Martha had told Mahala shortly after she came to live at the hotel that a maid had vouched for Rex's whereabouts the night of the murder. Still, who knew what that was worth. Rex was a known drunk and womanizer, and Mahala didn't expect the company he kept to be any more reputable.

Mahala also knew from Nancy, who had been Kawani's closest friend chosen to raise Mahala just before Kawani died on her childbirth bed, that there had been a mysterious drifter who had plagued Kawani shortly before the murder. A man whom Michael had refused as a partner for mining his gold.

Mahala was drawn to her father's handwriting, so neat, tall and slanting. She caressed the paper and read again, "Receipts from the Dahlonega mint, stamp mill and Aurarian bank, with payments shown to Rex Clarke, Clarkesville, whose signature shall bear witness along with these papers that one-fourth proceeds were delivered to him. Should the spring of our friendship dry up and hope for future partnership be buried, honesty will at least be proved and my assets found to be in order."

The way her father referred to Rex Clarke was puzzling. He had obviously known the partnership was souring and had felt it important to prove his own honesty. But had things deteriorated so much that Rex had actually killed her father? How could she ever find out – especially the way her grandmother moved heaven and earth to keep Mahala away from the man? What if Rex had wanted to share information about the murder the night he had asked to speak with Mahala, before in a fury Martha had sent him out of the hotel?

Since then, Mahala had obeyed her grandmother's admonition. She had only encountered Mr. Clarke in public in the past year, and that infrequently. On the few occasions he had seen her, Rex had raked her with a leering grin and swept a bow. He had never been close enough to speak privately. Normally he sent his manservant into town on his errands. Mahala had never told Martha, but it did seem the servant frequented some of her same haunts. She often saw him when she went out walking or riding or passed him in the aisles of the drygoods store. It had crossed her mind that this could be purposeful, but as he never attempted to speak with her, she dismissed it as her own fancy.

Mahala ground her teeth in frustration. She knew the unknown would gnaw at her forever.

"Mahala?" a voice called from the parlor. Patience.

"In here," Mahala replied.

The blonde girl appeared at her door, looking apologetic. "I know you just got home and I really didn't want to disturb you, but we're unusually busy for a Tuesday. Maddie said I should see if you can come help me run dinners out – just for a few minutes. The customers are getting grumpy."

"Of course!" Mahala replied. "Go on. I'll be right there."

Quickly she put her papers back in the box and replaced it on her bed-side table. Then, tying on the apron Patience had left for her, she ran out the door and past Leon and a loudly complaining guest at the front desk. She had no desire to step in to try to aid her father's tall, gawky cousin. Any day she could avoid an exchange with Leon was a good day. He had made it clear from her arrival at The Franklin Hotel that he resented Martha bringing her into the family. Let someone else take his ire for a change.

Clay was one of the diners, waiting on his slice of apple pie. His bright grin, white, straight teeth against tanned skin and coal-black hair always lit up a room. The sleeves of his checked cotton shirt where rolled up above corded forearms, the collar open at the neck beneath his dark vest. As she delivered his order, Mahala asked teasingly, "Did you come by here just to see me?"

"Sure did. Just hoping for a glimpse."

"Well, I guess you got lucky. Enjoy."

"Wait." Clay grabbed her hand. She paused and looked down at him. "I sure missed you, Mahala."

She softened at the sincerity in his eyes. "I missed you, too, Clay."

"I know you're busy now, but I was actually wondering if you'll take a walk with me tomorrow evening – say, about seven-thirty?"

Mahala smiled. "O.K. As long as I can get free."

Clay gave her a bemused look.

"That's the new saying everyone is using, right? O.K? It means I agree!"

"I'll be counting on it." Comprehension dawning, Clay smiled back, looking into her eyes, and Mahala's stomach fluttered. Could he mean to pop the question already? She wasn't prepared!

She was so distracted she mixed up the next two orders and was more than glad to retreat to her bedroom fifteen minutes later.

As she pushed open the door to her room, a flash of movement caught her eye. The lace curtains billowed out. She frowned. Surely the draft from the door hadn't created that much of a disturbance. She walked over to the window and looked out into the side street but saw no one. Still, next time she ought to remember to lock up, she told herself.

Mahala closed the window and turned toward the bed. Her eyes fell on her father's strong box, lying on the floor, its contents spilling out.

"It was just so strange," Mahala said the following evening as she took Clay's arm to step off the sidewalk. "If someone were going to commit a robbery at a hotel don't you think they would have waited until everyone was abed and then made a crack at our safe?"

"I doubt that was the goal. It was probably a passing ne'er-do-well who spied an open window, an empty room, and perhaps a promising box."

"I can't imagine anyone could have seen that much with the height of the foundation and curtains in the way."

"Then you think it was someone from within?"

Mahala drew out the corners of her mouth. "I can't think who. Everyone was occupied, and if it was a guest, they would have had to pass by the front desk where Cousin Leon was helping a customer the whole time. There was a problem with their dinner bill, though, and the man was rather irate, which would have definitely been distracting."

"A mystery, I'll agree."

"My family seems plagued by them," Mahala said wryly.

"Well, you can be glad nothing was taken. And be more careful from here on out. I don't want anything to happen to you now that I just got you back." Clay tightened his hold on her arm and smiled down at her.

"Thank you, Clay. I will." Mahala patted his arm in return, reassuring herself that his highly protective nature was nothing new. Then she looked around, her attention returning to their progress through town. "Where are we going?"

"I thought tonight a visit to our old rendezvous would be in order," Clay told her.

"What? Well, I hope you have some friends waiting there. You know my house rules."

"I surely do." Clay's rolling eyes told her he recalled all too well the early days when Martha had learned Mahala was sneaking out to teach him to write and speak the Cherokee language. They'd once been seen outside town alone together, and since then Martha insisted they never leave the public streets without others in attendance. "Don't worry about it, Mahala. It will be all right."

A rumble of distant thunder belied his words. "I don't know, Clay. Look at that cloud on the horizon," she pointed out. "Perhaps we ought to stay closer to shelter."

"That rain's a long way off. Trust me. See? The sun is still shining."

Mahala walked on, wary now. She knew where they were headed now. They found the bridge over the Soquee deserted, no traffic or fishermen in sight, and slipped unnoticed to the weeping willow, which had grown

18

substantially over the years. Clay spread his linen jacket for her to sit on and took his place beside her.

"Remember all the lessons we had here?"

"Of course I do."

He was smiling at her in a way that made her uncomfortable, his eyes never leaving her face. He went on, "It was you who taught me our native language, and before that, from the time we first met, it was you who made me love our heritage. Do you know why?"

"No. Why?"

"Because I was no longer alone, and I realized that if you were Cherokee, being Cherokee couldn't be bad."

"Oh … thank you, I guess." Mahala folded her hands and tried to avoid Clay's dark eyes.

"I know I've told you how much I want to go to Tahlequah."

Mahala nodded.

"And I think you know I've always hoped one day you'd go with me."

Here it came. Mahala's heart began to thud heavily.

"But I'm no longer set on that."

Mahala's gaze swung to his in shock. "Y-you're not?"

Clay shook his head and reached for her hand.

"You mean, you no longer want to go?" she questioned.

"I do still want to, but not so much that I would choose it over you. Mahala," he continued, switching suddenly to the Cherokee tongue, "I know how you love your family, and they have already torn you enough. I should not be the one to tear you from them. I have loved you from the day I spied you past the candy jars in my father's store. You are the only one for me. I've waited this long to speak those words because I knew your grandmother would never approve. But now you are a woman. And if you will have me, I will learn to be a farmer. I'll go live with your grandfather so he can teach me. Or, if you want, we can live here, in town – and help both our families with their businesses. Please, just say you'll be my bride."

Mahala stared at him, wordless with shock. She could not believe that he was willing to give up the dream he had held dear for as long as she could remember – for her. He was taking away her reason for protest. And doing it so eloquently, so heart-wrenchingly, in their parents' tongue.

His face was so near, wreathed in hopeful agony. Could she wish for anyone more dear? Perhaps if she stopped thinking so much and just went with the feeling of the moment, the intensity of love she had been waiting for would surprise her.

Mahala laid her palm lightly on Clay's cheek. He took the gesture as permission and made a move toward her. This time she offered her lips. His mouth closed over hers in a wet, eager kiss. She waited for the passion, the joyous certainty. Instead, a queasy denial spread from the pit of her stomach. It was wrong, all wrong. Like she was kissing Jacob. She stiffened and pulled away, sure that Clay must feel it, too.

But he was smiling uncertainly … nervous … happy. "Do I take that as a 'yes'?" he asked.

She moved back, discreetly covering her mouth, then smoothing back imaginary loose hair. She saw that a light rain had begun to fall from a darkened sky. She couldn't meet his eyes. What had she done?

"Mahala? What's wrong? Did I do something …?"

"No, Clay, you've done nothing wrong. I have."

"What do you mean?"

He tried to touch her arm, but she pulled away, impatiently wiping a tear that had formed suddenly and rolled down her cheek. "I'm sorry," she murmured. "So sorry."

"For what? Mahala … I know you care for me. You can't have been pretending all this time."

"No – you're right. I do care for you. But not in the way I need to to become your wife."

She couldn't face him still, but his voice embodied all his emotions when he said, "And … that's what a kiss told you."

"Yes," she whispered, closing her eyes. She wasn't brave, she realized. If she was she wouldn't be so afraid to face the pain she knew her answer inflicted. "Forgive me. I've thought it all along. You've been more like a brother in my heart than anything. But I thought maybe I was wrong, maybe if …"

She let her voice trail off and waited for him to tell her she couldn't base so much on one kiss, that in time she would come to love him as he loved her. But he said nothing. Mahala opened her eyes and what she saw astonished her more than anything had so far.

Clay was walking away.

Mahala scrambled to her feet. "Clay, wait!" she called. And in Cherokee: "Come back, please!"

But he didn't turn around. She could go after him. She could take it all back – pretend if she had to. But her feet felt like the roots of the tree, for she knew she couldn't lie and there was nothing more to say, nothing else to do but watch the back of him disappear, framed by the branches of their weeping willow.

The following morning, exhausted from a sleepless night and with red-rimmed eyes, it was all she could do to help with the breakfast rush. All Mahala could think about was how Clay must be feeling. Guilt clawed at her insides. She had handled everything poorly, hurt and humiliated him, and perhaps estranged him forever. Would he be able to forgive her? She thought if they could just talk maybe she could make some progress towards restoration.

Once the dining room was well in hand and departing guests were carrying luggage to the porch, Mahala felt free to go. She snatched off her apron and hung it sloppily on a kitchen peg, ran to her room and collected Clay's light brown coat he had left with her the night before. Folding it over her arm, Mahala hurried out into the street.

She half-ran down the sidewalk, away from the three-story hotel garbed in porches like a woman in hoopskirts, toward Fraser's store, head ducked, oblivious to the bustle about her. Outside Fraser's store, she turned and almost ran into none other than the famed architect and horticulturalist, Jarvis Van Buren. "Excuse me, Sir," Mahala hastened to say.

"No harm done." The gentleman's hooded eyes narrowed and his high brows drew slightly downward. "Are you quite all right, Miss Franklin?"

It would do no good to vent her emotions here and now, to a man so definitely above her in station. "Yes, indeed, Mr. Van Buren. And how are things at Gloaming Nursery?" Mahala knew Mr. Van Buren was always busy on his ten acres adjoining town. In his early days as a Clarkesville resident he had traveled Georgia and North Carolina collecting specimens from abandoned Cherokee orchards, from which he had developed his own nursery, classifying and drawing over two dozen types of Southern apples. He wrote widely, attempting to convince Northern skeptics that quality fruit could be produced in the South, and not just apples, but peaches, plums, figs, cherries and grapes as well.

At her inquiry, a smile lit his face. "I happen to have in my jacket at this very moment a letter to the editors of *Southern Cultivator*, calling for a convention of all Southern pomologists in Athens, the week of commencement, in August." So saying, he pulled out a neatly addressed envelope and gave it a little wave. "I'm on my way to post it now."

Mahala smiled as well. "I'm sure you will meet with great success," she said. "A good day to you."

Mr. Van Buren lifted his hat. "And to you, Miss."

These were the moments when Martha's and Miss Pettigrew's training paid off, Mahala thought as she finally opened the door to the dry goods store. Inside it was relatively quiet, for which she was grateful. There were but two shoppers and no sign of Clay. She approached the counter. Behind it sat Mr. Fraser, slumping on a stool and staring uncharacteristically into space. Catching sight of Mahala, the balding man rose slowly, his expression congealing.

"What did you do to my son?" he asked with purposeful emphasis on each word.

"W-what do you mean?" Mahala questioned, taken aback. She had never known Clay's adoptive father to be anything but easy-going and cheerful.

"You tell me."

"I don't understand." All right, that wasn't the whole truth. But she wasn't about to relate the details of Clay's proposal to this angry man. She continued falteringly, "I – I brought back his coat. I need to speak with him, please."

"I'm afraid that will be impossible." Mr. Fraser crossed his arms over his chest. His face was hard, but Mahala thought she detected a faint quiver of his bottom lip as he spoke. "He's gone! Left out in the night for Indian Territory with but a note to say goodbye. His mother's devastated – can't rise from the bed – and I … I am left to wonder what you did to him to so break his heart!"

Mahala felt frozen with shock. Suddenly a sob bubbled up to her lips. She covered her mouth with one hand and laid the coat on the counter in front of Mr. Fraser with the other. Then she turned and ran out of the store, blinded by fast-coming tears.

Back in the hotel, Martha caught sight of her as she streaked through the foyer. Her grandmother, round face creasing in concern, followed Mahala into their parlor, catching Mahala's arm just when escape was imminent.

"What happened? What's wrong?" Martha demanded. Mahala had told her the night before that she had rejected Clay's proposal, but Mahala had given as few specifics as possible. Now, Mahala poured out the latest news, wanting nothing more than to escape to her bedroom and let out the agony of tears.

"I know you valued Clay as a friend, dear," Martha said, stroking her arm. "But this may be for the best. After rejecting him you could hardly go on as though nothing had happened."

In Mahala's opinion, Martha was much too calm and satisfied. She had never considered Clay a worthy suitor. Mahala pulled away and hurried to her chamber, shutting out the world. She sobbed into her pillow, berating herself for her foolishness. She could hardly bear the thought that most likely she'd never see Clay again.

At length a timid knock came at the door.

"I'm not coming out!" she cried. "Please go away."

"Mahala? It's Patience. Your grandmother told me what happened. Do you want to talk?"

No, she didn't want to talk, but she did want the comfort of an understanding friend. And Patience had always been understanding. She had been the first girl to not only not look down on Mahala because of her mixed race, but to actually esteem her. "It's open," she hiccuped.

Patience entered. Her round face looked pink and even a bit puffy. Another arrow of guilt pierced Mahala. Her selfishness had cost Patience a good friend, too.

The girls embraced.

"I never would have thought he'd do something like this," Mahala said. "I had thought he'd outgrown such impulsiveness. I was so sure we'd talk today and set things to rights."

Patience shook her head. "Mahala, I think he loved you far too much to settle for friendship forever."

"Oh, Patience, I'm awful, I know! How could I not love him? How could I cause him so much pain?"

"You can't make your heart feel something it doesn't."

"I tried, truly I did. But at least I could have handled things better."

"Perhaps."

"If I hadn't kissed him…"

"You kissed him? Before even answering his proposal?" Patience cried incredulously.

"I know! I know!" Mahala fell back on the bed in an agony of defeat. "And now I've caused him to run away rather than face the shame of seeing me again."

"You didn't cause him to do anything," Patience pointed out, reaching for Mahala's hand. "You can't take the blame for all his decisions. We all know Clay wanted to go to Tahlequah years ago. If he chose this moment to make his break, he must have felt that was best for him."

Mahala drug a sleeve across her face and focused on the other girl's expression. "How are you so wise at sixteen? I dare say you would have done far better with romance than I. We've lost a dear friend, and for that I'm sorry, but at least we still have each other."

Patience would not meet her eyes. Something in her manner caused Mahala to sit back up in alarm.

"We do have each other, don't we, Patience? My debacle with Clay hasn't cost me your allegiance, too, has it?"

"Oh, no, it's not that! What happened between you and Clay has nothing to do with me."

"Then ...?"

Patience looked back at Mahala, her eyes filling suddenly with tears. "Oh, it's no use. I shouldn't have come in at such an emotional time because I knew I couldn't hide it – and I can't lie to you, Mahala ..."

"What? What?"

"Last night my father told us there is simply not enough business in Clarkesville to support us during the winter and spring. The past two years he's lost money. At the end of the season, in November, we're moving to Athens."

Mahala stared at Patience. She felt as though her world was ending ... in one day, to lose not one best friend, but two. She would be all alone. What future did she possible have now?

CHAPTER TWO

August 1856
Chatham County, Georgia

n his room at The Marshes, the Rousseau rice plantation commanding 600 acres of Harveys Island south of Savannah, Georgia, Devereaux Rousseau slipped into the jacket his man-servant, Little Joe, held out for him. No matter how balmy the weather, one always dressed for dinner. Dev turned to the mirror to inspect his cravat. The mirror reflected his neatly combed dark hair and dark-lashed eyes in perfect contrast to his strongly molded features.

"Very nice, Little Joe," he said.

"Ain' nothin' to it, Mastuh Dev – specially next to polishin' all dem buttons on your uniform," said the young black man with a smile.

"Feels a lot more relaxed, too," Dev replied, flapping his arms to demonstrate.

He had been home a month now, but he still felt like a slugabed in comparison to his schedule at Virginia Military Institute. He had not come home last summer, but everyone had felt a break after the July Fourth weekend was advisable between his third and second classes, or second and third year. It had been heartily good to see everyone and relax at The Marshes, where the fields were almost ready for annual harvest. He would, of course, be helping his father with that duty, but it seemed so much less demanding now than it used to.

Descending the stairs, Dev pondered how incredibly well VMI suited him. He had found what he had sought, an escape from the lethargy of his pampered youth. Ease had been replaced with challenge, ruling with service, and orders with obedience. His mind was stretched by the intense instruction and his body hardened by drill. He had also found brotherhood and camaraderie. Too bad most of his new friends were residents of Virginia. Dev had been an oddity, a representation of "the deep South," and everyone had wanted to get to know him because of it.

He entered the library with an easy smile. His father, his portly form clad as usual with great flair, was there pouring himself a glass of Madeira.

"Care for a drop?" Louis asked expansively.

"No, thank you, Father. I was sure I told you I signed a petition swearing off alcohol," Dev said.

"Ah, just testing you, my boy!" Louis boomed and laughed at his own craftiness. "I'm proud of you, Dev, but then I always was. Glad you're sober and serious about your studies – not harassing new cadets and writing on buildings like I hear some of your classmates do."

"Not all the cadets had the privilege of a gentleman's raising," Dev said.

"Indeed. Not a better young gent than Dev Rousseau. And when people hear Dylan's bound to be a minister – well, they think I must be a saint of a father." Louis laughed and sipped from his glass. "Barring my fondness for the drink, of course."

"It has never interfered with your temper or judgment," Dev felt compelled to say, in all fairness.

"Lucky for everyone. Sit down. We've talked about your studies, your friends, and all that, but you haven't mentioned any young ladies, Dev. Is there not a Virginia belle who's tickled your fancy?"

Dev took a place in a wingchair facing Louis and smiled self-effacingly. "No, Father. I find I don't have much time for girls."

"Is that so? Do you think to marry late in life?"

"Not necessarily. I don't think about it much at all, actually. I'm only twenty."

"I know that well! But in the art of courtship your younger brother already exceeds you," Louis declared.

Dev was stunned. He'd always been the favored older brother, outmatching Dylan in every physical or social pursuit. Dev had no desire to compete with him in spiritual matters, so it didn't matter that Dylan had excelled in his ministerial studies. But it rankled to hear his red-haired junior might have slipped ahead of him with the ladies. "How so? Surely not some New Jersey girl!"

"No, no. I hope I've raised him with more sense than that. For a couple of years now he's been writing your distant cousin, Miss Carolyn Calhoun."

"Carolyn Calhoun?" Dev sat back, plundering into the depths of his memory. "Not the plump little girl who fell into the goldfish pond!" He sat forward, recalling the day the poor creature had humiliated herself by tripping backwards into the fountain during a game of graces at her Savannah townhouse. Her grandmother was older sister to his mother, but in Southern families of influence, marriages between cousins, distant or not, was not an irregular thing.

Louis laughed heartily. "The same, though no longer plump, little, or, I daresay, falling into ponds. I'm bringing her here tonight to see how Bishop Elliott's school has been polishing her up."

"Tonight?" Dev's eyebrows winged upward.

"Yes! Tonight. She, too, is home on a break. Like us, her family decided not to travel due to its brevity. I've asked them up for dinner and a few nights. This will give us the ideal chance to look her over. Dylan's faithful correspondence all but declares he considers her his sweetheart. Let's see if she will make a good minister's wife." Louis practically giggled with anticipation. He rolled his glass in his thick hands.

Devereaux frowned. Louis ought to know that his comments were like throwing scraps to one dog while ignoring the other. About that moment he heard carriage wheels on the drive.

At fifteen, Carolyn Calhoun had never been to Dylan's and Dev's plantation home. She thought it grander than Brightwell, her own family's long staple cotton farm, but maybe that was just due to her state of nervous excitement as she surveyed the columned brick mansion. If it were Dylan instead of Dev who was home for the summer, she would not feel this anxious. Dylan's light-hearted, thoughtful manner set her at ease. But his older brother had always been a mystery. It was too hard to tell what he was really thinking behind that polished, aloof exterior. He seemed to regard her with a certain detached disdain, ever since the first day he'd met her as she had completed her first successful polka at the dancing school with Dylan. She'd been unable to string more than two words together in his presence. Then she had not helped matters by stumbling into that pond the last time he had seen her. Carolyn sighed. Hopefully two years of boarding school had better taught her how to conceal her own unwanted emotions.

Carolyn's younger sister Eliza was still at Montpelier, where she had gone the year following Carolyn's arrival. She was now staying at the home of a friend. So it was just Carolyn and her parents, Lawrence and Olivia, who stepped down from the Rousseaus' carriage, which had picked them up at The Marshes landing. Carolyn adjusted her dress. It was held out over a new cage crinoline. Her blonde hair was already done up for evening under her straw hat, fashionably full over her ears, knotted into a simple bun in the back.

"You look lovely, dear," her father said, sensing her apprehension. "We shan't let the rice side of our family unnerve us. Come, take my arm."

Carolyn smiled at him appreciatively. She loved her father. He was so positive and youthful, so full of life. He had always taken excellent care of the ladies in his family, never bemoaning the lack of a son. But Carolyn knew he would not be adverse to her marrying a Rousseau, and her mother was positively set on it.

Lawrence escorted his wife and daughter up the steps. The door was opened by the butler, but petite, lively Henrietta Rousseau was not far behind, her dark eyes shining as she called out a merry greeting to her "dear nephew Lawrence and his Olivia." Her rose-colored gown brought out the color in her cheeks. Louis joined her, offering his hand to Lawrence and bowing to the ladies. Carolyn noted that his inspection of her person was discreet but thorough.

Inside the entrance hall, the soaring ceiling provided some relief from the oppressive heat. On a large pillar and scroll table a full bouquet of roses spread their fragrance. As the butler hurried away with Lawrence's hat and the ladies' reticules, and another servant bore in the family's trunk, Carolyn noticed Devereaux approach from a side room.

"The steam boat ran a little late," Louis was commenting. "I hope you were not overly inconvenienced."

"Not at all," Carolyn's father replied. "Thank you for waiting your carriage."

"Of course! It would be too far to walk, even without luggage. Ah, here is Devereaux!"

As the young man greeted them, Carolyn and her mother curtsied. She felt his eyes linger on her and wondered what he thought. She would never be tall like Olivia, she now realized, but Carolyn at last possessed a woman's gentle proportions, and she had worked hard to bring her demeanor from shy and awkward to calm and graceful.

Dev's scrutiny made all inner quietude begin to flee, though, and she found she could not meet his eyes. His presence still had a damaging effect. He was more confident and handsome than ever, his military bearing a compliment to his poise.

Henrietta ushered them into the parlor for lemonade and shortbread. Carolyn felt mildly relieved that Dev did not follow them. She gratefully quenched her dry palate with the tangy-sweet drink while their hostess made small talk, exclaiming over how their presence would punctuate the monotony of the long summer on the plantation.

Shortly, they were shown to their rooms, spacious chambers with floral paper on the walls and massive mosquito-draped canopy beds. The home was so gracious and beautiful, it was not hard to imagine living here. Carolyn checked her thoughts as she sponged off in her undergarments at the basin, determined not to fall prey to her mother's assumptions. Dylan's letters *had* been faithful and warm – indeed the brightest part of her life at boarding school. He kept her up to date on his studies at Princeton and had even bared his struggles with religious and political matters. But while Carolyn was sure there was no other girl in his life, he had not made any declaration of his feelings for her. If he should so choose, he could have nothing to do with her after his graduation with no imputation on his honor and no harm to her reputation.

Carolyn donned her periwinkle silk organza dinner dress with the gathered front corsage, admitting to herself that she would be surprised, though, if Dylan did not pursue her once he had his degree. But, could the affection between them bloom into love? And could she ever put aside the dizzying reaction Devereaux provoked to one day be his brother's wife?

She patted rosewater into her hair and left her room, knocking on the door of her parents' chamber to see if they were ready to go down to dinner.

The Rousseaus were waiting in the parlor. As protocol demanded, Louis offered his left arm to Olivia to escort her into the dining room. Lawrence offered his to Henrietta. And that left Carolyn with Devereaux. She daintily perched her fingers on his sleeve and returned his smile with a fleeting one of her own.

The dining room looked lovely, painted a pale green with white molding and chair rail. Candles gleamed on crystal. A small black boy stood to one side, methodically tugging a rope attached to a large overhead palmetto fan. Dev seated Carolyn to his left. As soon as the men had also taken their places, a side door opened and a serving man brought in chilled tomato bisque soup. It was delicious.

"So, Miss Calhoun, when you leave us you return to Montpelier," Louis addressed her. "How do you like it there at Bishop Elliott's school?"

"Very well, Sir."

"And this will be your last year?" Henrietta inquired.

"Two more, Ma'am."

"We hope to take Carolyn abroad following next year's harvest," Lawence told them.

"Oh, how exciting," Henrietta cried.

Carolyn looked up and smiled her agreement.

"A perfect finish to a young lady's education," Louis agreed.

"Or a young man's, I think," Devereaux put in suggestively, causing everyone to laugh.

"If it will keep you from going off to Kalamazoo, we might just consider it," Louis told his son.

"You will join the army after graduation, then?" Olivia asked Devereaux.

"I am not yet sure, though my father hopes I will come home and be content with a stint in the Republican Blues or the Savannah Guards," Dev replied.

"Those companies are certainly top notch, and have the benefit of many years of respectable service," Lawrence said, "but there is another you might consider, though it is new. The Oglethorpe Light Infantry was formed last year by GMI grads to keep up their skills – mostly young professionals from the Independent Presbyterian Church. But they really turned some heads during their first parade this past January. They're the only company to drill by Hardee, and really shaped up since Francis Bartow accepted the captaincy."

"Francis Bartow, the politician?" asked Henrietta as a servant set before them an artfully boned and stuffed roast leg of mutton.

"Yes, Ma'am," Lawrence replied. "The same. He had terms in both our House and Senate, and before that, dazzled the courts solving difficult forensics cases with Law, Bartow and Lovell. Very sharp."

"But with no military training," Dev commented.

Louis fixed him with an impatient stare. "Nevertheless, the good families of Savannah are taking notice. And it could be that Captain Bartow would welcome an experienced lieutenant."

"It bears watching," Dev agreed.

"As much as we want our son home with us, we don't want him to sell himself short," Henrietta put in gently, as though she were making both a statement to the guests and a reminder to her husband. "He has a very promising two years ahead. This next year he'll get his class ring —"

"—the biggest of any school around!" Louis put in with a chortle.

"And he hopes to be a speaker at the institute's annual anniversary in November. It is considered quite an honor."

Carolyn looked from the proud mother to the unaffected son, who was calmly eating his mutton. He looked up and added with a smirk, "*Mother* hopes I might be chosen speaker, but what *I'd* value more than anything is the opportunity to become a sergeant. I'd get to sit in the guard room and wear a sword instead of standing post in the cold with a musket!"

They all laughed.

"You must never receive demerits, to justify such lofty goals!" Lawrence teased.

"That word is not even a part of my vocabulary," Dev joked back.

Carolyn smiled to see that he did have a sense of humor … and this was the most she had ever heard him talk. He must really like military life, she thought.

"Devereaux has sworn off intoxicating drink during his time as a cadet," Henrietta informed them. "And never frequents the taverns and hotels in Lexington. He even avoided trouble in Thomas Jackson's class." She went on to explain, "Jackson's Professor of Natural and Experimental Philosophy and an instructor in artillery as well. Dev tells us he must be quite brilliant, but he is a horrible teacher."

"What exactly is Natural and Experimental Philosophy, anyway?" Olivia inquired in complete puzzlement.

"To break it down, we use Bartlett's three volumes on Mechanics, Optics and Acoustics, and Spherical Astronomy," Dev told her. "Very difficult to understand under the best of circumstances."

"To be sure!" Olivia exclaimed.

"Professor Jackson does not explain, and we most certainly never *discuss*, the lessons. We learn them and recite them. Some of the cadets perform ridiculous antics just to get a reaction from him. The most he ever does is give a subdued smile."

"Unfortunately some of the students also take their shenanigans too far," Louis told them. "Like drawing caricatures on the blackboard of the man with enormous feet – and calling him 'Square Box' because of it – or pulling out the linch pins on the cannons during drills. I am very relieved to say my son has never been involved in such behavior."

"Certainly," Lawrence agreed heartily. "But even if you should excel beyond your wildest dreams, Devereaux, would you really want a position in the army now? With all the trouble brewing?"

"You have a point," Dev admitted. "Right now it may seem we're in a lull, but I don't think it will continue. Should the North persist in excluding representation of our agrarian economy to the benefit of their own industrial interest, my path in two years may be exceedingly clear." The furrow on Dev's brow suddenly lifted, and he looked at the women gathered at the table. "Perhaps we should save such discussion for the drawing room. We are monopolizing the conversation – and have not yet heard from Miss Calhoun on the subject of *her* schooling."

"I?" Carolyn said faintly, taken by surprise. Everyone looked at her with murmurs of agreement. She said, "There is not much to add to what has already been told, I'm afraid. I like the school and have learned much – even astronomy – but nothing so unique as optics and mechanics."

Dev laughed. "For that you can be grateful."

"That's not altogether true, though, Carolyn," Olivia pointed out. "Carolyn has become quite an amazing pianist."

Carolyn wanted to cringe in dread of what she knew was coming next, but she managed to smile as Henrietta said, "Oh? Perhaps you would play for us after dinner."

Her instructor at Montpelier had reminded her many times over the course of her studies that insisting she could not play before company was an act of selfishness. So as nervous as the thought of sitting down at a keyboard before Devereaux made her, she responded, "Of course, Aunt Henrietta."

31

And thereafter she could not enjoy the delicious strawberry ice that was brought forth for dessert. The butterflies in her stomach were much too intense. In anticipation of her concert, the gentlemen even forewent cigars and brandy in their drawing room. Devereaux escorted her straight to the piano bench.

I will not fail. I will not fail, she told herself. *This is my chance to show him I am no longer a clutzy child!*

"Would you care for music?" asked Henrietta. She came forward with sheet music in her hands. "Beethoven?"

"If you like."

"First, why don't you play your spring recital piece?" Olivia suggested.

"All right."

Carolyn's fingers rippled over the keys, getting the sound and feel of the instrument in a few scales, then a Foster warm-up song, "Jeanie With the Light Brown Hair." She strove to block out the attentive faces of her listeners. Finally she moved into "Concerto No. 1 in E Flat Minor" by Franz Liszt. When she was done, her parents and the Rousseaus broke into enthusiastic applause.

Devereaux was standing, coming over to her side. "Beautifully done," he complimented. "Would you like me to turn your pages?"

"Oh, yes, of course," Carolyn said, flushing pink. She put one of the Beethoven arrangements up on the stand.

He smiled, waiting for her to begin.

Carolyn played two notes and a chord, hopelessly botched. "Oh, dear," she said. "Let me start again."

Devereaux was watching her carefully, as if judging her reaction to his proximity. She had to ignore him. Carolyn pretended she was back at school and that he was her music instructor standing near. That way, she got through the song tolerably well, and the second one flawlessly. She breathed a sigh of relief when she was done. While everyone clapped again, Dev helped her slide back the bench. He briefly took her hand to help her round it and across into the center of the room. She quickly pulled away and went to sit beside her mother.

"Thank you, dear. That was lovely," Henrietta said, reaching over to pat her skirt. "You are becoming quite a young lady. My Collette also excelled at piano – among many other things, of course. She is now happily married and a mother herself. Have you any sweethearts in Montpelier or Macon?"

"No, Ma'am," Carolyn murmured, blushing again and furiously wishing she was not so given to the habit. She didn't dare look at Dev.

"Our son Dylan seems awfully fond of her, though," Louis boomed cheerfully.

"Now, Mr. Rousseau," Henrietta pretended to scold, although Carolyn saw the smirk she was trying to hide.

"What?" Louis declared with mock innocence. "Two years of constant missives? What other conclusion am I to draw?"

"Oh, leave the poor girl alone. You're embarrassing her," said Henrietta. "What kind of host will she think you? And speaking of that, you must show our guests around the plantation tomorrow morning."

"It would be my pleasure."

"And ours," Lawrence agreed. "I understand you follow James Hamilton Couper's example of crop rotation."

"Yes," said Louis, "though not so extensively as he. Rice is so lucrative it is with great pain that I force myself to plant anything else. But, in the end I do find a greater yield. I plant a year of cotton followed by a year of cane in each field following every two years of rice."

"Ah, so you gentlemen are already thoroughly familiar with the intricacies of raising long-staple cotton!" Olivia exclaimed.

Carolyn bit her lip, hoping her mother's thought pattern wasn't as obvious to the Rousseaus as it was to her.

"Yes, Ma'am," Devereaux replied. "The cotton has just begun to open. And of course it's almost time to harvest our rice as well. We're about ready to let off the harvest flow. If you had come but a week later you would observe the cutting."

"But then you would doubtless be too busy to entertain us, so I say we've come at just the right time," Olivia said, smiling sweetly.

Dev bowed his head in polite acknowledgement. Then his gaze was directed to Carolyn as he asked, "Would both of you ladies find a tour of The Marshes interesting?"

"Yes," Carolyn replied. "Very much." In view of Dylan's struggle with the issue of slavery, she was curious to see how the bondsmen here were treated, and what their living conditions were like.

"Very well, then," Dev said. "We'll set out right after breakfast."

It was a restless night that Carolyn spent in that fine bedroom, continually distracted by the thought of Devereaux Rousseau just down the hall. When she rose it was with anxiety about the time she was to spend in his company. She was glad the question of costume had been decided by the fact that their tour would be conducted from horseback, for that was one less thing to fret over. She donned a tailored summer habit, bone colored with tan trim and a big, netted straw hat that did nice things for her oval face and dark brown eyes. Then she descended to the dining room.

Hearing voices, she went in to find everyone at table except for Dev, who had already eaten in the interest of selecting their mounts. He came in as they were polishing off their eggs, bacon and fruit. He was garbed in a full-sleeved white shirt with light gray vest, coat and dark breeches. Black riding boots reached his knees.

"I believe I've found gentle enough yet responsive mares for the ladies," he said as he escorted them to the front porch. Just in front a black groom stood with the horses under discussion. Carolyn, admittedly no great horse-woman, was relieved to find Dev was right about her animal. She felt she could handle the mare without embarrassing herself.

Louis had decided to let Dev conduct the tour, so once Lawrence and Dev were also mounted on stallions, they set out.

"We can begin in the fields," Dev said. "But I don't know how much you wish to know about the rice process. I don't want to bore you."

"I'm sure Mr. Calhoun can converse adequately on the subject, but Carolyn and I know nothing, do we, dear?" Olivia called over her shoulder. "So anything you tell us will be quite fascinating."

"Very well. The entire crop is currently immersed in the fourth and final flooding of the rice fields. When we let the water out using our system of ditches and gates the ground will be allowed to dry before the slaves come through with sickles. They leave stubble on which the stalks are laid, then the sheaves are bundled and stacked," Dev told them. "They're carried by ox cart to the canal that runs through the land."

"You have lockgates to keep the canal water fresh," Lawrence observed as they passed the buildings surrounding the house and the fields came into view.

"Exactly. We use flats to take the crop to the threshing mill. Many planters use the old method of beating the stalks and letting the grain fall through slits onto the subfloor of a threshing house, but here at The Marshes our steam mill can put out 1,000 bushels per day."

"Impressive," Lawrence murmured. "Do you use Bermuda grass on the banks of the rice fields?"

"We do. It gives great protection against freshets when there's washing."

"Yes, I agree. Have you gotten into the Guana craze?"

"We tried it some, but Father still swears by cane leaves and stalk and rice straw that's been processed in the animal pens on the rice, and seaweed and mud marsh on the cane and cotton fields – plowed deep, mind you, about twelve inches."

As Lawrence nodded and the men continued to talk, gesture and point, Carolyn stared into the distance. She wasn't bored, she just had no idea what they were so enthusiastic about. And she couldn't see much, either. The glare of the rising sun on the flooded fields was blinding.

Her mother edged her mount up next to Carolyn's and whispered, "They certainly seem to be speaking the same language."

Carolyn nodded and smiled. "I wish I understood it," she said.

"Why?" Olivia said jokingly. "Do you think they would have the faintest idea how to make a quilt or how to preserve fruits and vegetables?"

Dev noticed them talking and drew closer with a smile. "Rather bright today, isn't it, ladies? My sister always used to say how magical it looked when we'd flood the fields, like the ocean had come right up to the house."

"She was right, Mr. Rousseau," Olivia said. "It's an impressive sight."

"And one that you've beheld long enough, no doubt. Let's go by where the rice will be processed."

Dev showed them the threshing mill of which he had spoken, along with the two-story pounding mill, the next step in the harvest process. While he and Lawrence went inside to examine the timber pestles and wooden mortars, Carolyn and Olivia waited.

"I'm impressed with him, Carolyn," Olivia said in a low voice. "He's very knowledgeable and mature for his age. His father has groomed him well."

Carolyn said nothing.

"You might put forth some effort into impressing *him*," her mother added a second later, just before the men emerged.

She smiled when Dev glanced their way, but she felt rather unnatural, like a hyena barring its teeth. He gave her a rather perplexed smile in return as he swung expertly onto his horse.

Dev led them to the slave quarters next. Carolyn's interest rose. She was pleased to see the cabins were neat and white washed with stone chimneys. Most of the residents were out in the fields where crops other than rice were planted, or at their various jobs as coopers, masons, gardeners and carpenters. Dogs watched them from stoops and chickens clucked and scratched in the dirt. Gardens to the rear of the homes added splashes of color.

"Our people supplement their rations with their produce," Dev said, "and of course they are allowed to sell excess produce and livestock to us or at market. Their work day is short. They often get done in five hours. Then they are free to crab, trap, fish or tend gardens or their own stand of crops, mainly corn."

"Five hours?" Carolyn echoed. "And I thought rice slaves worked harder than those at cotton."

"No, Ma'am. We're a far cry from the cane plantations of Louisiana. That's one reason my father quit raising cane for profit. It was too hard on the Negroes. We find that the incentive of having their own time is very motivational."

Carolyn couldn't help looking surprised.

"Come see the hospital. I think you'll be impressed," he invited with a smile.

When they reached the whitewashed building in a grassy clearing, this time Carolyn and Olivia did venture inside.

"We have steam boilers we use for heat," Dev said proudly. "Much more effective than fireplaces."

While he showed Lawrence the rooms designated for the men, a slave nurse showed the ladies the area set apart for care of the women, both general and lying-in. The nurse explained that when needed the Rousseaus' doctor came out to tend serious cases.

They went together into the nursery, where countless black children in shapeless cotton dresses were being tended by some old women. As soon as they caught sight of Dev, they all jumped up and down and clamored around him. Carolyn found herself pressed back against the wall in the tide of little bodies.

"Massuh Dev! Massuh Dev!" they shouted, hands held out. One mischievous boy of about six began turning Devereaux's pockets inside out.

"Whoa!" Dev cried. "Do you think I'm the general store or something?"

"But you always bring us peppermints when you come," piped a tiny girl with enormous eyes.

Dev scooped her up and felt for an exaggeratedly long time inside his coat pocket. At last, to cheers, he produced a bag of peppermint sticks, which he gave to the nurse before departing, leaving the poor inundated woman to break up and dole out the treat.

Olivia was much impressed by the scene, laughing as she mounted her mare. "They were adorable," she said. "I see so many similarities between The Marshes and the way we run Brightwell. Is our tour complete already, Mr. Rousseau?"

"For now, if that suits you. I think my mother is anticipating a luncheon chat and perhaps a time of rest this afternoon. I need to look over the cotton picking and some of our lesser crops. Would you care to accompany me, Mr. Calhoun?" Dev asked.

"By all means," Lawrence agreed enthusiastically.

"Then after we drop off the ladies we'll go back out. Although we may wish we'd had a nap, too, later tonight," Dev told them, a sparkle in his eye. "We thought if you'd like we might have our own little rowing party."

"Oh, definitely!" Olivia exclaimed.

Carolyn hoped there were large rowboats. She did not want to be alone with Dev.

But alas, her wish was not to be granted. After an afternoon spent visiting while Hennie Rousseau labored on her shell artwork, a rest, and another impeccable dinner, they rode in a wagon through the orange grove to the river's edge. There two small boats were drawn up to shore beside a few canoes – one row boat seating four and the other two.

"Louis, we'd love to hear some tips on tending citrus groves," Olivia said as they got out of the wagon. "We've been thinking of starting one at Brightwell. Isn't that right, Mr. Calhoun?"

Lawrence nodded.

"Mr. Rousseau can tell you all about it once we get out on the water," Henrietta volunteered.

Dev glanced at Carolyn. "Shall we?" he said.

Carolyn smiled faintly.

Dev pushed the smaller rowboat part way into the water and held it for Carolyn to get in, offering her his other hand. She gripped the sides as he climbed in facing her and shoved off. Silvery light from the rising moon glistened off droplets flung from the oars as Dev swung them in an arch and started rowing. He leaned forward as he pushed against the current – too far forward, in Carolyn's opinion. She was obliged to scoot as far back on her seat as she could without falling into the hull, envisioning legs and petticoats flying up in disarray. She bit down on her lip to avoid giggling as she pictured it.

Dev took her two gestures together as nervousness. "Are you scared of me, Miss Calhoun?" he asked with a teasing gleam in his eye.

"N-no. Of course not." *I'm scared of me*, she thought. *The way your proximity makes me lose all sense.*

"I really am an upstanding sort of chap."

"I don't question that."

"Then perhaps you can stop looking at me as though I'm going to bite you – and relax your grip on the sides of the boat. Oh, don't be vexed with me. Tell me what you think of The Marshes."

Carolyn took a steadying breath. They had reached the center of the river, and Dev let them drift slowly. A caressing gust of breeze lifted her curls and brought the sound of their parents' conversation.

"It's beautiful," she said honestly. "And seems very progressive in many ways, though I'm hardly an expert on such things."

"You mean the steam mills and such."

"Yes. Those were impressive, as was the quality of care for your workers."

"You thought to find it otherwise?"

"I – no. I just wish there was some other way."

Devereaux appeared to consider for a moment. His dark hair ruffled over his broad forehead. "Last year the Honorable Amelia Murry, lady in waiting to Queen Victoria, was dismissed from court after writing a statement publicly praising Hopeton plantation. She wondered if black people in the North or in any other country were as well cared for. Once, in fact, a slave who lived at Hopeton who had saved his whole life to buy his freedom changed his mind and begged Mr. Couper to let him stay. I'd like to believe the same thing could occur here. Yet it's much more sensational to accuse all of us of brutal dictatorship – to let the entire blame rest at our feet despite the fact that the English started the system, the blacks sold each other to the New Englanders, and the New Englanders sold us the slaves. And both the Yanks and the Brits are all too eager to gobble up our slave-produced cotton. You surely agree, Miss Calhoun, considering your background."

Carolyn raised her eyebrows, a bit taken back by Devereaux's statement and the fact that he didn't ask her opinion, but assumed it. "I … believe there is truth in what you said, but your brother … he thinks not of defending slavery, but about its future."

"And what does he write you of that?"

Oh, dear. She hadn't meant to cause dissention between Dylan and his family. She should have held her tongue. She answered, "It is his fondest hope to establish a mission church near the slums of Savannah."

"And thus to raise the spiritual awareness of the blacks."

"Yes, believing that will aid in their identity as eventual freedmen."

"And you think such lofty reasoning could only be found at Princeton?"

"I didn't say that. But he …"

"My father has always allowed freedom of worship among our slaves. As much as he feels them to be part of our family, and their needs well met by our system, he recognizes the winds of change. Offering them Christianity – and even education, for those who show interest and promise – will indeed help prepare them for the future."

"You mean you …?" Carolyn's voice trailed off again as she watched Dev man the oars, muscles and white shirt rippling with effort. "But it's against the law!"

"Shh!" he said with mock ferocity, a finger to his lips as he pretended to glance around.

Carolyn burst into surprised laughter. Dev grinned. She saw her mother turn from their nearby craft and smile in a pleased manner.

"She probably thinks we're talking about parties," Dev said in a conspiratorial manner.

"Let's let her think so," Carolyn replied, gratified that Dev would joke with her.

"Now that we've gotten that out of the way, and you know us not to be repressive ogres despite the implications of my brother's righteous missives —"

"I didn't say that, and he doesn't – he doesn't write that way at all!" Just when she was starting to feel comfortable with him!

Dev didn't respond, merely completed his sentence. "— we can truly talk about more pleasant matters. Like limes."

"Limes?"

"Did you always hunt them along the riverbanks?"

"Well, sometimes."

"I love limes. And you should taste the oranges here. When you've come back home, when we're *both* home next, come back in October. In fact, next year I'll still be away, but I'll have some sent down to you. They are the biggest and juiciest along the Ogeechee River!"

"Is everything at The Marshes the best?" Carolyn teased.

"Most certainly, except we are decidedly lacking in young ladies. We'll have to remedy that, don't you think?"

Carolyn hoped he couldn't see her blush in the moonlight.

CHAPTER THREE

December 1856
Clarkesville, Georgia

Mahala could hardly believe it. For weeks, nay, months, she had hoped for it despite herself – and now it had actually come: a small, stained envelope all the way from Indian Territory, addressed to her in Clay's handwriting. Wrapped in her wool cloak, she stood outside the post office in an agony of indecision about where to go to read the letter. At the hotel, even behind her closed bedroom door, she was likely to be interrupted. She was called on often now that Patience was gone, even though it was the off-season. And it was too cold and wet to linger outdoors.

Her feet took her to a place that had lately become her sanctuary in more ways than one – the Methodist church, set among the graves of former members and majestic oak trees. Mahala now attended regularly and had become special friends with the middle-aged pastor's wife, Mrs. Burns. It was certainly a different sort of relationship from the one she had enjoyed with Patience, but Selma Burns offered a quiet wisdom and a soft Southern humor that filled in the cracks in Mahala's heart. The older woman was helping her unlock the mysteries of her mother's Bible, and Mahala did not doubt it was God who had sent Selma in her hour of need.

As she walked up the pathway, she raised her hood against the light drizzle that had begun to fall. As she expected, she found the door unlocked. She entered the wooden structure, looking around at the white walls, plain wooden benches, and three-sided gallery for the colored people. The window sills were decorated with pine boughs and red candles in celebration of the Christmas season. It was still cold enough inside that Mahala could see her breath, but that didn't bother her. Here, away from the noise and bustle and the rain outside, she could give full concentration to Clay's letter.

She went to the third bench from the front on the right side of the center aisle and sat down. With shaky hands she put back her hood and drew out the envelope.

Since Clay's departure, Mahala had gone over Clay's proposal a hundred times in her mind. She had since decided that while she might have handled things differently, her answer – and probably the outcome, too – would have been the same. But that hadn't stopped her from missing him every day.

The fact that little had transpired between Jack Randall and herself during the summer and early fall had not helped her melancholy. She had irrationally hoped that he might be a source of diversion, or even comfort, in Clay's absence. But it had been a busy season at the hotels. And when Jack took his usual tact – shallow and teasing – during their first brief encounters, Mahala had put up her guard with a layer of disinterested politeness. She'd not tell him about Clay. She'd not let him in again the way she had the year before, then be left standing alone.

Mahala slit the top and pulled out a folded sheet of paper. Not surprisingly, the writing was in Cherokee.

Tahlequah, Oklahoma Territory
October 14, 1856

Mahala, As you can see, I am here. When I arrived, tired, hungry and out of money, the lady of this place, Lowe's Boarding House, took me in. At first I did some repairs for her in exchange for board. Now, I have a job clerking at a grocer's. Is it not ironic, you might say, that I am doing the same thing here that I did there. Well, I guess one does what one knows. At least now I am among others like me. Everyone is kind, especially once they hear my story.

It is a nice town, though there are still some tensions between the two parties, the settlers who came first and those who came only after all political efforts failed. But they have managed to build churches, schools and homes. The Supreme Court meets in a square brick building which also houses the newspaper, the Cherokee Advocate. *The whites even send their children to our schools. Some of the homes are very nice, like George Murrell's mansion. His wife was the niece of Chief John Ross. Chief Ross himself lives a few miles southeast at Park Hill, in a house called Rose Cottage. It's said they can accommodate forty guests at one time! The driveway is lined with rose bushes, and he has hundreds of apple trees.*

You may know I have written to my parents before this. But I wanted to write to you, too. I felt too angry and hurt to speak further after we last talked, but I probably should not have left in anger. To leave suddenly seemed the only thing to do at the time. I hope you can forgive me enough to write me a letter. It seems you were too much a part of my life to cut it off entirely, even if you continue as sister rather than wife. You are my Cherokee sister, Mahala, and I still wish you could see through my eyes every day.

Clay Fraser

Mahala looked up, wondering what Clay had meant. He wished she could see Tahlequah and its people, or he wished she could see life – *his* life, *his* feelings – through his eyes? Or maybe … both. How she wished she could talk with him in person, if only it were possible and doing so might not reveal more than she wished to respond to.

She was just thinking how she would word her reply when she became aware of a movement behind her. She whirled around on her bench as Rex Clarke slid into the next pew back! Her hand flew to her thundering heart as she met his cold blue eyes and mocking grin.

Fumbling to fold Clay's letter, Mahala stood up, all too aware of their isolated location. "H-how long have you been here?" she asked.

"Ever since you came in and read that letter," he replied. "Oh, don't look so surprised. You didn't think I came in here to offer prayers, did you? Sit back down. I've been waiting a long time to speak with you out from under your grandmother's imperious nose. Who was the letter from, anyway? That young Cherokee buck that used to follow you around everywhere?"

"None of your business," Mahala snapped, angered at his audacity. "Why should I listen to anything you have to say? If anyone's been doing the following lately, apparently it's *you*."

"Guilty as charged." The winter light glinted off Rex's dark blonde hair as he bowed his head in acknowledgement. "But you can't blame me, surely. I may have followed you, but I am *not* guilty of another crime I'm popularly accused of."

"You mean … murdering my father?" Mahala asked, drawn in despite herself. She sank back down on the bench.

"That's right. And you should know the real story. The last time I saw Michael Franklin was just before his fist hit my face in the Habersham House Hotel. It's true I wasn't of a mind to let that pass. That plus my belief that he'd not been – shall we say – *forthcoming* about my portion of the gold put me in a pretty bad humor. But by the time I recovered enough to go after him, he had left town."

"Who's to say you didn't follow him home?"

"Your cousin Leon."

"What?"

Rex nodded. "That estimable gentleman saw me re-enter your family's hotel with my eye swelling out like a cantelope. Half an hour later, the maid – a friend of mine – knocked on my door, having heard what happened. She was all concern and let's just say she took good care of me until morning."

Mahala blushed hotly at his unapologetic statement and blatant stare. She preoccupied herself by placing Clay's letter back in the envelope. "Yes, I've heard of her," she said. "Unfortunately she's no longer around to support your story."

"But she did, when questioned by the authorities … and at peril to her own reputation."

"You've told me nothing new," Mahala said.

"I told you your cousin witnessed me returning to my rooms. I believe it was he who sent Lila up to check on me."

"Lila?"

"Lila Swift. Her name should be in your hotel records. I was sorry to see her go."

"Grandmother could hardly do otherwise."

"Funny thing. Lila told me before she left that it was your cousin who was most eager to get rid of her."

"Well, they're both advocates of moral behavior, and had the hotel's reputation to consider. Any like-minded person would agree." Mahala looked at Rex distastefully, but he didn't appear to be the least bit censured by her disapproval. In fact, he smiled. She added, "There's no proof you didn't sneak out unseen and pay *Lila* to lie for you."

Rex shrugged. "I guess not. Thus, the town's suspicion. Maybe that's why I've devoted my career to law … always searching for proof."

"Helping criminals get away with their misdeeds could hardly be considered a quest for the right," Mahala scoffed.

"You really are a bold thing, aren't you? So like your father. But I rather like that."

"Why did you track me down to tell me what I already knew?" Mahala persisted.

Rex leaned forward. "Maybe because I couldn't bear for such a lovely young lady to think me a killer. All I can do is throw myself on your mercy and hope you believe my story."

He reached out, and his fingers brushed her cheek. A wild shiver of fear shot through Mahala, and she jumped up. This was more than a man past his prime who deluded himself into believing he was still a lady's man. Mahala sensed Rex Clarke could truly be dangerous, and she dared not find out in what ways.

"You've said your peace," she told him. "Now don't follow me again – or have your man do so – or I'll report you to the sheriff."

Raising her hood over her head, Mahala left the church, her heart beating the frantic rhythm of escape. She looked back once to assure herself Rex had not exited behind her, then ran home in the rain.

At the door, Mahala shook the water off her cloak. Leon was at the front desk and looked at her distastefully.

"You remind me of a wet dog," he commented.

"Thank you, dear cousin."

"Could you not clean the mud from your boots before entering the lobby?"

Mahala looked down. She had indeed left red footprints on the rug, something she normally would never have done in a calm state of mind. "Oh, I'm sorry! I'll clean it up!"

She exited and scraped off her boots on the side of the porch, getting a wet bare head in the process. Then she tiptoed back through the foyer to the door of the private parlor, calling back to Leon, "I'll come back and clean the rug just as soon as I've changed my shoes." She paused with her hand on the knob. "Oh, Leon, someone told me you saw Rex Clarke come back in here the night my father was killed. Do you remember?"

Mahala watched her cousin's face go blank with surprise. "Why are you asking about *that?*" he inquired.

"Just curious," Mahala said lightly.

"Who would have said such a thing?"

Knowing she was coming a hair's breadth from a lie, Mahala shrugged and shook her head as if she could not remember. "So – did you see him?"

"That was a long time ago but no, Mahala, I don't recall seeing Mr. Clarke at all that night."

Late that night, when Mahala was sure Leon had gone, she crept into the hotel office with a sputtering candle in hand. She went to the book shelf where she knew hotel transactions from years past were filed. She pulled down a notebook labeled "1835-40" on the spine, sat down at the desk, and began thumbing through. Her grandfather's purchases, payments and receipts were neatly totaled in separate columns. Asking Martha about Lila Swift would have been so much easier, but she didn't want to upset her grandmother should her encounter with Rex come into the conversation.

She found the first entry of payment to Lila in February of 1838, along with a note: "Forward half of pay to Mrs. Sophie Swift, Athens Road, Hollingsworth." Aha! Perfect. Just what she needed.

Mahala ripped a sheet of paper out of the top desk drawer, dipped the quill in ink, and began to write.

Christmas passed, a lonely one for Mahala even though her family came into town for a weekend. It was good to see them but again made her question her decision of staying in town another year. Clay was gone. She had no prospects except the hotel business. It helped only a little to remind herself that not much would be different had she stayed on the farm.

After the holiday, the slow month of January was even harder to bear. Mahala thought she would welcome anything – even the chaos of the summer season and Jack Randall's haughty face – to break the monotony of life. There was talk about town of the chartering of a railway line – The Clarkesville and Tennessee – that was supposed to be constructed soon between Clarkesville and Hightower Gap, and on to the Tennessee copper mines. Jack was said to be in on that investment, along with John Stanford, Phillip Martin, George Kollock, William Alley and George Phillips. Mahala actually found herself hoping that business might draw him to town again soon – sooner than he would normally come to open his hotel for the season. But she reminded herself it was none of her business – *he* was none of her business. She spent much time reading the Bible and visiting with Selma Burns, who urged her to use this time to draw closer to God.

"He will not leave you alone, Mahala," the pastor's wife told her gently. "Trust in Him."

Then, something happened. As Mahala worked a lunch rush near the end of February, it suddenly seemed that lanky teenagers and children were everywhere, surrounding a skinny farmer and his wife, whose waist was suspiciously thick under the hitched-up band of her wool skirt. Mahala had to put two tables together to accommodate the group.

As she was doing so, the woman asked, "Be you Miss Mahala Franklin, per chance?"

"I am," Mahala answered, straightening in surprise.

"My name is Rachel Jones, and this is my husband Paul. We come from down Hollingsworth way." The woman reached inside her reticule and drew out an envelope, which she shoved towards Mahala. "I believe you wrote this to my mother, Sophie Swift."

"Why – yes," Mahala agreed, staring at her own handwriting.

"Mama's passed on. I reckon I'm the one you'll want to talk to about my big sister, Lila."

"Oh! I see." Mahala tried to contain the sudden excitement that bolted through her. "I hope you didn't come all this way just on account of the letter."

Rachel shook her head, the lines about her mouth deepening. It would be difficult to guess her age, for she'd obviously led a hard life. "Mr. Jones needed supplies for spring plantin'. I convinced him to bring us all along."

A little girl with frayed black braids tugged on her mother's sleeve. "Ma, we're powerfully hungry."

"All right, Beth, sit down," Rachel said.

Mahala smiled at the child and asked, "Would you like some chicken pie?"

"Yes, Ma'am."

"Fine. Shall I bring everyone a serving?" Mahala inquired of the parents.

"Yes, Ma'am," said Mr. Jones. "And hot coffee for me and the missus, and my oldest son here."

"Of course."

"I eat quick. Have to," Rachel explained with a glance at her brood. "There some place we can talk private-like?"

"Yes, the family parlor. We can go there as soon as I bring out lunch," Mahala said.

As she hurried back to the kitchen, Mahala could hardly contain her curiosity. She found Maddie poking judgmentally through a dish of chicken pie.

"Look at dis," Maddie fussed. "Not done yet. Gwana hafta go back in de oven."

In all the years at the hotel, Mahala had learned that Maddie was never satisfied with her culinary efforts, no matter how delicious her food. She would invariably find fault with something, even if it be imagined. But Mahala did not have patience for the woman's finickiness today. "No, no!" she cried in alarm. "I've got a whole big family out there eager for supper."

"But de vegetables still be hard. See?" Maddie jabbed a fork into a carrot.

"If you put it back in, the crust will get too dark," Mahala bargained. "Look at it now – a perfect golden brown."

"Well ..." Maddie hesitated.

"Come on. Help me dish some up," Mahala prodded. "And I can use a hand getting it out there, too."

Once the reluctant cook had assisted in carrying dinner out to the Jones family, making her lengthy apologies about the quality of the vegetables, Mahala whisked Mrs. Jones across the foyer and to the family living quarters. She was grateful the ever-watchful Leon was not at his post to spy her conference with the woman. She felt he was always trying to catch her in a mistake or find something that he could criticize about her to Martha. At least, that was the only explanation she could find for the odd combination of attention and distaste with which his gaze followed her.

Mahala gestured the rumpled middle-aged woman to the sofa, where Mrs. Jones sank down wearily. But there was a fighting spirit in the tone of her first words.

"Let's just get one thing straight right off, Miss Franklin," Rachel announced. "If you're digging around to stir up trouble for poor Lila again, I won't have it. She's had enough grief. What happened is in the past, and I aim to keep it that way, so if it's ill your interest will do her, you'll be gettin' nothing further outta me."

"Oh, no, Mrs. Jones," Mahala assured the woman, perching on the chair near her. "I assure you I'm only hoping to confirm a few details for my own satisfaction."

"Nothin' legal-like?"

"Certainly not. You can surely imagine how unsettling it is to have a mystery surrounding one's father's death. I thought perhaps if I could contact your sister, get her whereabouts beyond a shadow of a doubt the night of the murder, that would be a first step. I'm not sure how much you know about the case."

"I know everythin'," Rachel said resolutely.

"Then … you know your sister was supposedly – er – with Mr. Rex Clarke the night of the murder," Mahala said.

"All that be proved by the authorities long ago."

"Yet suspicions remain."

"What sort of suspicions?" Rachel asked, shifting warily and placing a hand on her abdomen.

"Well, about Mr. Clarke. About … whether he paid your sister for her testimony."

Mrs. Jones shot indignantly up in her seat. "No, Ma'am, he did not!" she exclaimed vehemently. "Not that I care what happens to that no-account piece of trash. Hangin's what he deserves, but not for murder – for takin' advantage of poor daft young girls!"

"Perhaps you would tell me the story from your point of view," Mahala suggested gently.

"Sure'n I will. Lila got the bad end of things, that's what happened. All she was tryin' to do was put food in our mouths. Mama was a widow with a buncha little'uns and no one to go to. Lila was the oldest so it was decided she'd go up to Clarkesville and try to find a job. Mama wanted to hang onto the farm iffen she could until my older brother was of an age to take over an' turn a profit. While Lila was gone Mama farmed what she could with our help, but even with what Sister sent home we was dirt poor. Then there was the trouble, and I can tell you for sure she got no money out of it."

"Then why did she vouch for Rex Clarke? Was she an honest enough girl to sacrifice her reputation just for the sake of goodness?"

Rachel heaved a sigh. "She was that," she said. "Honest. And hard-working. But I'm afraid she also weren't very smart. See, the way she told it, that Clarke had been flirtin' with her ever since she started working here, always telling her how she was just his type of gal, pretty, sweet and simple. Tellin' her about that fine mansion he was buildin' and sayin' as how she ought to have a place there."

Mahala nodded. She was well familiar with The Highlands, a beautiful estate built by Rex's doctor father. Clay had taken her there delivering some meat when she'd first come to Clarkesville. It had been the first time she had met Rex.

"Lila thought he meant it respectable."

"She thought he would marry her?" Mahala asked in amazement.

"I know. You an' me, we'd know better. But that night she went up to his room to take him towels and water after she heard he'd been hit by your daddy, and he sweet talked her right into his room and she gave him what he wanted. She thought if she could show him she could take care of him … well, he'd take care of her."

Mahala shook her head sadly. "Obviously he didn't." *The scoundrel*, she thought. No wonder Martha wanted her to stay away from him.

"No indeed. She came back here humiliated and real sorry, but it was too late. She'd lost her job an' folks wouldn't look at her on the street. She was a fallen woman. An' Rex wouldn't have nothin' to do with her. Laughed in her face when she told 'im he ought to marry her. My poor mama, sick as she was, bundled all of us up and took us up to town, straight to Mr. Clarke's door. She humbled herself to beg for train fare, for that was all Lila could see straight to do – go west. He did give it, but grudgingly," Rachel concluded.

"And she went to California?" Mahala prompted.

"Aye, she did. Worked a while in a saloon an' sent money home, poor thing. Then she met a decent sort of miner who offered to care for her, and that's why I beg you not to write to her. I know she would tell you straight everything I just said, but stirrin' in it would bring up lots that oughta stay buried. They're set up proper-like now, with children who will have fair prospects if their ma's past don't come up to bite 'em."

"I understand," Mahala said thoughtfully. "I can see no reason for you to lie to me. Writing to your sister will not be necessary. Thank you, Mrs. Jones, for coming to see me. What you have shared has been very helpful."

"I do hope so, Miss Franklin. Some good oughta come out of the mess. I hope you find him who killed your pa."

"Me, too," Mahala replied. "Maybe some day ..." She got up to lead Mrs. Jones to the door. "I won't keep you further. Will you be needing a room for the night?"

"We'd be much obliged."

"Just have your husband check in at the front desk once your meal is done. There's a nice suite Mr. Franklin can give you for the price of a regular room. Tell him I requested it."

"I thank you very much."

Mahala offered her hand to the worn little woman, whose calloused palm slipped into hers and gripped firmly. She watched Rachel Jones walk back to the dining room and thought that, for better or worse, by all appearances, Rex Clarke was indeed innocent of her father's murder. But where should she look for the guilty party now?

If the killer was but a nameless drifter, the money was surely long gone and the mystery would probably remain unsolved. Maybe it was time she accepted that.

CHAPTER FOUR

May 1857
Savannah, Georgia

It was a day of crowning achievement for Jack Randall. At twenty-eight, he had finally become sole owner of his own ship, the new pride of the Randall and Ellis fleet. She was an Atlantic passenger sidewheel steamer, two hundred and thirty feet long with a twenty-six-foot beam and a seven-foot draft. Her single vertical walking beam engine and compartmentalized hull – of Randall iron from his Northern branch of the family – were the newest and best, just like those being built for Charles Morgan's operations in the Gulf by Harlan and Hollingsworth. That should make his father smile.

It seemed on this bright May day all of Savannah had come out to see her, from raggedy little slum boys who dreamed of being sailors to elegant ladies considering future pleasure voyages. But it was on his family gathered on the wharf that Jack focused as he stood with his captain, Jeremy Northrup, on the portside deck, rear of the paddlewheel and two funnels. His Ellis grandparents were there, William standing as straight as his bent back and gold-handled cane would allow. Next to him was Richard with Sunny, his stepmother. Their children had grown tall. Bryson looked bored. Jack guessed he would pursue a military career in a few years. Sylvie was blossoming at fourteen, already attracting male attention but still exuding a winful childish charm that kept Jack wrapped around her little finger. She waved brightly and bounced up and down, her ankle-length hoop skirt bobbing. He waved back just as Alan, twelve, hit her with his India rubber ball.

As Sylvie turned to scold her brother, Jack's eyes swept over Aunt Eugenie and Uncle Stephen. Their son Carl was with them with his new bride, the daughter of the owner of the law firm for which the stodgy young man was now employed. Even cousin Ella Beth was there with her husband and their two-year-old son. She smiled when she saw him looking in her direction, and Jack responded with a nod. She looked content, if not happy, he decided. It was said she and Lieutenant Draper lived a modest and quiet life on Abercorn Street, just as she had long ago predicted when she realized her crush on Jack had come to naught.

Jack waved to get the attention of the crowd, then placed his hands on the rail. He broadcast his voice to be heard by all. "Thanks to everyone for coming," he said. "It is your fine support that has allowed this newest addition to the Randall and Ellis fleet. You have let us carry your cotton, rice, timber and produce to the Carribbean, England and New England. You have journeyed with us in Southern waters for business and pleasure. Now we will be pleased to take you in luxury on your trips to New York. You are all welcome to come aboard and tour the ship and to partake of refreshments, but first, she must be properly introduced to the city of Savannah. I name her for the lady nearest and dearest to my heart."

Jack motioned to the two sailors who were holding the ropes to the canvas which covered the name plate on the side of the ship. The veil slowly raised as the men walked back across the deck.

"I christen her *The Evangeline*."

Applause and cheers went up. Jack smiled when he saw his father and grandfather brush tears from their eyes. It had, after all, been his mother Eva who had brought Richard from New York to work with her father's shipping business in 1835.

The hired band began to play as the gang plank was lowered. Within minutes guests would swarm aboard.

Jack turned to Jeremy, who looked resplendent in his captain's uniform. "I'm proud to give you a worthy ship to sail," he said.

Jeremy chuckled. "It does put a little salve on my wound over losing *Eastern Star*," he replied, affectionately remembering the wooden sailing vessel that he'd served as first mate on that very 1835 voyage.

"It was time she was retired."

"Aye, but it always hurts to see a good ship make her last journey."

"Yes, but soon enough your mind will be busy with *Evangeline*'s maiden voyage. Have you got the passenger list?" Jack asked.

"At the ready, young Jack." Jeremy saluted and held up a folder which he had tucked under one arm. "Once the people see the velvet drapes and spacious cabins, I expect I'll have my hands – and the ship – full."

"I hope so. I still worry some over the tensions with the North."

Before Jack could say more, he was surrounded by his family, who embraced and congratulated him.

"I'm happy for you, Son," Richard said.

"A lovely gesture ... the name," Sunny commented, placing a hand on his arm. Her dark hair glistened in the sunlight. She was still a beautiful, stylish woman, though fine lines creased at her mouth and between her eyebrows with her varying expressions.

"Thank you," Jack replied.

"The ship compliments her memory," Grandmother Ellis agreed.

Sylvie jockeyed for a place next to Jack, reaching out to take his arm. "If you're going up North on her maiden voyage, take me with you!" she declared. "I want to see if Yankees are as bad as everyone says."

Jack laughed. "Sorry to disappoint you, little sister, but I'll be leaving soon for North Georgia."

"Success with the railroad venture?" Richard asked him.

Jack frowned and said briefly, "Unfortunately we've hit continual snags in our plans. I'm beginning to wonder if there will ever be a rail line through Clarkesville – at least one put in by The Clarkesville and Tennessee. No, it's the hotel that draws me north."

"Oh, why do you keep going off to that silly hotel?" Sylvie whined. "You'd think you like the company of those mountain people better than ours." Then her expression grew suddenly suspicious. "You haven't met a girl up there, have you, Jack?"

Jack laughed again. He felt several family members, including Ella Beth, waiting expectantly for his answer. Pushing a pair of unusual blue eyes out of his memory, he tweaked Sylvie's nose. "I've met a great many girls there, but none so winning as you."

"Let's keep it that way," Sunny suggested teasingly, "until I can find you the perfect Savannah girl."

"Where has she been all this time?" Richard asked her.

Jack saw Ella Beth and Lieutenant Draper move off toward the forecastle. He took that as a cue to say, "Time for a tour, everybody!"

Walking along the deck of the long, low, white boat, Sylvie clinging adoringly to his arm, he began pointing out the masts which could be rigged schooner style at need. With all the success he enjoyed here in Savannah, he wondered to himself, why *did* he long for the peace he seemed only able to find in the hills of Habersham? And why had he felt more at home there than anywhere since childhood? Even his success at business had not made socializing with the elite of Savannah any easier. He had not fit in as a boy, unwillingly uprooted from New York. And he did not fit in now. His father had settled, sacrificed his convictions by marrying a slave-owner. But Jack had never let go of the beliefs he'd embraced growing up among his father's Northern family and during his time at Princeton. No one here knew he and Jeremy found ways to spirit endangered slaves to safety aboard their ships. If they did, the crowd around him now would be demanding his imprisonment instead of congratulating his success.

There were too many things he had to keep close to his heart here in Savannah. In the rolling hills of North Georgia, among the plain-spoken folk, there were moments he could be himself.

Sautee Valley, Georgia

Nancy Emmitt walked into the quiet house and placed their overnight valise at her feet. She looked around, listening to the distant sounds of Ben getting the horse and wagon into the barn. Everything was, of course, just as they had left it before their trip to Clarkesville. The laundry that she and Mahala had washed was still stacked on a chair in the corner of the kitchen, waiting to be ironed. The wildflowers Mahala had picked their last day were in the vase on the table, slightly wilted. But oh, nothing was the same. Nor would it ever be.

For just before going back to Clarkesville this year, Mahala had told them all over dinner that, after much thought and prayer, she saw her future in town. She would continue to visit, and they should, too. But without a husband, or any appealing prospects for one, there was little use in her residing in farming country. At least at the hotel she was guaranteed a living, and Martha needed her. It was true Leon was hotel manager, but Mahala and Martha made the final decisions and held the purse strings. That had been Martha's design all along.

For the past year Nancy had clung to the dying hope that the daughter she had nursed at her very breast would come back to her, for a year at least, maybe two – goodness, Nancy would have taken six months! – find some nice farmer and settle onto the adjacent land. Now that dream was crushed. Mahala had even spoken privately to Jacob. She had thanked him for the care he gave her grandfather and told him that once Henry passed on, should Jacob wish to buy her lot, she would sell it to him at a pittance.

Oh, Nancy could see Mahala's reasoning, of course, but that didn't take away the pain, the illogical sense of abandonment. She was like a mother bird with all her chicks now flown from the nest, and how her heart did ache!

She sighed, barely resisting giving in to self-pity and sitting herself down for a good weep. Might as well get busy and keep her mind occupied. She fetched some kindling and got a fire going, placing her iron in the ashes while she cut up some ham and potatoes. Tossing them with some parsley, salt and pepper into a pot full of water, Nancy hung it over the small, crackling fire to simmer. Later she would thicken up the mixture into a nice soup broth, and they'd have it for supper with the apple pie Maddie had sent home with them.

Nancy spread an old quilt over the table and brought over the laundry pile. She took the iron by the handle using a wrapped-up rag and started pressing her best Sunday meeting dress. Next was Ben's good white, tucked shirt. Time was, she'd had a whole heap of wee skirts and shirts to iron. She used to complain about how long the laundry process took. Now she'd be grateful for just one more set of clothes to press. But Maddie now pressed Mahala's fine dresses in the kitchen of The Franklin Hotel.

Nancy smoothed out her grandmother's best linen table cloth which she used when company came. She slid the iron slowly over its rumpled surface, pressing down. As she did she thought about the finality of her aloneness. Oh, there was Ben. He was a good man and she loved him. But the past year had been somewhat awkward, looking at each other over the dinner table, sitting alone together in the evenings. Sometimes it seemed they had run out of things to say. Nancy had kept her façade up with the hope Mahala would stay on come this past visit.

"Oh, no!" Nancy cried suddenly. Her mind had drifted too long while she let the iron linger on one section of material. She jerked it up to find a stiff brown spot, while the room filled with a singed smell.

At that moment Ben came in. "Are you all right?" he asked from the door.

"No! Look what I've gone and done – ruined my grandmother's table cloth! My best table cloth!" Nancy exclaimed, holding up the cloth for him to see.

"Oh, dear," he said upon sight of the iron-shaped mark.

Nancy burst into tears.

Ben came forward and took her in his arms. "There, there," he murmured. "This isn't all about the table cloth, is it?"

"Mahala – she – I thought she would stay!" Nancy admitted on a sob.

Ben patted her back. "I know. Let it out, sweetheart."

He stood there a long time holding her while she cried. She appreciated that he did not say anything. Nancy felt a closeness begin to bond them, and she clung as though he was her lifeline.

"It's just us now," she said at last.

"Yes. But that's how it started, remember? And it wasn't all bad." He peered into her tear-stained face with a coaxing little smile.

She didn't have it in her to laugh yet, but she shook her head.

"We're gonna have time now to get reacquainted, do some things we didn't have opportunity to when there were always children around," he continued. "What do you say we take a little trip? I hear Atlanta's quite the boom town."

"Oh, Ben, we can't afford that," Nancy protested weakly.

"Sure we can."

"There's no call for it."

"If it will put a sparkle in your eye there's plenty of call for it," Ben told her.

"You're good to me."

Ben nodded. "I want to be." He took her hand. "We're not all alone, you know. We see Henry and Jacob every other day. And Seth and Sam are not far away, either, with their families. We can stop in and see them on our trip. Would you like that?"

Nancy nodded.

"We've done our jobs now, Nancy, except for prayer and occasional advice. It's time to be grandparents and to think of one another."

"I know you're right, Ben. It's just going to take me some time. Be patient with me?"

"Of course."

Nancy gave her husband a slight smile of thanks, and with a sad sigh, settled back into his embrace.

It was a bright, breezy June morning as Mahala and Martha set out from the hotel to attend church. They wore their best day dresses of pastel silk organza, with beflowered bonnets tied under their chins.

The night before, in an attempt to salve Mahala's regret that she had hurt the Emmitts with her decision to live permanently in town, Martha had confided her intention to bequeath the inn and the bulk of her assets to Mahala. It was something Mahala had suspected she had intended all along. Mahala did not have to be warned to remain silent on the subject. She could only imagine the extent of Leon's hatred should such knowledge become public. Martha had never promised him anything, or even hinted at a promise – but Leon's continued attitude of competition and dislike showed them both that he still hoped to one day finagle himself into an inheritance.

Now, Martha took Mahala's arm and they locked elbows for their stroll. Not because Martha needed support, Mahala knew. She was reassured by the strength she felt in her grandmother's stout little frame. It was good to know it looked to be a long time before that will they had discussed would go to probate court. No, the gesture was one of affection.

"What was it your mother mentioned the other day about more gold mining in the Nacoochee Valley?" Martha prompted.

"Oh, about Josiah Robinson Dean?"

"Was that his name?"

"The man who's buying access to hundreds of acres along Hamby Mountain by promising people a share of his profits? Yes, that's him. Mother said he's trying hydraulic mining. He actually plans to build a ditch to divert Dukes Creek three miles up the valley and shoot it over the top of Whitehorse Gap. Hard to believe, isn't it?"

"Yes, it is. What a mess that will make of all that beautiful land."

"Just what I thought," Mahala replied, glancing around at the other churchgoers walking to the Episcopal and Methodist churches on the rise above town. "But to him it's all dollar signs. I guess this will open up thousands of new acres for mining."

"I suppose. Do you think Nancy will be all right, Mahala?"

"What?" Mahala diverted her attention from a broad-shouldered man walking ahead of them as they turned onto Water Street.

"Your mother. Will she be all right? I fear she had hoped you would stay on with them."

"Yes. Me, too. I admit I am concerned about her. But I think Papa will take good care of her."

"I hope so," Martha said. "I did hate to see her looking so sad as they left." At Mahala's surprised look, she added, "What? You still think I'm a heartless monster?"

"No! No, of course not." Mahala squeezed the older woman's arm to reassure her.

"Mahala, are you looking for someone?"

"What? No. Why would you think that?"

"Well, because you seem so distracted. You keep glancing around."

Mahala hadn't realized until that moment that was exactly what she had been doing. And it *had* been in the back of her mind this morning that it was about the time of year for Jack Randall to return to town. But what did it matter? All she was to him was his summer flirtation, and a competitor at that. She was too smart for such —

"Good morning, ladies!"

The direction of her thoughts caused her to nearly jump a mile when Jack himself suddenly spoke, falling in right beside them.

He observed her reaction and added, "Pardon me. I didn't mean to startle you."

"Good morning, Mr. Randall," Martha said politely.

"How are you this fine Sunday?" he inquired.

Flushed, Mahala answered, "Fine, thank you. Did you just arrive back in town?"

"Only yesterday, in fact. I find things delightfully unchanged, Miss Franklin. That is – if it's still 'Miss Franklin.'"

"Why wouldn't it be?" Mahala inquired blankly, taking in his gray morning coat, black trousers and silk checkered vest. A tiny emerald stick pin – just the color of his eyes – secured his cravat.

Martha gave an almost imperceptible jerk on her arm.

"Well," Jack said hesitantly, turning with them onto Jefferson rather than continuing up the hill along Water, "as I recall there *was* a young man rather keen on your affections in the past … though come to think of it I didn't see him much during the summer."

"He … moved away." She frowned a little, unable to keep from feeling accusing that he had not sought to discover that fact a year ago. "At the *beginning* of the summer."

She was sure Jack caught her subtle message but chose to ignore it. "I see. And how is your friend Miss Blake?"

"She moved, too."

"Ill luck lately," Jack commented with what sounded like genuine sympathy. "Must have made for a lonely winter."

Mahala glanced up at him in surprise. His eyes met hers, and they were devoid of sarcasm. In fact, there was a gentle depth to them she'd not seen before. "Rather," she murmured in agreement.

A faint smile lifted the corners of his mouth, and for a moment she thought she sensed not only sympathy – but empathy.

"And you?" she inquired.

"I've had quite a good year, actually," he replied, and at her urging, related a bit about his new ship, *The Evangeline*. He measured his steps to theirs, even as Mahala slowed hers in rapt imagination. His enthusiasm as he described the majestic steamer was infectious. As was the very manner in which he carried himself, his magnetism and charisma. And besides, it really was too beautiful a Sunday to be coolly polite as she should be.

"Oh, I wish I could see it – the ship – but the ocean, too. It must be amazing," Mahala admitted wistfully.

"You've never been to the coast?" Jack looked as if he couldn't fathom that.

"Never." Mahala shook her head.

"Perhaps we can remedy that one off-season," Martha put in.

"Really?" Mahala asked.

"If you come you've but to let me know and I'll find rooms for you with my family and take you out on one of my ships," Jack offered.

"That's very kind of you."

"It would be my pleasure. I enjoy seeing land lovers on the sea for the first time," he commented.

"Probably to observe how ill they become," Mahala joked.

"You think me that cruel?" Jack questioned laughingly.

"Well…"

"Not you, Miss Franklin. I don't believe the waves would faze you one iota."

"Thank you … I think."

"Well, here I am," Jack said at Green Street, nodding his head toward the shady lane. "I presume you're going on to Methodist."

"That's correct," Martha answered. Mainly the "summer people" attended Grace Episcopal, with the locals frequenting the Methodist and Presbyterian churches. "A good morning to you, Mr. Randall."

"And to you. I hope our paths will cross more often this summer." Jack met Mahala's eyes, then bowed. Lifting his hat off his brown hair, with the highlights glinting red in the sun, he bid them adieu and jauntily went his way.

As soon as he was out of earshot, Martha turned to her. "What was *that*?" she inquired pointedly.

"What?" Mahala echoed.

"That exchange – that shine in your eye the minute he appeared at your elbow!"

"*Grandmother!*"

"I know he's a handsome man, but it's said that the finest women of Savannah can't secure his affections. You surely can't think you will succeed where they fail," Martha said rather snappishly.

"Of course not! I'm no fool. Anyone can see he doesn't have a woman in his life because he thinks them all beneath him. Of course I know I would never be the exception. He's all charm on the surface but cares for nothing but his own success. He's proved that many times in the past. Besides, who could stand to live with the man?"

Martha eyed her suspiciously. "Methinks you doth protest too much."

Mahala rolled her eyes. "Just because he was pleasant this morning doesn't mean I don't remember all his past goading comments."

"Can you assure me your heart is not already involved?"

"Involved with what? A dream? I think you know I'm more realistic than that."

"Every girl of nineteen dreams a little," Martha said. "And don't think it's my selfishness in wanting to keep you. I admit I'd be grouchy if any young man started flirting – you know that well enough from Clay. But if ever you must wear your heart on your sleeve, don't pin it there for Jack Randall, Mahala. I fear he'd only break it."

"I know, Grandmother." Mahala sighed. "But it *would* be nice to be friendly with him, instead of always going at each other. Just for business' sake, you know."

Martha pursed her lips as they climbed the church steps and greeted Rev. Burns and Selma at the door. The conversation was over, but Mahala's mind was still preoccupied as the piano music began. She could never tell her grandmother, but she had always thought rather wistfully that if she and Jack Randall didn't have to be competitors, they would make a good team. Speaking in a strictly business sense, of course.

Jack sat behind his desk at The Palace Hotel, smoking one of those dratted Cuban cigars his cousin George had gotten him hooked on in college, as his manager gave his end-of-day report. June had not yet closed and they had a full house. He had booked the last suite himself, merely with a pleasant conversation on his stagecoach ride up here. The French chef's dinner tonight had been a great success, and the band from Athens had agreed to come for the Fourth of July soirée.

"Very good, Roberts. You may go," Jack said, blowing a small bluish-gray cloud into the air.

"Thank you, Sir. Oh – and there's a young lady waiting to see you."

"Oh? Send her in."

Roberts had barely stepped out the door when a pretty figure in flowered muslin brushed past him into Jack's office. Jack spluttered in his haste to extinguish his cigar and rise from his chair.

"Uh – Miss Franklin!" he exclaimed as the young woman came to stand squarely in front of him. "To what do I owe this unexpected pleasure?"

"I need to discuss a business situation," she said simply, looking him in the eye.

"Well, please sit down." They both did. "What can I help you with?"

She took a breath. Her manner was not the open, happy one of the Sunday prior. Her face looked perfectly composed, but her rigid posture and a possible tremor to the hands in her lap gave Jack clues that her visit might not be altogether pleasant. He shifted a bit in his seat.

"You could first clarify a couple of facts for me. Am I under the correct impression that you came from a family of folk who could be called both genteel and Christian?"

The question took him aback. But he didn't need to explore the reaches of his own soul, or dwell on his indignation, to answer. Everyone knew his family was completely upstanding. "Of course," he replied rather defensively.

"Then I'm sure you will be familiar with the story in the Bible of King David, Bathsheba, Uriah and the Prophet Nathan. When David took Bathsheba from Uriah, Nathan likened it to a rich man with exceedingly many herds and flocks stealing the one ewe lamb of a poor man."

Jack was getting frustrated. The way women beat around the bush never made any sense to him. "What in the world is your point, Miss Franklin?"

"Tonight I learned the reason our most faithful and valued customers did not check in as scheduled. They are now under your roof, where you convinced them to stay in your conversation with them on the stagecoach."

Jack started laughing in disbelief. "So I am King David and you are Uriah – or is it Nathan – or did you decide to play both parts?"

"There is no need for derision."

"I think your analogy is a little extreme – and rather condescending."

"I did not mean to be condescending. I meant for it to be memorable. I understand – men reason well with stories." When Jack would have spoken again, his arching eyebrow predicting his words would be argumentative, Mahala raised her hand and continued. "I know we have more than one family as customers. But the Dyers have been coming to us for *fifteen years*. They always took our best suite. You have to admit you have a house full of wealthy customers, with the opportunity to gather far more in Savannah. Why steal away our most loyal family?"

"Apparently they weren't as loyal as you thought," Jack replied. "It was they who opened the conversation on their desire for greater amenities during their stay. I merely told them what my hotel offered." There. That had her attention. "Was it my fault that they changed their minds about where they wished to lodge?"

For a moment Mahala looked blank. Then she asked, "If a friend of yours in Savannah, another factor, took your best account, would you find fault with him for it?"

He didn't like the way she was trying to turn the tables on him. "I might not be happy, but I'd recognize it's a free market out there."

"Are not some things more important than profit?" she asked, biting her lip briefly. "Things like chivalry, respect – friendship?"

Was she asking him to be her friend? There were certainly emotions here that went beyond a business acquaintance. Her beautiful form, sharp mind and witty reprisals had always drawn his admiration. But he had plenty of reasons to end it at that. Wasn't his father's second marriage a perfect example of the compromise expected in a relationship? And wasn't Mahala the last type of woman his very father and all of Savannah would accept?

"You have repeatedly spoken to me about how we don't always need to be in a spirit of competition," she continued. "Yet how am I to let my guard down if this is what I am to expect?" Suddenly she stood up. "You decide, Mr. Randall. Kindness or competition."

Jack got to his feet. Without another word Mahala turned and left his office. He stood there dazed for a full minute. Then he sat down to examine the strange emotion he was feeling. Sadness. Good heavens, why? He had done nothing wrong. But her plea had effectively rebuked him.

In the middle of the night Jack awoke knowing what the heading of his mental compass should be. The emotion Mahala had roused in him served as his guide. If he followed it he would make a gesture of conciliation. Her trust would be purchased – but friendship could lead all too easily to other things. Contrary to popular belief, Jack was far from immune to the charms of intelligent, appealing women. And there was no doubt Mahala was one of those, having obtained a maturity of bearing that had only been promised before. He had only avoided entanglement thus far by very intentional steps. Now was the time for an evasive maneuver, for Mahala Franklin would socially be the least acceptable of all the females he had ever given a second glance. But there was something else potentially more dangerous than attraction. It was far easier to keep people at arm's length. Playing a chivalrous front and employing sarcastic bantering had thus far accomplished that. Bowing to Mahala's request now would give her power over him. The same sort he had always vowed to avoid.

No, he would go against the flow of emotion and treat her as logic dictated, just as he would any man in the same circumstance. He could no longer afford lighthearted flirtation. The time had come to get off the fence he'd been straddling.

So it was that when quite by chance the very next day he spotted her from the back of his horse, he forced himself to stop and get right on with the task of setting her straight. She was in the church yard, Selma Burns just across the way, both of them kneeling by gravestones plucking weeds. She wore a faded cotton dress but, unhappily for him, managed to look just as appealing as she had in her Sunday silk.

As she saw him approach, leaving his stallion to munch the long grass that grew along the bank, she wiped the back of a gloved hand across her glistening forehead, leaving a smudge of dirt. He almost forgot everything he was going to say.

Mahala rose to her feet. "Good morning, Mr. Randall," she said.

"Good morning. Now I see why the church yard always looks so neat."

"Yes. It's a lot of work." She glanced around, removing her gloves.

"I hope you are keeping an eye out for snakes and poison ivy."

"Of course."

"It's – fortuitous that I find you here, following our conversation yesterday."

"Oh?"

Jack was too distracted to continue. "You have – a smudge," he told her, gesturing towards her forehead.

"Oh." Mahala frowned and swiped it off with her clean hand. "Is it gone?"

"Yes."

She smiled in an embarrassed manner and prompted, "You were saying?"

"Yes. I've given much thought to what you said. You presented it in a manner that was worthy of the most cultured women of Savannah." Jack paused, taking in the faint flush that crept up her cheeks. He continued, "I want you to know that I hope to avoid causing you such direct offense in the future."

"I thank you," Mahala said with dignity, obviously holding back her pleasure.

But Jack wasn't done. "When I typically conduct business, I do try to think of the other person. But where emotion and logic meet, Miss Franklin, I must fairly warn you that logic always wins. I will give you as much respect as I would give any other business owner, male or female, by not compromising my good sense in decision making. To treat you otherwise would actually be to demean you. Do you understand my meaning?"

A change had stolen over Mahala's demeanor as he had spoken. She was now stiff, drawn up to her full height, her face impassive. He could easily imagine her as a chieftain's proud daughter.

"I understand perfectly, Mr. Randall," she said evenly. "Please excuse me now. There's much work to be done."

Turning on her heel, she walked across the burying ground to the plot adjoining the one where Selma Burns was at work, effectively ending the conversation. A tiny, indescribable sensation burned in Jack's chest before he intentionally snuffed it out. He had done the right thing. To lead her into a more personal relationship would only have been to invite heartache.

CHAPTER FIVE

July 1857
Savannah, Georgia

On her first morning home from Montpelier, Carolyn sat in the dining room of her family's Italian villa on Madison Square and buttered a biscuit. She smoothed on jam, thinking how quiet it was. She had grown accustomed to the chatter of her school-mates. Now they were scattered across the state and she would probably nev-er see most of them again. The thought made her a little sad, though she ad-mitted that while she had come to enjoy the society of many, she had made no real bosom friends at the institute. She was still something of a loner. But it was always difficult to close a chapter in one's life, especially when one did not know what was ahead.

Carolyn pushed that thought aside and reached for the newspaper. Since she was alone at the table, she could catch up on regional and national events neglected in the course of spring recitations and exams. But she had a copy of *Godey's* near at hand should her mother make an appearance. Ever the traditionalist, Olivia did not understand her daughter's intellectual turn of mind and was always reminding her that men found a home-focused woman most attractive.

Regardless, Carolyn felt compelled to follow events of national signifi-cance like the pro- and anti-slavery factions' struggles in Kansas. Pro-slavery Missorians had crossed the border to cast ballots in elections there. And last year a man named John Brown and his sons had fought such "border ruf-fians," killing five pro-slavery farmers in the Pottawatomie Massacre. Brown and other free-soilers, not feeling represented at the capital in LeCompton, had set up an unofficial legislature at Topeka. Both governments wanted their own constitution recognized at the national level.

In other volatile news, there was still discussion on the Dred Scott case, though Judge Taney's ruling had been handed down from the Supreme Court way back in March. Scott, who had been the slave of a U.S. Army surgeon, had originally sued for his freedom in 1846, stating he should be free since he had lived in both a free state and a free territory. Now Taney had declared that Scott was *not* free, citing the 5th Amendment barring any law that should deprive a slaveholder of his property. The court had also indicated that territorial legislatures had no power to prohibit slavery, despite the Missouri Compromise's promise of popular sovereignty.

The fallout from the case was enormous, with the Democrats divided on sectional lines, the Republican Party consolidating, and the Northern abolitionists in shock. They feared Taney would soon rule in any similar case that states had no power to prohibit slavery, and feared the situation would only embolden Southern secessionists. It seemed they might be right. While munching her biscuit and fruit, Carolyn eagerly perused an editorial calling for a federal slave code.

A rustle of silk taffeta in the foyer caused her to fold the newspaper and quickly slide it inside the magazine. She looked up with a smile as Olivia entered.

"Good morning, Mother."

Olivia stifled a yawn. "Good morning. You're up bright and early. Are you not worn out from yesterday's travel? I'm afraid your late arrival quite set me back." She took her place as a servant efficiently moved from the sideboard to pour hot tea.

"No, I'm all right. You're probably still weary from nursing Father."

"Perhaps. What is that – April? Why such an old issue, Carolyn?"

"Oh, I've a lot of catching up to do. I now know that I should favor bold, geometric prints, lean toward lavender and 'stone,' as they called it, and that—" Carolyn bent to read – "'no lady with any pretensions to taste should ever wear a dress of crimson, scarlet, or any of the violent plaids.' '*Violent.*'" Carolyn stressed the word, made a face and giggled. "Oh, and for fall clothing, fringe and black velvet trim seem to be the rage."

Olivia smiled and nodded. "We do have some shopping to do," she agreed.

"Yes, for my European wardrobe." Carolyn smiled. "I'm afraid I did in several dresses at school with ink stains. Sorry." She cringed.

"It's all right ... but Carolyn, we do need to talk. About Europe."

"Yes?"

"Your father, he ..."

Carolyn felt a sense of alarm at her mother's words and tentative, almost nervous tone. She knew her father had been stricken with scarlet fever over a month ago, which was why he had stayed at Brightwell rather than come into town. But according to her mother, he was recovering well. Now Carolyn asked anxiously, "You don't still fear for him, do you?"

"No. The doctor assures us he will be all right. But I do still worry about him. He's so weak. I'm afraid a major trip would be very taxing, possibly risky. Then there's also the fact that he fears the depression will effect the cotton market. We may have to take a loss this year when harvest rolls around."

"I see," said Carolyn. "You are saying we should cancel the trip to Europe."

"Not completely cancel – just postpone," Olivia hastened to assure her, reaching across the table to take Carolyn's hand. "I'm so sorry, dear. I didn't want to disappoint you."

"It's all right, Mother. You know I'm a home body, anyway. I don't need Europe," Carolyn offered. It was true; she would live, but she *was* disappointed. There would have been so much to experience and learn in Paris and London. She struggled to set the vision aside graciously.

"Oh, my dear. You are such a good girl. I so hated to tell you. But we do have an alternative plan in mind."

"What's that?"

"Well, we should proceed with a coming out ball – here, in December, I was thinking. That should give your father time to regain his strength. Then, I thought we could travel north … pass the winter social season in New York and Washington City. Maybe return through Warm Springs and perhaps even stop in Lexington to see Devereaux Rousseau."

"Devereaux Rousseau?" Carolyn questioned blankly.

"Well, why not?"

"I – I don't know *why.*"

Olivia smiled and released her hand, cutting a ripe melon. "Are you so sure you want to be a minister's wife?" she asked.

Carolyn was taken aback at the sudden turn of the conversation. "W-what do you mean?"

"Oh, you know exactly what I mean. Everybody knows your coming out ball will pretty much be a formality. Who could compete with the Rousseaus? But you don't have to settle for the second son, Carolyn. If you had a bit of confidence in yourself I think you could set your cap for Devereaux."

"Why would Devereaux want me?" Carolyn questioned.

"See what I mean? With that attitude, he won't. But consider your assets. You may not be a great beauty, but you have fine eyes and good skin. You are trained to help manage a plantation. You have breeding and money. You are the heir to the bulk of Brightwell. He could do much worse. And best of all, you are family."

"Devereaux has never shown any inclination towards me before."

Olivia looked disbelieving. "By my calculations, he wasn't entirely adverse to you last summer."

"But Dylan—"

"Sweet, I know. And devoted. He would make a good husband, no doubt." Olivia paused to sip from her tea cup, then continued confidently. "That is, if you want to share him with the congregation, having him called out at all hours, and always being willing to graciously open your home at a moment's notice. There will be endless callers who will expect their pastor's wife to be always available – a model of virtue – and active in charity work."

Carolyn stared at her mother with a sinking feeling. It was not good to hear voiced the very things that had been in the back of her own head. She knew she was best suited to quiet plantation life, not the social role expected of a minister's bride.

"Then, there's your father. Should another major sickness take him, I am not certain he would have the constitution to overcome it. Devereaux would be an excellent master of Brightwell."

"But he is already committed at The Marshes," Carolyn pointed out. "And Mother, you should not talk thus."

"I'm sorry, Carolyn, but when I was faced with the possibility of losing your beloved father, I was forced to look at things in a very realistic manner. I need you to take a husband who will continue to build our family's assets. Managing more than one plantation is a common enough thing, and can be easily accomplished with good overseers. But could you see Dylan as the future master of Brightwell?"

Carolyn could not meet her mother's eyes. In truth, she could not. Dylan would fully commit himself to his pulpit and congregation. He would not embrace the role of plantation owner because he had come to believe in the gradual emancipation of slavery. That was something she agreed with him about. She had written to him that she had often felt the plight of the slaves in her own soul, but like so many other Southern women, had not known what to do about it. But it was true that while she had often thought that she could work well beside him in his establishment of a mission church, would that be more true in ideal than in actuality? And was the future of Brightwell really at stake?

"There's always Eliza," Carolyn said.

"What?" Olivia asked.

"If I don't do as you wish … if things don't turn out for me as you hope … Eliza could marry someone who could run Brightwell."

"Eliza's a wild card. And she doesn't love Brightwell as you do. It's you I trust to marry well, but Carolyn, I am not telling you what to do. I just want you to think about these things. Do you truly love Dylan?"

"I – I don't know. In any case, he hasn't proposed yet."

"Nor will he until he can follow through. Clearly he's a good young man. But unless I was completely wrong last summer, I sensed sparks like fireworks flying between you and Devereaux." Olivia set down her tea cup and smiled at her daughter's startled expression. "Just think about these things. Please?"

Carolyn nodded, unsettled. She folded her napkin. "May I be excused?"

"Of course."

Carolyn started for the door but her mother's voice stopped her. "And Carolyn – I *am* truly sorry about Europe. Maybe we can take both you and Eliza next year, if you aren't already engaged."

Further disturbed, Carolyn nodded. As she mounted the steps to her room, she felt the pressure closing in on her. She knew the next year held major decisions, but she hadn't an inkling which way to proceed. Was her mother right? Would Dev take to her if she were only more confident? The thought made her stomach roll with a combination of excitement and fear. She had a feeling those fireworks her mother had noticed last summer had been entirely one-sided.

Carolyn gazed outside, where gray rain clouds had consolidated and begun to issue a steady tattoo of droplets. The shower would bring down the temperature. She thought of how fresh the garden would be afterwards. Grabbing up her journal and a big hat, she ran downstairs. She made the dash to the wisteria-sheltered gazebo with her dress, a fan-front white cotton with tiny black polka dots, only getting a bit damp.

She settled on a bench, content to spend the morning there thinking, writing and praying. She breathed in the scent of the feathery mimosa trees with their pink powder puff blossoms and watched the rain glisten on the althea shrubs.

Did she really have a choice in the matter of her future husband? It was true that no one besides Dylan came to mind as a possible suitor. But that could change, couldn't it? There were other eligible young men. Dylan had certainly never declared himself. Perhaps he did view her as only a cousin and a friend. Most likely she was not to know for sure for another two years, at least, when he would be done with school and have the prospect of a church appointment. In the meantime, would it be worth turning away other opportunities on a gamble? Shouldn't he give her some sort of understanding if he expected her to wait?

Carolyn shook her head in frustration. She opened her journal and began to write. She was so engrossed in recording her thoughts that she failed to hear running footsteps slogging across the wet yard, and when a figure pounded up the steps of the gazebo, she startled, dropping her journal.

She could hardly believe her eyes. The very object of her confusion stood before her, dripping wet and grinning sheepishly.

"Sorry I scared you," Dylan said, hat now in hand.

It had been so long since she had seen him, yet she felt the emotional closeness of their letters. These two things combined caused her to unthinkingly hurtle into his arms.

"Dylan!"

"Whoa! What a greeting," he said, sounding pleased as he embraced her.

"I'm sorry – I'm just – so surprised! You didn't say you were coming home this summer."

"Exactly. I wanted to surprise you."

Carolyn drew back and smiled into his brown eyes, taking in the neat feathering hair and dark red sideburns, the strong, cleanly shaven jaw. "I didn't think you so devious."

"Only where the outcome is good. And I'd say I was well-rewarded." He smiled back, then his gaze fell on her journal, lying on the damp floor. He took a step toward it, bending to retrieve it as he said, "Oh, your book! I hope I haven't caused any damage."

He was actually opening the front cover to inspect for water spots when Carolyn, feeling her face flame, snatched it away. "None whatsoever," she declared.

Dylan looked at her wonderingly, considering her response. She made herself lower the book from its protective clutch against her chest to the bench behind her.

"Er – you're looking quite well," Dylan said.

"Thank you. So are you. Would you like to sit down?"

Dylan hesitated. "Would your mother mind?" he asked. "Should we go into the house to see her first?"

Carolyn glanced toward the mansion. She saw her mother's lilac gown against the parlor window. A ruffled sleeve fluttered as Olivia waved. "I think she's fine," Carolyn replied. If they went inside, Olivia would most likely eavesdrop on their conversation. Better to stay out here. She sat down and smiled, prompting Dylan to do likewise.

"It is good you came today. Tomorrow we are going out to the plantation," she said.

"Yes. My mother heard from yours that your stay in town would be brief."

"Oh?" Carolyn raised her eyebrows. Should she be flattered that he was keeping tabs on her?

"Your father … how is he?"

"My mother says he will make it, but he's not yet strong," Carolyn replied. "So we have cancelled our plans for a European tour."

"I'm sorry," Dylan said. "I know how excited you were about that."

"Yes, well, I'm just glad Father made it through. I suppose it would be selfish of me to think of anything else. And it seems this winter and spring we are to travel in the North."

"Will you come see *me*?" Dylan asked.

"Do you want me to?"

"Of course. That is, if you wouldn't consider a stop in a New Jersey hamlet too boring."

"How could it be boring if you are there?" Carolyn asked, then realized how romantically that could be taken. She drew back a bit, folding her hands in her lap. "If it can be arranged, I'm sure we'd all love to stop."

Dylan nodded. "Good. Keep me informed. You do know how much your letters mean to me ... knowing there's someone here at home who shares so many of my views. I wouldn't say I've gone over to the other side by any means, but in all honesty, Carolyn, I've not had the courage to share my convictions about the future of the South with my family, either. Do you think that makes me a coward?"

"It's never cowardly to be cautious and gradual in one's approach. It's wise."

"Some things do take time. I just hope change doesn't also require war."

"Oh, don't let's speak of it, not when we have too little time," Carolyn said, touching Dylan's sleeve. "You know I don't say that because I have no interest in the political climate, but because ..." She let her voice trail off, for he was doing something very unexpected. He had taken her hand. She concluded faintly, "... because, like you said, we both already know each other's mind on the subject."

"And on many subjects."

Carolyn's hand was still clasped tightly in Dylan's. Her face – was it as red as his? Was he about to make a declaration? And did she want him to?

"It is my fondest hope ..." Dylan said, and she held her breath. He cleared his throat and began again: "When I think of the future – I can only wish for our continued friendship ..."

"Yes?" she prompted in a strangled voice.

"And – he looked away suddenly, releasing her hand – "that you might continue to write to me when I'm in school."

"Oh." Carolyn sank back on the bench. Had she imagined the intensity with which he had begun to speak? Maybe she had been way off track. There *had* been that word, "friendship." Was he discouraging her from hoping for more? Then why continue to write? "If you are sure that's what you want," she said.

Dylan jumped up and walked a few paces. "I would not wish to – *assume* your interest in continuing to correspond." He couldn't quite look at her.

"Nor I yours," she replied, confused by his mixed signals.

He didn't miss her vexation. "I *love* writing to you," he hastened to clarify.

Suddenly Carolyn laughed. "We are not so silly on paper."

"No." He turned and smiled gratefully, giving her the feeling that she had initially been right, that he had wanted to say more but was afraid of asking her to wait. His next words seemed to confirm it. "But you are no longer in school. You'll have your coming out. You'll be traveling. Things may change."

"Yes, I might actually have something interesting to write you about now."

"You were always interesting."

"Even when I couldn't polka?" Carolyn joked.

Dylan came back and sat down, taking her hand again and patting it. "Even when you fell into the goldfish pond and ran into your house crying."

"It's rather cruel of you to bring that back up," she teased him, though she knew he did not mean it that way. His touch was tender. She found herself wondering if there could be that passion between them – that electricity her mother had mentioned. She blushed as though he could read her thoughts and blurted out the first thing that came to mind. "Your brother – how is he?"

Dylan looked blank momentarily, then broke eye contact as he gently withdrew his hand. "Quite well," he responded. "All his wishes came true this past year – sergeant, anniversary speaker, standing first in his class. But then, that's no surprise."

"You're not jealous? Not as well as you're doing at Princeton?" Carolyn asked in wonder.

"Jealous? There's really no point. It's just a fact of life Devereaux excels at everything. But I will admit to being glad we're not at the same university."

"I was rather glad when Eliza came to Montpelier," Carolyn commented.

"Eliza looks up to you, and you're different enough that there's no competition."

"You and Dev are different, too."

"Yes."

A silence fell that Carolyn didn't know how to break. Dylan was watching her carefully, as if waiting to see whether she would press further. She had never known him to speak ill of anyone else and she sensed that while he didn't want to now, he would not lie to her, either, if she asked him more about his relationship with his brother. But somehow she didn't want to hear more.

"Will you stay to dinner?"

"Will you play the piano?"

She smiled. "If you wish."

"Then I'd love to."

Again they fell silent. Carolyn rubbed her finger gently up and down the spine of her journal, wondering fleetingly if they had said everything already in letters. Everything that could now be said, anyway. They looked at each other evenly, eyes meeting, measuring.

"Perhaps we should go inside and let your mother know," Dylan said suddenly.

"Know what?" Her heart skipped a beat.

"To set an extra place – for dinner."

"Oh! Yes, of course." Carolyn rose, tucking the journal closely under her arm.

Dylan offered to escort her. As they stepped out of the gazebo, the sun came out. But in Carolyn's heart, the fog of confusion remained.

CHAPTER SIX

Mid-November, 1857
Clarkesville, Georgia

Martha had grown concerned about her granddaughter. Mahala had worked with her usual efficiency and pleasantness throughout the busy summer and early fall months. No doubt of that. But there was also no mistaking the apathy which marked her personal life. So one afternoon Martha had come forth with her remedy. Mahala should accept Patience Blake's invitation to visit in Athens.

So one Saturday when the poplars still clung tenaciously to the last of their golden leaves, the scent of wood smoke hung on the damp, earthy air, and probably the last of the season's apples passed by loaded onto a schooner wagon bound for market in Athens or Elberton, Mahala embraced Martha at the stage stop.

"I'll see you in two weeks," Mahala said.

"If you find you need to stay longer, just send a message. But mind you're home by Christmas," Martha told her.

With a kiss placed on the older woman's cheek, Mahala allowed the driver to help her up. A vacant seat faced an elderly couple. Mahala was delighted with the unusually few passengers and settled down, giving a smile to the lady. The woman was quite large and was clad all in gray, giving her the appearance of an inverted mushroom. Her husband stared drowsily at Mahala without acknowledgement.

"One more passenger and we're set to go," the driver leaned his head inside to tell them, patting the exterior with his gloved hand.

Mahala scooted over to make room for the next person. Presently the high-sprung coach tilted as a tall man climbed aboard. When Mahala saw who it was, she cursed her ill luck and looked away with a sigh, barely restraining herself from the unladylike practice of rolling her eyes. Of all people … Jack Randall.

Hadn't she done her best to avoid him these past four months? He had continued to greet her with that same polished enthusiasm, all cheer and smiles, but Mahala had drawn the line at politeness. He had made it all too clear that day in the cemetery that his friendliness was intentionally shallow and would never be anything more genuine. Mahala had no use for games. Why now must she be squeezed into a bumpy stagecoach beside him all day? It would take at least ten hours to reach their overnight stop at Mrs. Nash's, and another three the next morning to Athens. She could not imagine being closeted with the man for that long.

When he saw her sitting there, he smiled expansively and removed his hat. "Of all the traveling companions I could not have wished for another, Miss Franklin," he said.

"I can't imagine," she retorted dryly, bypassing civility entirely.

The old woman's bug eyes darted between them with new interest.

Martha had come around to Mahala's open window, her lips pursed at the sight of Randall. She acted like she didn't notice him and reached inside to take Mahala's hand.

"Take care of yourself, my dear," she said as the driver climbed on top of the stage, Jack's luggage having been secured. "I love you."

"And I you."

With a final pat Martha drew away. She blew a kiss as the driver called to the team. Mahala's heart lurched with uncertainty and they were off.

Mahala pulled her hands inside her cloak and looked out the window, determined not to engage Jack in conversation. But he spoke first.

"Shall I have the pleasure of your company all the way to Savannah?"

"Now what would I be going there for?"

"I don't know. Why are you going anywhere?"

"I suppose you think country bumpkins like us *haven't* anywhere to go. I'm to Athens, if you must know, to visit Miss Patience Blake."

"Ah, yes, Miss Blake! Well, I hope you have a delightful stay."

Mahala turned to him, out of patience. She had no wish to banter all the way to Athens and arrive flustered and irritated. Better to end any notions of conversation now. "Forgive me, Mr. Randall, but why should you pretend it matters to you?"

Jack looked blank.

She continued, "You made your sentiments quite clear earlier this summer. I'm not one of your belles who would continue to be charmed by your show of gentlemanly enthusiasm when I know you could care less. I would suggest we ride in silence."

"Whew." Jack felt his mop of brown hair. "For a second there I thought my scalp was the latest recorded at Chopped Oak."

At the mention of the famous local tree which earlier in the century had been a tally point for whites killed by the Cherokee, Mahala turned beet red. She felt like steam could come out of her ears. The eyebrows of the old lady across the way, who had brought out a volume under the pretense of reading, went to the top of her forehead. Thankfully at least her husband was oblivious to Mahala's humiliation, having drifted off to sleep.

"You are incorrigible," Mahala hissed, scooting as far away from Jack as possible. "Quite obviously *not* a gentleman."

She stared out the window, her heart pounding in anger. Why, oh why, did he have this impossible effect on her? Why could she just not remain calm and impervious?

A few minutes passed in silence, then Jack slid closer to her on the seat and said just above a whisper, "I'm sorry. That *was* a cheap shot. I don't know why we always are at odds, Miss Franklin. I think the reason I can't leave you alone despite my own resolve to do so is that you are such an excellent debater. Even though we are competitors – and thus have that barrier between us, not to mention being much alike in nature, I think – you are by far the most interesting woman to talk to I've ever met."

Mahala turned to look at him, her eyes wide with wonder. She never knew what this impossible man might come out with next.

"Forgive me," he said earnestly. "Can't we call a truce? Wouldn't it be better than riding all this way fighting – or in stony silence?"

Mahala hesitated. He was holding out a hand. Finally she touched the tips of his fingers in a half-hearted shake. "Only if you drop the chivalrous front *and* refrain from any more mean statements. If, that is, you are *capable* of finding some sincere middle ground."

"Ah!" he declared, raising a finger to punctuate her own lapse of civility.

Mahala smiled in a gesture of surrender. She looked down.

"I truly didn't mean to insult your heritage, Miss Franlin," Jack continued. "In fact, I believe that's a large part of what makes you so interesting. I have often pictured you in earlier days as a fierce Cherokee princess."

"There was no such thing as a Cherokee princess," she pointed out.

"See? I badly need educating. Do you still speak the language?"

Mahala nodded reluctantly.

"You do? Say something in Cherokee. Say my name."

"No," Mahala replied.

"No? Why not?"

"*Tse-gi,*" she muttered, looking at the opposite wall of the coach.

"What?"

She looked at him. "*Tse-gi.*" As their eyes met, a chill ran down her arms and her heart seemed to stop. That was why she hadn't wanted to say it. "Jay-ge" came out far too soft, too endearing, in her native tongue, and there was no way she could effectively alter it. Jack seemed to sense it, too, for the air hummed in a suspended moment of awareness.

Then he dropped his gaze. "*Tse-gi*," he repeated softly. Then with a lighter tone: "Mahala – I know the English for that one. Michaela. You are named for your father. Why didn't you go by that when you came to live with your grandmother?"

Mahala shrugged. "Why should I? I've always been 'Mahala.'"

"Yes, but Michaela … it sounds stronger. It suits you."

She tried not to be flattered. "Are you named for anyone?" she questioned back.

"I'm actually William Jackson Randall, the first name for my mother's father in Savannah. Everyone just thought Jack fit me better, I guess."

"Your grandfather was the one who began your shipping business?"

"Yes." And Jack proceeded to tell her about its history, the years of shipping local crops direct without the Northern middlemen to eat into planters' profits. He also spoke of the various ships they had owned throughout the years, including mention of his father's role in the company.

"It's pretty much Father and me now. Grandfather has grown too weak to spend much time in the office, though we keep him apprised of everything, of course."

"And your younger half brothers? Have they no interest in the business?"

"No. I expect them to pursue careers of their own. I was out of the house when they were still quite young. I live with my grandparents when I'm in the city. I hate to think it, but that lack of bonding may have discouraged their involvement with Randall and Ellis," Jack said. "My little sister, though –" he laughed –"She's very much like her mother, but for some reason she adores me. She's quite the little beauty. I rue the day she'll come out into society."

Mahala smiled. "What's her name?"

"Sylvie. And her mother is Sunny."

"Yes. Mrs. Randall." Mahala laughed in remembrance. "Lovely names. But I expect growing up you missed your mother very much," Mahala observed. Her tone was careful, remembering his sensitivity the last time they had spoken of Jack's family, and low, keeping the conversation as much as possible between the two of them. "I know Nancy Emmitt was the best mother ever, but there was always – is still – a longing in me for my true mother. They say I am much like her."

It was Jack's turn to smile. "I can't imagine," he said, but in an endearing rather than nasty way. Then he turned serious. "You were very lucky, Mahala, to have had so many people to love you."

She stared at him, not certain what to say. She wondered if his statement signified he had felt a lack of love in his own life. But even more, she wondered if he realized he had called her "Mahala" instead of "Miss Franklin." Apparently not, for he merely gave a faint smile.

"Yes," Mahala said. "I'm sure that is true. I have always felt wanted ... sometimes even torn, which is *not* so good."

Jack looked uncomfortable.

"I take it you know about that?" Mahala prompted gently.

"Yes, though not in the same way. I have a great deal of family still in New York. That is, in fact, where I plan to spend the holidays."

"Oh. Do they want you to stay up there?" She tried to hide the fact that the prospect filled her with unreasonable alarm.

"Not so much that as they still have a great deal of influence on my way of thinking."

"That must not set well with the Savannah folks."

"Exactly so."

Mahala sighed. "I just don't understand why North and South can't get along. Just let each other be."

"Like the Cherokees?" Jack asked. Mahala darted him a frowning glance, and he held up his hands in mock surrender. "Now you have to admit it's true," he added.

"Yes," she said. "It is. I suppose my comment was rather naive, wasn't it? I *am* aware of all the complicated issues. I just hope a solution can be found. So you ... you don't own slaves?" Mahala ventured.

Jack shook his head. "No, although my stepmother and my grandparents do. The people are, of course, very well treated. Some are like family members."

"Like Zed and Maddie," Mahala said with a fond smile. She couldn't imagine life without them.

"Your grandmother's servants?"

"Yes."

"Do you never see an incongruity in owning them?" Jack asked. "I mean, considering the way *your* people were treated?"

Mahala straightened a little defensively. "That's hardly the same. Zed and Maddie have happy lives with us. We live together peaceably. They wouldn't go even if they were freed."

"Are you sure about that?"

"Yes."

"Even if they stayed, might they not want to be *able* to make their own choices? Like ... the Cherokee?"

Mahala frowned, uncomfortable at his line of questioning. She glanced across the way and met the old woman's eyes. In her uncharitable state of mind Mahala decided she looked more like a frog sitting on top of a mushroom than just a plain toadstool. She looked at the lady until the other passenger dropped her gaze back to her novel.

"Did I just break our truce?" Jack asked.

She softened. "No. It's all right. I've just never thought about it that way. But you are right. Most people do consider Negroes a secondary race, much like they did my people. You've given me some things to think about, things I would not have expected from a lowcountry member of the gentry … even one with Northern ties. You are a very unusual man, Jack Randall."

He gave a rather secretive grin and muttered, "You have no idea."

They passed the rest of the journey with idle chatter about the hotels, Clarkesville and Savannah. As evening began to drop its cloak over the countryside, Jack commented, "See? How nicely we have done during our truce. You're actually as pleasant to chat with as you are fun to fight with."

Mahala shook her head, at a loss as to how to explain in a non-romantic manner that a little genuineness was all she had wanted in the first place. She told herself not to stake too much on the progress they had apparently made today. She had thought they would be friends several times before, then competition had reared its ugly head. Or was it something else? Could it be that Jack was drawn to her despite himself, yet for some reason, when she started to get close, he would find a way to push her back? Could it be that competition was just an excuse, a cover for some defensiveness that went far deeper? Mahala bit her lip. She must not expect too much. There was simply no predicting how she and Jack would relate when next they met.

He helped her down from the stage at Mrs. Nash's.

"Oh, I can hardly stand!" Mahala exclaimed, holding both hands out to steady herself.

"Come inside, Mahala, and I'll get you a cup of coffee. You'll be right in no time," Jack offered.

"Oh, that would be very nice, thanks!" Mahala agreed, pleasantly surprised again. And liking the way he spoke her name.

As Jack went off, Mahala settled into a comfortable armchair in the parlor of the boarding house, a relief after bumping about on the rutted roads. Toadstool lady was passing on her husband's arm. She tugged him over and said when she passed before Mahala, "Mark my words, young woman, one day the two of you will end up killing each other, or willing to die for each other. I'm not sure which."

Patience's family lived above the Front Street bakery near Franklin College, which made business steady and mornings early. Each day of her stay Mahala was awakened well before she wanted to be by the tantalizing smells of sweet rolls and sourdough loaves baking in Mr. Blake's ovens.

The first day was filled with the excitement of catching up and the joy of shared recollections. Patience was quick to inquire into all aspects of Mahala's life. She especially wanted to know the latest about Clay.

"We are still corresponding," Mahala admitted, "though letters are rather infrequent between here and there. He is doing well, still working for the grocer, saving and looking for an opening to one day start his own business."

"So he has completely forgiven you?" Patience inquired eagerly as the two girls sat on her bed in their nightgowns.

"Yes, I think so. He avoids discussing that day he proposed but seems to have accepted my feelings at that time."

"At that time? Have they changed, then?"

Mahala plumped the pillow she held. "I've thought much about it since my time has been so lonely. I do long for him at times, Patience, but I've realized it is not because I love him. It would not be right to give him false hopes – which I think he could easily have still, from what he hints, should I give rise to them."

"Are you sure? Have not many relationships based on friendship and companionship been quite successful?"

"Would *you* settle for that watered down rendition of love?" Mahala insisted.

Patience blushed prettily, her long red hair framing her face. "Well – no."

Mahala sensed it was time to turn the tables. "Has some university student bought one too many sweet rolls?"

"No, indeed! As if any of them would seriously consider me. Oh, they flirt aplenty, but they are mostly sons of the well-to-do, and me just a simple baker's daughter."

"Then, there's no one?" Mahala asked disbelievingly, for she sensed she had been on to something.

"Well … there's John."

"John?"

"A young law clerk. He comes from an ignoble background but his employer has been so impressed with his intelligence and determination that he has offered to foot most of John's expenses at university. In exchange, John is to contract a number of years under his employment."

"Patience, that's very exciting!"

"Yes, I know."

"And how serious is he about you?"

"Very, I believe. We will just have to wait a while, a good many years, actually," said the girl sadly. "But I know it will be worth it."

Patience reached out to impulsively hug Mahala, who was touched by the gesture. But she couldn't help the seed of jealousy that had dropped into her heart.

That was the best conversation of their visit. After that, it seemed John was with them everywhere they went, whether at home, touring the town, or attending church – for his name was so often upon Patience's lips. At times she would catch herself and make a visible effort not to dwell on him for some time, but she was so in love with the young man that her thoughts inevitably circled round to him again.

That Friday Mahala met Patience's intended. They packed a picnic to take to the park, and John Sprite joined them on his lunch break. Before lunch he took them on a tour of the Franklin College campus, showing them the 1832 Greek Revival chapel and the two library societies, Demos-thenian and Phi Kappa, rivals which were housed in two handsome build-ings facing one another. John was a quiet, serious sort, squarely built with a cowlick on one side of the light brown hair sprouting from his forehead. He wore wire spectacles which he continually pushed up with one index finger. But he waxed eloquent when telling them about the university.

As they left the campus and walked to the park, Mr. Sprite asked Ma-hala what she thought of Athens.

"I am so impressed with the many fine homes," she replied, "and the numerous centers of learning – not just the university."

"Indeed," John agreed. "We have a thriving town here. Business has really exploded since the Georgia Railroad linked us with Augusta in 1841 and Atlanta in 1845. Then there are, of course, the cotton mills. You know we are often referred to as the 'Manchester of the South.'"

"No, I didn't realize that."

Patience squeezed John's arm. She said proudly to Mahala, "And *I* of-ten refer to *Mr. Sprite* as my encyclopedia. His memory for facts and details is amazing. That is why he will be so successful in law. Tell us about the latest case you are helping with, John, dear."

John smiled and began a description of his current labors which lasted almost their entire hour together. At the park, Mahala listened to his droning voice and resignedly ate her sandwich. It was a good thing she didn't have anything interesting about herself or her life to relate, she thought, since she was never asked. But she couldn't completely fault

John's personality. No, she could see why Patience loved him, for he stared at her with such adoration. He would be a faithful husband and a good provider. Patience was simple enough in her expectations to never find him plodding.

But Mahala couldn't help but feel there was one less person in the world who truly needed her now. She was ready to go home before she had thought to be, but with no real expectation of future satisfaction there.

CHAPTER SEVEN

December 1857
Off the Eastern U.S. coast

On *The Evangeline*'s second day at sea Carolyn carefully tucked a warm blanket around her father and adjusted his scarf to protect his face from the chilly breeze. He had drifted off to sleep on deck, after insisting he preferred the fresh air to a nap in the cabin with Olivia. Satisfied that he was adequately sheltered and amply touched by the afternoon sun, Carolyn walked to the railing. She followed it along to the rear of the ship, where she could see the rippling wake behind them, while still keeping Lawrence in view.

Always having been tall and slender, Lawrence's zest for life had made him seem robust and strong. But now a pallor seemed to linger about him. Combined with the fact that he had still not come back up to a healthy weight after the illness, a hint of weakness hovered, and it greatly troubled Carolyn. Last night when they had docked at Charleston, Lawrence had elected to stay aboard ship rather than to go into town to sample its pleasures, quite opposite the decision he would have made a year ago.

Stress over the cotton market had not helped. As feared, prices for the crop had fallen dramatically below last year's rate. The last of the bolls had now opened. It had all been dried, whipped, moted, ginned and bagged – all with the greatest care to preserve the quality of the delicate long staple cotton that would produce fine cambrics and laces for the wealthy. Despite another painstaking year of care and harvest, they had only gotten 45 cents per pound. This year, they had actually lost money.

Carolyn sighed.

"You are troubled, Miss Calhoun?" asked a voice beside her.

She hadn't been aware that Jack Randall, ship owner, had joined her at the rail. She had been a baby when Aunt Sunny had married Jack's father. In the ensuing years they had crossed paths a few times, but the tall, handsome young man before her was a virtual stranger. All she knew about him, besides the fact that his firm exported Brightwell cotton, came by hearsay.

She smiled. "A little, I suppose," she said shyly.

"Is there anything I can do for your father?"

"Oh, no. Thank you. He's fine. It just seems he should be stronger by now."

"He was ill this summer, correct? That's not really been so long. Scarlet fever is a vicious opponent."

"The doctor says his heart may have been weakened permanently. But maybe being away from the plantation will do him good," Carolyn shared, surprised at the way the man drew her out. Maybe it was the fact that they were rather like cousins by marriage. "When he's home he tries to do too much. Maybe he can rest at my aunt's house over Christmas."

"So you are going to visit your mother's sister, then?" Jack asked.

"Yes. That is correct."

Jack nodded and a silence fell. Carolyn was still usually too timid to carry a conversation long with attractive young men, but there was a maturity about this one that set her at ease. He had the confidence of a man much older than his years – and he was already a good ten years or so her senior.

She asked, "You are also going to visit relatives?"

"Yes," Jack replied. "My uncle and aunt and their families."

"I had heard you had a great many Northern relatives – on your father's side," Carolyn said.

"What else have you heard about me?"

Carolyn glanced up and flushed. "That you – also have Northern sentiments," she offered hesitantly, afraid of angering him.

But Jack merely smiled. He *was* handsome, she thought, although he did not have the effect on her Devereaux did. She had also heard more than one young lady plotting to attract his notice, though she wouldn't tell him that, of course.

"Do you find that quite horrifying, Miss Calhoun?" he questioned.

"Well – I guess it would depend exactly what the sentiments were," she said, tucking her gloved hands inside her cape for warmth. "Don't worry – I shan't inquire. But I think if we knew each other well enough we might find a common love of the Union and the principles for which it stands, despite certain … exceptions."

"I take your 'exceptions' to refer to a repression of the South in some political and economic spheres."

"Exactly so," Carolyn replied, staring at him with a bit of wonder. From what she had heard of his disregard for women, she would have expected him to believe himself above discussing politics with one. And she would have guessed him to have no patience with the concept of states' rights.

Jack turned to look out to sea. The sun was just beginning to lower in a partly cloudy sky. He seemed to be speaking almost to himself as he said, "Yes, I have a few misgivings about my visit North this time. I haven't been back since my grandparents died, she within a few months of him. Things will feel different. My cousins could no longer be considered moderates."

She was touched at this glimpse of the aloof entrepreneur's vulnerable side. "I hope you will find that familial bonds transcend any sectional differences," Carolyn offered softly.

"Are you not worried about relations with your aunt?"

Carolyn shook her head. "She is a Southern sympathizer through and through, despite her marriage to a Yankee."

"And where does she reside?"

Carolyn gave the location of the residence, adding that her uncle by marriage was a well-known judge.

"That is not far from *my* uncle's house," Jack pointed out. "Perhaps we will see each other over the holiday."

"Perhaps. We shall take in all the popular sights and amusements before moving on to Washington and Virginia."

"What lures you to Virginia?"

"You may recall that Devereaux Rousseau is in his last year at VMI," Carolyn told Jack. "He has written to us that Crawford's equestrian monument of Washington is to be unveiled in Richmond on February 22 and asked us to come. I believe your family is acquainted with the Rousseaus?"

"Yes," Jack said, searching her face curiously. "But obviously not as well as yours."

Carolyn blushed again. "We are distantly related," she offered.

"I see."

"Your – uh – ship is quite grand," Carolyn blurted. "I'm glad we booked passage with you. We are all very comfortable."

"I'm glad to hear it. You can just let me know if there is anything you lack," Jack said with a slightly amused smile.

"Carolyn?" A voice carried faintly to them on the breeze. Down the deck on his chaise lounge, Lawrence was stirring.

"Please excuse me," she said hastily. "I must see to my father."

"Of course. It's been a pleasure, Miss Calhoun," Jack replied, bowing slightly.

Carolyn turned and hurried across the deck to see if Lawrence was ready to accompany her downstairs.

Christmas 1857
New York, New York

Jack did not see Carolyn Calhoun during his stay in New York. That was all right with him. He had indeed admired her nature and bearing –

sweet and level-headed, much like Eva's had been – but it had been clear to him that the girl already had feelings for Devereaux Rousseau.

Things had changed in New York. Every last one of Jack's cousins had married and were now all parents, too. The new family members were constantly on hand. It seemed one party would just clear out when another would arrive, so that the house, while now devoid of the permanent occupancy of George, Geoffrey and Grace Anne, was never empty. Jack had trouble keeping all the spouses straight. And then there were the toddlers and babies. Someone was constantly thrusting a squirming bundle into his arms and exclaiming over how natural he looked when in truth he felt twelve again and just that eager to get rid of the little person. He thought if he ever did have children of his own he could easily skip the first three years of crying, nappies and drool.

Then there were the expected political conversations. The men wanted to know the mood of the Georgian elite, the working class and the slaves. They inquired if he had made inroads enlightening his family members. Jack did not like to talk about his Ellis relations. The Randalls and the Ellises were so different he knew he could never explain them to each other, and he didn't like feeling the need to justify any of his kin. He loved them all and preferred to keep those feelings close to his heart.

In light of the painful realization that he no longer fit in with his Northern family, Jack was glad that Jeremy Northrup was also staying at the Randall home.

On Christmas Eve just before dinner Jack, Jeremy, Houston, George and Geoffrey all congregated in the gentleman's parlor for drinks and cigars. The Randall men were discussing a new contract at the foundry. Jack was distracted by strong memories of the night, here in this very room, when he had practically begged his uncle to let him stay in New York after his graduation. How different things might be if Houston's response had been impulsive rather than diplomatic, Jack mused. But he couldn't say he regretted his years in Savannah – and Clarkesville. They had been rewarding in many ways.

Suddenly, he heard Houston say, "Jack, I have a peculiar Christmas present for you. And for Captain Northrup."

"Oh?" Jack asked. "How can we not be curious at that?" He watched as Houston rose and went to the bell pull. A moment later the butler appeared in the doorway.

"Is he here?" Houston asked.

"Yes, Sir. Waiting in the kitchen."

Jack wondered at the Irish butler's pinched look of disapproval. But Houston didn't seem to notice. He rubbed his hands together, smiled in anticipation, and said, "Good. Send him in."

"As you wish, Sir."

The butler soon returned with a startling sight – a huge black man dressed in a brown sack coat and trousers, with a black tie knotted about his massive neck. He held a Derby-style hat in his hands. Jack and Jeremy rose uncertainly.

Houston asked, "Do you remember Jim, Jack?"

For a moment, Jack didn't. Then the dark eyes met his – a thing rather remarkable in itself – and the memory of a beaten, cowering runaway in the hold of *Eastern Star* came rushing back. This now-confident man had been the first slave he and Jeremy had helped escape to freedom. He laughed in surprise and stepped forward to shake the man's hand. Jeremy did likewise.

"How long has it been?" he asked in disbelief at the transformation. "Five years?"

"Six, Sir," Jim replied, showing his white teeth. "Six years since you an' de good Cap'n here he'ped me on my way to freedom."

"I'll be," Jeremy muttered.

"I employed Jim at the foundry," Houston told them. "I never mentioned it in letters for safety's sake. He has been such an exemplary worker that I promoted him to welding foreman."

"That's wonderful," Jack said. He turned to the ex-slave. "And how do you like it in New York?"

"I like it fine, Mistuh Randall, but in truth I owes everything to yo' uncle and cousins. Dey took me right in an' gave me a good job where many would have turned away an' hired a white man instead. It ain' easy for an ex-slave to find good work here. But de Lord, He use your family. Now I got a wife an' three children. Every day I wisht I could thank de two of you again, standin' up in front ob you lak a man. An' now, I get de opportunity." Jim took both of their hands again in turn, shaking them gently. "Thank you," he said. "Thank you."

Seeing the tears of gratitude in Jim's eyes, Jack felt himself tear up, too. He abruptly cleared his throat and blinked a few times.

"I wanted you to see the fruits of your labors," Houston said softly, "the fruits of your risks. To see with your own eyes that they are not in vain. The others you have sent us are also well-situated. Some have gone on to other states or Canada, but I was able to find employment for a couple of them as maids, stable hands, and what not. Jim can read, Jack – Jeremy. He teaches the men under him on his free time."

"That's wonderful," Jack murmured again, smiling at Jim. "You have done well for yourself, just as we said before that journey North."

"Because you gib me de chance to."

After Jim was ushered out by the stiff-lipped butler, they were called in to dinner. Jack carried his expected conversations with the ladies on either side of him – charming belles no doubt meant to tempt him – but he felt dazed. He could tell Jeremy had been as moved by the sight of the ex-slave. Once their eyes met and held with quiet understanding. They might not belong here, but through the Randall family they had been a part of something bigger than themselves. Something that mattered. Whatever happened in the future, that would always be true.

Later, as Jack mounted the steps, he heard George call his name and turned to see his cousin, his old roommate from Princeton, hurrying toward him as his family donned cloaks by the door. George held out his hand, and the two cousins met on the stairs to shake.

"I just wanted to say goodnight, Jack, and … I'm glad you came. I know things have changed, but you are always welcome here with us. You know that, right?"

"Yes, George, I know that."

"Good." George started to turn away, then hesitated. "I mean, should you ever find circumstances force a change … you are part of our family. The ties between us, they go deeper than the years, and farther than the distance between North and South."

Jack found he couldn't speak. Wordlessly he clasped George in a brief half hug.

"Merry Christmas, Jack."

"Merry Christmas."

February 1858
Richmond, Virginia

On Monday the 22nd of February, an icy mixture fell heavily from the skies above Richmond. Carolyn peered out her window of the Exchange Hotel warily. She was loathe to leave the snug comfort of the Greek Revival building, which had opened in 1841 and been tastefully refurbished by John Ballard, its current owner, in 1851. Snow lay on the Gothic pedestrian bridge connecting the Exchange with the Italianate Ballard House across the way, and Franklin Street below was a slushy mess, churned by countless hooves and wheels.

Still, the statue dedication would proceed, for this was the 126th anniversary of George Washington's birthday. State governors and dignitaries had been arriving for days. On Saturday the VMI cadets had escorted General Scott from the Exchange to a reception at the Capitol, and had also seen Secretary of War John B. Floyd from the depot to his lodgings. Despite that, the Calhouns had not gotten to visit with Devereaux yet. But he was promised to join them for dinner tonight after the ceremonies.

Bundled in wool paletots and scarves, with fur hats and muffs, Carolyn and Olivia were escorted by Lawrence to join the procession leading to the Capitol grounds. Carolyn judged it to be a good two and a half miles long despite the weather. She proudly noted that of all the companies of cadets present, the group of over a hundred from VMI had been chosen to head the column. In the note they'd received from Dev he had confided that General Scott had remarked that the boys of VMI drilled better than the cadets at West Point.

The statue was situated northwest of the Capitol building, which was a brick over stucco, magnificent Greek temple begun in the 1780s. Nearby were other historic buildings: the two-story Federal Executive Mansion and the Old Bell Tower. But today all eyes were on the veiled monument. Everyone was eager to see the results of Thomas Crawford's seven years of labor. Crawford had died the October previous, but his widow was to be in attendance.

The surrounding ground was pretty well flat, but they found a slightly raised spot beneath a barren tree and there huddled together. Carolyn was amazed at the precise manner the cadets paraded, eyes front, though the mud and slush were ankle deep. She thought she saw Dev at the end of one line, sword held at attention, but from that distance she could not be sure.

John Thompson, editor of the *Southern Literary Messenger*, gave the opening ode. He was followed by Governor Henry Wise, whose speech hinted that the North was to blame for the problems of sectionalism. He called Washington's name magical, for before it he said "Feud and Faction stand abashed: – Civil Discord hushes into awed silence: schisms and sections are subdued and vanish; for, in the very naming of that name, there is … the strength and beauty of *National Union*."

Carolyn shifted uncomfortably and burrowed deeper into her coat. Freezing flakes landed on her eyelashes and nose. Her mind drifted to their recent travels. From New York they had gone down to Princeton, where they had spent one night. Dylan had showed them proudly about the university, and they had shared dinner at their inn. She had found him as devoted to his career course as ever. In the one private moment they had claimed he had confided that he had become convinced that even happy slaves deserved freedom – that it was their inalienable right, just as it was his. The blacks he had met while in the North had showed him what success they could achieve given proper dignity and education.

Carolyn understood why he did not wish to speak of such things before her parents, and she appreciated his gratitude for an understanding ear, but she could not help but wish that he had taken the moment to share more personal thoughts. He had, though, kissed her hand, and his brown eyes had glowed with devotion. When they parted they had embraced, and she was sure he had not wanted to let go.

Her attention was drawn back to the present. They were about to remove the veil. Everyone was still with anticipation. As the bronze figure cast in Munich was revealed, an unexpected ray of sunlight shone through the falling snow, illuminating the mounted leader in a moment of unforgettable nobility. A collective gasp went up. The incredibly life-like horse and rider were fixed on a six-pointed star. Some said that was a nod to Washington's Masonic membership. On each point would be erected smaller statues of prominent Virginians. Only Thomas Jefferson and Patrick Henry had been completed to date.

It was beneath Henry's gesturing arms that Virginia Senator Robert Hunter took his position to give the principal oration.

"This statue is not merely a monument to Washington," he said, "but an altar erected to Heroic Virtue itself."

"Carolyn," her mother whispered in her ear.

"Yes?"

"Your father does not look well. I think he had best get out of the cold."

"Of course."

They turned to begin slowly edging their way out of the massive crowd, the words "there is a promise in which we all confide, that the good which men do shall live after them ..." trailing behind them.

Once back in the hotel, Carolyn rang for a bath. The poor staff was overworked, so it took some time for the brass tub and hot water to arrive. But at last she gratefully eased herself into the steaming liquid foaming with rose powder. She was about to doze off when a knock came on the adjoining door.

"It's me," Olivia called. "I must speak with you."

"One moment." Carolyn hastily rose and donned a robe. "Come in!"

Olivia entered, looking a little peaked. "Oh, I'm sorry. You should have said you were in the bath."

"It's all right. What is it?"

"Your father has fallen asleep. Before he did he said how he wished we did not have a dinner engagement. I think I should honor that."

"But Mother —"

"I said *I* should honor that. *You* should go with Devereaux."

"Alone?" Carolyn squeaked. She pulled the tie of her robe tighter as if said person might burst through the door immediately.

"Yes. There's nothing improper in it. You'd just be right downstairs. I will walk you to the lobby to make our excuses and leave you in the care of your *dear cousin*. I'll have dinner sent up for your father and me. We'll set an hour, and if you are done early, visit in the parlor. If I'm any judge of character Devereaux won't miss us a bit."

"Oh, dear," Carolyn moaned. "Oh, dear, oh dear."

"Now don't take on so," Olivia said, striding to the armoire and throwing the doors open. "You should wear the new amber silk we bought in New York. You can borrow my topaz set to compliment it."

An hour later Carolyn was elegantly coiffed and gowned. Mamsie had come in to expertly arrange a fall of ringlets. Olivia had rubbed tinted balm on her lips and brushed her skin with powder. Carolyn kept tugging at the neckline of her dress, which she had felt from the beginning to be too low. Olivia lightly slapped her hands away. She strode to the door and opened it.

"A woman uses all her charms," she said. "They are our tools to get us where we want to be in life."

Carolyn thought if her mother had showed half as much determination to primp and press her and give her daughter time alone with Dylan, he might have spoken about something besides emancipation. And she would have had a far better chance of holding up her end of the conversation than she did with Dev. She gave a hesitant glance in Mamsie's direction.

The old woman looked faintly sympathetic, despite the merciless lacing she had just given Carolyn's corset. "Go on now, sweet girl," she said.

Carolyn followed her mother. Before they even finished descending the stairs she had seen Dev in the crowd below. He was taking his leave of another cadet who wore a sword of leadership like his own. When he turned and saw her he actually froze in place. He looked surprised.

"See?" her mother whispered. "Already we are off to a grand start." She gave Carolyn a little nudge in the back.

At the foot of the stairs, Dev greeted them with smart military propriety, clicking together his heels as he bowed over their hands. Carolyn caught a glimpse of the huge class ring, gold with a red and black face and an arm with a sword emerging from a shield. Every button on his dress uniform was polished to a high shine. He made a good expression of dismay when Olivia explained her husband's fatigue, but it was true that he did not seem to mind escorting Carolyn alone.

As Olivia bid them enjoy their meal, Dev offered his arm.

"So it's to be just us," he said with a smile.

"Yes, I'm afraid so."

"Afraid again?"

She blushed and felt irritated. But she forgot about it when she entered the dining room on his arm and almost every woman present glanced their way. Dev pretended not to notice, but he raised his chin a notch.

They were seated and studied the menu. In reality Carolyn was casting about for the first topic of conversation. Dev relieved her of the responsibility.

"Do tell me about your travels," he said, pushing his menu aside. "How was your time with your aunt, and where did you go after that?"

"It was a good visit and a happy Christmas. While in New York we went to the Astor Library – which I found quite fascinating – and the Egyptian Museum. When we left we went next to Princeton."

"Ah, yes – and saw my brother. How fares the earnest minister-to-be?"

Dev's tone bothered her a bit, but she responded, "Very well. He sends his greetings."

"Did you stay there long?"

"Only two days. Mother was impatient to be off to Philadelphia, where we saw the sights. After a week in Baltimore we took the train to here. We decided to go back up to Washington later this week and tarry there. We didn't want to rush our time there, but we didn't want to miss this occasion, either."

"And I'm so glad," Dev replied. He reached out to touch her hand, but at that moment the waiter arrived, so she withdrew.

"*Monsieur* is ready to order?" asked the fellow.

"Yes," Dev said.

When Dev glanced at her she replied, "I – I haven't quite decided yet."

"Then allow me." He proceeded to request a chain of dishes in French, from soup to dessert.

Carolyn sat resigned. She told herself it didn't really matter. Even if she had the presence of mind to make a choice she'd be too nervous to do more than pick at the food, anyway. When the waiter left, Devereaux resumed the conversation.

"So now that you went out of your way to come here, what do you think? Was not the horse and rider incredibly realistic?"

"Oh, yes! And the cadets – you did such a good job!"

Dev smiled in thanks. "Want to hear about our adventurous journey here?"

"Of course!" Anything to keep him talking.

"We left at seven in the morning on the fifteenth, marching eight miles to a point on the North River Canal. They had two boats waiting for us. It was so cold we were shivering in our boots. Our boats got so frozen up on the river we began to wonder if we'd make it through. The canal was floating with these big sheets of ice. One of the cadets fell out of the boat and split right through one."

"No! Really? Was he all right?"

"Yes, we pulled him out and went on. The canal flowed into the James and the Kanawha Canal, which took us into the city. I have a feeling a lot of us may be going home with colds."

"And hopefully nothing more serious!" Carolyn said in concern. "But you certainly look well now."

"Well, thank you." He grinned and she blushed again. "I did think the ceremony today exceedingly long, didn't you?"

"A little. My mother worried about my father, so we left early."

"Lucky you. I think my feet are still thawing."

Carolyn laughed. "I hope you had a change of socks. If you need anything, you have but to speak to my father ..."

"I'm fine, thank you." Dev met her eyes as French onion soup was set in front of them. He seemed to appraise her before turning his admiration to the steaming liquid. "Ah, this is a sight better than cornbread and Goshen butter."

"Is that what they feed you?" Carolyn asked, aghast.

"Well, sometimes ... for breakfast. But this is indeed a real treat tonight. I tell you, never was a man more ready to return to the comforts of home."

Carolyn sipped her soup a moment. "Oh, that reminds me," she said, "I wish to thank you in person for the oranges you sent us this past fall. They were delicious."

"Just as I promised." Dev grinned.

"Yes." She wouldn't say how touched and surprised she had been that he had kept his word over something so small.

But he seemed to read her mind. "It is my hope," he said, "that much more than oranges will pass between our families in the future ... starting with a summer visit to our mountain home. Would you come?"

Carolyn stared at him, transfixed, trying to determine the meaning and depth of his words. But she didn't have to think about her answer. "Yes. We would come."

CHAPTER EIGHT

July 1858
Habersham County, Georgia

As the carriage bore them through the verdant hills of North Georgia, Carolyn gazed raptly out the window. Her first glimpse of distant mountain ranges had filled her with delight. The Rousseaus had made good on their promise, even sending their personal coach all the way from Habersham County to Athens so that they would not have to endure the strains of a crowded stage. They had just passed through Clarkesville on their way to Forests of Green.

But everyone was not delighted with the journey. Still the ever-active one, Eliza shifted in her seat and moaned, "Oh, my aching bones. I need to stretch. I'm so tired of traveling. It feels like we are going into the very wilds. Are you sure this isn't still Indian country?"

"Don't be silly," Olivia responded.

"I still don't see why we're spending summer and fall *here* instead of in Europe."

Henrietta sighed and fixed her younger daughter with a displeased look. "Because securing a proposal for your sister is more important than a European tour. Besides, the mountain air will do your father good."

Lawrence offered his wife a small smile when she glanced at him. He had passed a rough winter, though spring had returned some color to his complexion.

"What if Dylan doesn't pop the question?" Eliza asked sulkily.

"It isn't Dylan I'm speaking of," Olivia said concisely, looking out her own window.

"Mother!" Carolyn gasped. "What would lead you to any assurance that Devereaux ..." She trailed off. Even saying his name as part of a discussion of matrimony seemed preposterous – despite his attentions in Richmond. Then, she told herself, he had been severely deprived of female company, and she had simply been available.

"Yes, they've both known Carolyn forever and have had plenty of chances to make their feelings known," Eliza pointed out most helpfully. "Things will probably just go on as before and we'll have wasted all this time."

"That's quite enough from you," Olivia told Eliza sharply. "Your whining attitude does not become a young lady of your breeding. It just serves to confirm my suspicion that the school at Montpelier failed utterly when they decided to open a section to men. Anyway, you will have plenty to do. You ought to be thrilled at the prospect of riding horses and climbing mountains all season. And you, Carolyn, are not much better, with your continued insecurities. Haven't you learned anything about feminine wiles? You have but to play your cards right to get one of those boys on their knee before November."

"Dylan is going back to school in September," Carolyn said calmly.

Her father began to chuckle.

Olivia turned to him in annoyance. "Oh, what's so funny?" she asked. "You ought to give me a little support."

"I do, I do!" he exclaimed with a half smile. "But Carolyn is hardly an old maid."

"Still, it's high time a Rousseau declared some intentions where she is concerned – and I'd much prefer Devereaux. But if I must, I'll settle for the younger one."

"I wasn't aware you were setting your cap, *Mrs.* Calhoun," Carolyn's father said teasingly.

Olivia bopped him with her fan.

"Forests of Green," the black driver suddenly called down from his perch above and before them, next to Mamsie.

Carolyn glanced out to see they were turning onto a narrow lane. The sunlight danced through the tree limbs. Up ahead she caught sight of a queenly white house.

Like Eliza, she was bone weary from travel. She'd gotten scarcely a wink of sleep the night prior in the Athens inn, due to the freight-train-volume snoring of a next door guest. But despite that, and despite her uncertainties as to the future, anticipation spiraled up inside her. She didn't want to speak it aloud for fear of breaking some silent magical spell, but in her heart she *did* possess a sense of expectancy, as if all the letters, all the meetings, might have been leading up to this visit.

And now as the black-shuttered, white-columned manse drew near, she almost felt as if she were coming home. A strange sense of belonging came over her, for she automatically loved the serene, private beauty of the place.

A bevy of activity greeted their arrival, breaking that serenity. Hunting dogs barked, servants scampered, and Henrietta appeared on the front porch. The carriage stopped, and a footman let down the steps. Lawrence climbed out, then helped the ladies down.

Henrietta rushed to them, embracing them all in turn. "Oh, I am so glad you are here! What a joy! How beautiful you girls look! I am so sorry to give you such a paltry welcome."

"Oh, are the gentlemen out?" Olivia inquired.

"Yes, all three gone over to G. H. Waring's at Annendale. They got word that a new Morgan horse had just come in and Mr. Waring might sell it. Believe me, I protested. What manners! But there was no stopping them ... too afraid someone else might get wind of the deal if they waited. I must beg your forgiveness."

"There is nothing to forgive, Ma'am," Lawrence said graciously, "for I would have done the same thing."

"That is good of you to say," Henrietta replied, as though she didn't quite believe him.

Carolyn actually felt relieved. Now she could take in her new environment before adding the unsettling elements of Dylan and Dev to the equation. She took a deep breath and smelled the spicy pungency of boxwood.

"Come in," Henrietta urged them.

The foyer lacked the grand elegance of The Marshes, but again, Carolyn loved it. A rug partially covered polished heart pine floors. Flowers from the garden created showy bouquets on tables with petticoat mirrors on either side of the hall. Henrietta led them into a parlor where shell and hair artwork mingled with pastoral paintings on stucco and plaster walls, painted a light blue. As she took a seat on a plush settee, Carolyn glimpsed another room adjoining this one, but with horsehair sofas, armchairs and hunting prints: the gentlemen's parlor or study.

They were served fresh lemonade and tea cakes. Carolyn felt like she could drink the whole pitcher before she succeeded in washing all the dust from her throat – and a handkerchief for a good nose blowing would come in handy, too – but she restrained herself and sipped delicately. Henrietta was watching her and smiling.

"Dev told us about your lovely visit in Richmond," she said, "but it's been so long since *I* have seen your girls, *Miss* Carolyn and *Miss* Eliza. We shall have a grand time. I have all sorts of things planned – parties and excursions galore."

"It sounds wonderful," Olivia said. "Let us compliment you on your home. It's so beautiful."

Henrietta smiled. "It's our oasis – and we hope it will be yours, too."

Carolyn waited for her to add "for the season," but she didn't.

"What do you grow here, Aunt Henrietta?" Lawrence asked.

Ever the farmer, thought Carolyn.

"Oh, corn and sorghum. Some wheat. Lots of vegetables." She smiled brightly.

"I look forward to a tour."

"Of course. Mr. Rousseau will be as delighted to oblige as he was on Harveys Island. But first I am guessing you might like to be shown to your rooms," Henrietta said.

Carolyn nearly sagged with relief.

Their hostess led them up the large staircase. Expecting to share a room with her sister, Carolyn was pleasantly surprised when Henrietta assigned them each their own, with an adjoining door. Their parents were just across the hall.

"There seems an inordinate number of bedrooms," Olivia observed in awe.

"Yes," said Henrietta, "the house just rambles on forever. There are actually six, five upstairs and one down, behind the gentleman's parlor. We like to have company, so when we do, Dev takes the lower chamber. He's still on military time, he says, so he doesn't mind getting up when the servants stir about. Just let me know if there's anything you need. Come down when you're refreshed."

With many thanks, Carolyn's family retreated to their quarters. Carolyn's room was painted a light green, which made her feel as though she were part of the woodsy world outside her window. Her trunk was already waiting at the foot of the high bed.

Carolyn unhooked the bodice of her traveling dress and let it and her hoop and full petticoat fall to the floor. A small cloud of dust poofed up when the garments hit. She bent down to unlace her boots and strip off her sticky, dingy stockings. She sighed with relief upon finding cool water in the wash basin.

After a sponge bath, Carolyn turned back the white coverlet on the bed and fell across lavender-scented sheets, ignoring the heap of discarded clothing. She was asleep almost immediately.

When she awoke, the sunlight slanted in the window from an angle, highlighting tiny dust motes in the air. She stared groggily for a moment at her surroundings before realizing where she was. The house was so quiet the only sound she could hear was the ticking of the mantel clock. She stretched, feeling much revived. The sense of expectancy stole over her again.

Rising, she dug in her trunk until she found a taffeta dinner dress. She tried to shake all the wrinkles out, then gave up. Donning her hoop, she dropped the gown over her head. Later tonight Mamsie would come and hang everything up, but she had been shown to the servant's quarters and no doubt told not to disturb their rest until called. And Carolyn did not have the patience to wait for her. She slipped a painted tortoise shell comb into her hair and earrings onto her ears. With her feet in comfortable slippers, she pushed the door open.

She tried Eliza's door first, then her parents'. No answer. Thinking she would find them downstairs, Carolyn descended to the foyer. A view into the parlors showed her they were empty. Across the way the dining room was vacant, too, as were the front porch and yard. It seemed this time of day even the servants were in their quarters or outdoors about their chores.

She stood for a moment in indecision. She did not feel at liberty to explore alone. Carolyn's eye fell on the piano in the front parlor. She had noticed it before. It was a particularly nice, new Steinway grand. Maybe she would quietly peck out a little tune until she saw a servant pass in the hall. She sidled over, feeling like an invader, and touched an ivory key. Sitting down, she gently rippled out a few scales. The instrument sounded just as rich as it looked.

She paused, then played the introduction to a popular love song by a lady named Sallie Ferry. She and Eliza liked to belt it out with great drama and exaggerated flourishes when at home. Now, Carolyn played and sang quietly.

Dev was in his downstairs room gloating over the papers of his new Morgan horse, Revere, when he heard the music. A second later a sweet voice began to sing:

I cannot love another,
For when in youth we met,
The flame I tried to smother
Lives in my bosom yet.

He smiled. The lovely young Carolyn had awakened from her nap and been drawn to their piano like a fly to sugar water. He rose and crept from the room down the hall.

Tho' other hands caress thee,
And other hearts are thine;
No other lips can bless thee,
With warmer prayers than mine.

Leaning in the door frame, Dev beheld the singer. She was lovely indeed, though a bit rumpled, he thought. But the tendrils of blonde hair that escaped from her braided chignon created a soft frame for her milky face.

"With a voice like yours, I can believe it," he said.

The engrossed musician's fingers jerked over the keys in a compulsive start, and her head snapped up.

"Oh!" she cried. Her face turned bright pink.

Dev was too amused for mercy. He came forward, adding, "I almost think you must have had someone in mind, you sang those words so tenderly."

Carolyn stood up, sweeping her skirt off the bench and against herself in a protective gesture. "No!" she replied. "You – you should have told me you were there."

"I did." Dev watched her frown and added more compassionately, "I'm sorry. I didn't intend to scare you. Your voice drew me right down the hallway." He reached for her limp hand, the one not holding the dress, and raised it for a kiss. "A pleasure to see you again, Miss Calhoun."

Her eyes grew big as saucers, and she pulled her hand away in obvious flusterment. Then, seeming to collect herself, she gave a small curtsy.

"And you. Thank you for having us. Your home here is beautiful."

"Have you seen it yet?"

"Only this room – and mine," Carolyn offered shyly.

Dev couldn't help again warming to the girl, as he had in Virginia. She was undeniably pretty, but seemed to have no airs about herself. Instead, she seemed perfectly swept away by his mere presence, a fact which flattered his masculine ego. "Then allow me to show you."

"Oh, I'd like that. Perhaps we'll come across the others. I have no idea where everyone went."

"My parents took your sister and parents down to see the pond. Did you not find the note? Your mother said she slipped one under your door."

Carolyn looked bemused. "Oh … no. I probably brushed right past it in my hurry to go out and find them. Not hard to do with these big crinolines now." She smiled.

"No doubt."

Dev was about to offer his arm when he heard boots on the stairway – hurrying down. Carolyn glanced at him curiously. The next second Dylan appeared in the doorway, red hair tousled and waistcoat halfway buttoned. Dev guessed that Carolyn appreciated his brother's eagerness to see her, for she displayed a rare natural smile and hurried across the room into Dylan's opening arms. As Dev watched them embrace, he felt slightly irritated at the freedom of expression Carolyn exhibited … so unlike her awkward response to *him*. The two were laughing joyously, and Dylan even chanced a quick little peck on her cheek, which did make Carolyn color up again.

"I think I must have dozed off," Dylan was saying, "then I heard this angelic music. It took me a minute to realize I wasn't dreaming."

"You were not here to greet me," Carolyn said sadly, the closest Dev had ever seen her come to petulance.

"I'm so sorry. I truly wanted to be, but father made me come along with Dev. I think he was hoping the both of us together could talk him out of his purchase, but alas, it was useless." Dylan shot Dev a grin. "He's a sucker for nice horseflesh. Forgive me, please?"

Carolyn surveyed Dylan's pouty, pleading face and softened. "Oh, how can I not," she said, resigned. "Besides, I can't start off our visit by being mad at you."

"I couldn't stand it if you were."

"I was just about to show Miss Calhoun the house and grounds," Dev broke in, impatient with the exchange.

"Oh, good, let's," Dylan agreed. And it was he who offered his arm. Dev drew his mouth into a flat line as he turned to lead out of the parlor. Then Dylan added, "Let's not stand on ceremony. If I can call you by your given name, as long as we've all known each other, shouldn't Dev, too? After all, we *are* cousins – once removed, I suppose."

Devereaux glanced back. Carolyn was blushing yet again. Her eyes darted briefly to his face, then down. "Of course," she said.

Dev resolved not to say it any time soon.

"Let's go into the gents' parlor first," Dylan suggested, wheeling Carolyn back that way.

Dev was obliged to follow. He did so grudgingly. It wasn't like his brother to be this confident and assertive. He clearly felt his past correspondence with Carolyn gave him entitlement. It was quite the opposite of their normal manner of relating to women. Dev found himself uncomfortable in the role of second fiddle.

Next they moved across the hall into the dining room and then into the library, where Carolyn exclaimed over the handsome bookcases and fine collection of volumes. He took her enthusiasm for politeness. He couldn't imagine such a bashful innocent as much of an academic.

Determined to take the lead, Devereaux stepped up to gesture into the butler's pantry. He pointed out the collection of jars and containers, saying, "This is where my mother supervises the canning each year. Behind this room is our kitchen."

As he entered, the plump, turbaned cook looked up. "Oh no you don't," she immediately exclaimed. "You cain' come in here, Mastah Dev. Ah'm makin' my stuffed goose. Cain' nobody see."

"Esther wants to surprise us," Dylan said by way of explanation to Carolyn.

"Det's right," Esther said. "It's my secret recipe – de purtiest bird you'll ever set eyes on in Georgia."

"We'll go out through the side door," Dev insisted, walking past the big beehive oven and inbuilt shelves that held massive pots and pans.

His path clearly did not please Esther, who frowned and muttered, "Only comes aroun' when dere's somethin' ta snitch. Jus' go on wid ya."

"I'm not snitching anything today," he told the sassy servant, not appreciating the light she cast him in.

Dylan placated her. "It's all right, Esther. We won't look." He quickly led Carolyn through the room and out onto the side porch. He gestured to a long settle bench along the side of the house, telling her, "This is where the servants sit to rest and cool off. Twice a week a wagon comes with cuts of meat from town and pulls up here in the side yard. Esther decides what she wants. In the fall, we can supplement that with turkey or deer shot here on our property. That is, Father and Dev can. I'm not much of a hunter."

Carolyn smiled. She and Dylan followed Dev across the yard into the nearby mint garden, where everything was carefully marked along neat paths. It was beginning to annoy him the way the girl kept clinging to Dylan, as though his younger brother was a knight in shining armor there to protect her from … what? *Him?* She obviously had only a partial understanding of Dylan's character, which was not surprising, he thought, considering it had been gained primarily from letters. Honest and true Dylan might be, but time in his company would reveal to anyone that he lacked a knight's bolder qualities. Dev just wondered how long such a revelation would take.

They had come to the formal garden, planned and lovingly tended by Henrietta. One perfectly manicured section was entirely devoted to roses. Another area was given over to a more casual profusion of native plants. Orange and pink butterfly weed hung over the path, attracting winged visitors. Black-eyed Susans were about to bloom. There were salvia, hydrangeas, carpets of white and purple phlox and tiny primroses.

"Oh, I could lose myself here for hours," Carolyn sighed.

"If you do, I'll know where to find you," Dylan teased.

As Carolyn twirled in delight, Dev, who was standing at the entrance to the rose garden, stepped back to snap off a perfect red bloom. He knew just what to do.

"Carolyn," he called, breaking his own resolution.

As expected, she stopped and turned abruptly at the sound of her name. He approached her and reached out to tuck the stem of the flower into a braid at the side of her head. As he did, her big brown eyes floated up to his face. She seemed moved – by the gesture or his nearness, or both. She touched the tender petals with a gentle hand.

"Now you are ready for dinner," he said. "And we're glad – I'm glad – it will be the first of many here at Forests of Green."

"Thank you," she murmured. Their eyes met. "Me, too."

Beyond her, Dylan's face came into focus, the lips compressed.

August 1858

Inside Selma Burns' English-style cottage, which had been built on the land of a wealthy church member, Mahala placed her glass on the table. She sat back and smiled at her hostess.

"Thank you, Mrs. Burns. It's been lovely, but I really must go," she said. "Grandmother and Maddie will have a cow if I'm not back in time for the lunch rush."

"I'm glad to hear business is good."

Mahala lifted a shoulder. "We're not quite full, which we normally would be this time of year ... except for the popularity of The Palace."

"Ah, yes," Selma sighed. "That Jack Randall. I hear he and his father went to Gainesville this year for the meeting of stockholders in the Georgia Air Line. If there's anything afoot to make money off of, he seems to be involved. Have you seen much of him this season?"

"We have met in town a couple of times. So far he's been good to his word and avoided offending me. But to be honest ... I also wonder if he's simply *avoiding* me. We've chatted, but we've not had the opportunity to really talk again since that time in the stage. I felt as if we had truly connected then, but ... apparently it didn't make a lasting impression on *him*."

"Or maybe it made too much of one," Selma said dryly.

"I would be presumptuous to think so."

"Oh, I don't know about that. So he can be very charming, hmm?"

"When he's not being sarcastic."

"And rakishly handsome."

Mahala sealed her lips. She had already told her wise friend far too much.

"Just don't let him rattle you. Keep your heart at a distance. I just don't trust him, Mahala."

"You or me, either." Mahala stood and slid her chair in. Her hostess did likewise.

Selma asked, "Aren't there other young men paying you attention?"

"The few who do my grandmother quickly finds fault with. She dismisses most of them as money grubbers. She seems to think the only men who would settle for a half breed would only do so to one day inherit a hotel."

"Mahala! Surely you don't really think that!" Selma exclaimed.

Mahala shrugged again. "Maybe she just wants to keep me with her. It *would* complicate living and working arrangements should I wed."

As they stepped out onto the porch, Selma slipped an arm through hers. "Think positively," she encouraged. "Have you ever considered that she just feels you haven't found one who is good enough for you yet?"

Mahala smiled. "It's true Clarkesville is not exactly brimming with eligible young men of my class ... whatever that is." She did, however, know what it was *not*. Martha would never approve of a common laborer, and the "summer people" were out of reach. That left precious few choices, even before throwing in her Cherokee blood. She sighed.

"Don't despair," Selma said. "I have a sense about this. The Lord has a plan for you. Remember that precious verse – 'For I know the plans I have for you, saith the Lord, plans to give you a future and a hope.'"

"'A future and a hope,'" Mahala repeated. "I'll remember."

She hugged Selma goodbye and untied *Unagina* from the hitching post, where the horse had been craning her neck to reach some long shoots of grass. Mahala mounted and waved before turning the mare down the drive and onto Tallulah Falls Road. The Burns' property was located just south of Forests of Green and just north of The Highlands.

Mahala had just gotten up to a gentle trot when suddenly *Unagina* threw back her head and reared. Trying to calm the animal, she realized that what she'd first thought was a stick was not. Right in the middle of the road, a six-foot black snake began to move lazily towards the trees.

"Whoa, Gina," she urged, trying to slowly draw the mare back.

Unagina fought her, then plunged forward onto the far side of the lane, breaking into a wild run. Mahala tightened her thighs on the horse's sides and pulled at the reins. Suddenly *Unagina* slowed and came abruptly to a halt, though Mahala sensed it did not happen in response to her instruction. The mare heaved and shuddered, shifting her weight to one side. Speaking calming Cherokee words, Mahala gingerly dismounted. She patted the twitching flesh, carefully looking the horse over. As she lifted the left front hoof she saw that Gina had thrown a shoe. In fact, one of the other shoes was loose, too. How could Zed have been so careless? He always kept the horses in the livery in top condition.

After a few minutes' search, she found the missing piece of curved iron a few yards back. Mahala put it in the saddle bag and sighed. There was nothing for it but to walk all the way back to town.

"See, that's what you get for not listening," she told the horse as she led her along by the bridle.

As if on cue, her stomach rumbled, reminding her that lunch would be long past by the time they got back to the hotel.

At length they reached the entrance to The Highlands. Mahala looked up the long drive. Her stomach flipped over as she spied a man on horseback riding down it toward her. Rex Clarke. It would seem her bad luck was only beginning.

"Come on," she hissed to Gina, trying to hurry the horse up a pace. Then she realized that was totally pointless. Unless she mounted and forced the mare to trot, which she would never do while Gina was unshod, Rex would be upon them in about a minute. She resigned herself and sent a prayer heavenward.

All too quickly he pulled alongside her, grinning with delight. "Why, Miss Franklin, what a nice surprise! Is your horse injured?"

"She threw a shoe just up the road."

"Ooh, tough luck. You've got a ways to go 'til town. Tell you what, come on with me back to the house. I'll have my man hitch up the buggy, and I'll drive you in."

Alarm bells went off inside Mahala's head. "No, thank you," she said. "We'll make it just fine." Then she saw he was preparing to swing off his horse. She added quickly, almost panicked, "No, no, don't let us stop you. We'll be all right."

But Rex showed no sign of heeding. Bridle in hand, he came around to her side. She saw that his skin had grown more florid over the past few years, and his eyes were bloodshot. Even his clothes looked a bit worn – not like the dapper outward image he had always tried to project. No time to think about that now, though, for he was actually reaching for *Unagina*'s line.

"Oh, come on. Don't be silly. I'll have you home in time for lunch and another of my slaves can follow with your horse."

"No!" Mahala drew back abruptly, pulling her mare's head out of Rex's grasp. The horse snorted in protest. Rex looked incensed. *Oh, God*, she prayed as full realization of the danger she was in came upon her, *please help me. Please send someone – anyone!*

She tried to quicken her stride, head held high and looking straight ahead, hoping he would let her go, but he was not about to. A hand snaked out, grasping her waist and turning her, almost making her fall.

"You're an uppity little wench, aren't you?" he snarled. "Cocky, just like your daddy. Well, he might have got away with it, but not you!"

Mahala grabbed for the saddle and hoisted herself up, knowing it was her only chance and praying God might give the lame mare wings. She felt

Rex clawing at her skirt as it slipped from his grasp. Then she heard the sound of carriage wheels. She was poised to ride for town, but the sound came from the opposite direction. She turned *Unagina*'s head and urged her toward the approaching buggy.

A black man was driving the vehicle, one she recognized as belonging to Louis Rousseau, though she did not know the fair young woman sitting inside. It didn't matter. Praise God, He had heard her and sent help!

"Whoa!" the slave called, halting his rig.

Mahala reined in right in front of them. "Please – I need help!" she cried. "My mare is lame and – and–"

The man's eyes went past her to the entrance of The Highlands. "Det man bother you?"

A sudden sob bubbled up in Mahala's throat so that she couldn't speak. The girl in the buggy was climbing down.

"Here," she said, "It's all right. Just you get up with me."

Though clearly skittish of *Unagina*, the blonde raised a hand toward Mahala, urging her to dismount. Mahala did. But she had to grab for the girl's arm as soon as her feet hit the ground. Detesting her weakness, she was nevertheless shaking so badly that she clearly needed some support. The girl helped her into the vehicle. Meanwhile, the driver tied *Unagina* to the back.

As Mahala settled onto the plush seat, she looked down the lane – only to find it deserted. "Where – where did he go?" she asked.

"The man who was with you? Up that driveway, I believe."

Mahala covered her face with a trembling hand. She felt the buggy sway as the servant made the knot behind them secure.

"Are you all right?" her companion asked.

Mahala lowered her hand. "Yes, thanks to you," she replied. "I'm Mahala Franklin."

"Carolyn Calhoun."

"Very, very pleased to meet you."

"Do you need some smelling salts?"

Mahala laughed out loud. She had always scorned smelling salts. "Yes, thanks." She took the proffered little net bag and waved it under her nose as they lurched forward.

"Better?"

"Much." Mahala looked up the driveway to The Highlands as they rode past. Rex Clarke was nowhere in sight.

Carolyn ventured, "That man, was he ...?"

"Yes."

Carolyn shuddered. "Will you report him?"

"I don't know. My grandmother will probably want me to if I tell her.'"

"So we're taking you to your grandmother? At what address?"

"The Franklin Hotel."

"Oh, yes!" Carolyn exclaimed with recognition. "You're *that* Franklin. Did you hear, Dewey?"

"Yes'm. De Franklin Hotel," the driver repeated.

"And you are ... a friend of the Rousseaus?" Mahala queried.

"Oh, yes – the buggy. Our families are related," Carolyn told her. "I am staying with them until late autumn. I was actually going into town to look for some fabric for a masked ball they are giving next month."

Mahala couldn't hide her curiosity. She studied the other girl's pretty face and fashionable dress with a tinge of envy. "A masked ball?" she echoed.

"That's right. It's so exciting, isn't it? What a change from summer in Savannah – when no one would *dream* of dancing outside, or even leaving open their shutters for fear of the fever. Dylan says they are forever thinking up interesting things to do here. I love it. You are very lucky to live here."

"You are very lucky to attend masked balls," Mahala observed with a faint smile.

"Why don't you come?" Carolyn asked impulsively.

"Me? I'm not invited."

"You are now."

"But why? You hardly know me. And it's me who owes *you* a favor now, not the other way around," Mahala pointed out.

Carolyn waved a small, white hand in a gesture of dismissal. "Posh," she said. "Forget it. I just think you should tell on that awful man, whoever he was. Who was he, anyway?"

"A lawyer named Rex Clarke, known for drinking and gambling – and womanizing."

"Indeed. I'm glad to know his name so that I can avoid him. Please tell me you'll report how he treated you. I'd hate to think of him trying it again."

Reluctantly Mahala nodded. "All right," she said at last. "And thank you, Miss Calhoun."

"Carolyn. Please call me Carolyn. And please come to the ball as my guest. I don't know anyone up here except my sister, and she is impatient with the whole idea. You'd be doing *me* the favor."

Mahala hesitated again, not sure how to speak her mind. "In case you didn't notice," she said slowly, "I'm half Cherokee. Not exactly on a level for mixing with the Rousseaus ... or their guests. Yourself included."

"I think I can decide who I want to mix with. Aren't some Cherokee very successful? Haven't they married into some prominent white families? Not that any of that matters. God looks on the heart, and so should we."

"But you don't know my heart."

"Goodness, I've never heard anyone argue so hard against attending a ball, unless it was myself a couple of years ago. Just give it a chance. Don't you want to come?"

"Well … yes. I admit I *am* curious. I've always wanted to see Forests of Green."

"Oh, it's lovely. We'll dance on the lawn, but the house will be open, of course. I can show you around. It's Saturday night in three weeks. Eight o'clock. Remember it's a masked ball, so you won't have to worry about being recognized – well, as long as you keep your face covered and wear long sleeves. Oh, and it's Shakespeare. You must pick a character and try to dress like them."

As they entered town, Mahala's face fell. "I haven't read much Shakespeare. And I don't know if I can come up with a costume."

"I have a volume I can drop by to you when we come into town for church Sunday," Carolyn offered. "Pick someone, and I'll help you with the costume. The Rousseaus have a trunk of clothes for things just like this. We do this sort of thing a lot on the coast."

"I hardly know what to say."

"Just say you'll meet me Sunday."

"All right. Oh – who are you going as? I wouldn't want to pick the same person."

Carolyn laughed. "I doubt you would. The invitation I'll give you says you're not to tell anyone who you are – or who your character is – until they guess. Then and only then can you remove your mask. I'm picking someone no one would expect for me. Lady MacBeth. But you mustn't tell anyone – and you must pretend not to know."

Mahala searched her limited mental store of Shakespeare knowledge. "Didn't she murder someone and then go crazy?"

"Exactly. Everyone knows I'm shy in company, unambitious and generally very boring."

It was Mahala's turn to chuckle. "You're awfully hard on yourself."

"You'll see. There's no more of a Plain Jane than I."

The vehicle had stopped. The driver came back to help Mahala down. As he transferred *Unagina* to the hotel hitching post, Carolyn said, "I'll come by Sunday after church."

"Would you have lunch with me – and my grandmother?" Mahala inquired. "I can have Zed drive you home afterwards."

"I'd be delighted." Carolyn had an endearing dimple when she smiled. Mahala wondered how she could be so modest. The blonde girl rubbed her palms together and tried very hard to look evil. "Now I'm off to find some red silk cloth – 'Here's the smell of blood still: all the perfumes of Arabia will not sweeten this little hand!'"

Both girls laughed.

"Where should I look?"

"Try Fraser's. He has more cloth than my uncle's store does," Mahala suggested.

Carolyn waved as they pulled away. Mahala felt a youthful excitement she hadn't in years. And all over a silly ball. What was she thinking? She had no business mingling with "the summer people," no matter how nice Carolyn was.

But for once she decided to brush aside her logical half. Her life had been dull and lonely long enough. Maybe, just maybe, she was about to turn a corner.

With a smile she turned to go into the inn and explain to Martha how what could have been a tragedy had become an opportunity. Maybe even a Godsend.

CHAPTER NINE

Early September 1858
Clarkesville, Georgia

The plans were carefully laid, the costumes selected. Mahala and Carolyn had visited twice at the hotel. It was strange, thought Mahala, how it seemed they already knew each other. She had never met such an unassuming member of the gentry. And Carolyn actually seemed fascinated with Mahala's life, asking all sorts of questions. The first was whether Mahala had reported Rex Clarke's attack.

"Yes," said Mahala. "I told Grandmother, and she took me down to see the sheriff. He said he would talk to Mr. Clarke. He said he'd give him only one strong warning."

"That's good," Carolyn replied. "Between your grandmother and the Rousseaus it will serve him well if word spreads and no one will give him the time of day, much less a case to try!"

As open as Carolyn was, Mahala had found herself telling about her background, her unusual family situation, the lost friendships with Clay and Patience, her work at the hotel – and even her competitive relationship with Jack Randall.

"Oh, I know *him*," Carolyn had said. "His father is married to my aunt! We sailed to New York on his ship *Evangeline* last December."

That had led Mahala to a bevy of questions of her own. She had only ever dreamed of such travel. She wanted to know all about it, and admittedly, how Jack behaved in other circumstances.

Despite their budding friendship, it was a surprise when Carolyn asked if she could come to the hotel to get ready for the ball. "You want to come *here?*" Mahala had asked blankly.

"Yes. It will be a grand surprise. Dev and Dylan will be expecting me to emerge from somewhere within the house. They'll never guess it's me if we arrive together in a buggy."

Mahala could see her point. Still, she had persisted doubtfully, "But are your parents all right with that?"

"Of course. After we first met I asked Aunt Henrietta about you, and she said the Franklins were good Christian people."

"She did?"

Mahala had wondered if the woman's commendation would extend so far as to invite her into their home. She said nothing else but resolved to keep a low profile at the party.

Now Mahala stood in her bedroom surveying her reflection. If she let herself dwell upon it, she would surely be overwhelmed by her own folly. She felt like a child playing dress-up.

Her character was Beatrice from "Much Ado About Nothing." She had been drawn to the girl's feisty independence, her scorn of the need for a man. She had certainly held her verbal own against the equally independent Benedick.

Mahala had to admit that she did look rather grand. Carolyn had managed to assemble a costume reminiscent of sixteenth century Sicily – a square-necked red gown with puffed and slashed sleeves, worn over a white linen kirtle with a small neckline frill embroidered in black. A corded girdle looped about her waist. And her black hair was braided with red ribbons and partially pinned up. She had a black fabric mask to tie around her head when the time came.

A knock came at the door. It was Martha, who looked her over with undisguised pride. "You are truly beautiful," she pronounced solemnly.

"Do you not think me truly foolish, too?" Mahala asked, her insecurities about to get the best of her.

Martha clasped her arm. "Why is it the few times you have had the opportunity to look in the mirror and see yourself done up like a queen, you suddenly want to cower? Why are you only brave in an old dress with a scrub brush? Go to the ball, Cinderella, and hold your head up high. No one deserves it as much as you."

Mahala stood looking at her grandmother in wonder. Could Selma have been right? All along, Martha just wanted her to hold out for the best? It did make sense when she thought of how Martha had helped her daughters marry "up." She had just assumed the same principles would not apply to her because Kawani had been her mother.

And there was truth in what Martha said. She *was* afraid to let herself be a woman – be a girl, even – dream a bit. She was too afraid of hurt or humiliation.

Suddenly Mahala launched herself into Martha's arms, thinking she had never loved the woman more.

Martha patted her back. "Don't look a gift horse in the mouth," she added in a low voice. "If this young lady wants to be your friend, let her. Heaven knows you need one. And she has access to many things you would not alone."

At that moment a throat cleared in the hallway behind Martha. The two separated to see Carolyn standing there. But Mahala's mouth dropped in astonishment.

"Your hair!" she cried. For Carolyn's beautiful golden tresses had disappeared, replaced by long red curls peeking out from beneath a white veil with a gold fillet.

Carolyn smiled. "It's only a wig. Am I pale enough, or do I need some more make-up?"

"No, you look – perfectly ghostly."

Mahala took in her new friend, who was clad in a green silk chemise and undertunic as befitted an eleventh century Scottish queen. Carolyn had tied a red scarf around her waist.

"I suppose that's supposed to symbolize the blood," Mahala said, pointing to it.

"Yes. Is it too obvious?"

Mahala smirked, already having been told about the curious love triangle between Carolyn and the Rousseau sons. "I suppose that depends on how quickly you want to be unmasked."

Carolyn laughed.

Minutes later, they were climbing into the carriage with Zed at the reins. Carolyn forced a big black hat and a silk-trimmed cloak upon him.

"What dis be for?" he cried suspiciously.

"Your costume," Carolyn insisted. "You can't give us away. Besides, it lends you an air of drama."

The old man harrumphed and clucked to the horses. He was certainly not in a position to argue. When Martha had learned that two of *Unagina's* shoes had been loose enough to throw, and that carelessness on his part had almost cost Mahala dearly the day she'd visited Selma Burns, she'd lit into Zed with her first threat ever to send him from Clarkesville. Though the stable hand had tearfully protested that he'd never been neglectful, Martha had refused to hear him out. He'd promised greater vigilance.

Mahala felt sorry for the poor man. He had enough work on him to keep three men busy, and he was getting on in years. She leaned forward to pat his shoulder. "Thank you, Zed," she said, wanting him to know she did not hold him responsible for her accident.

Her turned to smile at her, and proceeded to drive slowly and carefully.

The moon was coming up full, and the heat of the day dissipated with evening's damp. The trees cast mysterious shadows along the red road. As they left town, Mahala heard a chuckwill call in the thicket.

"Will your sister be upset when she can't find you tonight?" Mahala asked.

"Oh, Eliza – no. She probably won't even leave her room until later. She's not much into parties. All she can talk about is going to that new medical college for women – The New England Female Medical College."

"Really? She's truly going?" Mahala asked in admiration.

"I doubt my mother will let her. She's perfectly horrified at the idea. She says 'who would want a woman doctor?'"

"I imagine a great number of women would," Mahala said.

Carolyn shrugged.

"Do you not think it would be ever so much less embarrassing to see a woman instead of a man?"

"I don't know," Carolyn admitted. "I avoid it entirely."

Mahala frowned, digesting that. Rather than make a judgment on her friend's decision, she asked, "So … there's not a young man Eliza wants to see tonight?"

"No. She's determined to achieve her goals in life before marrying."

"And what of your goals? That is, if you'll permit my asking …"

"Oh, of course. I *want* us to be friends, Mahala. You can ask me anything and I hope I can do the same of you. No, nothing is much clearer. Dylan and Dev are both attentive. We have talked about many things, but nothing definite has been spoken." Carolyn sighed.

"It must happen soon, if it's Dylan you hope for," Mahala said. "For you said he'll soon go back to school."

"Yes. But truly, I don't know *who* to hope for."

Mahala said nothing, realizing she had only barely met Devereaux, and her judgments even of him were necessarily shallow.

"How beautiful," she murmured instead, turning her face towards the trees lining the Rousseaus' driveway. The limbs were hung at regular intervals with lanterns. While the full moon made extra illumination unnecessary, the lights sparkling among the branches looked like magical fairy lights.

The house was lit top to bottom with the open grassy area in the midst of the circular drive hung with more lanterns for dancing. The piano had actually been moved onto the porch. Its notes were accompanied by two fiddles, a bass and a flute. People in brilliant costumes – everything from "A Midsummer Night's Dream" fairies to kings and soldiers – milled about on the lawn and in and out of the house. A liveried servant opened their carriage door as they pulled up. Masks in place, the girls alighted.

Since it was a masked ball, their hosts were not waiting to greet them. Instead, the servant bade them make use of the downstairs bedroom – which had been cleared for guests' *toilette* – and enjoy the refreshments in the dining room and the dancing on the lawn. A midnight supper would be served *al fresco*, under the trees. Tables robed in white damask and floating chiffon, crowned with silver candelabra, were set to one side.

They walked toward the dancing and stood watching a Cromarties reel. The gaily costumed participants were very expressive when it came each couple's turn to stroll down the set. Some twirled, some polka-stepped, and some marched military-style to meet their partner. Mahala and Carolyn joined in the laughter.

Just to her right Mahala immediately identified Devereaux, though he was hanging back in the shadows as if to preserve his anonymity. Why he would pretend to try, she could hardly tell. His white robe, sandals and laurel leaf circlet said that he had predictably chosen the guise of Caesar, and no one else could carry it off so easily. His height and breadth gave him the bearing of royalty, and his dark, wavy hair shone like a Greek god's.

She turned away before he could observe her perusal, but not before he had caught her passing smirk of amusement. Immediately he approached. Oh, dear. So much for keeping a low profile.

"Good evening, ladies," he said.

Both women curtsied.

"I saw you over here looking smug. Is my costume that silly, or do you suppose you know my identity?"

Of course Carolyn knew. But when she remained silent, certainly to delay her own surprise a bit longer, Mahala decided to respond. Most likely he would not recall her voice, for their few meetings had been very brief. Besides, they could hardly stand around like mutes all night.

"You are our host, Mr. Devereaux Rousseau, O mighty Caesar."

Dev removed his mask. "I guess it was to be expected that I couldn't hide for long." He grinned, then frowned in concentration, surveying her garb. "But you ... I'm at a loss."

"As you are supposed to be." Mahala smiled, enjoying the banter.

"Well, whomever you are, would you honor me with a dance?"

"I ... I don't know."

"You don't know? It's the Gothic, very appropriate for tonight, don't you think?"

"I'm not familiar with it," Mahala blurted, then realized she had made a mistake. Anyone who frequented ballrooms would know all the dances.

"You're not? It's – very easy."

"All right," she agreed. As she took her persistent host's arm, and he excused them, Mahala smiled at Carolyn. The smile she got in return looked a little stiff. Hoping she had not irrecoverably offended her new friend, she went off with Devereaux. He quickly explained the steps and they got into line facing each other. All the while he was studying her curiously. And she was trying hard to believe this was really happening.

"You don't talk like you are from the low country," he said as the music started. "That leads me to believe you live around here."

Mahala merely smiled. Forward and back went the lines of men and women. The women passed under the arches of the gentlemen's arms and repeated the steps. The head couples circled and completed their sachet in a race to the end of the set.

"Say something else," Dev demanded.

"Everything looks beautiful tonight," she replied.

"Especially you."

Mahala felt flushed. If Dev knew who she was, he wouldn't be looking at her so ardently, she thought. And as flattering as it was, she wished he'd stop, for she could only imagine how dismayed Carolyn must be. She glanced around to find her in the crowd, indeed watching. At least she'd been joined by a man in a shirt, doublet and hose.

It was their turn to be one of the head couples. Mahala snatched up her skirt to run around to Dev's right side, then they grabbed hands and made a laughing mad gallop down the row, easily beating the other couple.

"Good job!" Dev cried. "But are you going to be this quiet until midnight?"

"Maybe my dress will turn to rags if I speak before," she jested.

Dev laughed. "But how am I to get to know you?" he asked pleadingly. "At least tell me if we've met before."

"Briefly."

"I know who you are. You're the granddaughter of Mrs. Martha Franklin."

Mahala's stomach dropped in surprise. "Yes," she admitted.

"I didn't know you were coming."

"I *was* invited," Mahala replied.

The music was ending. Dev stepped close to her to bow. She made a curtsy.

"It's all right," he told her, apparently having sensed her uncertainty. "I'm glad you're here. We need new faces to spice things up a bit. And speaking of that, aren't you going to take off your mask?"

"But you haven't said my name."

"Mahala Franklin."

She trembled slightly at the sound. "And my character."

"Oh."

Mahala burst into laughter. "You don't know," she said.

"I don't. But I'd surely like to see those beautiful eyes."

"I'm sorry. They *are your* rules."

"Quite right, Miss Franklin." He offered his arm and led her back to the spot where Carolyn was still standing. As soon as they arrived, Mahala realized with dismay who her companion was. And it was clear from his sardonic smile that he recognized her, too.

"Good evening, Miss Franklin," Jack said. "Young Caesar here didn't figure out who you were?"

"He did, but not my character," she replied.

"It would seem our costumes bear some similarities," Jack pointed out.

"Yes, they do," Carolyn exclaimed. "Could it be that you are people from the same play?"

"Why don't we conspire upon it while we are dancing?" Jack asked her. "Maybe you can whisper a clue in my ear. That is, if you will honor me, Miss Calhoun."

Dev's head turned sharply. "*Miss Calhoun?*" he repeated.

Carolyn laughed in delight.

"And Lady MacBeth," Jack added, reaching back to untie Carolyn's mask. He took it and tucked it into his pocket as Dev watched. "Did you not know a lady from under your very roof, Mr. Rousseau? Apparently – you did not."

Mahala had the sensation that Jack intended for more than one meaning to apply. And for some reason that was unsettling – to her as well as to Devereaux, who frowned slightly as Jack led Carolyn off to waltz. He held her at a respectable distance and twirled slowly, but with a tender respect. She laughed gaily at something he was saying.

"I would have never pegged her for Lady MacBeth," Dev murmured.

At that moment a portly older gentleman asked Mahala to dance. Dev looked momentarily irritated, but relinquished her attention gracefully. Mahala allowed the man to escort her onto the dancing lawn. She made small talk while looking over his shoulder, watching Jack and Carolyn and wondering where Dev had disappeared to.

As the dance concluded, a Spanish waltz was announced. Mahala waited on the sideline, noticing that Carolyn had already been claimed by a dashing black-haired gentleman. Then she saw Jack approaching. She felt a rush of conflicting emotions. He bowed before her and asked if she would be his partner.

"That depends," she said coyly. "Did Carolyn tell you who I am?"

"I already know who you are," Jack said meaningfully.

Uncomfortable, Mahala prodded, "I meant my Shakespeare character."

"She was amazingly impervious to charm *and* cajoling," he said with a grin.

"All right, then." Mahala offered him her hand.

He pulled her quickly into the circle facing another couple. "Having a good time?" Jack asked.

"Yes. I was very touched that Carolyn insisted I come. As you know, this is quite above and beyond my daily life."

"She's very thoughtful," Jack agreed.

Mahala felt inexplicably irritated at the comment. But she smiled as they waltzed forward to greet their opposites, then she turned under the gentleman's arm. Another forward and back and she returned to Jack.

"It's rather silly, though, if you ask me," Mahala added.

"What is?"

"Shakespeare. People plotting murder, going mad left and right, and committing suicide by eating hot coals or letting asps bite them."

They parted, then came together again.

"In its condensed package it may be a bit extreme," Jack said, "but if you consider our daily actions in a milder form, wouldn't you agree there are some similarities?"

They formed a right-hand star with the other couples, then reversed their direction. Their eyes met, and Mahala fought down the silly lighthearted sensation of rising attraction.

"Maybe."

Jack swept her into his arms so firmly she was startled. He waltzed back to back with the other man, then the ladies passed back to back as they swirled around each other in a graceful progression through the circle. Jack made the group waltz easy.

"You like Shakespeare, then?" Mahala asked as they began the movements again.

"I like real life action."

"Then why are you here? For surely this is a make-believe night."

They danced with the new couple, smiling politely. When they were again in closed position he answered. "I came to see how Miss Calhoun was faring. When we met aboard my ship last year I was impressed by the same sweetness of character that must have drawn you."

An unexpected sensation – totally different from what she had experienced only moments ago – burned suddenly inside Mahala. Knowing they were about to face yet another couple, she answered impulsively, and a little waspishly, "Well, anyone who truly knows her well knows her feelings are already engaged."

Jack smiled at the other lady and frowned at her. "I realize that. If the two who so admire her – who shall for obvious reasons go unnamed – weren't such numbskulls, they would have both proposed a long time ago."

Surprised at hearing that from one so fiercely independent, Mahala could only believe it confirmed Jack's own attraction to Carolyn. She had not expected to find them acquainted, much less connected. But then, what did she know? She hardly moved in their circles.

"Why so sour all of a sudden? Surely you're not jealous," Jack said teasingly. "You can hardly have believed I came to see *you*, when I had no reason to think you'd be here."

Mahala's temper flared. "Don't flatter yourself," she snapped.

Jack sighed in a martyr-like fashion. "Why does everyone find it so hard to believe I could be an admirer of those of the opposite sex in merely a friendly, unattached sort of way? 'Because I will not do them the wrong to mistrust any, I will do myself the right to trust none ... I will live a bachelor.'"

Jack's words didn't fully register amidst the movements of the dance. "*What* are you rambling about, Mr. Randall?" she asked. Then she giggled as one of her character's best lines came suddenly to mind. She quoted aloud to herself, "'I wonder that you will still be talking ... nobody marks you.'"

"What was that?" Jack nearly stopped the right-hand star, staring at her.

"I'm sorry?" she questioned blankly, thinking she had now offended him.

They reversed directions, but his eyes were still on her. As if testing her, he said with wonder, "'It is certain I am loved of all ladies, only you excepted.'" He took her into his arms again.

Realization was dawning fast. She quoted faintly the only other line she had memorized from her character's part in the play, though it sounded far less witty now. "'I had rather hear my dog bark at a crow than a man swear he loves me.'"

Their gazes locked, they stood still. It was a good thing the music was ending.

"Beatrice?" Jack asked.

"Benedick?"

The irony was choking. Jack pulled the string of her mask, and it dropped to the grass. Then he removed his own.

"Well, now we know each other," he said. As he tucked away his mask, he asked, "Did you read the end of the play?"

Mahala only stared at him mutely. In fact, she had been too busy with work and preparing her costume to do so. Jack didn't smile or explain. He just walked off.

A few minutes later, Carolyn found her and they went into the house to get some punch. Then Carolyn took her on a tour, including her own beautiful guest room and the fragrant rose garden. All the while Carolyn chatted happily, telling Mahala how she had known Dylan even with his hair blacked and some sort of oil on his skin, though she hadn't been able to guess the part he was dressed as. Listening absently, Mahala felt like she was in a daze. She kept mentally returning to that moment at the end of her dance with Jack.

"And was Devereaux's face not priceless when Jack unmasked me?" Carolyn was asking.

"Oh – yes. Carolyn, what happens at the end of 'Much Ado About Nothing'? Between Beatrice and Benedick, I mean."

Carolyn looked at her blankly, then she said, "Why of course they finally admit they are madly in love and live happily ever after."

Carolyn lay on her bed at Forests of Green, face down. She was fairly suffocating – not in the covers, but in her own confusion and misery. Tomorrow Dylan would leave for his last year at seminary. And still he had not spoken. She wondered if Devereaux had been around less if he would have. At first Dylan had not seemed put off by his brother's presence and attentions to Carolyn. But as the weeks passed he had become less forward, almost resigned. In all fairness, Devereaux had given them little time alone. Their outings had all been group affairs. The few times Dylan had gone out of his way to arrange something for just the two of them, Devereaux had inevitably appeared.

She thought back to the night of the Shakespeare ball. It had been Dylan who had been the last unmasked, declaring during the supper before all assembled that he was Antonio of "The Merchant of Venice."

"Ah, the faithful friend and supporter," Dev had declared, standing and clapping an arm about Dylan. "And the best of brothers."

Everyone had then toasted the hosts.

Faithful friend. Was that supposed to have a special significance in the eternal scheme of things? Carolyn wondered. She was forever asking God for a sign, but so far none had been forthcoming.

A whisper of a sound made her turn over on the bed and squint in the evening light. A small white piece of paper had been slid under her door. Her heart rate picked up a notch.

Rising, Carolyn went and knelt to retrieve it. She stood, unfolding the paper. In masculine hand she read:

Meet me tonight on the widow's walk. 10 p.m. D. R.

She knew the handwriting was not Dylan's. Her heart thundered now. What was Devereaux suggesting? And should she oblige? It was surely not proper. But she already knew she would go.

In his shirtsleeves, Devereaux sat on a bench atop the narrow widow's walk crowning the mansion's hipped roof. He jiggled a leg impatiently and tried to content himself with watching the half moon rise.

Would she come?

He had written the note on impulse, though he had wanted for some time to see how she would respond to him alone, without the distraction of his steady little brother. If his internal sensors were correct – and they usually were where women were concerned – it was he, Dev, who stirred her.

He still wasn't entirely sure he wanted it that way. As far as attraction went, Mahala Franklin was much more his type. He sucked in his breath at the thought of her. Earthy and strong, with a cutting beauty and a tongue to match. But Mahala was fantasy. His family would never approve. Carolyn was reality. He felt his parents' subtle pressure toward her. She *was* comely, in a sweet and quiet sort of way. He generally didn't think much of the shy, fainting type, but knowing he elicited such admiration from the girl was rather gratifying. As a wife she would be easy to manage. That would have its advantages.

He wished they grew rice at Brightwell instead of cotton. Oh, well. It was still a pretty parcel.

It was not completely out of his mind that Dylan was leaving tomorrow – and might actually make some sort of declaration to Carolyn before departing. He was not yet sure if he wanted to circumvent that, though he had to admit the thought of Dylan living with her beneath his nose rubbed him the wrong way. He would just see what happened tonight, and go with his feelings. If she came.

She would come.

A movement confirmed it. Carolyn's head appeared in the trap door. He jumped up to help her climb atop the roof. He was surprised to see that she wore her hair loose. It curled down her back past the curving waist of her golden gown. It struck him as a vulnerable move – and an appealing one.

"You look like a wood sprite," he blurted out.

She smiled with pleasure.

"I didn't know if you would come. It occurred to me after I slipped you the note that I should have written something about star gazing, so you wouldn't think me a rogue," Dev said, gesturing to the handsome brass telescope behind him. "You said you enjoyed astronomy at Montpelier?"

"Yes, I did." She looked interested, and faintly relieved.

"I wanted to show you something. Come. You don't need the telescope to see this." Dev drew her along the roof so that they were looking northwest. He braced her with one arm and pointed with the other. "There. See? Just below the Dipper."

"The comet?"

117

"Exactly," Dev said, looking from the streak of light that appeared to be about two feet long from the distance to Carolyn's face. "Do you know about it?"

"Only that there is one. But do tell me."

Devereaux smiled. "It's Donati's Comet, named for the Italian astronomer who discovered it in early June. It's the most brilliant since the Great Comet of 1811. It was first seen in 1556. Charles the Fifth was so alarmed at its appearance that he abdicated his throne and lived the rest of his life in a convent."

"No! Really?" Carolyn exclaimed, turning to look at him.

"Indeed. It's supposed to be visible every 292 years, but it ventured too near some of the remoter planets and was drawn off its course. Here, if you wish to see it closer, look through the lens." He helped her get situated, then added, "The tail is six million miles long, and it is now about 87 million miles from us."

"Oh, what marvels it must have traveled through," Carolyn breathed in quiet awe. She stepped back from the lens to ask, "Aren't comets supposed to be portents of war?"

Dev nodded. "So it's said. Though some would argue that the Dipper – the Great Bear – has it under its foot, so this time we'll be all right."

"Let's hope that '*some*' are right."

"Yes."

"Are there more comets?"

"That is, I think, the fifth discovered this year. Two or three others are still visible. I think I can find one of them for you, though I don't know its name." Dev adjusted the lens, panning slowly for a moment, before drawing back for Carolyn to gaze again. "There."

"Ah, I see. The view is certainly remarkable from up here."

"Clear, isn't it? Like sitting on top of the world. That's why I wanted to bring you up. We'll have to come back in a couple of weeks during the day to enjoy the leaves at their peak."

"I'd like that." Her face popped up, glowing in the pale light. Her hair swung over her shoulder. "I'm going to look at the moon now, all right?"

"Have at it." Dev chuckled. He watched her in silence, thinking that she *was* rather a prize. There really wasn't anyone else eligible who had caught his eye.

"It seems to be stuck," Carolyn said suddenly.

Dev bent in close to adjust a stubborn gear. She raised her head to thank him just as he raised his, placing their faces only inches apart. Her words died on her lips. Dev made a split decision, if it could even be called that – a reaction, really. He swooped in and sealed her lips with his. They straightened, mouths joined, his one hand going to her neck and the other to her waist. He didn't even move his mouth, really. It was certainly not what he'd term a passionate kiss – not yet, anyway – but the second he drew his face back a fraction her knees buckled and he found himself holding her up.

He was about to pull her to him when she groped behind her for the bench. He released her, a little cheated, and she sank down weakly. She looked from him to the moonlit hills in a dazed manner.

"Are … are you angry?" he ventured.

She raised a hand to tell him she needed a moment. Then she asked, "Why did you do that?"

"I like you?"

"You *like* me? You like all women."

"Hey, now, that's not fair. I've never —"

"You've certainly charmed a lot of them. Why am I to believe I'd be anything special? Because I'm Dylan's friend?"

Her directness amazed him. He had expected romantic sentiments, not accusations. "If I didn't have feelings for you I never would have kissed you. If I've overstepped my bounds, you've but to say so."

Carolyn shook her head, a hand at her heart. She seemed confused and again unable to speak.

"Do you find me offensive then?" Dev demanded, knowing she did not but hoping loyalty to his brother would not cause her to pull away from him.

She stood up suddenly, and he saw there were tears in her eyes. "Don't toy with me!" she exclaimed. "Don't – don't toy with me!"

Carolyn snatched up her skirts and started climbing down the ladder into the attic.

"Wait, Carolyn. I'm not!"

But she was gone, disappearing through the hole into the house.

In his bedroom, Dylan turned over on his feather mattress at the sound of footsteps in the hall. A door quietly closed. A few minutes later heavier, though still stealthy, steps were heard on the back stairs, continuing down another flight. He knew exactly who it was and where they'd been.

A minute later he heard muffled sobbing. He rose on one elbow, a sense of agony piercing him. Whatever had happened, whether Carolyn now felt she loved or hated his brother, it was clear that her feelings for Dev were just as strong as Dylan had suspected … and feared.

The knowledge had risen slowly, over weeks of quietly watching every blush, every glance. And he hated it. For this was one thing he had wanted for himself. Despite his growing depression over the situation, he had wanted it so bad he had even managed to talk himself into laying it all on the line tomorrow morning. He had told himself it was just his reticence – for who wouldn't be reticent when feelings ran so deep, and so much was at stake – that had stood between him and Carolyn's acceptance. He knew she cared for him, after all. He ought to give her the chance to say so, having heard his own ardent declaration. And if she cared enough another year or two of waiting would be little enough to ask.

Now he knew he could never do it. There was no room in his life for someone so moved by another man – certainly not by his own brother, who would always be in close proximity. Devereaux had won again. As always.

The following morning Dev took Revere out for a canter. The semi-coolness of the early hour and the time on horseback cleared his head. The manner in which Carolyn had held herself away from him last night, combined with Dylan's interest, had upped the anty another notch. He had decided that he would see her before breakfast and declare that she had engaged his affections as no other lady ever had, and that he would be honored to court her, if she and her father were willing. He would make her his. The possibility of defeat never entered his mind.

He was, however, surprised to see a feminine figure approaching as he brushed down Revere in the stall. Not Carolyn, but her mother. Now this might be interesting.

"Good morning, Mr. Rousseau," said the poised, stately Olivia.

"Good morning, Ma'am. You are up early."

"Yes," she said vaguely. "I did not sleep well, what with all the comings and goings of the night."

Dev paused, brush in mid-air. "Oh?"

"Don't act innocent, young man. I know everything."

"You know everything?"

She nodded, but instead of expanding on the subject, asked unexpectedly, "Why do you groom your own horse? Don't you trust your servants to do the job well?"

"Of course. I merely enjoy taking good care of what's mine."

"I'm counting on it."

"Pardon me?" Dev was growing exasperated.

"My daughter, Mr. Rousseau, whom I found in tears after ten last night. Absolutely undone following your trifling."

Dev stood up straight and said firmly, "Now listen here, Ma'am, I hardly consider a peck of a kiss to be trifling – begging your pardon," he added as a nod to respect.

"Then you surely underestimate the weight of her feelings for you. Am I to assume you do not share that burden of affection?"

"On the contrary, Ma'am, I find Miss Carolyn very pleasing."

Olivia pursed her lips. She watched him a minute. Dev felt that she must consider various cuts of meat with the same degree of scrutiny. Finally she said, "There are many of the old school who still believe that a kiss is a liberty that should only be taken *after* a proposal of marriage. If you act quickly perhaps a certain gentleman of that persuasion will not be too offended."

"Mr. Calhoun? You mean you – he –?" Dev couldn't believe the direction the conversation was taking. He had not planned to move *that* rapidly.

"We greatly value our relationship with your family, and would be pleased to see more of you in the future. We can only do so if Carolyn's ruffled feathers are soothed and her father satisfied. So you see, some form of permanent settlement must be reached. But of course I would not urge you to act against your own inclinations."

"I am never pressed into acting against my inclinations," Dev replied succinctly. He didn't like being pushed around, even if he was not opposed to the general direction.

"I'm sure that's true," Olivia said in a slightly sour tone. "Well, now you know where we stand on the matter. The rest is up to you. Carolyn is in the garden, should you wish to seek her out."

Having thus spoken, Olivia turned and walked away.

The page of her journal blurred before her even in the golden morning sun, so weary were Carolyn's eyes. She doggedly scratched out a few more lines before shifting on the wrought iron bench. Stretching out her legs, she flexed her hand and looked around.

She had felt blessedly hidden in the perennial garden, but she saw it was not so. A masculine figure came into view, causing her to quickly straighten, drawing her legs back under her seat. The effect the sight of Devereaux had on her insides made her feel suddenly certain of what she had just written in her diary. She loved him. Adored every inch of him from his black riding boots to his wavy dark hair, hung on every pronouncement from his lips, feasted on every smile. More than anything, she longed to get into his head and understand his thinking – to know him beyond the charming surface.

But was her love of the sort to last years, or merely the fickle stirrings of youth?

And had he come to take back his doings of their previous meetings, or to lay a foundation?

She snapped her journal shut and sat waiting, watching him approach with her heart hammering beneath her muslin bodice.

He stopped before her and surveyed her for an instant. Did he note the shadows beneath her eyes, the tremor to her hands? If he marked it he gave no indication. She determined that he should speak first.

At length he did. "Miss Carolyn – Carolyn … it was not my intention to give you offense last night. If I did, I'm here to ask your forgiveness."

"You did not offend me … merely confused me," she confessed softly.

"Will you tell me how I can provide clarification?"

Stubborn man. She would not beg to know his feelings. "No, Sir, I cannot. That is something your heart must tell you."

He perched beside her, hat in hand, turned toward her. "You must know my heart, Carolyn. I don't go around blithely kissing women, regardless of what you might think. I had not thought to be drawn to you – and I'm not unaware of the ties between yourself and my brother. But I find I must tell you I do care for you, Carolyn, and I hope you return the feeling."

He paused, waiting.

Her lip trembled. "I do."

"Those words are in fact the very ones I'd hoped to hear – in answer to another question."

What was he doing? Oh, saints above, he was getting down on one knee, a posture she had never thought to see him in! She scooted back, hand at her breast. She had trouble getting a breath.

"In fact, Carolyn, I can see that we have much in common, even beyond our feelings. I can imagine a happy future together. I would like you to consider becoming my wife."

"W-what?"

"An engagement. It can be long if you like, to give us more time together. What do you say?"

"I – I say I'm honored." She smiled as he took her hand. Then suddenly another face flashed before her. If she accepted Dev, would she be closing the door on something else that was truly meant to be? Could she so easily alter, perhaps extinguish, a three-year relationship? Ought she to give Dylan at least a chance to speak – a chance to fairly choose between them, if both wanted her – before she committed to a lifetime as Dev's wife? *Dev's wife.* The thought filled her with a paroxysm of wonder. It was more than she had dared to dream of. But a tender sweetness of affection, a sense of loving obligation, filled her when she considered dear Dylan. She should not act rashly and regret it later.

"But I'd like a little time – to think," Carolyn heard herself say.

"You would?"

"Yes, I would – I need to. This is such a surprise. Give me a day or two to get my bearings – please."

Devereaux frowned and released her hand. He obviously had not expected a delay. His reaction made Carolyn more sure she was right.

He looked faintly worried as he said, "A day or two. That's all?"

"Yes. I promise." Carolyn thought she was surely as eager to settle this as he was.

Dev stood up. He looked little-boy endearing as he asked his next question. "Do you think you could give me a hint as to which way you might be leaning?"

Carolyn laughed, touched at the unexpectedly vulnerable side of him. She stood, too. "My feelings are very positive," she said, wanting to make contact with him but only brave enough to twist the button on his waistcoat. "But to be quite fair, one's feelings are not always a predictor of one's actions."

"Then I will pray in this case they shall be."

Devereaux was, of course, more bold than she. He leaned down and planted a kiss on her forehead before taking his leave.

At the library window, Dylan moved back out of view as his brother approached the house. The stage left at ten. How could he make it through breakfast with everyone?

It was as difficult as anticipated. His mother and Olivia planned a picnic to Currahee Mountain, which they would conduct on the coming Saturday. Dylan could imagine Dev and Carolyn basking together in the autumn sun on the cliffside rocks, Dev plying her with flirtations. Even now Dev kept trying to catch her eye. Though she tried to seem impervious, there was a tell-tale color in her cheeks. It seemed everyone was oblivious to Dylan's eminent departure.

Having completed his meal, Dylan excused himself and headed toward the stairs. He ad gotten as far as the landing when he heard Carolyn call his name. He turned and waited for her to climb up to the level he was on.

How foolish he had been to believe she would be his, he thought. He should have known anything he set his heart upon – save the ministry, he thought wryly – Devereaux would want, and get.

"Are you all packed, then?" she asked.

"Yes. My trunk will be brought down directly."

"And you're to leave before ten?"

"Right away."

"I had thought we'd have time to talk," she said faintly, wringing her hands.

"We've talked a lot this summer. It's been fruitful, don't you think?" Though Dylan was not one normally given to sarcasm, he couldn't keep the edge of it from his voice now.

"I ... I don't know. I had assumed we'd have a final visit ... a private good-bye."

"I suppose this is it. Was there something more we needed to say?" He allowed himself to open the door only that much.

Carolyn hesitated, her lips parted. She reached out tentatively and took his hand, her fingers barely holding his. She looked so sincere he knew that she wasn't playing with him. His heart wrenched as she spoke. "Only that I thank you for the summer ... and to assure you that my affections for you ... have not altered. Dylan, please say something. You look so unnaturally cold. Have I done something wrong?"

No, he thought, *you have only followed your heart*. He couldn't blame her for that, couldn't let his hurt become anger. For a moment he thought of speaking, because what if her heart led her astray? What if Dev, once he had won her, soon cast her aside like a toy he had tired of?

Dylan reached out and pulled her to him, holding her close with her face buried in his shoulder, praying no one emerged from the dining room below. Suddenly he realized she was weeping. Hope flamed in his heart. If it was from longing ... He quickly put her away enough to gaze at her face. When he saw sadness and regret there rather than yearning, he sighed, briefly closing his eyes against the pain.

"Shall – shall I continue to write you?" Carolyn asked, clearly confused by his manner.

"No, I think not." He patted her hand and backed away from her slowly. Then he turned and jogged up the flight of stairs to his room.

That very afternoon she would tell him, Carolyn decided. Time to move on with the future. She trembled with nervousness while she waited on the bench in the foyer, knowing he was due downstairs any minute. The men were going deer hunting. Even now her father and Louis – her future father-in-law, she realized – were selecting guns from the locked case in the gentlemen's parlor.

When she heard Dev's step on the landing, she put aside the book she had been pretending to read. She rose as he came into view.

His face brightened upon sight of her. "Carolyn," he called out.

"May I speak with you a moment?" she asked, twisting her hands in her skirt.

"Of course. What is it?"

She backed into the parlor, bidding him follow with her eyes. But she misjudged her direction and her shoulder hit the door jamb. He gave an amused smile at her clumsiness.

"You o.k.?"

"Yes." Carolyn rubbed the offending spot. Now that they were inside the room, goodness, she did not know how to do this! "I – I wanted to speak to you regarding ... regarding what you asked me this morning."

"You already have an answer?" Dev asked eagerly.

She nodded.

"Well, are you going to tell me what it is?" With an attempt at patience, he reached for her hands.

She stared at their joined fingers, noting his square thumbnails, the dark hair, the size of his hands. All very different from Dylan's. But Dylan had not wanted her. At least not enough. Her palms grew sweaty.

"I – I will marry you," she stated.

His response was swift and exuberant. "Yahoo!" he exclaimed, and suddenly snatched her up and swung her around.

Carolyn laughed in flusterment. When her toes touched the rug he peered into her face.

"Can I kiss you?" he asked.

"What? No!"

"No?" Dev sounded shocked.

Carolyn put a hand on his chest. "Please, not now. I – I don't think I could stand it. In a good way, I mean." There had simply been too many emotional moments in the last twenty-four hours. She was sure if his lips touched hers now she would faint.

The dark look dissolved at her words and a slow smile, much like a Cheshire cat's, spread across Dev's finely chiseled face. "Very well, then," he said. "I'll respect your tender sensibilities for now. But I won't let you off the hook for long. You've made me very happy, Carolyn. You won't regret this."

As he released her, she had a wild, fleeting notion to make him promise.

"We'll announce it at dinner tonight." He grinned triumphantly and fairly bounded out of the room.

Carolyn was left standing there, the heir to all a girl could dream of – untold riches and the most handsome, charming fiancé in the world. But a heavy sense of confusion settled over her when she realized that among all Dev's fine words, not once had he spoken the three she longed to hear most.

CHAPTER TEN

October 1860
Clarkesville, GA

 'll give you a better price on that," Thomas Franklin said from behind the counter.

Looking up from some fine blue wool she'd been fingering in her uncle's store, Mahala smiled in appreciation. Thomas had always been kind to her, despite the continued coldness of his son. She could only guess it must be Leon's mother, Amy, who had always held herself rather aloof, who had fed his prejudices. That and his poor choice of friends. Abel Quitman, the boy at the hotel she had met her first morning in town so long ago, was now well known for his drinking and fighting. He was a common laborer who went from one odd job to the next, but Leon seemed devoted to him. Not that either of them had many friends to choose from, she thought.

She was still stalling her decision by peering out the rain-flecked window at a calvacade from the successful Waring horse farm on its way to the fair in Athens when a voice spoke behind her. "You should definitely go with that one."

Mahala turned to behold Jack. "You have a way of sneaking up on me," she said with a smile.

"Sorry." He smiled tightly. He was holding a dripping umbrella, and one lapel of his overcoat was turned awkwardly under, attesting to haste. Hmm. Not like him. And where was the witty comeback?

In the last two years – ever since the Shakespeare ball – they had enjoyed a sort of truce. Their exchanges, whether she came upon Jack fishing at her favorite spot by her willow or they met in town, had still been lively. Lively, and more warm than before. She truly considered them friends now, though Mahala maintained the sense that Jack guarded himself from going beyond the surface, getting too emotionally close. His weapons of defense were humor, sarcasm and long absences.

Mahala still told herself this was all right with her. A warm friendship – that was always what she'd said she wanted. For her to expect more from a man like Jack was unrealistic.

"The blue would be nice with your eyes," he said now, "but I'm sure you already know that. Shall I take it to the counter for you?"

"No, thank you. I'm quite capable. I'm sure you came in to look around for something," Mahala said, lifting the awkward roll off the table and under her arm.

Jack took it from her. "I found what I came in for."

"You want blue wool, too?"

"I want you."

"*Me?*"

Even before Mahala's astonished question, Jack had realized how his statement sounded. He looked vaguely uncomfortable for a second, but impatience quickly overrode that. "What I mean to say is, if you'll come with me to my office in the hotel, there's something I really need to discuss with you. Something business-related."

Mahala studied his face. There was none of the usual lightness there. Instead, he looked transparent, drawn. She was completely overcome with curiosity but sensed that it was not the time to pry further. "Well ... all right," she agreed.

Jack gestured to the aisle in front of him. "Shall we?"

Mahala preceded him to the counter, where Thomas cut the desired yardage. Once Mahala had drawn some bills from her reticule, Jack carried the fabric to the door and attempted to hold it open while simultaneously opening his umbrella for her. She was smiling at his struggle and offering to carry the wool again when Leon ran up to the entrance, ducking out of the rain. He stared at them a minute, eyeing them both in a disapproving manner, before brushing past them.

"Pleasant fellow, isn't he?" Jack mumbled.

"Only to my grandmother and rich customers," Mahala replied, pretending to take him literally.

"You should be rid of him. You don't need him."

"There are many who would balk at a visible female manager," Mahala replied.

"True enough." Jack handed her the open umbrella. "Still, you don't deserve that disrespect."

Mahala was pleasantly surprised by his comment. They passed down the sidewalk to The Palace Hotel, where a doorman whisked away Jack's coat, hat and umbrella. He tried to take Mahala's wraps as well, but she told him, "I'll keep mine, thanks. I can't be long."

Jack led her to his office. Leaving the door cracked open as protocol dictated, he put her wool down on his desk. But instead of taking the seat behind it, he gestured for her to take one of two leather wingchairs facing the desk. He took the other one. A fire crackled on the grate. Mahala removed the damp thickness of her cloak and waited expectantly for him to speak.

"I just received a letter that my father has suffered an attack. The doctor says it was his heart. I'm to leave for Savannah in the morning."

"Oh, my goodness, Jack!" Mahala exclaimed. "Is he all right?"

He paused a moment to steady his emotions. The sight of it made her stomach tighten with surprise and pity. Then his jaw firmed and he said in a controlled manner, "He has been ordered to bed rest and is very weak. There is some concern about him having another episode. Needless to say, I should go see him – and there are matters of business that need attending to."

"Of course." Mahala was sympathetic but wondered why this concerned her. His next statement addressed her uncertainty.

"The season is almost out, but not quite. There are still several of my best families here whose bills will have to be settled, and several seasonal employees who need to be let go. After a thorough cleaning around the first week of November, I cover all the furniture and close the top story. I'm asking if you would oversee all that."

"*Me?*" Mahala was totally aghast.

"Yes. I believe I can trust you to be honest, tactful and efficient."

"But – do you not have a manager with those same qualities?" she queried, her voice faint with amazement.

"Unfortunately my manager was bereaved of his wife this past week," Jack answered levelly. He looked her in the eye. "So will you help me out?"

What could she possibly say? How could she refuse – even though accepting would undoubtedly put a strain on her and possibly even raise questions about a conflict of interests. But his trust in her was touching. She could hardly shove the olive branch back in his face.

Jack misunderstood her hesitation. "I will, of course, pay you, if you will but keep a log of your hours on my behalf."

That pushed Mahala to the edge. "You most certainly will not!" she exclaimed. "I refuse to be your employee, Jack Randall!"

He was smiling at her indignant tone and flashing eyes. "What will you be, then, Mahala Franklin?" he teased in a low tone that suddenly gave her butterflies.

She fidgeted with her gloves. "Asking a favor as a friend is one thing, but don't go waving money in my face," she replied.

"If that's the way you want it, I'll be in your debt. Come, let me show you the books."

Mahala followed him around his desk and watched as he drew a key off his ring and opened a locked drawer. He laid out two ledgers, one for customer accounts and another for employees, plus his check book. Her eyes bulged.

"Are you not worried I'll steal you blind?" she questioned.

"Like I said, I trust you."

"*That much?*"

Jack surveyed her thoughtfully. "I've got to trust someone. You seem a logical choice, given your experience both in the hotel business and in the past."

He was referring to her father's lost fortune. Soberly she turned her attention to the desk. Jack went over each column and made some notes for her as to what he expected. As she had always guessed, The Palace was operated at a pretty surplus. What she couldn't do if she had the capital of the Randalls!

When Jack was content that Mahala understood everything, he placed the key in her hand.

"Guard this carefully," he said. He began to tug a second key from the ring, adding, "I will tell the employees and servants that you have *carte blanche* while I am away – so long as you don't go redecorating." He paused with a twinkle of humor. "Here is the key to my office. It will remain locked unless you are here. All right?"

"Of course."

"Write me if you have any problems."

"Will you return before the end of the year?" she asked.

"That's doubtful. But the manager should resume his duties by December. You can give the keys to him when he returns to town."

"All right." She had everything. It was time to go, but she hesitated, drawn to the man in his vulnerable state. "Mr. Randall – Jack – I ... I want you to know I'm cognizant of the honor you do me in asking this favor."

He studied her. "And what of the honor you do me?" His voice was unusually soft.

Mahala dipped her head. "I will pray for your father."

"Thank you."

The next moment, Jack's hand gently caressed the hair knotted at the back of her neck. She started, but he did not withdraw. For a long moment, he gazed into her eyes, his mouth upturning in a tender smile. "You really are something, Mahala," he murmured. She saw his gaze drop to her lips and knew instinctively that he was about to kiss her. Her heart started hammering like a runaway train.

"Jack –" she began. Facing him like this, all the emotions for him that she normally managed to deny rose up within her. She didn't know what she was going to say, just that she was possessed of an irresistible urge to break through the barrier that normally lay between them.

But she didn't have to say anything. In an instant, she had already shown him too much. Something flickered in his eyes, and he stepped back from her.

"It's a good thing I don't see you too often," he said, flippantly, smiling, "or I'd surely be a casualty of your charms just like the Indian boy." He turned his back as he stepped behind his desk.

Feeling like she had been punched in the stomach, Mahala gasped. She snatched up her cloak and the bundle of wool and moved quickly toward the door.

"Well, you'd better hurry back to Savannah, then!" she called over her shoulder, her voice coming out breathless, angry. And far too unsteady. "Because right now the idea of killing you is very tempting!"

Mahala ran through the pouring rain to the hotel, letting herself in with a banging door. Leon was down on hands and knees mopping up muddy water – the leavings of recent guests.

"Where have you been?" he asked suspiciously as she paused a moment to catch her breath.

Mahala was not in the mood for another stupid man. She stalked to the family's door without answering.

"Stop! You are leaving more footprints!" he demanded.

"Oh, hush up!"

Mahala slammed the door to the parlor, too. She sat down on a chair and started unlacing her boots, but tears suddenly blurred her vision. Why, oh why, did Jack Randall have to be so confusing ... to finally treat her like an equal, open up to her, and just when she was adjusting to the idea of their finally being on the same team, throw in a romantic move in the same breath with an insult? For clearly he thought her undeserving of his attraction to her.

Why had she returned a barb for a barb? Why had she not called him on the carpet and demanded to know why he would rather insult her than embrace her, when she saw – she *saw* – the truth in his eyes!

Because she was a coward. No, because she was not a fool. She could never speak her true feelings to a man who could scorn them.

Mahala brushed away tears. She realized what she hated most was that if Jack had said nothing to hurt her feelings, she would have welcomed his kiss. Even still, with her body quivering from insult, she longed for his embrace, his tenderness, more than anything in the world. And there was nothing she could do about it.

Upon arriving in Savannah, Jack went straight to his father's house. He found the family at dinner – all but Richard, of course, who took his meals in bed. Sylvie fairly flew into his arms. He caught a vision of blue ribbons and silk and the comely face and figure that the local beaux were crazy over before she began weeping rather theatrically on his shoulder.

"Oh, Jack, I'm so glad you're home! We've needed you so!"

He awkwardly patted her back. "Isn't there a special one among your suitors yet to comfort you?" he couldn't resist asking.

She drew back and replied with childlike sincerity. "No, Jack. There's just no one like you. Beside you, they all seem so shallow."

Jack smiled. "I thank you for your good opinion. How is Father?" His eyes went to Sunny, who had appeared in the dining room door. Her face looked drawn, though her hair was carefully arranged and her gown tastefully chosen, as usual.

"Not so good. He gets up sometimes and comes to sit downstairs, but after a couple of hours he's so tired," Sylvie replied. "But the worst of it is, he doesn't seem to *believe* he will recover, and without that hope, well ..."

Sunny nodded to confirm her daughter's words. Jack put an arm around her as she added, "Thank you for coming so quickly."

Alan, fifteen, also joined them in the foyer. Jack shook his hand. He knew that Bryson at eighteen had just entered the Georgia Military Academy and was away from home.

"I guess you want to see your father right away," Sunny said.

"Yes. I do."

"Sylvie, tell cook to set a place for Jack. We'll be back down in a minute," Sunny directed. She slipped her hand onto Jack's arm as they mounted the stairs. He tried not to show his surprise.

"How are you holding up, Sunny?" he asked, having long ago forgone the habit of calling her 'Stepmother.'

"All right, I guess. I'm frightened, though, Jack. I don't want to be a widow again."

Jack frowned. Giving up on life was not like his father. Richard must truly feel his strength diminished if he wasn't even putting forth much effort to encourage his family. In the bedroom, his suspicious were confirmed. Although he was sitting up with a bowl of soup on a lap tray, Richard looked thin and rather ashen. He grinned, though, as Jack hurried forward to embrace him.

"My boy!" he exclaimed joyfully. "Well, the one good thing out of all this is that it brought you home."

Sunny, smiling at the reunion, quietly slipped out the door, closing it behind her. Jack took a seat next to the bed.

"Yes," he said, "and I am dismayed to hear you are being very worrisome to the womenfolk."

Richard's face looked pained. "I do regret that."

"How bad is it, really?"

Richard set his soup bowl aside. Jack helped to settle the tray on the bedside table. "To be honest, since the attack, I have no energy. When I get up and do much of anything, this old heart of mine labors like a wheezing horse – and I sound about like one, too."

"You'll gain strength," Jack told him in what he hoped was a confident tone.

"I pray so, for Sunny's sake. But Jack, there's more. Don't ever repeat this to anyone, but the night of the episode, just before it happened, I dreamed of your mother. She came and laid her hand on my forehead and called my name like she was trying to wake me from sleep. So I thought – I thought I was to go join her."

"Well, you weren't," Jack snapped. He knew he only sounded impatient because Richard's revelation rattled him.

Richard knew it, too. His father's face creased into a sympathetic smile. "I'm sorry to upset you, Jack. I think no son or daughter is ever prepared for the illness or death of a parent, no matter how old or strong the child may be. And strong I know you are – and you will need to be. Until and unless I recover, you are the acting head of our family. You *are* Randall and Ellis. The others – and the public – will look to you. I want to ask you to remain here for the foreseeable future."

Jack thought of the hotel in Clarkesville, now in Mahala's capable hands – and of Mahala herself. What a cad he'd been. What a fool. The truth was, he had never been so attracted to any woman. He was drawn to her like a Monarch to butterfly weed. He couldn't stop himself. But when he'd seen something in return on *her* face, it had scared him silly. What would he do with a woman like Mahala – besides the obvious? He couldn't let her in. If he did, he knew without a doubt she would invade every pore, sink into his bloodstream, until she would be all he could think of. It was only with distance between them that he was successful in maintaining his perspective. Reining in his thoughts, he replied, "I had already anticipated that."

"Good. In all honesty, Jack, it would appear we're to be in for some rough waters ahead. Last year that undercover New York reporter wrote that scathing account of Joseph Bryan's slave sale on Johnson Square. And that fanatic John Brown tried to seize the arsenal at Harper's Ferry, West Virginia, to arm slaves – until Robert Lee showed up with the Marines. Those things really fueled the fears of people around here. You know that," Richard said. "And things have not improved since. The mayor just had a bunch of free black sailors arrested for tampering with the local blacks. With the split in the Democratic Party, everyone's feeling protective and leery of what might happen in the election. Francis Bartow spoke at a rally last month. I think he's actually hoping Abraham Lincoln will be elected so there will be another push for secession. A lot of people agree with him. I would hate to think what a split from our Northern family might mean, but Jack, I want you to be thinking about all the ones here who would be relying on you."

"And *you*," Jack said stubbornly. "You're not going to give up the ghost just like that. Not now that *I'm* home." Jack stood up, inwardly determined that he would not be left alone with the responsibilities and decisions his father had implied. "Now why don't you rest. I'm going down to get some dinner."

Richard clasped his hand. "I love you, Son."

"And I love you."

Jack turned away, a bit choked. As he did, his eye fell on a large painting above the mantle that he had never seen before, not having been in his father's bedroom in many years. He froze. He recognized himself as a boy, standing in short breeches with a hoop and a stick by a fountain. Memories came rushing back. Himself bitterly rolling that hoop into Sunny's painting. The canvas falling to the ground, leaving streaks on her dress. The sad way his family had gazed on the ruined painting. And he had never realized why.

His father spoke from the bed. "Yes, Jack, that's the portrait that Sunny did in the park that day. She has always cared for you. She just didn't know how to show it."

Jack lingered a moment, feeling ten again, his shoulders slumped. Then he nodded. Without turning around to look at Richard, he went downstairs. He found Sunny alone still in the dining room, sipping a drink across from an empty place setting – his. Well, he had never questioned that she was a lady.

He sat down quietly and placed the napkin in his lap. Instantly a servant appeared at his side with the first course.

A moment later Sunny said, "You see what I mean?"

"Yes. I've not seen him like this since … well, since Mother died," Jack admitted softly. "He is truly ill, Sunny. We'll have to encourage him, but with little steps."

"About that, Jack, well, I was hoping … I'm not very good with sick people, and I think having you around, bringing in information from the business and the world he loves … well, what I'm trying to say is, I was hoping you might actually stay here. With us. We – I need you." Sunny's normally strong voice trailed off lamely, and her dark eyes hung hopefully on his face. "Please."

"Of course, Sunny. I'll stay."

A smile of quiet relief spread across her face. "Thank you, Jack."

"That's the last family checked out of the third floor," said Maureen O'Beaty, Jack's Irish housekeeper. Mrs. O'Beaty supervised the maids at The Palace. "Have I your leave to start closin' it up once the cleanin's complete, Miss Franklin?"

"Of course, Mrs. O'Beaty," Mahala replied. She finished recording the recent payment in the ledger and looked up with a smile. She had already found the housekeeper to be independent and reliable. She could only guess that it was only Jack's innate sense of hierarchy that had kept him from leaving the business in O'Beaty's hands. Then again, maybe the woman could not read and cipher. "Thank you. Once the job is done, let me know. I'll have end-of-season pay for the employees."

"Yes, Ma'am."

As the woman left the office, Mahala pondered the fact that Jack used no slaves at The Palace. Oh, there were blacks, whom many assumed to be bondsmen and women, but he paid them a fair wage. This definitely made a statement about where he put his values in relation to gain. His words of several years previous came back to her, when he had questioned the contentment of her grandmother's two slaves. Shortly after that conversation, when Mahala had returned to Clarkesville from Athens, she had asked Maddie what she would do were freedom offered. Mahala clearly recalled her response.

"Why, take it, ob course," she had said instantly. "Not det I be goin' anywhere. Your grandma take good care ob us, feeds an' clothes us, an' gibs us money for special things. An' Ah lub doin' what Ah does, cookin' for folks all day. But it be something' jus' to know we be free."

Mahala guessed the full pay would come in handy, too. The couple could buy their own home or livestock, or purchase the freedom of a family member. But there was not much she could do about all that. Martha had been adamant that she had no inclination to free anyone. Wages would cut too much into their modest profit margin.

Mahala sighed, locking up Jack's desk. She had only been coming here just under a week. She still felt like an intruder into his domain, as though at any moment someone might arrive and drag her out by her collar. Mahala was careful, though, not to relay her insecurities to Jack's employees. They were already curious enough... though quietly so, thankfully. She didn't want to imagine what they thought of her new business liaison with their employer. She hadn't even wanted to come here, not after the way he'd treated her. But she had given her word, and she hadn't been about to pay him another visit to go back on it. She despised herself for it, but neither could she rid herself of her attraction to the man. Despite everything, there were things about him that she still found both intriguing — and admirable.

Drawing her cloak about her head and nodding to the footman, she passed out the front door. A new moon hung above lantern-lit buildings in the chilly early November night. Her stomach growled, reminding Mahala that she had skipped dinner to give time for Jack's affairs.

Once she reached home she headed straight for the kitchen. Maddie always had leftovers wrapped up in the coals. But just as she entered the deserted hotel dining room, she heard her grandmother's voice call to her. Mahala turned. Martha was framed in the doorway to the office, golden light from the oil lamp creating a soft silhouette.

"Mahala, I need to speak with you," she called.

"Can I grab a bite to eat and come right back?"

"Now, please."

Unclasping her cloak, Mahala did as she was asked. Upon entering the office she was surprised to see Leon seated there, one long, thin leg crossed over the other. He did not bother to get up, but merely gave her a slightly smug look.

"Sit down, Mahala."

Confused, Mahala did so, though Martha remained standing. She did not get a good feeling about this.

Her grandmother said, "Leon tells me that you have gone to The Palace Hotel four or five times this week. Would you please explain what that is about?"

Mahala glanced at Leon, who did not meet her eye but stared imperiously ahead. "Jack — Mr. Randall — was called away due to his father's grave illness. In the absence of his manager he asked if I would help tie up a few loose ends at the season's close. That's all. What, do you have spies following me now?" she could not resist throwing Leon's way.

"'Jack,' is it?" he answered sourly.

"And do you not see that as a conflict of interest?" Martha wanted to know.

"I don't see how. I'm merely settling a few accounts and letting go a few workers, all on my own time. Look, I don't like being called in here like a criminal," Mahala fumed, sitting up straight. "Mr. Randall asked a favor of me as a business acquaintance. There is nothing more to be made of it."

"And is Jack paying you, or do you dispense your favors freely?" Leon asked.

"*That* is too much!" Mahala cried, jumping to her feet.

Leon shook his head. "Awfully defensive, aren't you?"

"Leon, I don't like your tone, or your insulting insinuations," Martha said suddenly. "I listened to your feelings, but you will not speak this way to Mahala. You are walking a fine line. Be careful. Now please go."

"But —"

"I *said* please leave. I will settle this."

Scowling, Leon looked from one to the other of them, then barged out of the room.

As Martha took a seat behind her desk, Mahala braced herself for a further onslaught. But to her surprise, her grandmother looked up with an almost pleasant expression. "I have good news, and I don't want to forget to share it with you."

"What is that?" Mahala asked suspiciously.

"Rex Clarke is leaving town."

"For good?" Mahala asked in wonder. She had heard that the renegade lawyer had slowly lost business as the citizens lost any remaining good opinion of him. Drinking and gambling had been one thing. Assaulting a young lady of good reputation was quite another. Though it had taken a couple of years, Carolyn's prediction had, it seemed, at last come true.

"So it's said," Martha responded. "Supposedly he's packed up and moved to Darien. Maybe his father's family down there can keep him afloat for a while. Servants are closing up the house as is. It appears the family will keep it for the time being. Maybe some other members will summer there in the future."

"I hope they are a better sort," Mahala said. "It's a beautiful house. It deserves a good owner. It will be sad to see it all closed up."

"Yes, well, I'm just glad the scoundrel is gone at last, aren't you?"

Mahala smiled. "Yes. Very glad."

"So *is* he paying you?"

"What? Who? Rex?"

"No, silly. Jack."

"Oh." Just when she had warmed to the new subject and begun to hope her grandmother was prepared to let the old one go. She should have known better. Martha had merely diffused the emotions in the room with a temporary change of subject. But she would never let a matter drop until she was satisfied. "I refused payment," she said rather sulkily.

"When were you going to tell me? You do realize this whole scene with Leon would have been unnecessary if you had only informed me first. Your silence made you indeed look suspicious."

"I realize that now," Mahala said, "and I'm sorry. I kept meaning to tell you, but we've been so busy. I guess, too, I wasn't sure how you'd feel about it, so I delayed ..." Her voice trailed off as she recalled how confused her feelings had been when Jack first asked her for her help. Who was she fooling? Her emotions were still a mess.

Martha sighed and put a hand on the side of her head. "Oh, Mahala, what have you gotten into?"

"What do you mean? It's not a big deal. He simply needed some help, Grandmother."

"I am speaking of the big picture. You have feelings for Jack Randall, don't you?"

Mahala cast her gaze downward. She could not lie to her grandmother. "Yes," she admitted softly. "I think I love him … despite the fact that I hate him half the time, too."

"And do you think he cares for you – could ever love you in a permanent way?"

Mahala shook her head. "I think he has feelings – I glimpse them sometimes, even though he doesn't want me to – but what does it matter? We both know we are not in the same class."

Martha rose and came around her desk. "And he will not forget it. Life is not a fairy tale, Mahala," she said, holding out her arms. Mahala miserably stood and leaned into her grandmother's sympathetic embrace. Martha gently smoothed her hair and sighed, "I did so want you to not spend your affections on someone who could never return them."

"I know, Grandmother. I tried, but I could not help it."

CHAPTER ELEVEN

November 8, 1860
Savannah, Georgia

inning a cameo at the collar of her pink, brown and white silk taffeta gown, Carolyn surveyed her reflection. With her golden hair done up and pearls dancing at her ears, she thought she looked very mature and composed – like a young matron who had it all. Appearances were very important, for Dylan was coming to dinner tonight, and he must not suspect that she was aching inside.

For the hundredth time, Carolyn longed for someone to talk to. Mahala Franklin would have been her first choice, for even though Dev had kept them in the city this year and last summer's visit had been shortened due to wedding plans, she and the half-Cherokee girl had a special connection. Mahala seemed to be able to read her mind. She could say a lot in the simplest statement. And she was the soul of discretion.

But there were some things Carolyn could never say to another living being – most especially to an unmarried young lady. Still, last summer, and since then – by reading between the lines in Carolyn's letters – Mahala had surmised that all was not well between Carolyn and Devereaux.

Dev had been the very embodiment of charm during their engagement, paying her courtly attention and sending her thoughtful presents. If she sometimes had sensed he was playing a part she had told herself she was too critical, for what had she to complain about? When he flirted with other women at dances they attended, she had reminded herself that engaged people no longer had the social privilege of solely focusing on one another. She had ignored the warning signs, for when his handsome face and dazzling smile had turned on her, she had been overcome with amazement that *she* was his chosen, envied by every other woman in Savannah.

Olivia had "prepared" her for her wedding night by reminding her that it was a wife's duty to meet her husband's physical needs, even though such experiences might not always be pleasant for the bride, especially at first. Of what those experiences entailed little was said. Thus Carolyn had gone to their first intimate encounter trembling with fear – of the unknown, and awe that she was to be so vulnerable to one she still felt she knew only on the surface. She wondered if Dev's mother had had a similar talk with him,

138

for before Carolyn had absorbed what happened between them, it was over. Then after a kiss and a thank you, he had explained that in consideration of her "delicate sensibilities" he would withdraw to the adjoining bedchamber. She had been left to wrap herself in a blanket, tears of confusion and longing easing out of her eyes. She was too uncertain of what she truly wanted or needed to go after him.

But then, on their honeymoon, Carolyn had dared to hope. Dev had taken her to Europe – at last! They had left less than a week after their late November wedding last year and toured England, Scotland, Ireland, France and Italy. With just the two of them together most of the time, Dev had focused on her and clearly enjoyed her delight in their surroundings. She had tried to be the adoring, sweet and simple bride she knew he expected. At times, she had felt his affection in return. She had told herself she only imagined it was the doting warmth of a master with a pet instead of the admiring flame between mental and emotional partners.

Then, in late spring, they had returned to Georgia, to The Marshes, where Dev had wanted to look things over and visit with his parents. But it had not been long before the simmering political climate and the lure of the Oglethorpe Light Infantry had drawn him to town. Dev had joined as lieutenant in early winter of 1858, about the time the company had been incorporated by an act of the state legislature. He quickly fell again into the routine of drills and parades, and talked constantly of the men of OLI. He loved to wear the dark blue dress uniform with its fringed epaulets, buff-colored waist and cross belts and brass buttons, and he had great respect for the captain, Francis Bartow. Bartow obviously valued the training Devereaux brought to the unit as well.

Carolyn found herself with many hours alone at her parents' town home on Bull Street. Her parents were at Brightwell, and Eliza had enlisted the monetary support of their Northern aunt for medical college – a fact that Olivia tried hard to keep hush-hush. They stayed here because Dylan spent much time at the Rousseaus' Savannah mansion. He was doing exactly what he had set out to do – pastoring a small Presbtry in the country and a tent mission in Yamacraw. It seemed she was the only one with no purpose.

Yes, there was *that*, too – people expectantly looking at her waist, seeking for signs of rounding now that her first year of marital bliss was up. Was she to add barrenness to her list of failings? Or would no seed grow where fulfillment lacked?

Tania, the maid Olivia had given to Carolyn upon her marriage, appeared at the door. Her dark face impassive, she said, "Mistah Dylan be in de parlor, Ma'am."

"Thank you."

With one last glance in the mirror, accompanied by a sigh, Carolyn straightened her spine. She brushed past the servant, who came in to tidy up. Carolyn didn't like her much. She was sullen, but polite enough that it was hard to find occasion for rebuke. Of course, anyone would fail in comparison to Mamsie, whom Carolyn missed terribly. There had been no chance of Olivia parting with the loving old woman. Just one more change in the past year.

She found Dylan examining the new wax fruit she had recently made from a set of molds, his broad shoulders to her.

"You like them?" she asked teasingly.

He swung around quickly. "Of course! Very realistic." He awkwardly set a banana back atop an apple in the china bowl.

Carolyn suppressed a smile and, with a quick turn of her hand, quietly arranged the pieces at a pleasing angle.

"You are the artist, I presume?" Dylan asked.

"If you can call that art – which I doubt. Just another way for ladies to pass their time."

Dylan's face brightened, and for a moment he looked eager and boyish, as he had often looked before her marriage. "You should come out to Yamacraw – take in a service there. I think the females would benefit from the example of a gentlewoman. There is much you could do to help."

"Thank you, but I … doubt Dev would like that."

"Oh." Dylan paused. "Where is the old bother, anyway?"

"Out with some friends, taking in the excitement."

"Yes, it's a regular festival out there. Secession is the buzz word."

"I was afraid of that." Carolyn gestured to the sofa. "Won't you sit down?"

"Thank you."

They took seats opposite each other.

"Secession is all Dev has been able to speak of since word of Lincoln's election arrived yesterday," she continued. "He's been anticipating it ever since the Democrats split and the Republicans united behind Mr. Lincoln – President Lincoln now, I guess."

"Yes, no one can stand the thought of them being in power, turning the tide of decisions in favor of the North – even though Lincoln vowed not to disturb slavery where it already exists. It's just the final straw folks have been waiting on for decades."

Carolyn nodded. "I'm afraid so. But Dylan, if we are hesitant about what leaving the Union may mean, I think we're the only ones in the city … well, except for Jack Randall, perhaps."

"There are still many people with Northern ties and families."

"I fear ... what if they don't let us go peacefully?" Carolyn questioned in a faint voice.

"Then, Dev will go to war."

Carolyn swallowed. "Surely it won't come to that. Would you go, too?"

Dylan laughed. "I'm a preacher, Carolyn, not a soldier. I doubt if they'd have me."

"Well, it won't be an issue," Carolyn insisted firmly. "It *won't*. They simply must let us go peaceably. I've been doing some reading. We have every legal and historical precedent – and clear statements in national documents – acknowledging that states are sovereign and have every right to remove from the Union. Did you know the colonies became states in 1776 and did not agree to unite until 1781? Then, after the Revolution, North Carolina and Rhode Island didn't even join the *new* Union the others formed, not until 1790!"

"My, you have been doing your research," Dylan commented, looking rather impressed.

"That, and listening to Dev." Listening, because that was all she could do. She could never have this sort of discussion with her husband. He quickly became impatient with her and always seemed to feel the need to have the last word, to show he knew far more than she.

"Well, I agree with you. And as you said, even the Declaration and the Constitution call the states 'free and independent' and say they retain their sovereignty. Nowhere does it state they cannot leave the union," Dylan pointed out. "Some states even wrote in when they accepted the Constitution that they preserved the right to resume their own powers if they be injured or oppressed."

Carolyn nodded. "The Yankees must believe it, Dylan – look at how we urged Texas to secede from Mexico – and how mad New England merchants got early this century about Jefferson's Embargo Act. Mad enough to consider secession."

"And just fifteen years ago, when John Quincy Adams and New Englanders felt the same way about the admission of Texas," Dylan threw in. "Did you know even Lincoln himself stated – regarding the Texas issue – that any people had the right to rise up and shake off existing government, and form a new one?"

"No ..." Carolyn gasped. "He said that?"

Dylan nodded in satisfaction. "He did indeed."

"So he must honor the legal right of southern states to withdraw ... peaceably." Carolyn sat back, a hand at her heart, relieved. "Oh, that makes me feel better. Lincoln would not violate the Constitution and his own beliefs by allowing hostile action against us."

Dylan drew in one side of his mouth and gave a thoughtful half-shake of his head. "I surely trust that will be the case. But there's a lot of pressure, Carolyn – many who believe the Union is inviolate. And that doesn't even consider the influence of the abolitionists. A politician is so greatly subject to those who elect him."

Carolyn stared sadly, anxiously again, at her brother-in-law. Then she heard the front door open, and the next minute Devereaux appeared, an intense excitement about his face.

"I could hardly get through the crowd," he said, not taking time for greetings. "I came by to say I can't take supper tonight – at least not until much later. Prominent townspeople have been giving their views to the legislature. Now Bartow is to address the crowd at the Masonic Hall. It's good you're here, Dylan. You won't want to miss this. It will be a key moment in our city's history."

"But Dev, we can hardly leave Carolyn here to dine alone," Dylan protested, glancing at Carolyn. He asked her, "Would you like to come, too?"

Dev looked incredulous. "Did you just come down the same street I just came down? Because the crowd is really worked up – hanging secession banners and giving orations, pushing and shoving, some of them drunk – and it's a sea of top hats. It's too rough for ladies."

Carolyn swallowed, noting that her husband had not even acknowledged her presence. Now that she was his, there was obviously no need to defer to her wishes, except for occasional public show. Better he go on. Trying to force him to a calm supper would be like trying to cage a pacing tiger. He would only turn on her later with his particular brand of coldness.

"It's all right," she said. "I don't mind dining alone."

Dylan looked uncertain. However, his brother wouldn't take kindly to him staying to an intimate supper with Carolyn. So they both rose and followed Dev into the hall.

"I'm sorry," Dylan murmured as he shrugged on his coat.

"It's fine. You can tell me about it later."

Dev turned from accepting his hat and gloves from the butler to give them a quick once-over. He dropped a quick kiss on Carolyn's cheek. "Don't wait up," he said.

Then the men were gone and to the closing door she murmured, "Of course not."

They both could be annoying, thought Devereaux as his driver pressed their buggy north along Bull Street. Carolyn with her needy glances and Dylan with his continuing deference to her needs. One would think he did not take care of her, go where she wanted to go, stay home with her when his friends were out of an evening, and shower her with presents. Why did women feel the need to dissect their men? Why did they always want *more*?

And here was Dylan, who would have given it to her on a silver platter. Honestly, they would have made a great pair, the two of them, discussing every nuance of their emotions and so absorbed in each other and their charitable causes they'd have scarcely noticed the world was aflame around them. But that thought made Dev uncomfortable, so he pushed it aside, telling himself it hardly mattered now.

"Ah cain' hardly get through de crowd, Mast' Dev," the driver called from above.

Dev saw that they were at Wright Square. Once past the courthouse it was only two blocks to the Masonic Hall. "That's far enough," he said, swinging the door open. "We'll walk the rest of the way. Find a spot and wait near here until we return."

They set out at as brisk a pace as possible. Dev was concerned that the building would be packed to the gills, which it was, but people made way for a lieutenant in the OLI. He could hear Bartow's impassioned voice already raised in oration before they ever entered the room.

"If any man is to peril life, fortune and honor in defense of our rights, I claim to be one of these men," he was saying.

Dev smiled. If anyone could stir his phlegmatic brother's heart, it would be the dark-haired, chivalrous and eloquent young leader. Joining several other soldiers, they took a place near the back of the enthusiastic crowd.

"I do not wish to destroy the government," Bartow continued. "I am a Union man in every fiber of my heart ... but I will peril all – ALL – before I will abandon our rights in the Union or submit to be governed by an unprincipled majority."

Shouts and cheers erupted. By the end of the speech, Dev was certain that every man in the room had been convinced to take the lead in the secession movement ... well, maybe except for his brother and Jack Randall, whom Dev brushed up against on their way outside. Both of those two wore concerned expressions. Clearly the time for hesitancy had passed. Dev decided not to let the moment go.

"What did you think of the speech, Randall?" he asked. He was eye to eye with the half-Yankee shipping merchant, who was giving him that faintly condescending look he had always abhorred. He had no idea why his father insisted on maintaining business with Richard Randall. Dev had always felt that another firm, free of the taint of Northern ties, should ship Rousseau rice.

"I'm sure all here would say it was a brilliant oration," Jack replied. "After all, any one of us might be the Grand Rattle."

Dev smiled sourly. He knew Jack referred to the secretive secessionist Rattlesnake Club which had recently started putting announcements in the paper, stating that it was time for members to "come out of their holes."

"Not *any* one of us," he corrected pointedly.

Jack merely shrugged and grinned lopsidedly, offering a hand to shake Dylan's. "Captain Northrup tells me your services in Yamacraw are becoming quite popular," he said. "Apparently some of the black sailors are attending?"

"Yes," Dylan said, smiling. "Come yourself, any time."

"I might just do that."

As evening had descended the people mobbing Savannah's streets and squares had lit bonfires and torches. The flare of light from a nearby rocket someone fired off illuminated a man with curly dark hair, beard and mustache who was just leaving the Masonic Hall. Dev recognized the city's mayor, Charles Jones, Jr. Only a year or so Jack Randall's junior, he was a young but capable leader. Dev was surprised when Randall and Jones recognized each other with a wave.

"You know him?" Dev asked Jack.

"Some of our years at Princeton overlapped," Jack replied.

"If Georgia goes out on her own I suppose you'll become very important to Mayor Jones," Dev said, "considering your family owns the largest and most versatile fleet of ships along our coast."

"Yes," Jack said musingly, staring at him, "I suppose so. Well, please excuse me, gentlemen. My father is ill and will be at home eagerly waiting to hear the evening's news."

"Oh, of course," Dylan said. "I hope he is well soon, Jack."

"Thank you." With a tip of his hat, Jack strode away, powerfully shouldering through the crowd.

Dev watched him go speculatively. If Jack was at the helm of Randall and Ellis when Georgia seceded, and possibly went to war, it would be interesting to see what transpired. Randall might show his true colors at last. Dev wouldn't mind seeing the haughty Yankee sympathizer finally receive his social comeuppance.

"You don't like him much, do you?" Dylan asked.

"He rubs me like a piece of sandpaper."

"Funny," Dylan observed. "I would have said the two of you are much alike."

Dev stared at his brother incredulously. Dylan's time spent in the pulpit was making him increasingly bold of tongue. Dev decided to let it go with but a shove and a playful ruffle of Dylan's bright hair. As different as they were and as little as he understood Dylan, he had but one brother and he did love him. He wanted Dylan to share the spirit of this moment with him, when

Georgia was perched on the brink of becoming her own Republic. This night was the stuff history was made of.

Appropriately, a nearby band chose that moment to strike up Dan D. Emmett's catchy new tune, "Dixie." The citizens clapped, cheered and sang: "Oh, I wish I was in the land of cotton! Old times there are not forgotten! Look away! Look away! Look away! Dixie Land!"

"Are you never afraid, Dev?" Dylan asked unexpectedly.

"Afraid? Of what?"

"Of making a dreadful mistake?"

"All great moments are preceded by a leap of faith, Dylan."

"Is that was this is, do you think?"

Dev put an arm around the shorter man and pulled him along toward home. "I think Georgia is about to find her wings to fly – and we along with her."

"Oh, it's flat! It's flat an' thick!" Maddie exclaimed despairingly, poking an unforgiving finger at the surface of her Christmas pudding.

"It is *not*," Mahala said, pausing in stirring the sauce that was to top Maddie's plum concoction.

"Now, look, Miss Mahaley! It sit lak a pone ob corn bread, an' Ah bet it taste like an old shoe."

"Maddie, why are you so hard on yourself? Nobody finds fault with your cooking except you."

"Hmph." With a lip poking out, the old woman plopped the dish disrespectfully down on the counter.

Mahala sighed. She should just let Maddie ramble on uninterrupted. In all her years at the hotel, she had never convinced the servant to just be happy with what came out of her oven.

Martha hurried in, dressed in emerald silk. "Is everything ready? The dining room is all decorated. The holly cuttings from the church yard look beautiful with the silver candelabra, Mahala. I declare I'm glad we have your adoptive family to share holidays with, otherwise they would seem so lonely – or I'd be forced to have over Thomas' family." She laughed. "Oh, well, it isn't like we won't see them on Christmas Day."

"I'm sorry your daughters don't come more often to visit," Mahala said.

Martha smiled. "You really should go get changed, dear. Let Maddie finish up the pudding."

"Dey be here! Dey be here!" Zed exclaimed, running into the crowded kitchen.

Mahala practically threw down the big bowl in her haste to tear out the door. She was so excited to see Nancy, Ben and Jacob – and especially her grandfather – that she could hardly wait. She fairly flew to the front porch, where Nancy was helping Henry up the steps.

"*Ududu!*" Mahala flung her arms around him. She felt his tough old hands smoothing her hair and patting her back. "Oh, I'm so happy you're here! I've missed you so!" She kissed his wrinkled cheek.

"And I have missed you. Your brother is a good farmer but not nearly so easy on my old eyes."

Jacob laughed behind them, and Mahala turned to hug him, Nancy and Ben all in turn. Martha had appeared on the porch to graciously welcome everyone. It was gratifying, Mahala thought, to have them all together and getting along now, having accepted her decision to live in town.

As baggage was carried upstairs by Zed and Jacob, the others were shown into the parlor. A fire crackled merrily. In the new trend of England's Queen Victoria, they had set a small evergreen on a table and decorated it with tiny candles and ropes of popcorn and cranberries. The mantle and window sills were graced with swags of fruit and fragrant greenery. On the dining room table was the traditional arrangement of paper whites, red cedar and nandina berries.

"I never thought I'd see the day we celebrated by dragging a tree in the house and dressing it up like a lady going to a ball," Henry commented. He leaned stiffly back on the sofa as Nancy placed some gifts under the said decoration. Mahala guessed his joints must be giving him some pain.

"Have you been taking your tea and vinegar?" Mahala asked him. The root of the hydrangea and gravel plant, taken with water and apple cider vinegar, had always helped Henry's arthritis.

"Yes, and taking dried poke berries, too," Henry said. "It is just the drive over. I'll be fine once I stretch out."

"What's this little package?" Nancy asked suddenly. "It looks like it came in the mail."

"Oh, it did – for Mahala. I forgot to tell her about it," Martha replied.

"Oh?" Mahala went over to inspect the tiny brown-wrapped parcel. She lifted it off the branch where it nested. There was nothing to indicate where it had come from. "Perhaps Patience sent it," she said.

"I assumed so," Martha replied.

"Well, I don't see why you should wait," Nancy told her. "We're all curious, aren't we? And Patience is not here. Go ahead and open it."

"Really?"

"Yes, go ahead," Martha urged.

146

Mahala obliged, tearing the paper away from the box, which turned out to be a fine leather case. She lifted the lid carefully. The minute she saw what was inside she knew that the gift was not from Patience. Such an expensive, finely detailed item could only have come from one person, and the realization caused her stomach to feel like it plunged to her toes.

Her family was growing curious due to her still and quiet reaction. They gathered around as she drew out the dainty silver oval on a long, delicate chain and laid it across the palm of her hand. Centered amidst scrolled etchings were her initials. She touched them and sprung open the cover. Inside the hands on the miniature timepiece proclaimed that it was seven o'clock.

"Ooh," Nancy breathed.

"Well, who is it from, Mahala?" Ben demanded suspiciously. "Isn't there a note with it?"

"No – nothing."

Martha drew her hands onto her hips. "I know who it's from, and it will just have to go back. Of all people Mr. Jack Randall knows a young lady could never accept such an expensive gift from a man."

"Jack Randall!" Nancy exclaimed. "Wh-what makes you think it is from him? Is there something you didn't tell us, Mahala?"

"I minded some business for him when his father fell ill in Savannah," Mahala replied. Then she added softly: "I – I can only guess he meant this as a thank you, seeing as how I refused to be paid."

"Well, he'll just have to find some other way to thank you," Martha declared. She took the necklace from Mahala and put it back in the box. "If you can't bring yourself to send it back, *I* will. Maybe that would make a point. Do you not agree, Mrs. Emmitt?"

Nancy looked dazed. "I do," she replied. She looked carefully at Mahala. "Do you think this man has serious intentions toward you, Mahala?"

Mahala shook her head. "I don't know. I don't think so. *No.* It must just be a thank you." Her gaze followed Martha's hand to the top of the mantle, where the box was deposited, then her eye fell on Henry's face. Her grandfather was smiling, and the oddest thing was, he looked tender – and pleased.

She puzzled over that as they all went to the table for Christmas Eve dinner. Ben cut the turkey, and they had sweet potatoes, cranberries and nuts, peas and rolls. Turning the topic away from the mysterious present, Martha inquired about happenings in the valley, and Nancy told how J.R. Dean had gotten the England family of Nacoochee to sign a ten-year lease on their property for a one-eighth share in his gold mining operations. The Hamby Ditch was seven-and-a-half miles long and was expected to cost $50,000 to build.

"But I'm afraid all that's going to be dull news soon," Nancy said. "Tell us what you've heard from travelers from the coast about the secession movement."

"News of great magnitude just came this week, in fact," Martha told them. "On the 20th, South Carolina seceded."

"What!" Ben burst forth.

"We'll be next," Jacob said in a prophetic tone.

"In fact I hear before it even happened our state called a convention to discuss a confederation with South Carolina, Florida, Mississippi and Alabama," Martha confirmed.

"The last paper I saw told how our governor has been preparing for possible hostilities," Ben said.

"Yes," Mahala agreed, cutting her turkey into bites she did not eat. "My friend Mrs. Carolyn Rousseau keeps me informed of what's happening. Her husband is in the Oglethorpe Light Infantry. She says the governor has reorganized all the volunteer regiments and consolidated them into the First Regiment Georgia Volunteers. He's been getting cannon and arms from up North and encouraging people to make military equipment here in the state."

"I bet the people in Savannah are wild with excitement, being in the center of everything," Nancy said.

Mahala nodded. "Apparently banks are curtailing business and the merchants are hard up for money. And there's to be a meeting January 16 that will decide everything."

"Does your friend think the state will secede?" Ben asked.

"Yes. She says that's all the talk. Maybe the U.S. government will finally learn the lesson that they can't push everyone around," Mahala stated, remembering Henry's stories of the days just before the Trail of Tears.

"Now Mahala," he interjected, "do not forget the part the state of Georgia played in the tragedy of our people."

"Maybe – but the national government started it all, way back at the beginning of the century. Did you not say so?"

Henry nodded reluctantly. "Perhaps. But there is much danger in simplifying such weighty issues."

Mahala fell silent. Her grandfather's words of caution caused her mind to turn again to Jack. What must he be thinking and feeling? Surely he was one who now weighed many such "weighty issues." She wished very much that she could talk to him tonight – listen to his views and struggles.

And the first thing she would ask him was if he was the one who sent the watch. But who else could it be? She did not want to send it back. Was that because she secretly longed to believe it was not just a form of payment but a token of his affection?

Later that evening as she kissed Henry goodnight, she asked softly, "Grandfather, when we were discussing the watch earlier, why did you smile?"

He patted her hand. "Because in your words and eyes I saw that you, Mahala, dear child, have finally met your match."

Mahala gaped momentarily, then shook her head. "If you met him, Grandfather, and saw how rich, how impossible this man is, you wouldn't say such things."

"Time will tell," was Henry's only response, with a quiet chuckle at his own cleverness of expression. "Time will tell."

CHAPTER TWELVE

January 3, 1861
Savannah, Georgia

arolyn awoke slowly to the steady tattoo of rain on the roof. She turned over and nestled into her pillow, wanting to go back to sleep. But today was important. The niggling memory of it stirred her to wakefulness alone in her big bed. She opened her eyes. Today Devereaux would go to Fort Pulaski in the harbor, to seize it along with forty-nine other men from the Oglethorpe Lights, fifty from the Savannah Volunteer Guards, and thirty-four from Chatham Artillery. They would beat any Federal forces to Cockspur Island and thus secure the mouth of the Savannah River.

She popped out of bed and hurried to the door adjoining their bedrooms. Pushing it open, she found the chamber empty. A sense of incredulous panic seized her. He wouldn't have gone without saying goodbye, would he? Even Dev wouldn't do that – not on so momentous an occasion.

Carolyn ran to the bell pull. She was yanking on stockings under her chemise and rolling the tops down on garters when the tall, slender Tania appeared.

Immediately Carolyn asked, "Mr. Rousseau – where is he?"

The eyebrows elevated, as if Tania knew any good wife ought not to need to ask such a question. "Downstairs, eatin' breakfast, Miss Carolyn."

Impatient with the taciturn maid, Carolyn insisted, "Well, help me – help me get dressed. I must hurry." Didn't the woman know what was afoot this morning? And didn't Dev realize how much she would have wanted to spend these last few minutes with him?

Shamed and irritable, she buttoned her petticoat. As she hooked up the front of her corset, Carolyn thought of the chain of events that had led the militia of Savannah to take such a big step today. Following South Carolina's secession, President Buchanan had assured the state's leaders that there would be no change in the status of military forces around Charleston until problems could be settled. Yet on December 26, Major Robert Anderson had transferred his U.S. troops from Fort Moultrie on Sullivan's Island to Fort Sumter in the middle of Charleston harbor. The next day as word of the situation circulated in the sister city of Savannah, angry citizens had gathered on the streets. Civilian and military leaders had met, all saying the same thing: that if it happened in Charleston, it could happen in Savannah. Days later, the Savannah *Republican* had received a copy of Georgia Senator Robert Toombs' telegram to Alexander Stephens, warning that a virulent anti-Southerner had been made secretary of war and that the time was ripe to secure Savannah's harbor. Governor Brown had arrived in town, and Col. Alexander Lawton of the 1st Volunteer Regiment had been given the nod for action. As disunionists elected three ardent secessionists to represent them at the state convention – one of them being Francis Bartow – the militia packed their knapsacks.

Tania dropped a soft wool dress over Carolyn's head.

"Hurry, hurry," Carolyn whispered as the maid buttoned up the back.

Carolyn grabbed her long braid, frayed though it was, and wound it around at the back of her neck, haphazardly sticking in hair pins. Then she ran out the door and down the stairs.

"Have the carriage made ready," Carolyn instructed the butler, who was standing in the foyer. "I will be going out with Lieutenant Rousseau."

He went off to relay her order.

She found Dev eating the last of his ham, clad in his dark blue uniform with buff trim and brass buttons. His tall, white-plumed shako, the brass nameplate proudly proclaiming "OLI" in Old English script, rested on the table in front of him. He looked up with a smile as she paused in the doorway.

"Finally awake, dear?"

"You could have called me. You *should* have called me."

"But you were sleeping so soundly." He actually looked nonplussed, perplexed even.

"Would you have let me sleep right past your departure?" Carolyn asked, moving slowly into the room.

"I probably would have kissed you before I left. Why so upset? I'll be back soon. Once we get the fort in order we're to rotate shifts of duty out there."

"That doesn't matter. You of all people know how momentous an occasion this is," Carolyn said. "Anything could happen now. Every day is unpredictable. And you wouldn't even spend the last few moments before you go with your wife?"

"Well, here we are," Dev said in a quickly cooling tone, laying down his knife and fork and looking her in the eye in the manner meant to intimidate her.

Carolyn faltered but held her ground. Her voice only trembled a little as she asked, "Do you have no idea how I love you, Devereaux? No idea at all?"

Dev rose slowly. He came around the table and embraced her, though she noticed his arms were stiff.

"And I love *you*, of course."

Stiff words, too, and stiff material as she laid her cheek wistfully against it. Carolyn listened for the beating of his heart and wished the sad, empty feeling in her own would go. If he couldn't love her – devotedly, passionately, as she yearned for – then, ah!, what blessed relief it would be not to care. Would time at least grant her that small mercy?

"I'm coming to the wharf to see you off."

Dev pulled back. "Not in this downpour!" he exclaimed.

"Yes, I am, and you cannot dissuade me. I've already called for a carriage."

Dev sighed. "Very well then, Carolyn."

She trailed Devereaux into the hall, where his faithful servant Little Joe handed him his knapsack. "Sure'n I can't go, Massuh Dev?" Joe asked woefully as the butler gave Carolyn her cape.

"Sorry, Joe, you know you can't."

"What'm I gonna do 'round here?"

"Make sure Mrs. Rousseau is safe." With that vague directive, Dev clapped the tall black man on the arm and turned toward the door.

Looking out into the rain at the waiting carriage, Carolyn raised the thick hood of her cloak. The footman was holding the vehicle door open, getting drenched. She made a dash for it. Dev came after her, yelling to the driver, "OLI barracks on Liberty Street." He jumped in and the door shut.

"Will your parents be at the wharf?" Carolyn asked.

The carriage lurched forward.

"No. They said their goodbyes last night." *As you should have*, was the rebuke implied in his tone.

"Promise you'll write me."

Dev smiled. "The first chance I get."

Carolyn didn't know if that was hopeful or not.

"You're not to worry about me," Devereaux added. "We don't expect any trouble from the tiny caretaker force on duty in Pulaski. And once we're in there, we can defend Savannah forever."

Carolyn smiled faintly. "It sounds like a good plan."

"You'll rest easier at night knowing your husband is in the fort that guards Savannah."

"I'd rest easier at night if my husband were by my side," she blurted.

Dev's cool mask came down. He had long known she was sensitive about their separate bedrooms, not because they were convenient, but because they represented their separate lives. Was she that repulsive then? Carolyn felt fat and awkward, thirteen all over again. Why didn't she maintain her dignity and leave well enough alone?

Because it just wasn't well enough. And she just didn't understand.

The vehicle slowed. They had reached the barracks.

Apparently not wanting to leave her on a sour note, Dev leaned forward and said, "I will be back by your side before you know it."

"Promise?"

"Sealed with a kiss."

Dev's lips briefly – all too briefly – joined with hers. Then he sprang out of the carriage as if eager for the adventure ahead. He waved as she pulled away.

Broad Street to the wharf was lined with people on their porches and outside buildings holding black umbrellas, obviously too excited about giving the militia a good send-off to be discouraged by the weather. The wharf was jam-packed with conveyances like hers. Carolyn sat for a good long time listening to the rain on the roof and waiting. She peeked out and saw the U.S. government's sidewheel steamer *Ida* bustling with activity. Each soldier would have a trunk, cot and bedroll, and every few would be allotted a mess chest. The boat had also been loaded with Chatham Artillery's battery of bronze guns – two twelve-pounder howitzers and four six-pounders.

At last Carolyn heard the roar of the crowd as the OLI men approached in their navy uniforms and shakos. They marched like the professionals they were, officers along the sides with their swords. She picked out Dev right away. Even in such handsome company he stood out, with his dark hair, square jaw and tall, fine physique. She wondered how many feminine hearts had fluttered even today at the sight of him. Hers was fluttering, too. Here was where he shone – in authority, in the midst of excitement. He moved with a confidence and eagerness even military discipline could not hide.

He didn't see her, of course. He was occupied with keeping the men in formation as they passed through the enthusiastic crowds.

Why had he married her, she wondered suddenly. For clearly this was where his heart belonged. Had it been for her inheritance? Or just to win her from his brother? And had she married the wrong man, then? For even now she hardly knew him. At least that was what she had to believe, for believing the opposite – that what she knew of him, what she had of him now was all there was, all there would ever be – left a black vacuum of hopelessness inside her heart. And she had to have hope.

Mid-January, 1861
Clarkesville, Georgia

Trekking back towards the Clarkesville square along Washington Street, Mahala thought the frosty ground beneath her boots felt as hard as her heart.

The winter landscape was equally as bare, with sprinkles of brown leaves clinging here and there to denuded branches.

During the winter, there were far too many long hours alone. The isolation and introspection went against Mahala's grain. She longed for excitement, love, friendship – anything. Her visit with Selma had helped some. They had spoken of all that was going on in the world. Even now the Georgia delegates – including Habersham County's Baptist minister Singleton Sisk and the Presbyterian minister Richard Ketchum – were in session in Milledgeville, deciding whether the state would leave the nation or not. For two hours she had felt alive again, connected to someone and something outside herself. But as soon as the door of the new parsonage had closed behind her, the rest of the day had stretched ahead long and bleak.

No need to stop by the post office. She had received a letter from Carolyn three days ago.

Yet as Mahala passed the little building, the now very aged Mr. George Blythe caught sight of her. Mr. Blythe was too old to run the mail wagon, but the postmaster, Alexander Erwin, allowed him to help in the post office and take care of deliveries and errands about town.

"Oh, Miss Mahaley!" he called cheerfully, his breath making a white puff above his scarf. "I got a package for ye!"

Mahala turned. "A package? For me?"

"Well, in truth it be addressed to yer grandma, but half a second an' I'll fetch it."

Mr. Blythe had been about to lock the door, but now he ducked back inside. Mahala waited by the street. Almost as quickly he reappeared with a small parcel in his hand.

"Maybe a late Christmas present," he conjectured, handing it to her.

As soon as Mahala read the address in the neat, masculine hand, her heart picked up its pace.

"Thank you very much, Mr. Blythe."

"Right welcome. Good evenin' to ye."

The old man raised his hat as Mahala turned away, now hurrying toward home with a purposeful step.

She found Martha in their private dining room setting out napkins and silverware.

"Ah, there you are," her grandmother said, turning back to the sideboard to reach for the tea pot. As she did Mahala quietly set the package on the table. "And how was the Rev. Mrs. Burns today? – What's this?"

"Mr. Blythe just gave it to me."

"Oh, well, what is it?" Martha repeated, pouring hot water over tea strainers squatting atop china cups for the two of them.

Mahala did not reply, merely shrugged out of her coat and went to hang it up. She placed her bonnet on a peg of the hall tree and patted her hair before returning. Martha was busy tearing the wrapping away, her mouth pursed. She had read the address. Mahala watched as the older woman removed the familiar leather case and snapped open a letter.

"What does he have to say for himself?" Martha muttered. Then she read aloud: "'My dear Mrs. Franklin, it was with great bemusement that I received this watch in the mail from you. Some mistake has obviously been made. What would I have to do with such an object? And who else could use it, with your granddaughter's initials on it? I am sure the only way I know how to dispose of it is to return it to her in hopes that she will at least be able to get some use out of it. Kindest regards, Jack Randall, Esquire.'"

Mahala bit her lip at Jack's cleverness.

Martha slapped the letter on the table. "What a scoundrel! He admits to nothing. 'Great bemusement,' my foot! He thinks to get around me."

Mahala still held her peace. She had learned silence often worked best when Martha was in a tizzy. But as her grandmother brought dinner to the table, she couldn't resist a glance at the case. Martha did not fail to mark it.

"Well, you might as well take it to your room. It *is* a valuable time piece, and I'm not one for total waste. But you are never to wear it in his presence – *never*, do you hear?"

"Yes, Grandmother," Mahala replied dutifully, as though she were ten. Her heart soared with triumph, but she left the case lying on the table as she consumed her beef tips and rice. Best not to appear too eager.

After the meal, Mahala took the watch into her bedroom. She opened the lid of the box and gazed at the silver time piece. She had to believe Jack's affection for her had motivated his determination for her to have this gift. Surely sheer stubbornness would not have made him go to so much trouble. Maybe over time, his inbred views of class and propriety would melt with a softening heart. She could be patient. She just had to have hope.

And right now she had an opening, though one Martha would have to remain ignorant of. She took out a bottle of ink and a pen, along with her best stationery, and sat down at her desk. Dipping the nib into the black liquid, she wrote:

Dear Mr. Randall, I thank you for the return of the beautiful silver time piece. I shall indeed make good use of it. Its receipt brought to mind your father's illness. Is he better now? I truly hope so. Sincerely, Mahala Franklin

That night, she lay for a long time listening to the buffeting of the January wind against the inn, thinking of Jack. How she missed him, exasperating man that he was. She now recognized that she would be bored with any

155

man who failed to stir her emotions and engage her intellect like Jack. And she admired him – his courage and convictions.

Oh, God, she prayed, *please let him write back.*

It had been two days ago – January 21st, to be exact – that Jack had received the telegram. "Pulling out with iron only. Stop. Port authorities searching S-bound ships. Capt. Northrup."

Jack's heart had nearly stopped for a second, then beat fast with a rush of gratefulness for Jeremy's alertness. Because of the importance of this mission, Jack had asked the older man to take the firm's only non-steam vessel to New York and back. If the plates, straps and screws from his family's foundry had been confiscated, the loss would have been difficult, time-consuming and much more expensive to replace. He was eager for the iron shipment to be safely in Savannah's harbor – and thence to the ship yard, where the iron would be applied to his new coastal passenger packet, *South Land II.*

At that very moment his father leaned on his door jamb, a bright smile on his face. Though he still tired easily, and became short of breath even from climbing stairs, he was at least back at work. And his outlook was more positive.

"She's just docked," Richard said of the company schooner.

"Excellent! What's the latest on the trouble with New York authorities?" Jack asked. New York's governor had ordered city police to seize vessels deemed contraband of war, and twenty-eight cases of Georgia-bound muskets aboard the steamer *Monticello* had been withheld. Savannah was irate.

"Apparently Robert Toombs telegraphed his protest to the mayor."

"Oh, that will do a fat lot of good," Jack commented.

"And Governor Brown will be telegraphing Governor Morgan, to be sure. What will happen remains to be seen."

"It sure happened fast – like they were just waiting for us to secede."

Richard nodded. He slid some mail onto Jack's desk, which Jack rifled through. A small envelope with a fine feminine script caught his eye. He slit it open as his father said, "Probably were. Now we've cut our ties from the Northern states. In a way I hate it, but in another, the excitement of independence is intoxicating. This will mean good things for us, Jack, as a firm – as a family."

"Will it? Doesn't the severed tie with your brother and sister dampen that intoxication just a little?"

"Oh, nothing has been severed, Jack. We will always love each other – even if they can't openly ship us iron."

156

"Don't you think you're being a little too optimistic?" Jack asked as he pulled Mahala's letter from its envelope. "The New York police were looking for contraband of *war*."

"Premature. The governors will settle it. There are always hot heads."

"Like the ones shooting off guns and skyrockets Saturday?"

Richard sighed. "You are still the most argumentative boy."

"Boy." Jack laughed. He scanned Mahala's brief lines and the smile remained on his face. So she had liked the necklace. He hadn't been sure if sending it back to Savannah was solely the grandmother's doing. He was glad it was. Good. Maybe he had smoothed over his foolish, uncalled-for behavior last time he'd seen her. He had not been able to rest remembering the look on her face, the quaver in her voice, at the hurt he'd caused her.

He folded the note and placed it in his breast pocket, where it was sure to crinkle as he undressed that night, reminding him to write her back, even amid all the excitement. Maybe he'd tell her some of what was going on, though doubtless the curious girl kept herself fully apprised.

"What's that?"

"Nothing important."

Richard frowned suspiciously, but before he could speak again, a wind-blown figure appeared behind him in the door. Richard turned to see Jeremy Northrup's pleasant grin. He laughed and clasped the captain's hand.

"Northrup – I can't say as I've ever been happier to see you!" he exclaimed.

Jack stood and shook his friend's hand as well. "We owe you a hearty bonus," he added.

"I can't take all the credit," Jeremy admitted. "Your cousin George heard rumors of what was afoot before the searches began. He warned me. We had just finished loading the iron. I telegraphed and set sail."

"Good old George," Jack said with a grin.

"He sent a letter for you." Jeremy fished in his pocket. He held out an envelope.

"For me?" Jack glanced at his father.

"For you."

Richard drew up his bottom lip and shrugged. "Go ahead, Son. I've told you I consider you acting head of Randall and Ellis. I have paperwork waiting."

"But don't you want to know what he says?"

"If it requires counsel, you know where to find me."

Jack let him go, resisting the urge to force his father's involvement for his own good. Most people commented positively on Richard's new serenity, but Jack found it inexplicably disturbing.

Jack and Jeremy discussed a few items of business over coffee brought up by the new clerk, Andrew Willis. Willis, who lived with his widowed mother, was from impoverished gentility and thus possessed a pleasing combination of manners and humility. One hardly knew he was there, and the work was always done.

"Well, I reckon that covers it, then," Jeremy said when he had a grasp of his employer's expectations.

"All right, Captain. And thank you again," Jack said, sincerely meeting the other man's eyes.

Jeremy nodded. He pushed his cup farther onto Jack's desk and stood up. Jack opened George's letter, but he looked up after a minute when he realized Jeremy was still standing there, fingering his battered seaman's cap.

"Is something wrong, Jeremy?" Jack asked.

"Well, yes, Young Jack, there's something very wrong. In this country. When I was up North, all I heard talk of was preserving the Union and quashing the rebellion. 'Rebellion,' that's what they called it. Never did two sections see things so entirely different, and not just slavery. But slavery's a big part of the states' rights the South is clamoring for, and well, I reckon we both know where we stand on that. Here's the thing. I don't think they'll let Georgia and the others go without a fight. You know how deep my loyalty to you goes, Jack, and to your family, but I don't have family. Georgia's not my home. So that leaves me with conscience ruling."

Jack laid the paper flat. A queasy feeling had started in the pit of his stomach. "What are you saying, Jeremy? Are you quitting on me?" He could hardly get the words out. In the office, Jeremy had been the best of employees. On the open seas, he'd been a mentor. Most of all, Jack had thought they were the closest of friends. And he didn't have many of those.

Jeremy immediately hung his graying head. "I reckon I am. I'm sorry, Jack. I just can't have peace with it any other way."

He wouldn't meet Jack's eyes. Silence reigned for a few minutes.

At length Jack said, "It seems your mind's made up – so I won't attempt to bargain or plead."

"I thank you, young Jack. This is powerfully hard for me."

Jack didn't need to mention what a bad way Jeremy was leaving *him* in. "Come by tomorrow for your check. I'll see that it's ready, even if I'm not here." Jack didn't think he could bear another awkward scene. He got up, passed around the desk, and held open the door.

Jeremy paused in front of him. He finally looked into Jack's face. "If we go to war, is there any chance of you joining your Northern family?"

Jack felt like a scratchy pebble was caught in his throat. "I don't know," he said roughly.

"Well, if you do ... look me up. I'll probably be in New York, too. Seems a place of opportunity."

Jack nodded brusquely. The older man started to walk by him, when suddenly Jack remembered his first sight of a smiling young officer on *Eastern Star*. He hooked Northrup in a rough half embrace, admitting, "I'll miss you."

"And I you, Jack. I don't regret a minute. We've had many a fine year working together – and much of eternal value to show for it," Jeremy said, nodding and smiling. He quickly brushed a tear from his eye and headed for the stairs.

CHAPTER THIRTEEN

April 15, 1861
Savannah, Georgia

xamination of a wartime market had convinced Richard that sterling would be the wisest investment for surplus funds – and a wartime market it was. Three days prior Confederates had opened fire on the Federal forces occupying Fort Sumter in Charleston harbor. Prepared for a naval assault but not for one from land-based guns and mortars on three surrounding points, Robert Anderson surrendered after a thirty-four-hour bombardment. Although only one man had been killed – and that an accident during the withdrawal – Richard guessed Lincoln's response would be swift and severe. He would look upon the situation as no longer just a shipping tiff between two ports, but an act of aggression – never mind that Yankee troops had made the first move by seizing the strategic fort.

It was all the bank clerk could talk of while transacting business. Richard rubbed his arm a bit. It had been aching since dawn. He wished the young man would hurry. Jack was picking up the women so they could all go to lunch together.

Yes, after the governors had gotten involved – despite much stalling on the part of New York's leader – and Georgia had demonstrated her seriousness in holding four barks and a schooner with New York registry, the arms taken from *Monticello* had at last been released. But shortly thereafter, other events had transpired that had created far greater excitement in Washington. Virginia had seceded, taking with her other pivotal states. And on February 18, Jefferson Davis had been elected president of the new Confederacy. Now the North had a specific target much more concrete than a handful of independent, solitary states.

When Stephen Mallory had become secretary of the Confederate Navy, Richard's contacts had relayed Mallory's plan: a small (of necessity) but technologically advanced navy, comprised of steam cruisers and ironclads, the best to break the blockade Lincoln was sure to impose. Open lanes by sea would be vital to the Confederacy, especially considering the irregular railroad system throughout the South. In past decades each state had wanted to retain control of its own railroad system and had resisted linking with that

160

of other states. Now, if the war went on for any amount of time, that was sure to pose a hardship. Davis had touched on the need for a Richmond to Atlanta rail route in his inauguration speech, but resistance was already being thrown up by states' rights activists suspicious of too much government interference.

Boy, did Richard wish he had started his own foundry. Between iron plates for ships and cast iron for cannons, rails and cook pots, what money he could have made! But he'd have to do with what he had: Georgia's small but most impressive shipping flotilla.

Obviously, some adjustments would have to be made to the boats.

He knew the president had been authorized by Congress to buy or construct ten steam gunboats for coastal defense, and that retired U.S. naval officer Josiah Tattnall had been appointed commodore. Tattnall was pulling together a mosquito fleet of any boat he could get his hands on. Naval representatives had already sent out tentative feelers in Richard's direction. Unbeknownst to Jack, Richard had given them hope by agreeing to a meeting later this month.

A prick of guilt jabbed him. He said he considered Jack acting head of Randall and Ellis. And he did. Heaven knew his father was losing his memory and could only be considered a consultant at best. And his own health now limited *him*. But Jack was stubborn and might need a little prodding to explore ways they could work with the Confederate officials. This was one last thing he could do to help navigate the firm in the right direction.

There was that idea again – "one last thing." The feeling of finality, of quickly passing time, seemed to pop up even when he tried to act normal. But acting it was, for he felt tired – and old.

That morning at breakfast, he had read aloud to Jack the stirring tale of how a Lieutenant Hall had run the newly-purchased *Huntress* eight days in stormy weather south from New York, for the first time flying the Confederate and Georgia flags together. It had stirred Jack's boyhood derring-do, as he'd hoped.

He would talk with Jack tonight. For sure he would.

"Here you go, Mr. Randall." The obsequious clerk had at last returned with his receipts. "Smart, you and your son pulling all monies out of the New York bank and putting them into sterling – not bonds. I wouldn't tell just anybody that. Don't want to appear unpatriotic, you know, and mark me, I have every confidence in our new Confederacy, but with silver, who can go wrong?"

"Thank you, Mr. Hammond." Richard stood, pocketing the papers, and shook the clerk's hand.

"A pleasure doing business with you, Sir – as always."

Richard backed away from the nodding and smiling little man. He left the office for the lobby, which was humming with people. Across the way he saw his wife, daughter and Jack enter, looking worried. He had held them up. He lifted his arm to wave. As he did, a gripping pain shot down the limb and into his side. He couldn't move. He stood there paralyzed like a fool. When he was able to grab his chest, he did, simultaneously falling to his knees.

Everyone was looking at him, but he was too internally focused to care. What was happening? Another episode? Would this be the last? He couldn't breathe, it hurt so bad. He did hear Sunny call his name. Alarm was on her face. Jack bounded ahead of her, clearing a path for her and Sylvie with his broad frame.

A second later his family surrounded him, Jack yelling for a doctor while easing him to the floor.

"Richard, is it your heart?" Sunny asked in a sobbing voice. Then she exclaimed, "Oh, God, help us! He's turning gray! Richard, hold on, honey."

His vision temporarily blacked out. He struggled for breath, then opened his eyes to see Sylvie spluttering with fright, her big, warm tears falling on his hand. He tried to reach for them, even as he felt the most powerful force in the universe sucking him away.

With his last strength he focused on his son and whispered, "Take care of them."

A whisper of a breeze rustled the live oaks in Laurel Grove Cemetery. Spanish moss stirred above Jack as he sat with his back to the large tree overlooking his father's fresh grave, the letter Jeremy had brought him from George several months past clutched in his hand. He merely held it, one booted knee drawn up, staring expressionlessly ahead while his horse munched grass some distance away. He didn't have to read it again. He knew the contents by heart.

> *Dear Jack, this is the last iron shipment we can get out to you. New York businessmen are known Southern suppliers, so they are cracking down hard. From here on out, I fear the content of any Southern-bound ship will be searched. I regret the end of partnership between Randall Iron and Randall and Ellis Shipping.*
>
> *But this does not mean the end of our relationship. Georgia has gone out on her own, but that does not mean you have to go with her. Decide carefully where you will place your alliances, for once pledged, they cannot easily be retracted. Let conscience be your guide. My home and my father's home are always open to*

The Gray Divide

you. We would do all in our power to see you established here. Enough said.

Your cousin, George

A family member's final lifeline thrown over the chasm of a renting nation.

There was no doubt in his mind that George and Geoffrey would answer the call to arms if the need arose, leaving Uncle Houston to manage numerous and lucrative government contracts. Apparently he could still fit into that picture any way he wanted to. He had many good contacts in the shipyards and firms of the U.S.'s most bustling port. The opportunities were endless.

Jack got up and walked to his father's grave. "But you made it clear what you wanted me to do, didn't you?" he asked aloud.

Even Richard's will had borne out his expectations. Sunny had been given the house, servants, and wharf properties, which would generate a small continual income. She and her three children had also received comfortable financial sums. But Jack had been left his father's share of Randall and Ellis, stocks and railroad shares – the bulk of the inheritance which promised substantial future provision, handled rightly. And Jack knew why. His father's legacy tied him like honeysuckle vine to the Georgia soil.

Oh, he could cut it all loose in one fell swoop and run like mad to New York, but what kind of fool would do that?

He knelt before the headstone, a hand on the mound of fresh earth. Richard had been separated from Eva even in death, for Colonial Park had been closed to new burials in 1853. It galled him something fierce to not see their headstones side by side, in fact made him fire mad, until a still, small voice whispered in his head, asking: "Does it really matter where the body lies?"

Jack bowed his head and cried out inside: *Must there always be division? This awful pulling asunder? I think my spirit is being ripped apart – conscience from duty!*

Incredibly alone, he felt hot tears well up in his eyes, and for the first time he longed for a woman's embrace – not for passion, but for comfort. Some small part of him recognized fleetingly that the longing was deeper and higher, reaching up toward the blue skies, but he was too confused to analyze that.

There came no direct answer to his question, only another breeze and the resounding memory of his mother's voice. "Do you love me, Jack? …Then you've got to love the South. …It's part of you, too."

His mind skimmed over the smell of salt and marsh, the clank of moorings and the creak of his office chair, the soft drawl of familiar voices, the color of autumn on the North Georgia hills. Then he heard a step behind

163

him. His bowed head and slumped shoulders jerked up. Sylvie stood there, soft face and dark eyes anxious, looking much too young and vulnerable in her black dress. Funny, but he had never noticed before that she favored their father, too.

She obviously realized she had interrupted a struggle of momentous proportions, for her face crumpled with sorrow and sympathy. "Oh, Jack," she cried, biting her lip.

Jack couldn't find his voice, but he held out an arm to her, and she ran to him. Sylvie wept, and Jack realized his own tears finally mingled with hers. They huddled together by their father's grave, joined in misery.

He smelled the sweetness of her dark hair and felt the petite frailty of her frame. In the flower of youth, she had lost her protector. Her brothers were away at school and only mildly interested in her welfare at best. It was to him that Sylvie looked. And for so much more than money. It wasn't about money, really. Not at all. It was about the ties of blood that ran deeper than any words, any feelings. It wasn't about duty. It was about love.

A few days later Jack was in his father's office, clearing his desk of personal effects. One day he might move into this more spacious room, but for now he would leave it as it was, taking what he needed to his own office and letting the rest remain. He could come in as needed for reference – or reflection.

He thumbed through a file containing his father's recent correspondence. The sight of Richard's script caused him to pause a moment to clear the moisture from his eyes. He just couldn't believe Richard was gone. At home, he kept expecting to hear Richard's voice, where instead he was greeted only by women's weeping and tones muted with sorrow. Every day he left the pink mansion, his parting view of Richard's top hat on the coat rack sent a dagger to his chest. And here at the firm, he kept getting up to seek out his father to ask some question, only to remind himself with the sense of loss bitterly renewed that Richard was no longer but a room away.

Jack came to a recent letter bearing a signature that made him abruptly halt. Stephen Mallory. He jerked out the paper and perused it quickly. As he did, his brows lowered. His father – in discussions with the Confederate Navy about the possible lease or purchase of Randall and Ellis ships? Apparently Richard had disclosed quite a number of details on each model and had been open to the thought of at least establishing a partnership – if not selling outright! Jack was so confounded he hardly knew what to think.

He was still mentally spluttering when a knock came at the door and the smooth, thin face of Andrew Willis peeked in.

"Mr. Randall? Someone is here to see you. I know you are not taking appointments, but this man says he had a longstanding date with your father for today and well ... he seems rather *important*." The clerk swallowed apologetically.

"Who is he?"

Andrew ventured forward and placed a crisp calling card before him. Augustus Blinkwell, CSN. Jack frowned. The name was certainly unique and sounded oddly familiar. It couldn't be ... He shifted the letter back before him and skimmed it again. There it was, in the final paragraph! Augustus Blinkwell was the agent who would be sent to represent Mallory and Commodore Tattnall. Apparently the specifics of that meeting had been arranged in another communication. Apparently the meeting had been arranged for *today*.

"What shall I tell him, Sir?"

"Nothing. Show him in here in five minutes."

Andrew gave a nod and hurried out. Jack needed a preparatory moment. He took out one of his favorite cigars and lit it, leaning back in his chair thoughtfully. By the time the clerk appeared again with a portly balding man in tow, Jack had schooled his thoughts and expression. He banked his cigar and stood to offer his hand.

"Mr. Blinkwell? Jack Randall."

"A pleasure."

"Please have a seat."

His caller dumped a black satchel by a wingchair and pulled a handkerchief out of his pocket. He proceeded to pat away the evidence of the exertion of the stairs. Then he said, "Forgive me, Mr. Randall, but I was given to believe my appointment was with the senior Mr. Randall, Mr. *Richard* Randall. As I came in I could hardly help noticing the black ribbon upon the door. And now ..." He paused to wave a plump hand at Jack's mourning attire. "Am I to assume that, sadly, your father—"

"— has passed away," Jack completed abruptly.

"Oh, I'm so sorry."

"Thank you. Now if you wish to proceed with any conversation about the business of our family's firm, I am the one with whom you must speak. Do you still wish to do so?"

"Oh – yes, of course. Thank you," Blinkwell hastily replied, though he looked rather crestfallen at this development. Perhaps Jack's reputation had preceded him.

"Please sit down," Jack said again, and this time the man did. "Now, what can I do for you?"

"The question, Mr. Jack Randall, is not what you can do for *me*, but what you can do for our new country."

Ah, thought Jack, Mr. Blinkwell recovered his equilibrium quickly. He raised his brows and gestured for his guest to continue.

"Our opponents are preparing to swoop down on us, not only on land but at sea. Their navy is buying gunboats, paddle wheel steamers and iron-clads hand over fist."

Jack had already been apprised of that truth, as Randall iron was being used in some of the contracts. He remained impassive.

"Unfortunately Secretary Mallory does not have the same options. Our agents are having a h– an awful time finding any decent boats to purchase. We just sent an engineering officer to New York, Philadelphia and Baltimore and all he came up with was one steamer – the *Caroline*, but an outbreak in Baltimore aborted purchase negotiations. We also have men in Canada, but I fear the Yanks have beat us there. We need steamers, Mr. Randall, to counter them. We expected a cabinet blockade. Instead they are posting squadrons off all our major ports, as I'm sure you are aware. We can't outrun them. We need speed – steam. In short, Mr. Randall, your father had offered us the hopes of an arrangement with Randall and Ellis – something that would be of benefit to your family as well as the Confederacy, and, even more specifically, the security of your home city. Commodore Tattnall's flotilla would be greatly bolstered by the addition of any of your steamers."

"And what sort of arrangement did you have in mind, exactly?" Jack asked. He was always willing to hear a man out.

Augustus Blinkwell sat forward slightly, clamping his hands on both knees. "The outright purchase of one or all of your shipping vessels – however many you will part with. I'll even take the schooner."

Jack's eyes widened, then he burst into laughter, leaning back in his chair. His visitor seemed slightly unnerved by his reaction. "I'm sorry, Mr. Blinkwell ... you actually want me to sell my entire business away to the Confederate Navy?"

Blinkwell spluttered, "Under the circumstances, I'd consider it better than the whole fleet sitting at anchor."

"And just why would it be doing that?"

"Do you mean to say you have no intention of supporting the cotton embargo?"

Jack smiled. "I have every intention of doing what is best for my family's business – whatever that may be. But even if I were to forgo running cotton this fall, there are plenty of other exports to keep us busy. And if the blockade is effective, the *imports* would be all the more valuable."

"If your captains, inexperienced in military situations as they are, can make it past the gunboats."

"Oh, my captains are very experienced." Jack thought fleetingly, regretfully, of Jeremy Northrup.

"And the overseas connections to make it happen?"

"That's not a problem, either. I can do for Savannah international shipping most of what Fraser, Trenholm in Charleston is setting up to do for the Ordnance Bureau. Only I can do it on my own."

Augustus cleared his throat and shifted in his chair. Taking a different tact, he said in a conciliatory voice, "I'm sure that's all true. But you have yet to hear the price I would offer you, Mr. Randall. I assure you it is substantial."

Again Jack smiled. He already knew the Confederate Navy to have an almost nonexistent bank account, so he could be fairly confident that even if he had been disposed to sell, the offer would not have tempted him. "No amount would be substantial enough to will me to part with my family legacy – my inheritance," Jack responded calmly.

Augustus rapidly fluttered his eyelashes. He was living up to his name, "Blinkwell," Jack thought, and had to quickly divert his musings so he wouldn't chuckle. "I was afraid you might feel that way," Blinkwell said, "and understandably so. Randall and Ellis has long been a respected name in Savannah – an asset to the city. I can sympathize with your desire to maintain the status quo, especially in this season of fresh loss. So, I came prepared to offer you a second option, though I do so a little more reluctantly. A partnership. Your ships, my crews. And one-fourth cargo space."

"One-fourth to you?"

Another tiny throat clearing. "One-fourth to *you*."

Jack was too perturbed to laugh the man out of his office, which was exactly what he deserved. "And when your crews get my ships shot up or sunk by the Yankees, do I get one-fourth loss, too?" Jack stood up. "It would appear our negotiations are at an end, Mr. Blinkwell. You would do better to make your preposterous offers to Charles Morgan in the Gulf."

Augustus stood as well, his face turning bright red as he reached for his bag. "Charles Morgan is a full-blooded–" here he interjected several strong explicatives that caused Jack's eyebrows to raise – "Yankee, and him giving controlling interest to his New Orleans son-in-law is not going to convince anyone otherwise. It will serve him right if we confiscate each and every one of his–" more descriptive cursing – "steamers. And the same for you, Mr. Jack Randall."

"So that's what you want everyone to think of the Confederate Navy? So much for chivalry, gallantry and free enterprise – take what you want and never mind that you'd be trampling the rights of Southern citizens far worse than the so-called Northern oppressors ever did!"

"Only where disloyal, Yankee profiteers are concerned – it if were up to me," Blinkwell said, his eyelids again fluttering rapidly. He put a finger near Jack's face. His voice lowered to a rasp. "You should have been honored by my offer, Randall. It was your chance to show everyone where your loyalties lie. But your pride and greed will cost you everything. You may enjoy a few lucky voyages at the outset, and turn a pretty penny at the expense of the people, but before long they'll begin to question why Randall and Ellis has refused to support our military. The whisper is a powerful thing. You will one day find yourself desperate to renegotiate."

Jack walked calmly around the shorter man and held open the door. "First of all I do nothing 'at the expense of the people,' which you would already realize if you knew me. And second, if the day ever does come when I decide to strike a deal, it will be because it is best for my family – *and* the citizens of Savannah. And you can rest assured it will not be with you. Good day, Mr. Blinkwell."

The small boardroom of Randall and Ellis Shipping was filled to capacity with broad-shouldered and not altogether immaculately clean men. Voices rumbled and cigar and pipe smoke hung heavy. Andrew Willis raised the windows, but the late April air was already rather humid and thus his action was not very helpful. The captains and pilots of the Randall ships began to hang coats on the backs of their chairs and loosen their neckties. When Jack entered bearing several file folders – followed by an unfamiliar blonde young man – the room quieted. The stranger circumspectly took a seat while Jack stood at the head of the long table.

"Good afternoon, gentlemen. Thank you all for coming. In light of recent events – both nationally speaking and regarding my father's passing – I felt it was time for us to meet and discuss our future plans."

"And may we all offer our condolences again on that score, Mr. Randall," said Dean Howell, *Fortitude*'s captain.

Jack nodded to the sturdy, salt-and-pepper bewhiskered sailor. "Thank you. I hope to have as good a working relationship with all of you as he did. You already know me. I've overseen everything through my father's illness. But it's time you know my plans here at the outbreak of hostilities. Beginning this week, you will all enjoy a paid leave as your ships are taken to the yard – all except the schooner *Regale–*" Jack nodded to her aging captain – "which will set sail tomorrow, taking her exports to Liverpool in lieu of New York. The others will be refitted with telescoping funnels, turtle-back decks and lower masts. Any state rooms will be renovated to cargo space. While dry docked *Fortitude, Evangeline* and *South Land II* will be painted a dull gray-white. All this is to equip them to better run the blockade."

As Jack had expected, murmurs immediately arose among his employees.

"Cargo space!" *South Land*'s captain, John Billingsly, cried. "We make a pretty penny running folks up and down the Southern coast. Using Wassaw Sound and St. Augustine Creek there's no reason we can't continue to do so – even should a Yankee fleet appear off the Savannah."

"We'll make a prettier penny bringing in supplies from the Bahamas," Jack pointed out, "using those same waterways."

"This war won't last. Then the *South Land* will have been dismantled for nothing."

Jack shook his head doubtfully. "We'd all like to believe that, but remember, I've seen the power of the North's manufacturing – and the supremacy of their navy – first hand. Most of you have, too. If I'm wrong, I'll gladly eat my words and swallow any loss along with it. But if I'm right, if the blockade is effective and the war stretches out … the profits for us will far outweigh the gamble."

"Then, you plan to continue commercially, instead of outfitting *Fortitude* and *Evangeline* as raiders?" Howell ventured.

"That's right. I know some of you may have heard the rumors that the Confederate government will be offering Letters of Marque and Reprisal to privateers. I will not be among those answering that call. It's not my desire to take up arms against the Yankees or to ask my crews of non-military men to attempt to capture Northern merchant ships. If you are interested in buccaneering, you'll have to seek out adventure with another ship owner. You may, however, face dangers in the future even as much as we may seek to avoid confrontation. Thus, Mr. Lawrence Birch here."

All eyes turned to the blonde young man, tan and good-looking, who rose to his feet and gave a dignified bow as Jack continued talking.

"Mr. Birch spent five years in the U.S. Navy in Southern Atlantic waters. He comes to us from Charleston highly recommended as one of the best pilots in the business," Jack told them. "When Captain Northrup left our company, he took his pilot with him, thus leaving the opening for Mr. Birch. He will be our invaluable teacher on the nuances of various ports and our advisor on military tactics. Starting this week, he will instruct all of you, especially you pilots, in a series of meetings. But his eventual post will be *Evangeline*."

"Under what captain?" Howell wondered.

"Mr. Birch will work with me."

"You're to captain *Evangeline*?"

"That's correct." Jack felt no need to defend his ability or background. He had been at sea and studied shipping and sailing his whole life. Now was at last the time to put his head knowledge into action. He felt confident that with Lawrence and *Evangeline*'s first mate as practical advisors, he would be a successful captain. It was an exciting bend in his road.

Jack continued in another vein, "You may also have heard rumors that my father was considering selling out or contracting with the Confederate Navy. You'll quickly realize if you haven't already that I'm not him. The offer they made me was an insult, tailored, I believe, to a suspected Northern sympathizer," Jack said, pausing to rub the back of his neck. "So you'll all be keeping your jobs. However, if any of you have patriotic urgings, now's the time to part ways with no bad feelings. If you have a problem hauling civilian cargo for a private shipper, go enlist."

He paused and met the eyes of each man in turn. They all looked back levelly – no faltering. "Good," he said. "So if no one wants to play pirate or soldier, we may proceed. In light of circumstances I expect we'll all grow quite rich. It may not be unheard of for a captain to net, say, $5,000, and a pilot, $3,500 or so – per successful round trip. There will be abundant pay for every sailor. You earn it, you pocket it."

Cheers and clapping erupted from the group. Grizzled faces lightened.

Jack couldn't stop himself from adding a bit smugly: "Substantially higher pay than your enlisted counterparts will be receiving, by the way."

"Hooray for Cap'n Jack!" Billingsly cried. As the captain of the smallest ship, he would be receiving the most substantial raise. But Jack also expected he would be the most harried.

It was a good feeling to be one of them, not merely their boss. Jack smiled and held up a hand. "Don't get too excited yet. If things pan out as I anticipate, you'll be earning every cent. There may be long periods of inactivity followed by runs entailing great danger."

"Do you not think the English will force open the ports?" one pilot asked.

"If they do, I'll be surprised. If the Brits had wanted to make a statement, they could have made it at the board table – by giving the Confederacy political recognition instead of relegating us to the status of belligerents."

"Give 'em a few months without cotton, an' they'll feel differently," the same pilot answered.

"We've shipped too much cotton out the past two years for that to happen right away," Jack replied.

"So we're to carry it out?"

"We'll carry in or out whatever best benefits this firm and the people of Savannah. I expect the Committees of Public Safety will ease up later this year, by the fall. I'll judge the cargo on a trip by trip basis. Initially, we'll focus on importing civilian cargoes. If the North does create an effective blockade, such items will be in high demand. Captain Harmon, should that be true, it will be difficult for you to outrun their steamers. Your eventual station may well become the Bahamas, bringing supplies from Europe to our steamers there. But we'll cross that bridge when we get to it. The U.S. Navy will have to make a move first. Any other questions?"

In the silence that followed, Jack looked around to make sure each man understood what was expected. Their faces were bright, registering eagerness for adventure – and wealth.

"Well then," Jack concluded, "I'd like to request you all return tomorrow for a session conducted by Mr. Birch. In the coming days, he will acquaint you with the new technology being installed on your ships. When the blockading fleet arrives, our goal will be simple: to not even let them know we're here."

CHAPTER FOURTEEN

Early May, 1861
Savannah, Georgia

s the small but proud *Ida* steamed away from Fort Pulaski, Devereaux had the feeling that it might be the last time he'd leave
Cockspur Island. Everyone knew that OLI's commander, Francis Bartow, was at loggerheads with Governor Brown over the
use of Georgia militia. Brown felt that these troops were exclusively his for use
within the state. Bartow held that they should be offered in service to the Confederacy as part of the provisional army. During his time as delegate to the
Confederate Congress, he had announced his intention to do just that with his
Oglethorpes. When the governor had blocked Bartow's gesture to Jefferson
Davis, the politician-officer had written directly to the president. What most
folks didn't realize was just how soon the boys might be leaving for Virginia.

The idea filled Dev with a swell of pride and excitement. He was ready to
go. Like most of the other men, the last thing he wanted was to be stuck on the
coast when the big battle came up North. There were more than enough companies to defend Savannah, noble duty that it was. Savannah's finest should
represent Georgia in Virginia.

Dev shrugged aside any uncertainty on that score. All winter and spring
preparations to secure the city had been made. Earthworks had been built
and manned from Hilton Head to Fort Jackson and from Red Bluff to Gen-
esis Point. Pulaski itself was readied by their very sweat and muscle. On May
Day, William Howard Russell, correspondent of the *London Times* – the same
who had covered the Crimean War – had come out with Commodore Tattnall and General Lawton to tour the fort. He had found 650 soldiers hard at
work, building sandbag traverses before magazine doors, mounting ten-inch
columbiads on ramparts, and storing ammunition and provisions. Everyone
had been dressed in their finest with every bayonet, barrel and button at a high
shine. The journalist had seemed very impressed.

Never mind that rumor had it that Russell had later pointed out the inse-
cure rear approach and the fort's accessibility to boats. Lawton had admitted
to these flaws but expressed confidence that the commodore would take care
of any Yanks by sea while the men in the fort managed them on land. Later,
the white-haired, rosy-cheeked Tattnall was said to have commented, "I have

172

no fleet, and long before the Southern Confederacy has a fleet that can cope with the Stars and Stripes, my bones will be white in the grave."

Dev just didn't believe it. While staring admiringly at Dev's jaunty uniform, the stocky, bearded Russell had personally congratulated him on a job well done. That's what he knew for sure. He could leave the fort with confidence and move on to what lay ahead.

Standing well away from the crowd, Dev propped a foot on a bench and leaned on one knee, looking ahead as they came near Savannah. Most commercial ships had abandoned port at the threat of a blockade, even though no Yankee cruisers had yet been sighted. He frowned when he saw the schooner *Regale* in the process of being unloaded, just in from Liverpool. If that selfish rascal Jack Randall would put his shoulder to the naval grindstone like any self-respecting Southern shipper, a grand old man like Tattnall wouldn't be forced to grasping and insecurity … even in rumor. Dev lost no love on Randall and didn't mind saying so openly these days.

"You look glum. Need some company?" Thumbs looped on belt, Hank Watson joined Dev at the fore prow.

Dev smiled. "Sure, Watson."

There was no denying the congenial private, short of giving him an order. Hank, with his lean, good-natured face under a straw-colored swatch of hair which fell to one side, would not be put off by aloofness or even surliness. He eventually won his companions around. The son of a man who had come up from nothing and now owned a chain of grocery stores, Hank seemed to notice no difference between a clerk and a planter. He was thus equally liked by all. He possessed a boyish enthusiasm that often manifested itself in mischief … pranks and impersonations and so forth, nothing mean-spirited. Despite his reputation as something of a clown, Dev had come to realize that Watson possessed a keen discernment.

"How's the wife takin' the idea of Virginia?" Hank asked now. Then he quickly added, "If I may ask, Sir."

Dev grimaced. "Not so good."

"She's not one of the flag-waving type eager for you to cover yourself in glory?"

"Not exactly."

Hank shook his head. "Got to say I'm glad to be single here at the outbreak of war. A mother's enough to worry about."

Dev could only silently agree. There were two ways a man could take his wife's reticence in such a situation. He could be touched and ultimately endeared. Or he could be resentful. Though he didn't like it in himself, Dev was resentful. He didn't know how to make Carolyn understand that he needed this opportunity. That his marital commitment had been premature, before he'd had the chance for action and glory. To see how his mettle would hold up under fire. It was something a man needed to know about himself.

And it wasn't all selfish and shallow. When he thought about the Yankees trying to force them to remain in the Union, raising troops to send down against them, a holy zeal burned in his chest. He would defend the South, Georgia, his lands and family to his dying breath.

Carolyn spent the afternoon of May 20 at Mrs. Lawton's "cartridge class," rolling little round bundles of flannel into various sizes for the different cannon calibers. Everyone tried to speak to her of the OLI's imminent departure. She wished she had not gone. She had thought that since Devereaux was out and about anyway, the activity would distract her. She should have known better. She could barely bring herself to politely answer the questions, and trying to look brave and patriotic made her face feel like it would break.

No one faulted her for leaving early in hopes that her husband had returned home. She put down the carriage window and allowed the breeze to fan her flushed cheeks. *Devereaux, oh, Dev,* she thought, *you're going to go off and get yourself killed before I even know you – before you even know me.*

She did not think the war would be short, or easy, but if ever she opened her mouth with those thoughts, she sounded like a bull frog among a chorus of songbirds.

She didn't want to feel that way, to be negative or unpatriotic. And certainly she had every reason to hope everyone else was right in believing that one battle would end the conflict. For ten days ago Lieutenant Hamilton Couper had assembled the corps at their barracks and read a dispatch stating that a bill had passed Congress that would allow military commands to enter service for the duration of the war – not just the six months to a year that had been common. Of course the brave Oglethorpes had heartily cheered their officers' suggestion that they do so. So when Dev went away, it was until the conflict ended – or he was sent home wounded or in a coffin.

And now, that order to go had come. Tomorrow morning, the men would entrain for Richmond.

Carolyn alighted from the carriage and ran up the front steps to the town house. As she entered, Little Joe was coming down the stairway with a small chest on his shoulder.

"Is he home, Little Joe?" Carolyn asked eagerly.

"He at de barracks, Ma'am. Dey havin' some sort ob meetin'."

"Still?"

Joe shrugged the other shoulder. "Ah guess de officers hab a lot to discuss."

Carolyn's face fell into lines of disappointed resignation. Untying her bonnet, she went upstairs.

After taking dinner in her room, she rang for a bath. She lingered in the foamy water as long as possible, then dressed in her prettiest nightgown and wrapper and sat down to brush out her hair. She wrote in her diary. She read the Bible. She prayed, trying not to run to the window every time she heard horse hooves. At length, darkness fell.

Leaving the door to Dev's adjoining room ajar, Carolyn lay on her bed, staring at the canopy. A mourning dove cooed softly from the garden. The clock ticked on the mantel. And the lonely minutes eased by.

Suddenly Carolyn realized she had fallen asleep. What had awakened her? A noise? She sat up and swung her feet over the side of the bed. There was no light in Dev's room, but she padded silently over to the door just to check. At first she thought the chamber empty, but then as her eyes adjusted she beheld a figure sitting almost motionless in the wingchair by the window. Dev was staring at her. His hands hung limply off the arms of the chair, touching his spread knees. On a small table beside him Carolyn saw a crystal glass. It was empty.

"Dev, what's wrong?" she asked softly, almost afraid to speak. "I thought … I thought you'd come over."

"What could possibly be wrong? I'm home."

Carolyn frowned. She didn't like his cynical tone. Suddenly she realized more than just his manner and slouching posture were strange. "Where's your uniform?" she asked in alarm.

"Folded neatly at the barracks where I left it."

"Why? Aren't you all to leave first thing tomorrow still?"

"Yes, the OLI is still going to Virginia, but not I."

"*What?*"

Dev rose, walking lankily over to her, looking down at her. "It was decided tonight that the business at hand was far too serious for married men to risk. All of us who are wed are to vacate our spots, to be filled by last-minute volunteers."

Carolyn blinked, her mouth agape, hardly able to comprehend what she was hearing.

"Your dearest wish has come true," Dev prodded her. "Can you not look a little bit happy?"

"Dev, I – I would never have asked for this – not like this," she spluttered. She reached for the open lapels of his vest. "I know what this meant to you."

"Do you?" He bent his face to hers, studying her in the darkness with an intensity that she found unnerving.

"Did you not plead your case, try to reason with them?"

"Oh, most eloquently. But first lieutenant or not, VMI or not, I was outvoted. The membership passed a resolution. The only exception is to be Bartow."

"There's got to be something we can do."

A ghost of a smile flickered over Dev's face like the shadow of beard darkening his jaw, and he gave his head the barest shake. He reached up to cup her cheek. "Just be happy," he said.

When he turned away from her, Carolyn was anything but. She stood there watching him go back and pour himself another drink, then look out the window with an empty resignation that was far more painful than blame or bitterness, for it hinted of permanency. She ached inside, feeling the chasm between them was wider than ever.

When Dev did not acknowledge her again, Carolyn turned and went back to bed. But sleep was not to be hers that night. She lay thinking and praying. By the time dawn's first gray light touched the windows, she knew what she had to do.

An hour later Carolyn peered out of the window of her carriage. She watched her footman confer with the guard at the door of the Liberty Street barracks. When the servant returned he came to her and said, "He not here, Ma'am. You want to wait?"

"Yes, yes. We'll wait."

But the minutes as they ticked by on the time piece about Carolyn's neck seemed interminable. She knew how valuable each one was. Her maid Tania sat quietly across from her, unhappy at their early morning errand. Finally Carolyn's vigil paid off. She bolted from the carriage and quickly crossed the distance to the hitching post, where the resplendently uniformed leader of the OLI was dismounting. As he tethered his mount she made sure to come up right behind him, for Devereaux had told her the captain was quite nearsighted.

"Captain Bartow?"

The gentleman turned. His face, the forehead high under the shako, the lower half clean shaven except for a mustache, registered surprise. "Mrs. Rousseau!" He recognized her from reviews and socials. "What can I do for you?"

"I know, Sir, that you are busy beyond words, but I would beg a few moments of your time."

If he felt inconvenienced, he would never have shown it. "Of course." Bartow graciously gestured towards the barracks. "Shall we go into my office?"

"Yes, thank you."

Carolyn tried to proceed with as much dignity as possible. Her comportment had great bearing on the outcome of this meeting. Bartow must take her seriously. She allowed him to precede her to clear a path, Tania bringing up the rear. The men who were already present began to cheer at the appearance of their leader, but they fell silent when they saw the women. Carolyn did not make eye contact with any of them, but she was keenly aware of their curious gazes following her whispering taffeta skirt.

She was seated across from Bartow at his desk. She held her back straight and met the officer's eyes as he said, "This must be pressing business, Mrs. Rousseau."

"It is, or I would not have presumed to have bothered you on such a day. You may already be aware that the membership of your company decided yesterday that married men should not proceed to Virginia. I am here to ask that you might intercede on behalf of my husband, Devereaux Rousseau."

Bartow's face fell for a moment. Carolyn wondered if he had not yet learned that he had been deprived of his first lieutenant. Or perhaps he merely regretted the loss. "Your husband has been a very valuable member of the OLI, a well-trained and capable leader."

"Then you agree he is indispensable to your task."

"The men like Lieutenant Rousseau, Mrs. Rousseau. If they stood firm in this matter despite that admiration, their feelings must have been quite clear. I would hesitate to disregard a motion the membership already passed."

"But Captain Bartow – forgive me – but you must. It's imperative that you reinstate him. This is his life, all he's trained for, worked for. To take away this opportunity now would destroy him."

"Sending him into battle might accomplish that as well, Mrs. Rousseau."

"Not like keeping him from it would. Please, Captain Bartow. Leaving him behind in Savannah would be much more devastating for him – for *us* – than the risks he'd face in Virginia. We have no children. There's only me, and you have my blessing to take him. I can only hope you will receive that as it's meant, in love for him, not disregard."

The captain studied her long and silently. Carolyn tried not to waver from his gaze. She had been too emotional, not logical enough for the former star lawyer. And maybe too insistent for his masculine ego. She had not presented her argument well.

Finally he said, "He did not send you here, did he."

It was more of a statement than a question, but Carolyn replied in horror, "Of course not! He would never –. You must believe I came of my own accord."

"I do. And I believe you must love your husband very much."

Carolyn nodded, her eyes filling with tears. "I do, Captain Bartow, but he is now of more use to you than to me."

"Very well, Mrs. Rousseau. I will speak to the membership on his behalf and tell them how much I need my VMI-trained lieutenant. I think they will listen." Bartow smiled slowly.

"You will?" Carolyn asked breathlessly, hardly believing her ears.

"I will. But you'd better tell him to hurry back here, if we're to get him suited up in time to make it to the parade ground."

"Oh, Captain Bartow, thank you," Carolyn cried, a hand at her heart as she rose.

"You are welcome. And I pray your sacrifice for the cause will not go unrewarded."

Not for the cause, oh, selfish woman that I am, Carolyn thought as she curtsied and hurried from the barracks, *but for me. And yes, I pray there will still be a reward.*

"Home," she said to the driver, "with all possible speed."

The door had barely closed on Tania's dress before they lurched into the street. When they arrived, Carolyn ran up the steps, calling Dev's name. The lack of response led her to his bedroom. Apparently he had still been asleep. One arm was flung over his face in the position of one who had imbibed too much alcohol the night previous. But upon seeing her running in fully dressed and with such an animated expression, he sat up and caught her hand, mildly alarmed.

"What's wrong?" he asked.

She looked at his tousled dark hair, shadowed jaw and handsome, aristocratic features, and her heart clenched in fear and love. "Nothing's wrong," she said on a sob. "If you will but get up and get dressed, you're going to Virginia today!"

"*What?*" Joy and disbelief blazed across Dev's face. "But how?"

"I have spoken with Captain Bartow just this morning. He needs you. He said to hurry."

"But – did he come *here*? Why did you not wake me?" When Carolyn hesitated, not answering, realization dawned. "You went to him? You did that – for me?"

"Doesn't matter," she said, brushing away a tear. "There's no time to go into all that now. You must hurry to the barracks and get your uniform for the muster at the parade—"

She was cut off from finishing as he grabbed her by both arms and pulled her toward him, landing a kiss soundly upon her lips. And not just any kiss, but the type that even as a married woman she had still been forced to covet. His mouth moved on hers with an intensity of feeling that made her breathless.

"Thank you," he whispered fiercely. Waiting until she met his eyes and saw his sincerity, he repeated, "Thank you."

Carolyn nodded wordlessly. Now she was the one who was dazed and he animated. She watched as he leapt off the bed and started pulling on a shirt and trousers, snapping up suspenders and hopping around shoving his feet into boots. She shook herself. He needed help. As he buttoned his waistcoat, Carolyn found a black silk cravat. He stood before her for her to loop it around his neck, his dark eyes shining as they fastened upon her face.

"Don't come to the parade ground," he said. "Or to the depot. The plan was to march up Whitaker to the mayor's house for a flag presentation. I think it might be easier for me to spot you there."

She nodded. "I'll see you there."

"All right."

With another quick kiss that left her lips tingling, he was out the door. She heard him yell, "Whoo-hoo!," an expression of joyful abandonment and patriotic zeal, as he swept down the stairs.

"Little Joe! Where's that trunk? Call for my horse! We're going to Virginia to lick some Yankees!"

Carolyn stood there with a sad smile, listening to her husband bounding about below until Revere's hooves clattered on the cobbled drive. It felt just like she had thought it would, like the right thing, the only thing, to do. Like the bittersweet hope of a new beginning coming at the same moment as goodbye.

She drew in a shuddering breath. She should go to her in-laws' house and see if they wanted to accompany her.

Carolyn did so, finding them almost ready to walk out the door for the depot, never having been aware of the hours in which Dev had not been an official part of the OLI. Carolyn decided to keep it that way. They were quickly persuaded to make haste to Whitaker Street. Henrietta thought the speech-making there would be much more engaging than a long wait at the crowded, smelly train station.

"Dylan was to meet us at the depot," she commented with a tinge of worry. "I hope he won't be upset."

"No, no," Louis said. "It will be good for Dev to have family both places."

They discovered that it was just as crowded in the streets as they'd anticipated the depot would be. It seemed all of Savannah was turning out to bid goodbye to the brave Oglethorpes. Along the route from the parade ground to the depot, sidewalks, windows and balconies were full.

At the home of Mayor Thomas Holcombe, several prominent young women waited eagerly with a folded flag. They had to park some distance off and walk in, but Mr. Rousseau was able to establish them in a good spot. Carolyn was ever so glad she was not alone. She would never have been granted the automatic respect and clearance reserved for the walking stick-waving planter.

"Carolyn, are you not excited? Is this not exciting?" Henrietta asked. She swished her silk fan avidly in front of her rosy face.

"Yes," Carolyn answered. "Very."

But she had a lump in her stomach the size of a cartridge roll, and all she could feel was intense longing for the man she was so sacrificially sending away to battle.

"I hear them!" Henrietta cried.

"Indeed," Louis muttered.

A brass band in the distance was playing "Bold Soldier Boy." The music echoed off the buildings along Bull Street, then the marching boots turned onto the cobbles of Gaston. At last cheers arose as the crisp uniforms came into view, Bartow at the head. Nine of Savannah's other companies had turned out in dress uniform for the last OLI review and now followed at their rear. Company A of "Bartow's Beardless Boys" were wearing full packs and field gear and carrying state-of-the-art .58-caliber Harpers Ferry rifled muskets. Company B, filled with more recent recruits who would be staying in Savannah, joined them. They came to attention as their leader greeted the ladies of the city and the crowd.

Carolyn was so busy looking for Dev that she paid no attention to the speech-making. At last she saw him on the far side of the ranks, sword held vertically at his side. She longed to get closer to him. How horrible it would be if he did not know they were here. She strained on her tip-toes for a better view.

Louis seemed to recognize her consternation, for he tugged her sleeve and whispered, "It's all right, Carolyn. I believe they will march in such a way that he will pass right before where we're standing. If not, I promise I'll get you to the depot before they leave."

Carolyn relaxed a little, giving her father-in-law a grateful smile. He patted her hand with a mixture of approval and pity.

The silken Stars and Bars had been presented. Bartow graciously thanked the givers. Handing the flag to the color bearer, he said loudly to all those gathered, "I pledge to you this day in their behalf that should they fail to bring back to you this flag it will be because there is not one arm left among them to bear it aloft."

"Oh, my," Henrietta murmured. She and Carolyn exchanged glances. Everyone else seemed encouraged by the sentiment, but for the Rousseau women, it had the opposite effect.

When Bartow offered that if any among his men had doubts about the weighty and dangerous task at hand, they could leave the ranks, naturally none did. The flag was unfurled amid deafening cheers. Laurel wreaths were placed upon shining bayonets. Carolyn had the feeling that history was a mighty wave, sweeping her unwillingly along in its tide. Her mind hung on the fact that this was really happening. This was not play or practice. Those bayonets might – would – soon be stained with blood. And some of those men they knew would never come home again.

The idea filled her with a rising sense of panic. She felt nauseous. She took a breath, then another and another, trying to fill her lungs with air. The command was given to order arms.

"Are you all right, dear?" Henrietta asked.

A journalist with a note pad rudely jostled her as he brushed past. Carolyn put a hand on her chest.

"Louis, she looks pale. Do something."

"Here, watch out. The lady's ill. Give her some room," Louis boomed to those pressing suffocatingly near.

Blessedly, a small space around them cleared.

"Do you need my smelling salts?" Henrietta asked.

Carolyn shook her head. The last thing she wanted was her husband's final view of her to be with a pouch of herbs to her nose. As the men wheeled and marched forward, the band bursting into song, she prayed for the Lord's strength and calm. Dev *was* passing near.

Just as he approached her, he called out, "Eyes – right!" And one hundred and six pairs of eyes turned their way. But what mattered was, *Dev* was looking at her, and with a tender devotion of expression she had never seen before. He smiled, and as he passed right in front of her, he mouthed, "I love you."

She thought her heart would stop. She wanted to throw herself into his arms, but she had to content herself with brushing his coat with her fingertips. Then there was the back of his uniform, then a blur of white and dark blue, then the OLI was gone, on their way to the field of glory.

Early June, 1861
Savannah, Georgia

Carolyn sat in bed with her breakfast tray beside her, her tea cooling and her toast forgotten. She held Devereaux's first letter from the field and prepared to read it for the third time.

181

May 26, 1861

My dear Carolyn,

It's Sunday afternoon, and following a fine sermon by Georgia's own Rev. Dock Stiles, I am sitting under the fly of my tent trying to catch an elusive breeze whilst writing home.

As you know, Gov. Brown was furious at Capt. Bartow for taking troops and arms out of the state. I'm sure you have read his virulent attack upon our commander as printed in all the Georgia newspapers. I have no doubt Capt. Bartow will reply as soon as time allows. Anyway, to avoid capture we had to alter our route by rail away from Augusta, which was on Brown's alert to look out for us. Instead we went through South Carolina. At every station we had quite a time keeping the boys on the train, as ladies came out to cheer us and pin rosettes on our coats. Finally we gave up and allowed the soldiers to mix with the crowds. In Charleston, we were treated like royalty. Bartow explained his actions in one memorable sentence: "I go to illustrate Georgia."

We arrived in Richmond on the 25ᵗʰ at noon. After being treated to a splendid meal at the Exchange Hotel – which brought back lovely memories of my dinner there with you, and good times with the VMI cadets – we were marched to a bunch of old houses that stunk and hopped with fleas. Bartow was livid. He got our orders changed so that we might camp on the eastern outskirts of town in Howard's Grove. Not much of a grove here, though. It's mostly hot with no trees.

Soon we were joined by the Atlanta Greys, a fine company from Fulton County eager to have Bartow as colonel, as is expected. They are under the command of a 29-year-old attorney, Thomas Couper. Other companies have been coming in – the Floyd Infantry, Pulaski Volunteers, Echols Guards from Warm Springs, and most recently, the Rome Light Guards in their fancy gray uniforms. They are most like OLI in background and bearing. We are an interesting crew from all over the state. VMI cadets are helping drill some of the units. Most do not have the experience that we do. The men are seven to a tent, packed in so tight the corporal of the guard has to pull the first man out each morning. Even with all these soldiers we are still waiting on several more companies to complete our regiment so that we can join the Alexandria Line.

As much as the men enjoy the attentions of hundreds of Richmond ladies who delight in our fierce Zoauve drill daily – never you worry on my score – they are eager for action. A Union force is tak-

ing shape near Chambersburg, Penn, threatening the mouth of the Shenandoah. We are to reinforce Gen. Johnston in that vicinity when we get our full strength – and guns. We are lucky to have our rifles. The others will have to settle for Model 1822 muskets. The soldiers grumble against Gov. Brown, saying he is willing to send poorly armed forces to be massacred just to satisfy his hatred of Pres. Davis.

But enough of military matters ... though I've come to realize you would not be satisfied without an update on such things. I think there is much about you that is surprising me. I don't know what you said to Bartow – I haven't asked him – but I must tell you again how indebted I feel to you. That you would lay aside your own preferences in my interest means more to me than words can say. All I can say is, I'll make every effort to ensure that you aren't sorry, to be a husband you can be proud of. Thank you, Carolyn. I'll write again soon.

Your loving husband,
Devereaux Rousseau

Carolyn smiled and held the letter to her bosom. It wasn't positively flowering with romance, but it was a start. He had acknowledged her, thanked her, thought enough of her to give a thorough report, and said he loved her. That was definitely progress.

She would write him back now. She got out of bed and crumpled her face up at the rising nausea. She held onto the bed post for a minute. It was no matter. Being as sick as a dog each day was well worth the joy and anticipation of carrying Dev's child. And his mother had been such a help, insisting Carolyn stay with her and Louis on Oglethorpe Square, and waiting on her hand and foot – despite Carolyn's protests – like she was a queen.

Carolyn got ink and paper out of her desk. She thought about what she would say. When she felt strong enough, she was making socks, uniforms, bandages and, of course, cartridge rolls. She was helping organize a great tableaux of the young girls at the Atheneum to raise money for the soldiers. Forts were being built on Warsaw and Green Islands, and their fathers had both joined the Home Guards and periodically went on patrol duty. None of that would seem too exciting to Dev, but hopefully any type of home news would be welcome. After all, this life here was what he had gone off to defend. And the news that should most please him ... well, it would just have to wait a while to be told, much as she was tempted to share the joyous announcement now. It would be better that he not be distracted, better that she be sure all was progressing well. But one day soon – perhaps the next letter – she could tell him that he would at last be a father.

After that Dev's letters came frequently. They were often short, sometimes started in one place and continued in the next, like the one that arrived
in mid-June when Carolyn had just sat down to start sewing Dev's new uniform. A bunch of ladies had gathered on Saturday at Mrs. Bartow's to discuss
making suits of the gray color the captain had suggested for the Confederacy.
Some of the women were quite ambitious, like the widow Charlotte Branch,
whose three sons were all in the service. She was making four uniforms. But
due to the fast turn-around time and Carolyn's "delicate condition," the other
women had urged her to take on only her husband's outfit.

But she was quick to lay it aside and read:

> *June 6, 1861*
>
> *Dear Carolyn, it's one in the afternoon and here we sit in the
> blazing heat beside the Orange & Alexandria Railroad tracks at
> Manassas Junction, waiting on a locomotive. The one that brought
> us here, arriving in the wee hours of this morning, needed wood, so
> they had to send for another.*
>
> *Our excitement began on June 3, when after dark sentinels
> spotted President Davis and Secretary of War Walker. They were
> shown to Bartow's tent. The next morning we got the written or-
> der to leave for Harpers Ferry. We were supposed to march out
> at eight a.m. but left around 1:30. That's how army life is – full of
> starts and stops, hurry up and wait.*
>
> *Continued June 14, 1861*
>
> *Shortly after I started to write before, the locomotive arrived.
> We traveled on the Manassas Gap Railroad over the Blue Ridge to
> the Shenandoah Valley – Strasburg, end of the line. I kept thinking
> of that song, "O Shenandoah, I love your daughter! Away, ye rolling
> river …" The scenery here is really remarkable, a part of the South so
> different from our coast but if I may say it just as beautiful.*
>
> *We had wagons to take us to Winchester on the Valley Pike but
> not enough. So the Rome Light Guards, OLI and Macon Guards
> gallantly volunteered to march. It was eighteen miles. I felt guilty
> for riding Revere so I walked part of the way, too.*
>
> *I am getting to know the men better – among them Sgt. Fred
> Bliss, Corporal Sanford Branch, his brother Lieutenant John
> Branch (quite an admirable young man), and even a farmer, Ber-
> rien Zettler, who took the place of a married man with a wife less
> vigilant than mine. And of course I already knew 2nd Lt. Ham*

Couper. Hank Watson keeps the spirits of his comrades high with his outrageous antics. I must know them all, and well, Carolyn, for as Bartow has accepted colonelcy I shall soon be their official captain.

We camped on the other side of Harpers Ferry on Bolivar Heights, within view of the railroad and carriage bridges and the Chesapeake & Ohio Canal. Our men fired on Federal scouts within 700 yards of the B & O Bridge. We must block any flanking movements by the Yankees. Yesterday orders came to march to Winchester so we struck tents at midday. We blew up the two bridges and burned the rifle works. It was a shame, for these structures were quite handsome. Now we eat cold food and wait.

I miss you all and covet your prayers. Love from your husband, Dev

It was this last sentence that Carolyn repeated to Dylan when he came to visit in town in late June. In recent weeks, Dylan had spent more and more time in the tiny parsonage that came with his church outside town. Carolyn had wondered if that fact had anything to do with her. But he did still oversee the Yamacraw mission, and while he had lay preachers to help, he spoke there a couple times a month. When he came into Savannah, naturally he stayed with his parents. It was expressly awkward when he discovered Carolyn ensconced on Oglethorpe Square, just across from his own bedroom. Carolyn didn't know what to do about it except to pretend that nothing was strained and try to act normal.

"I understand I'm to be an uncle," he said with a stiff smile when they met that first afternoon in the parlor.

Carolyn's face turned pink. "Yes," she said, "though it's early days yet." There really was no help for his knowing, she reasoned.

"Congratulations. Have you told Dev yet?"

"No. I wanted to make sure ... well, it was the right time."

"I see," he said, though clearly he didn't.

Carolyn wasn't about to go into the details of her pregnancy, which had been difficult enough so far to cause her some concern. Instead she said, "I just had a letter from him. Have you written him? I'm worried about him, Dylan."

"I think in your condition you should try not to worry. What does he say?"

"That he expects to meet the enemy soon. He asks for our prayers. I think a letter from you might be especially meaningful now."

Dylan looked thoughtful. "Right. I'll do that."

Carolyn wondered why he seemed reticent, almost resistive. His eyes swept briefly over her, not meeting her gaze, before he made his excuses and departed. She felt sad that he seemed eager to get away from her, sad her presence – and her pregnancy – apparently caused him discomfort. She didn't want to be the wedge between him and his brother. Especially not now, when something told her in the face of imminent danger Dev would be responsive on a new level to Dylan, should he reach out.

But yet another letter came with no news of battle. Dev was in Winchester, the official new captain of the OLI. Carolyn swelled with pride. Hamilton Couper had become first lieutenant and John Branch adjutant.

The men of the 8th Georgia Regiment were camped in reserve at the picturesque community of Hollingsworth, surrounded by grassy fields, wheat crops, Town Creek, a limestone grist mill and Abrams' Delight, the home of Isaac Hollingsworth. Col. Bartow had a room in the house, the same one occupied by George Washington in 1760. Nearby was Shawnee Springs. Those who drank of its waters were said to have to return. Upon their arrival, the Georgia troops had earned the nickname "goober grabbers" when they mistakenly pulled up clover, thinking it to be peanut plants.

There had just been a brigade review, and the troops stretched for a splendid mile and a half. The citizens came out each day to watch dress parade. According to Dev, Hamilton Branch was quite the ladies' man. After review the men played games with the enthusiasm of school boys. The only things dampening the ideal of the setting were measles and typhoid.

Still, Carolyn knew the calm could not last. It was only a matter of weeks, perhaps days, before Northern and Southern armies would clash in a battle that would change it all. She prayed fervently for her husband – and their child.

CHAPTER FIFTEEN

Between Paris & Manassas Gap RR, Virginia
July 19, 1861

iding at the head of Company B, the Oglethorpe Light Infantry of the 8th Georgia, Dev blinked sleepily and listened to two privates complain of their empty stomachs.

"If they expect us to march into eternity, they ought to feed us."

"Oh, suck it up. I tried to tell you when they said cook three days' rations, they meant it."

"Who can carry that much food, plus all this gear, too?" The man shifted his blanket roll and haversack grumpily.

Hank Watson said from behind them, "It sure don't take y'all long to get long faces. You were all right as rain when Lt. Col. Gardner told you where we're headed. Soon as he stops walking right beside you, you start belly achin'."

"Yeah, literally," someone laughed.

"I think it was more the three hours' sleep that did it," the first private admitted a bit shame-facedly.

Dev got off Revere and drew up close to the men. Doubtless they had not been aware their conversation carried to his ears above the clinking of canteens, the stomping of brogans and the chirping of crickets in the hedge. The men looked up and acknowledged him with smiles and the unfamiliar greeting of "Cap'n."

"I was just fixin' to say, I bet you wouldn't mind if these hungry boys can catch a cricket or two alongside the road, would you, Captain?" Hank jested.

Dev smiled as the men gave half-hearted guffaws. He answered, "We should reach Piedmont Station by noon. I have a good guess the locals will come out with lunch, and maybe you men can even get a nap in while we wait on yet another train."

The privates laughed more enthusiastically at that prospect. He didn't blame them for being weary. He was, too. The last two weeks had been trying. On the 2nd they had heard the Yankees were moving, and in response the 8th had deployed at Darkesville. There they had sat for four days, but General Patterson refused to budge and engage them. Dev had suspected

Patterson's orders had been given to distract Johnston's forces from aiding Beauregard at Manassas. Eventually they had brought up the rear on a hot Sunday march back to Winchester. The next several days had been a blur of striking tents, marching, dismantling fences, and more marching. When they had begun this latest jaunt many had thought it just another lark that would end in frustration. The OLI had no clue where they were headed until Lt. Col. Gardner, a handsome Mexican War vet in his late thirties, had ridden up and announced that they were marching to aid Beauregard, who was engaged at Manassas. Deafening cheers had answered him.

Last night at midnight they had crossed the Shenandoah, guided to the far bank by a blazing bonfire. Dev had had it easy on Revere. The men held their rifles above their heads in the waist deep water, some of the taller ones who went ahead crouching halfway down to trick shorter comrades coming behind. The joyous spirits that had prevailed as they dried out by the campfire had wavered with only a few hours' sleep in the tiny hamlet of Paris on the crest of the Blue Ridge.

"We'll be in the thick of it when we get there, won't we, Captain?" the soldier asked.

"Yes, Sir!"

Bartow's were big shoes to fill, but Dev hoped he could begin to prove himself a capable leader on the field of battle.

Up ahead he saw dual carriage gates that led to a handsome brick plantation house with a long veranda and a circular drive. A black female servant wearing a white apron was standing by the road, and she appeared to be speaking to the men of Company A, Rome Light Guards. Dev hastened ahead to hear.

"Missus says come up to breakfast. Come right up, Missus says, all of you come right up."

Looks of consternation passed among the men. They were such a mighty host, surely they could not be hearing right. Someone shouted, "The fool thinks we are officers!"

Dev had wondered the same thing, though he was annoyed at the private for his lack of manners. Companies A and B were the most nattily dressed of the regiment, so that even the non-enlisted men were sometimes mistaken for soldiers of rank. But the slave kept right on earnestly entreating them.

Dev swung onto Revere. "Come on then, men," he called. "Shall we investigate?"

Thus urged on, the ranks began to turn in at the gate. A refined lady stood on the house's veranda, nodding to them.

"Glad to see you, dear boys," she said. "Just pass round the house to the dining room."

"Thank you, Ma'am," Dev answered her as he tethered his horse, very curious now but following the direction of her gesture.

The men doffed kepis and shakos as they entered an open door. Dev followed them and his mouth almost fell open like theirs at the sight of tables groaning under the weight of biscuits, bread, ham, cakes and doughnuts of all shapes and sizes, and tubs and cans of coffee. At least a half dozen ladies stood ready to serve them.

One came up to Dev and said, "Good morning, Sir. We know your men don't have time to stop and eat, but we want you to take what you can with you. We know you have to hurry to the aid of General Beauregard." As she spoke the fair blonde woman who made Dev think of Carolyn offered him a napkin with a variety of refreshments.

"Thank you," he said, bemused. "What you are doing is very appreciated."

She smiled. "You're welcome. Coffee?"

Dev handed her his tin cup to fill. Nothing had ever smelled or tasted so good. Around him, in the process of stuffing their haversacks, the soldiers were grinning at the women.

"Again, on behalf of my men, I thank you," Dev said, bowing his way out and herding a bevy of Oglethorpes with him.

The ladies waved. "God be with you, gentlemen!" After that it was pleasant going. More women along their route came out to offer food and fill their canteens with water. They did have to wait for the train, and lunch was provided. Dev even got a snooze in before the tired solitary engine huffed into the station around nine p.m. There was still only enough room for the 7th and 8th Georgia.

It was hot even then, powerfully hot. Some of the men rode on the roofs of the car in the cooler air, despite the sizzling metal and the blowing cinders. Then a rainstorm drove them all inside. They arrived at Manassas Junction at dawn. As the men boiled their coffee in an open field, Dev saw Bartow ride up to the renowned General Beauregard. They spoke a few minutes. He had no doubt Bartow was securing their place of honor among the other regiments. Sure enough, after a four-mile march to a wooded campsite, the colonel – only just promoted to brigadier general – sought Dev out.

"We're to be on the right of the line, in the opening of the fight," he said. "I trust you will tend to the boys well."

"I will, Sir."

"I'd like to speak to them."

"Of course."

Dev hastened to gather the men. In the wavering light of snapping campfires, their faces looked expectantly, respectfully at their commander. Bartow talked in a fatherly manner, for indeed, at forty-four, he was old enough to be father to most of them, untried youths that they were. Dev listened with a curious sense of sadness, an awareness that this was the last night things would be as they had been. He had already thought Bartow's parting words before the general spoke them: "But remember boys, that battle and fighting mean death, and probably before sunrise some of us will be dead."

Devereaux had never been much of a Bible reader, but it was funny how impending battle and death brought out the religious bent in men. He had packed in such a hurry he had not brought along his Testament. So it was that when he had gotten a letter from his brother only days before arriving in Manassas, he had welcomed rather than scorned the entire 91st Psalm printed neatly in Dylan's hand. Now, he thought of the words of the psalm as he awaited their fate.

Dawn had seen Bartow pacing and on edge, no action presenting itself to their front. He had soon mounted his horse and ridden off to see what was happening.

The men of Company B looked questioningly at Devereaux.

"We'll soon be in the fight, don't worry," Dev assured them.

One man fiddled nervously with his cartridge box. "Waitin's the hard part, Captain, the knowin' it's coming but not being in it yet. I feel like a boulder's sitting in my stomach."

"Me, too," said another man. "I think I'm most afraid I won't prove myself worthy – make my family proud."

Dev nodded his understanding.

"Maybe someone should say us a prayer," Hank Watson suggested.

"How 'bout you?" another private shot back.

"I'm not much good about prayin' in public," Hank replied, suddenly embarrassed. "But, well … o.k. I guess I can."

Dev cleared his throat, unfolding his brother's letter from his pocket. He sure wished Dylan were here now. He was not so good at religious things, either, but as their leader, he felt compelled to speak up. "Well," he said, "before you do, how about if I share some words from the Psalms?"

There were murmurs of eager assent.

"Psalm 91." Dev read, "'He that dwelleth in the secret place of the Most High shall abide under the shadow of the Almighty. I will say of the Lord, He is my refuge and my fortress: my God, in him will I trust.'"

A larger knot of men began to gather 'round, eyes intently on Devereaux, some standing, some sitting. Dev's voice gained strength as his confidence rose.

"'Surely he shall deliver thee from the snare of the fowler, and from the noisome pestilence. He shall cover thee with his feathers, and under his wings shalt thou trust: his truth shall be thy shield and buckler. Thou shall not be afraid for the terror by night; nor for the arrow that flieth by day; Nor for the pestilence that walketh in darkness; nor for the destruction that wasteth at noonday. A thousand shall fall at thy side, and ten thousand at thy right hand; but it shall not come nigh thee ... For he shall give his angels charge over thee, to keep thee in all thy ways.'"

As Devereaux finished reading the psalm, a hush fell over the men. Hats were doffed and gradually heads bowed, so that as soon as Dev ended it seemed natural for Hank – no longer bashful – to lead right out in a prayer.

In a soft voice he said, "Lord, we come to you today on the eve of this great battle. We fear, God, but we're ready. Please go before us and shelter us under Your wing like the words of this psalm just said. Help us to drive back the enemy before us and do our country proud. Well, I guess that's it, Lord. Amen."

"Amens" echoed throughout the company. Dev shook hands, passed on words of encouragement. Eyes met with the knowledge that it might be for the last time. But when Bartow returned to the regiment, the OLI was waiting calmly, ready for his orders.

Fighting had commenced two hours prior on their extreme left. What soldiers who were still sleeping were awakened, and the 7th and 8th set off at the double quick in that direction. Actually it seemed they went in *every* direction, meandering about between hills and woods and various units. Bartow kept asking them, "Is this our extreme left?" All the while there was the dull rumble of cannon and the boom-BOOM of exploding shells.

Around ten the artillery grew louder, punctuated by the crackling of muskets and rifles. The sound caused Dev's pulse to accelerate. Orders came down for the 8th to halt while the 7th was brought up from behind. Dev heard the orders Lt. Col. Gardner received for the 8th. They were to support the nearby Virginia battery. Dev's portion of the column swung up a long slope. When they reached the top of the summit, they could see two Confederate brigades firing at several Union brigades. The sudden appearance of the long lines of blue and gray, bayonets gleaming and muskets flashing fire, had the same effect on Dev as it did on his men. Jaw dropping – if he would have allowed his natural reaction.

As they stood in a corn field with the stalks waist high, Dev dressed the line right.

From his perch on his white horse, Gardner said placidly to the officers below him, "Let the men load their guns and lie down."

Dev relayed the command to Company B, amazed at the lieutenant colonel's calm. Would he ever become so nonchalant in combat?

Shaking fingers shoved steel ramrods into rifle barrels, and Dev called, "Lie down in ranks!"

Most lay quietly, straining to see ahead, sweat trickling down brows. But Hank Watson and a couple others had spied an apple tree to the left of the line. And – *were they really? They weren't*, thought Dev disbelievingly as the men dashed over and started peppering the fruit with rocks and dirt clods.

"Watson! Boys! Get back here!" Dev and his lieutenants yelled.

But the apple-seekers did not hear. Some were actually starting to climb!

Behind Devereaux, Gardner stated, "I see a battery taking position over yonder; they will not need orders in a few minutes."

Berrien Zettler, the ex-farmer, gave him a confused glance. Dev guessed some of the soldiers didn't even know what a battery was. The next second, a cannon boomed, followed by a distinct whizzing. Awareness dawning fast, the tree climbers jumped down and scrambled for their lines. The shell exploded overhead. But the next one was much closer. The men covered their heads as they lay in the corn furrows. This one struck ground, and earth exploded all around them. Dev was covered with dirt. When he looked up, brushing off his uniform, he was astonished to see Gardner still calmly walking his horse along the front of the regiment.

The next shell found its mark in Company C. The Oglethorpes heard loud yelling in that direction. Grimly they hugged the earth, waiting. To their rear the regimental band absurdly tried to inspire them, seemingly competing with the din of battle. Dev was glad when they at last gave up. After the shot that hit the Macon Guards, Dev noticed the long-range fire was not very effective, so the worst part of it was suspense – wondering when they would finally receive their orders to advance. Amazingly, he found himself praying, and again his nerves calmed.

Then he heard horse hooves and Bartow's voice.

"Rise, 8th Regiment!" Gardner shouted.

Not a man hesitated. They were ready for the fray. Their aim: to reach the cover of a patch of woods adjoining a Union battery and from there to silence the guns. They formed up on a hill, where General Bee directed their deployment. A large field lay between them and the flank of the Yankee battery. The men went at the double quick, and then at a dead run, for dead they would be if they hesitated. Spurning a sheltering fencerow, Bartow led them right in front of the enemy rifles. Dev saw an Oglethorpe private go down. The sound of the zipping bullets reminded him of the whir of dragonflies in the marshes.

At last they were in the cover of the thicket – a growth of young pines and blackberry bushes. Gardner halted them. He seemed angry as he had the officers dress their lines, though at Bartow for his course of advance or the Yankees, Dev could not rightly tell. When the companies were reformed, the men eagerly obeyed the command to advance to the edge of the wood. There, they had another surprise waiting.

"Good golly, Captain, there's a whole line of Yankee infantry!" one man yelled.

He was right. And many of the bluecoats were well-ensconced behind fences, outbuildings and straw bales. Had Bartow not seen them? Or had he thought they would present no significant challenge? Dev knew otherwise, and now, so did everyone else. To take the guns, they would first have to route the infantry. They would have their work cut out for them.

And another sight brought him up short: the Stars and Stripes floating proudly above the Union ranks. For a moment he quailed, something inwardly rebelling. Then he thought of home, and Carolyn's face rose before him. He would fight any foe – even his former countrymen – to preserve the dream that his life had been and the promise of what it could be.

Everyone was bunched up in a protrusion of the thicket. Dev tried desperately to straighten and thin the ranks. Three companies were sighting their rifles, in places stacked a half dozen men deep. In their eagerness soldiers were loading and firing without waiting for sufficient clearance. Dev cautioned more than one wild-eyed private by slapping down his barrel before disaster could occur.

The Yankees were making their presence felt. Bits of pine and leaves fluttered in the air, and many bullets found their mark. Gardner had taken one in the lower leg. Declining offers of help, he dragged himself to a stump and continued calling out to the men from there.

Dev was dismayed to see several men under his command fall dead. One soldier was struck three times while right next to him his friend fired on. Adjutant Branch reeled and fell, shot through the arm and body. His brother Sanford dropped his rifle and ran to John's side, taking him to the rear.

The arrow that flieth by day.

Dev's shako flew from his head with a rush and a whiz. When he bent to pick it up, his heart nearly stopped. The bullet had passed about an inch above his scalp.

Down the line, Bartow's horse had been shot from under him. As he waved his sword in the air a bullet snapped off its blade. Devereaux saw him shouting to the captain of Company F. When a glance in the other direction disclosed the blue of Federal soldiers crashing through the thicket only about fifty steps away, Devereaux started yelling "Fall back! Fall back!"

But the line was so hopelessly snarled and the rattle of musketry was so loud that he was sure many could not hear him. A handful of men followed his waving sword deeper into the thicket, leaving behind them a sickening number of still bodies in the Oglethorpe uniform.

The destruction that wasteth at noonday.

He went back to the thicket that evening, after they had retreated and rallied, taken more abusive enemy fire, then finally watched Brigadier General Thomas Jackson – Dev's big-footed professor from VMI – miraculously stabilize the Confederate line on Henry Hill. They had all fallen in, men from various states, into a hodge-podge line of jubilee, chasing the Yankees from the battlefield, overrunning their abandoned camps where they had drunk the coffee and eaten their ham. Theirs had been the victory, but the cost was incalculable. Dev knew it as he walked among the scarred saplings – some hit up to twenty times – and demolished undergrowth. He saw it in the glazed, staring eyes of fresh-faced boys. He heard it in the rhythm of the thumping heels of a handsome private in the uniform of the Stephens Light Guards, who died a slow, unconscious death while his brains oozed out. Standing in frozen horror staring at the gruesome sight, he gradually became attuned to the moans of the wounded crying for water. And he joined many others filling canteens at the nearby branch and bringing drink to parched lips.

As darkness fell and the shock of wounds set in, the afflicted began to shiver uncontrollably. Dev found blankets on dead Yankees to cover his comrades while they waited for musician-orderlies to carry them to the nearby field hospital, set up near the creek in a willow grove. There the regimental surgeon probed for bullets and amputated arms and legs steadily, forever maiming many a strong young man.

The pestilence that walketh in darkness.

Dev found the whole scene sickening. The moments of exhilaration and pride had passed, and now this was what was left. In the inky blackness of the night he eventually stumbled back to camp, lying down by he had no idea whom and pillowing his head on his arm. Well, he had reality. And he didn't like it very much. And one thing more he knew before he fell asleep, his soul crying out to make sense of the whole day. It was a good thing he wasn't among the dead in the pine thicket, for he wasn't ready yet to meet his Maker.

July 22, 1861
Savannah, Georgia

Lingering behind closed shutters in the sultry heat of Savannah, citizens breathlessly awaited news of the action in Virginia. The temperature made Carolyn queasier than ever – that and her own anxiety. She wished for the hills of North Georgia but would never dream of leaving the city when reports of the 8th were expected daily.

Then came the afternoon she heard a knocking at the back door. Someone was at the servants' entrance. She didn't think much of that until voices stirred in excited hums throughout the house. She quickly set aside her book of poetry and rose from the fainting couch in her room. She was on the landing when she heard Louis speaking with Henrietta in the foyer.

"What did they say, Louis? What did they say? Tell me!" Henrietta urged.

Her husband was shrugging on his linen coat. "That a battle was fought at Manassas, and that Bartow was dead. Killed leading the 7th into the fight. Lt. Col. Gardner was captured, feared mortally wounded as well."

"Oh, dear heaven!" Hennie put a hand to her breast. "And the 8th?"

Carolyn did not miss his hesitation. She delayed descending farther, fearing that if he caught sight of her he would soften his answer past the point of truth.

"Badly torn up," he responded.

Carolyn felt her knees buckle and grabbed for the rail. The ever-emotional Henrietta broke immediately into loud sobs.

"Now, Hennie, don't take on so. You know how reliable the slave grape vine is. I'll just go down to the newspaper office and bring back an official report."

Henrietta grabbed his arm as he put on his top hat. "Louis, promise me – promise me that you'll look at the list and tell me right away. Whether his name is on there or not, you must tell me – the second you enter this house!" Louis nodded and hugged her briefly. Then the door closed behind him. Henrietta sagged weeping against the wall. Carolyn quietly descended and went to her mother-in-law.

"Mother," she said, "you must save your tears. Devereaux is probably fine." Her words sounded empty, for the possibility of the opposite was equally true.

Henrietta turned to embrace her. "Oh, Carolyn, I just can't help it!" she cried.

"Let's go sit in the parlor."

There they sat. At length Henrietta's tears dried and an awful stillness fell. It was pointless to read or talk. They listened to the mantel clock ticking and occasionally their eyes met, wide with fear. Carolyn's stomach had gone from queasy to aching. She put a hand on her still-flat abdomen and prayed silently.

When at last they heard a step on the porch, they both jumped up. In the seconds it took for the door to open she thought they both might faint.

Louis rounded the corner and stood staring at them, his face slack. Its ashen color made Carolyn's heart stop. Then he said, "He's all right. Our boy is all right!"

Laughing and crying again, they all three flew into a hysterical huddle, hugging and jumping and wiping their eyes.

"He's alive! He's alive! Thank God!" Henrietta exclaimed.

Louis produced his newspaper and read to them from the account of the battle, standing right there in the hall, Carolyn and Henrietta with their arms around each other's waists. They heard the story of the pine thicket, that place of slaughter where many they knew had died.

"Oh, poor Mrs. Branch!" cried Carolyn when she learned John had died and Sanford had been captured as he stayed by his brother's body. And "Poor Mrs. Bartow!" as Louis told them how the commander had indeed fallen as he brought the 7th into the fray, after the 8th had sustained the highest casualties of any unit present. His last words had directed his boys to never give up the field.

By the time Louis was done reading, and telling of the reactions he had witnessed about town, Carolyn's eyes were again streaming. Her joy that Devereaux was unharmed mingled with horror at the tragedy and pity for the loss of others. And then there was the dawning realization that this wouldn't be the last time they would go through this – the awful suspense and fear. She made her excuses and said she would retire to her room.

"Of course, dear Carolyn," Henrietta said, patting her arm. "You should go rest. This has been very emotionally taxing on all of us."

Carolyn climbed the stairs, thinking to do just that, hoping the ache in her stomach would let up if she could just lie down. But it didn't. It intensified, tying into a knot. She tried to breathe deeply and prayed for relaxation. She had just been too stressed.

After a while she wondered if she laid on her stomach if it would help. She moved to turn over but froze with a sweeping, unrealistic horror when she saw blood on the sheet under her.

Five days later, Carolyn's heart thudded slowly, painfully, with the minute-guns that fired as General Bartow's funeral cortege moved through the streets of Savannah. Henrietta went out to see the black hearse drawn by four gray horses pass on its way to Bartow's temporary rest at the City Exchange. She told Carolyn a small escort of OLI had brought the commander's body home, but of course Dev had not been with them. He needed to stay with the majority of the men. Henrietta also said that the Oglethorpe Barracks had been draped in crepe and that Savannah's other companies were to pay their respects at the funeral – which she and Louis planned to attend.

Carolyn, of course, would not attend the ceremony at Christ Church. Henrietta promised to make her excuses should she come in contact with the widow. She would say that Carolyn had been taken with a temporary but very debilitating illness, and since all the ladies in their circle had known Carolyn was pregnant, this would then be correctly understood among them.

She might be well enough now in body to attend, but not in spirit. She had so fiercely wanted this child, it felt as though part of herself had been ripped away. That child would have brought them together, herself and Dev, in a new and splendid way. It would have solidified the fragile ties that had begun when he went off to war at her request.

The day her in-laws went to the funeral, Carolyn sat in the arm chair in her room, holding Dev's portrait. It had been made one weekend he was home from Pulaski. How she wished he could have come home with Bartow's body. Nothing would comfort her now like his arms about her.

At length she heard the carriage return with Louis and Henrietta. She wasn't surprised that her mother-in-law, all in black, came to check on her. She *was* surprised to see a smile on her face.

"I've brought something to cheer you," she said. She reached into her reticule and pulled out two envelopes. "From Dev. He sent a letter to you and one to Louis and me by the OLI escort."

"Oh!" Carolyn cried and leaned forward eagerly.

Henrietta placed the letter in her hand. "I've already read mine, but if it's all right with you, I'll sit down and read it again, then maybe we can see if he told us all the same news," she said hopefully.

Carolyn hardly heard her. She was tearing into the envelope. "Yes, of course," she agreed absently, then started reading.

July 25, 1861
Camp Bartow, Virg.

Dearest wife,
Rest your mind, for I am well. We have just removed to a camp about four miles northeast of the sight of the recent battle at Manassas Junction. Before going, we dug a single grave and laid the

bodies of six slain Oglethorpes side by side into it. Others were left recuperating in the field hospital. We are a more sober crew now. We will fight again, but not with the same naiveté we entered this fray. I must be honest and say it was eye-opening, and while we did cover ourselves in glory – Beauregard himself raised his hat to us as we left the field, saying "I salute the gallant Eighth Georgia Regiment" – it was not what I had expected. I am proud of Company B, but Carolyn, the cost was so high. Some of the men think they should be able to go home now that we routed the Yankees. But I know there will be more, more to this war.

The men are listless, depressed and irritable – the let-down after all that excitement. Their wages are overdue. They are unhappy with the camp. The water is very bad here. I fear it and the heat will soon take a toll in illness.

On the up side, many have turned to religion. Tell Dylan he ought to be here – I told him! He'd have many more converts than at that little church at home. The soldiers who were spared, including myself, give the credit to God Almighty. This is especially true of Company K Oglethorpe Rifles. Not one died in the battle – the only company of the 8th of which this was true. They later learned that at the very hour we faced hell in the pinewood their citizens back home in Middle Georgia were gathered in Atkinson's Church, interceding for their soldiers.

I realize now there is much more I need to accomplish with my life. There is a different sort of man I can be. You have been patient with the selfish, arrogant ass I've been – forgive my language, but I don't know how better to describe myself. Give me time – and experience – and maybe I can become the husband you deserve.

Write to me, for I long for home and your sweet embrace. I will write again soon, too.

Love, Devereaux

Carolyn smiled faintly and sat contemplating Dev's amazing words, feeling the first spark of hope she had since before the battle and her miscarriage. Then she became aware that Henrietta was watching her. They compared their letters – at least, most of them. Carolyn didn't think Henrietta would understand Dev's saying he had been selfish and arrogant, for the elder Mrs. Rousseau had never found any fault with her perfect first-born. It appeared the content of the letters was much the same, except Dev had written more details about the battle to Henrietta and Louis.

"Well, then, I'll let you go. We both will want to write back and send our letters to him by the funeral escort."

"Yes," Carolyn agreed.

"And you will want to tell him about the baby."

Carolyn paused. "No," she said, "I don't think that would be a good idea."

Her mother-in-law couldn't have been more shocked if Carolyn had suddenly gotten up and danced a jig. "What do you mean?" she cried. "How can you *not* tell him? He has every right to know!"

"Yes, but it doesn't have to be now. Did you not sense the heavy-heartedness in his letters? He and the men have hit a very low spot, despite the recognition they have earned. I wouldn't want to add to his load. There will be a better time."

Henrietta simply couldn't conceive of such reasoning. Her *modus operandi* was to tell all, all the time, and as dramatically as possible. Her bottom lip briefly protruded. "If you won't tell him, I will."

Carolyn jumped up. "No! Please, Mother. Don't do that. What can he do except worry about me? I couldn't stand to add further anxiety and sadness to his shoulders. Is he not bearing enough?" She could see Henrietta begin to waver. "Please. I will tell him, but when the time is right. Please just give me some time."

Henrietta sighed. "Very well, though I don't understand you. If it were me, I would need the comfort of my husband's knowledge and the letters he could write me, even across the miles."

"I do," Carolyn said softly. "I do need that." But as tempting as it was, Carolyn knew it was not the right thing. She had the Lord to help her, and time would ease the ache. There was also the promise of one day receiving true love from her husband. She could go a long time on that alone. But there was one thing she did need, and preferably right away …

"Mother," she began tentatively, "there's something that would mean more to me now than anything, if you would be willing."

"What is it, dear?" Henrietta was eager to help if she could.

Carolyn smiled at the thought of cool mountain breezes, peaceful days and chats with Mahala Franklin. It would all be like balm on her heart. "Will you take me to Forests of Green?"

CHAPTER SIXTEEN

Late October, 1861
Habersham County, Georgia

ahala looked up and down the road as far as she could see in both directions. Satisfied that no one was in view, she turned *Unagina*'s head and squeezed her thighs on the mare's sides. Instantly they burst into a gallop, heading up the driveway of The Highlands. She knew the house to still be deserted, but nevertheless she slowed the horse to walk as they neared, again glancing around cautiously. There was no evidence of drifters. Instead, all was still – a scene of perfect beauty. The white Federal-style mansion was framed by hardwoods in their autumn glory. Drying leaves covered the lawn and the veranda. Empty windows reflected the mid-morning sun.

Mahala dismounted, tying Gina to the hitching post. She walked up the steps, pretending she was the owner of the estate, coming home from a long trip. She wished she could walk right in but had to content herself with peeking in the windows. Gentle rays of sunlight fell on occasional furniture, glanced off stark white sheet coverings and scattered on the hardwood floors. It looked lonely.

This place had always held a special appeal for her, ever since Clay had brought her here her first week in Clarkesville. It was the perfect retreat in which to read his latest letter, as-yet unopened and making its presence keenly felt in the pocket of her paletot. The rockers had been removed from the front porch, so Mahala settled on the top step. She pulled out the envelope, slit the top with her index finger, and unfolded the paper inside. When she saw Clay's handwriting, a bittersweet swell of emotion rose in her chest. Dearest Clay. Always faithful, even across the miles.

Tahlequah, Oklahoma Territory
October 7, 1861, evening

> *Dear Mahala,*
> *Well, I wish we could sit down together and have one of our good old talks. You always seemed so clear in your views, and I*

could use some of that right now. Everything here has been a mud-dled mess. As hard as some of our leaders are trying to keep white men's problems from dividing our people, that is exactly what's happening. We are being swept along in the tide of war despite cries for neutrality. It now appears the tide is carrying us into the Confederacy. I guess that's not surprising. The Federal soldiers have abandoned their western forts. They have not paid our an-nuities or sent representatives to try to convince the Cherokee to join them, as the Confederates have. The Choctaw and Creek to our south have joined the Southern states. And the battles at Bull Run and Wilson's Creek have made everybody here take a hard look at our position. We hear the Southern army is just outside Washington, D.C.

Some do grumble against fighting for the very states that kicked us out. But some of the things we have heard from North-ern politicians, even in recent years, have been threatening.

At the end of August we held a meeting here in Tahlequah. Our little town was overrun. What good business we did! Yes, I am still working at the same place. Mr. Murrell rather holds a monopoly on the grocery business in town, but I can't bring myself to leave the capital where all the action is. And I have made friends here. Anyway, 4,000 Cherokee men descended upon us. Stand Watie came with 50 or 60 of his militia that guard the remnants of the Ridge Party – armed, they said to protect themselves from assas-sination. Yes, the tensions still go that deep. The political murders of the early '40s are far from forgotten. Watie's group was vehe-ment about joining the Confederacy. But Chief Ross had already sensed the way popular sentiment was running. He outmaneu-vered Watie by himself calling for a treaty with the Confederates. The treaty was signed less than a week ago at Park Hill.

Meanwhile, Ross' nephew John Drew has been raising a regi-ment. Ross wants these men loyal to him – sadly, to protect him from Watie's group as much as to protect the Nation from inva-sion. Three companies were raised from Tahlequah alone. I joined up, Mahala. I know you will say "Why did you not just stay out of it?" I agree if it would have been possible to preserve neutrality that would have been best. But almost every able-bodied young man here enlisted, even the Keetoowahs (the secret society I told you about founded to preserve tribal rites and loyalty and main-tain relations with the U.S. government). Maybe that's not a good reason for me to enlist, but it does sound like the outcome of all this could be good. This treaty promises our sovereignty, that we will not have to fight outside our territory, and that the CSA will buy the Cherokee Neutral Lands for a good price. Our people have been trying to sell those lands to the U.S. government forever! If the South is victorious we will come out way ahead of where we were. Anything that will help our people, I am for.

Many tribes are here. While Drew enlisted men Albert Pike, the Confederate representative to the Indians, negotiated terms in the log council houses on the square. On the 2nd, the Osages. On the 4th, the Quapaws, Senecas and Shawnees. Today, officers were commissioned. You can tell your grandfather that after the ceremony I actually saw Ross shake Watie's hand and express a desire for harmony. So you see? That's progress, right?

Now, if Opothleyahola doesn't ruin the peace! He is a Creek chief who has been gathering pro-Union Indians about him, as well as blacks, both free and fugitive. Some of the Southern sympathizers fear having their men off in Confederate service while this gang is behind the lines. Pike has offered Opothleyahola a pardon for himself and his followers if they will join with the CSA. Pray it may be so. No one would relish fighting Indian brothers. Such actions could have long-lasting repercussions.

Write and tell me if men are signing up there in Habersham County and what the sentiment is. Will your brothers go? I hate to think of any change in that peaceful place. I miss the green hills and want to think everything is as I left it, including you.

I am glad you have a friend in Miss Carolyn Rousseau. I know some of the white upper crust are kind and that friendships and sometimes even marriages with them can be successful. (I think of Mr. Murrell.) But there are others who would not treat you so equally and would play with your affections. I think you know who I speak of. Try not to think me bossy for asking you to watch out for snakes in the grass. It is only because I care about you.

> *Your loving friend,*
> *Clay Fraser*

Mahala snorted. *Snakes in the grass!* Clay *was* bossy. He had a lot of nerve still trying to tell her what to do five years after leaving and hundreds of miles away! Her mention of news from Jack in Savannah must have really gotten his goat.

Then her irritation slowly ebbed. *Loving friend.* It must be as she suspected, that Clay had never gotten over her. A couple of times he had mentioned young women in passing – references like "Must go now. Taking Miss Bird to the social." She had thought such comments were inserted to test her response, but when she had never given him one, mention of that lady never occurred again. If she had to guess she'd say Clay had never kept a steady sweetheart.

That made her faintly sad. Even now she wished she could be what he had hoped for.

She folded the letter. Placing it back in her pocket, she rose and walked down the steps and around the side of the house. Squirrels chattered in the trees and scampered about the lawn, gathering acorns dropped from the massive oaks. She inhaled the scent of the boxwoods and paused to touch some forgotten blue gentian. By the kitchen, the herb garden was all ashoot and atumble. Mahala shook her head. Farther off, trailing vines and floppy green leaves hid pumpkins in various stages of development. They were too big to do much with presently, but she did stop to gather up an armload of butternut squash. She took it around front and deposited the cumbersome vegetables in her saddle bag.

Mahala looked around, and it seemed the empty mansion looked back. She felt like asking the house if it was glad to be free of its awful owner, but deciding that would be a bit too fanciful, unhitched Gina and swung into the saddle.

On her way to Forests of Green, she thought of the Cherokee people – of all these beautiful lands they had lost, and them now siding with the South. Would it really benefit them in the end? Mahala surely hoped so. So many promises had been broken already, no more valuable in the end than a bunch of fool's gold. She *would* share Clay's news with Henry. Maybe it would cheer him. In recent months it had seemed a shadow hung over him. He had grown more quiet and introspective. Mahala had sensed he was not feeling well. She had spent many hours with him this past spring during her visit to the valley, talking and sharing memories. She was glad that since then Ben and Nancy brought him in to town more often to lift his spirits.

There for a while, Jacob had talked about joining up. Both the 16th and the 24th Georgia Infantry regiments had recruited this past summer in Habersham and neighboring counties. Company C, Phillip's Legion, had also opened enlistment on June 11. With Marietta's William Phillips, son of Dr. Phillips of Farm Hill, in command, and the postmaster's son Alex Erwin second lieutenant, a good many local men from their late teens to mid-twenties had enlisted, including the Chitwood and Trotter brothers, the McCrackens, William Nichols and Levi Wyly. But, thankfully, many of the farmers just over the line in White had decided to stay put for the time being. Mahala had breathed a sigh of relief. Now her adoptive brother's restless energy was channeled into the harvest, though something told her it was only a matter of time until it surfaced again.

Forests of Green was an immaculate contrast to The Highlands. As Mahala rode up she considered the irony that she was now a frequent guest, where once she had but stared longingly down the drive after Jack's stallion. However, that didn't exactly put her on a par with the family. She had a feeling Henrietta merely tolerated her presence as an indulgence to her lonely daughter-in-law.

It was, in fact, Mrs. Rousseau who greeted her from the front porch. She had been reading a book there and rose as Mahala climbed the steps.

"She's in the butler's pantry," Henrietta said as she led Mahala inside. Then she called out, "Carolyn, your little friend is here."

Mahala merely smiled. She was at least three inches taller than the elder Mrs. Rousseau. She forgot about the comment as she entered the narrow room where her friend was ladling a thick brown liquid from a large cook pot into open jars. Her face was flushed a nice rosy color, presumably from the recent heat of the kitchen, and blonde wisps of hair trailed down her neck. It was good to see her looking healthy and industrious. When Carolyn had first arrived this summer following the loss of her child, Mahala had been alarmed at her wan, sad countenance.

"Oh, good! You can help me hold up this big thing while I get the butter out," Carolyn cried with no preamble.

"Butter?" Mahala moved to Carolyn's other side and lifted the pot indicated.

"Yes, pumpkin butter." Carolyn scraped the last remnants from the sides of the container and then waved the spoon. "Here, try it."

Mahala smiled and took the spoon. She licked it tentatively. "Very good," she pronounced.

"Of course. It's Esther's special recipe. I helped her make it. Will you take that pot back to her in the kitchen? Then I'll just seal up these jars, and we can go have lunch. Today is so beautiful I thought a picnic by the pond might be nice."

"Oh, that would be lovely!" exclaimed Mahala, delighted at the idea of being away from Henrietta's all-too-polite manner.

The territorial cook was no less skeptical of Mahala's intrusion than the mother-in-law. She snatched the pot suspiciously and seemed hesitant to surrender the picnic basket Carolyn had packed until the young mistress herself put in an appearance.

"As though I was going to run out in the yard with it and gobble it all down by myself or something," Mahala giggled as they set out across the back lawn.

Carolyn laughed. "Oh, don't worry about *her*. She's just that way. When I first came to Forests of Green she nearly scared me to death. She's just very loyal to the Rousseaus."

Speaking of loyalty … Mahala glanced uncomfortably behind them at the tall, slender young black man carrying their basket and blanket. Little Joe followed Carolyn around like a lost puppy. While Mahala was accustomed to the presence of Zed and Maddie, she was not accustomed to being waited on.

"We could have carried that," she whispered to Carolyn.

"I know, but it gives him something to do. He's been ever so long-faced since Dev did not take him to the war. He's forever trying to find things that will help me, since Dev told him to watch out for me." Then a little louder she instructed the servant: "Over there will be fine, Little Joe. Thank you."

After the young man had spread the blanket on a swell of ground and started back to the house, Mahala asked, "Why did he not take him?"

Carolyn sat down. "He left in such a hurry, there really wasn't time to discuss it. But I think it's good for Dev, though perhaps hard on Little Joe." She opened the hamper. "Are you hungry? I made chicken salad sandwiches."

"My, you have been busy this morning."

"Staying busy helps. I'm learning a lot about gardening and cooking and practical things. When Dev comes home I want him to be amazed at how efficiently I can run his household."

"That's admirable, Carolyn," Mahala said.

"I hope so." Carolyn shrugged. "Here, have one."

As Carolyn laid out pickles, apples and cake, Mahala started to pinch a bit of bread off to toss to the ducks swimming at the waterline.

"Oh, I wouldn't do that," Carolyn spoke up. "At least, not yet – or we'll have no peace. They're quite pesky. I brought extra to feed them after we eat. Do tell me if you've had any letters. Did you hear from Jack in Savannah?"

"Yes, actually – a few days ago." Mahala smiled.

"I'm dying for news from the coast. What did he say?"

"Well, let's see." Mahala rocked back on her heels and drew her knees up in front of her, glad she was in her riding habit and not encumbered by hoops. "I told you his half brothers enlisted in the Savannah Cadets. Alan is sixteen like most of the others in the company, and they let in Bryson, too – though he's nineteen. And you already knew how Jack had his ships refitted – though he had quite a time finding carpenters and mechanics since they were all enlisting. The blockade is not very effective. I think it was on September 18 or so he got his small packet in from Nassau, and then earlier this month one of his larger ships arrived from Liverpool. He's established regular sales on the docks, and the people just flock there to get things like rope, coffee and salt.

He told me salt went from seventy cents a pound in the spring to a dollar fifty a pound, and it's now selling for up to nine dollars a sack!"

"You're kidding!" Carolyn declared, swallowing a bite of apple with difficulty. "That's highway robbery!"

"Yes indeed. Jack said he's trying to bring his prices a little lower than other vendors so as not to take advantage of everyone." Mahala chuckled. "But knowing him he's still making a nice profit."

"Oh, everything he touches seems to turn to gold. Of course I guess there was that railroad venture that fizzled out."

"Yes, but one day there will be a railroad through Clarkesville, and when it comes, Jack Randall will be part of it."

"No doubt you are right. Does he think he'll be able to keep getting out of Savannah? Is he carrying cotton out?"

"Yes, most of them are now – well, what few there are to make the runs. He did say he was considering a Nassau to Charleston route."

"What? Would he abandon the people of Savannah so easily?"

"Oh, no. He would establish offices in both places and hire a Caribbean brokerage agent, and bring goods into Savannah by land. I bet he'd end up holding sales both places. He just seems to think Charleston would be easier to navigate for his bigger steamers, if the blockade tightens," Mahala explained, crunching on a sweet and tangy pickle. "Of course," she added, "the little packet will still use the inland waterways up the Georgia coast."

Carolyn looked at her speculatively. "You've never been there, yet to hear you talk I would never guess it. His letters must be remarkably long and descriptive."

Mahala blushed. "Not really. I've told you practically all he said."

"Are you sure?" Carolyn teased.

"Yes, I'm sure." Mahala smiled back. She did think briefly of the way Jack had openly shared his struggles during the secession crisis, and the flush of joy such trust in her had evoked. "Either way," he had written, "there will be sacrifice. Neither way will I really win."

Carolyn shook her head. "He might as well be writing a business report to a co-worker, then. What's the point? When will the man get around to what he *really* wants to say?"

"I wish I knew what that was," Mahala sighed.

"*Don't* you?"

Mahala shook her head. "I don't think *he* knows."

"Oh, he loves you. Why else would he write to you?"

"Because we're friends?"

Carolyn made a blowing sound with her lips.

206

Mahala said, "Honestly, I can tell more what Clay Fraser's thinking by reading his letters, even after all this time, than I can when I'm looking Jack right in the face."

"Clay Fraser, the Cherokee boy? Well, I guess he's not much of a boy now. He's still writing to you?"

Mahala nodded and filled Carolyn in on the situation in Indian territory. Carolyn listened with fascination, then said, "Well, I just don't know what to make of that! It's touching that the Cherokee would come in on our side."

"No offense, but I think they're just trying to find the path through all this that will bring the least harm to their – our – people."

"That's understandable." Carolyn nodded. "So you have two men who love you, Mahala. What will you do?"

Mahala laughed. "It's not exactly like I have a choice to make. I've already turned the one down and the other one won't have me."

"I wouldn't lay stakes on that," Carolyn replied, handing her a crumbly slice of pound cake. "Both of those men are smart and determined, and you are a beautiful and capable woman. If I were a gambler, I'd say you'll have a decision ahead yet."

Mahala smiled in appreciation. "And if I were a gambler, I'd say before another year is out your husband will be madly in love with you."

A shadow crossed Carolyn's face. Mahala quickly touched her arm and said, "I'm sorry. I've overstepped my place."

"Oh, no, it's not that," Carolyn replied. "It's just that it's so close to my heart. I'm very thankful I can talk with you about it, Mahala. There is no one else I could tell. I just – hope he isn't angry when he finds out about the baby."

"That you didn't tell him sooner?"

"Well, yes. And maybe he would assume I wasn't careful enough."

"No, Carolyn. He'll understand. But you *should* write and tell him, and right away."

"I know – I just can't bring myself to. You don't know how many letters I've begun and torn up. It's just so hard a thing to write down on paper, when our relationship is already so tentative. We've always been so – *proper* together before. It's like there's this invisible barrier I can't break through, at least not on paper."

"Maybe it's in your mind," Mahala suggested.

"Maybe."

"You'll know when the time is right. Just pray for an opening. Are his men in better spirits now?"

"Yes, in fact they were for a time quite hopeful that there would be a battle to capture Washington. They have been camped near Fairfax. Dev said that when they were on picket duty they could actually see the Potomac River and the unfinished spire of the capitol dome!"

"Oh, my," Mahala breathed. "Were there not Yankees very near?"

"Yes, very. Sometimes on picket duty they exchanged fire a bit. They could hear their drums and bands in camp. And one day they even watched a hot air balloon go up – one that the Yankees were using to try to spy on them. A Confederate battery opened fire on it, and the men on the ground frantically started reeling it in. Dev said they were so close by they could hear the Yankees on the ground laughing at how scared the balloon detail was."

Mahala laughed. "So why did they not advance on Washington?"

"President Davis came to camp and counseled with some of the generals. The generals wanted reinforcements. Disease has really taken its toll in the camps. Hamilton Couper is actually rather ill now. You don't know him. Anyway, President Davis could not supply the needed extra men. So I think they will wait to spring," Carolyn said. She started packing up the picnic items, leaving out a partial loaf of stale bread. "This month they are pulling back to Centreville. The place they were at would have been too difficult to defend."

Mahala brushed off her skirt, and the girls both stood up. Noticing their approach to the pond, the ducks waddled forward. Mahala started breaking off small bites of bread and tossing them. She and Carolyn laughed at the race to gobble down the food.

"So, anything else?" Mahala questioned. "At least, anything you want to share with *me*?"

"Well, there's been a bit of fuss about the man who became lieutenant colonel when they promoted Gardner to colonel. The men didn't think him a capable leader. They've written petitions but nothing's changed. It appears John Cooper will remain in place. The 8th also got a new major, Lucius Lamar of Company C."

"Why was Captain Rousseau not chosen?" Mahala asked.

"Oh, he's fine with it. Some of these other men have more combat experience, and he says he'd rather stay with the Oglethorpes anyway. He actually has more duties than a major would."

"Truly?"

"Yes. One of the mysteries of the military world. I don't understand it, but he loves it." Carolyn smiled faintly, flinging the last of her bread.

Mahala sensed her lingering uncertainties and impulsively put an arm around her friend, steering her on a walk around the pond. "And he loves *you*," she reminded Carolyn gently. "Remember what you told me, about the day he left? I couldn't dream up anything more romantic if I tried."

Carolyn laughed softly. "It *was* an amazing moment," she admitted. "I just hope if we ever get back to reality he doesn't forget."

Early November, 1861
Savannah, Georgia

As the tall, aging Saleem closed the door of Jack's grandfather's St. James Square house behind him, Jack paused on the front step and shook his head. He would feel a whole lot better now about leaving Savannah if his grandparents had been cooperative. They should be packing dutifully as Sunny and Sylvie were. Instead William had chosen not to believe him.

"Yankees? Here?" he had questioned.

"Yes, Grandfather," Jack had insisted. "A huge fleet has been sighted off South Carolina's coast. If the forts there on Hilton Head and Bay Point don't hold, they'll be here next."

"Did you confirm this report?"

"Of course. The Warsaw fort outside Savannah has already skirmished with the blockading fleet."

William had shaken his head and leaned on his walking stick. "Pulaski will keep them out," he had merely argued stubbornly.

"Please go with Sunny and Sylvie to my hotel in North Georgia, just in case you're wrong," Jack had begged. "Just pack and be ready, should there be a panic."

"At our age, jostling along in railroad cars and in a stage over rutted roads would much more likely bring on our demise than Yankees in Savannah," William had pointed out. Jack had been forced to grudgingly concede his point. He had unhappily remained silent as his grandfather had added, "No, Son, we'll stay put. Do what you feel you must with your sister and stepmother."

Jack had explained that he must immediately get his remaining ship in Savannah, *Evangeline*, out of port. It would not do to have the Union gunboats bottle up his most valuable vessel. They would sail to Nassau and there join the rest of the small fleet. Should the coast clear, he would return. If not, perhaps he'd have more luck running into Charleston, the South's dominant east coast port.

William had nodded and murmured his understanding, but Jack's heart had been pained to see the clouds of confusion that occasionally dimmed the light in his grandfather's eyes. The time had passed when he could rely on William for aid, support or advice. It was all up to him now, and him alone.

Sadly Jack pressed his hat on his head and descended the steps.

He rode the short distance to Wright Square. He was pleased to enter the house and hear the activity of packing. Footsteps sounded upstairs, and he was drawn by voices in Sunny's bedroom. The door stood open. He now entered without hesitation. Under Jack's childhood portrait stood Bryson, in the uniform of the Savannah Cadets, his face under his brown curly hair earnest.

"You're overreacting," he was saying to his mother. "There's no need to go rushing off to the mountains with your tail between your legs. We'll never let the Yankees get into Savannah."

"Jack thinks it's best," Sunny replied, holding a bonnet with streaming ribbons over the top of a hat box.

"Jack, Jack, Jack," Bryson mumbled.

Jack cleared his throat.

"Jack!" Sylvie ran to him and put her arms around his waist, her eyes shining with delight. He hugged her back despite Bryson's frown. He allowed her to cling to him, knowing his presence comforted the girl. During their last visit, his half sister had confided that of all the sons, she felt Jack most resembled Richard, in appearance and mannerism as well as in voice. He thought he saw the same reaction in Sunny. These days he would often catch her staring at him in a pensive, wistful manner. She smiled now, too. Whether he had wanted to or not, he had stepped into his father's shoes.

"It's a precaution, Bryson," he explained as gently as possible without patronization, not wanting to rile the overconfident nineteen-year-old. "I just can't feel easy leaving the women here while I'm in Nassau and the Union troops are this close in such great numbers."

"*I'll* be here," Bryson pointed out stiffly.

"I know, Bryson, but with the ladies gone you can better attend to your duties. Should they remain and need you, you might not always be able to get free."

Bryson said nothing.

"Won't you feel better with them in Clarkesville, too?" Jack urged. "And if I'm wrong, what's lost? They will have had a nice vacation."

"I suppose," Bryson mumbled. "But you're not the only one capable of taking care of this family, Jack."

"I know that, Bryson. I never meant to imply otherwise."

Jack tried to soften his tone, but there was still a crease between his half brother's brows as the boy turned to leave. Sylvie went to kiss him. "I'll miss you, Bry," she said. He smiled then and hugged his mother, who fretted over his safety and made him promise to write. By the time he departed he was noticeably cheered, tossing Jack a wave.

"Are your grandparents coming with us?" Sunny asked Jack hopefully.

"I'm afraid not. I had thought they would make a good escort for you, but the servants will have to do. I'll send Jonathan from the stable. He's big and very loyal. Have him help out at the hotel when you get there. And of course you'll take your maids."

"Yes," Sunny agreed.

"Do you think me crazy, Sunny?"

"No, Jack, of course not." She smiled. "I trust you."

"Good. I don't think the city will fall, but there could be trouble, and I don't want you caught in a rush or a riot."

"I understand."

"You have enough money?"

"Plenty."

"Once you reach The Palace, you've but to ask for anything you need. Mrs. O'Beaty will take good care of you," Jack promised. "You may want to visit the Rousseaus. I understand they are still in Habersham. If Mr. Rousseau has not heard the news of the Union fleet, please warn him. He may wish to be here to look out for his crop and workers. Sylvie might enjoy spending some time with her cousin Carolyn." He smiled at his sister. "And please tell them I've sent word to be on the lookout to Carolyn's and your Calhoun relations in Liberty County. They will probably not be as alarmed there, but I've tried to spread the news to all my clients."

"That was good of you, Jack," Sunny said. "We'll be certain to call upon the Rousseaus the day we arrive and give them your messages."

"Good. Thanks." Jack paused and smiled. "All set to go? Anything I can do?"

"Just be careful," Sunny said, coming up to him for a half hug and a gentle kiss on the cheek. She looked at him with new affection.

"Pray for a dark night for *Evangeline*'s departure," he said.

"Oh, Jack, if anything happened to you–!" Sylvie exclaimed in a sudden burst of fear.

"It won't," he assured her. "I'm too stubborn for trouble. And if the Yankees got hold of me, they'd send me back."

His joke elicited only a faint smile from the women.

"I'll write to you as soon as I'm settled in Nassau," he added.

"I don't like this – this separation!" Sylvie suddenly exclaimed and began to cry. "I'm frightened, Jack. When will we see you again?"

"I don't know. But I promise you will. I've got to get back to the harbor now. I've called all hands to *Evangeline*."

Sylvie walked him to the door. As much as he adored his little sister, her clinging and fearfulness was beginning to wear on him. He really didn't know how to lift her spirits. He couldn't imagine the needs a *wife* would have! He thought of Mahala. She seemed independent and feisty enough, but once an attachment had been made, would she, too, simmer with expectations and demands?

He turned to Sylvie, braced for more questions and tears, but suddenly her eyes had cleared. Jack wondered if this perfect little Southern belle had been playing him. Oh, he knew she loved him, but half the time he thought Sylvie's theatrics were performed for an audience that existed mostly in the girl's mind. Too, he had a sneaking suspicion that Southern women were far tougher than they allowed their men to realize.

"Jack, who is Mahala Franklin?" she asked suddenly.

"Who is – *what?*"

"Mahala Franklin. Who is she?"

He was confounded. "Where did you even hear that name?" he had to know.

Guilelessly Sylvie blinked. "I just saw it one time on an envelope you left lying on your desk."

"Have you been reading my mail?" Jack demanded, towering over the petite girl in a menacing manner.

She was nonplussed. "Of course not. I would never stoop to such a thing. Why, is she some secret love?" Sylvie asked, tapping on his chest knowingly.

"She's a business acquaintance – a friend," he replied.

"In Clarkesville?" Sylvie pressed.

Jack conceded reluctantly, "Yes. Her family owns The Franklin Hotel."

"Well, then, wouldn't she make a good companion for me, too?"

"Yes – no. I don't know. I really have to go." Jack kissed her forehead and jogged down the steps. When he turned to glance back, Sylvie was watching him speculatively. Maybe sending his sister and stepmother to Clarkesville hadn't been such a bright idea after all.

A deep channel led to Nassau's fine harbor by Hog Island. The harbor was open at both ends and lay parallel to the city, which bustled with sailors, free blacks, slaves and white "Conchs." The wharf area was crowded with ships of every description, so that Jack felt they were just a tiny part of the dizzying business. But a ship of *Evangeline*'s size and sleekness, even steaming quietly to dockside with the simple three pillars of "wisdom, justice, moderation" floating on the blue background of Georgia's unofficial flag, could not fail to attract some attention.

From his spot by the wheel, Jack saw Andrew Willis waiting for them, dressed in his neat gray suit and bowler hat. He fluttered his hand in a wave. Next to him, as if in purposeful contrast, was a swarthy black-haired sailor whom Jack recognized as the first officer of the *Fortitude*. It appeared that his chest was in danger of bursting the buttons off his muslin shirt. He stood almost at attention, like a bodyguard.

"I suspect you'll be glad you sent Willis ahead on *Fortitude*," his pilot, Lawrence Birch, said, coming alongside him once docking was complete. A bunch of sailors scrambled to set the gang plank down.

"I already am."

Jack had been to the Bahamas before, but only briefly. It would indeed be helpful that the young clerk had been able to scout out the area, though Jack had to admit he had some reservations on that score. Willis was just so timid. Jack hoped he had not been taken for a fool in renting a warehouse property.

His employee was eager to assure him otherwise. They had barely shaken hands when Andrew said, "Finding a warehouse, even a small one, is no small feat around here. But I've accomplished it, Mr. Randall – Captain Randall – and at a price I think you'll be pleased with. There's even an office in the building, though the cleaning I had to do, it would have made an Irish maid weep. I, in fact, nearly wept."

"All that can wait, Willis," First Officer Scott said, sticking his hand out. "These gentlemen look like they can do with a good meal – and perhaps a stiff drink. And if we hurry we can join Captain Howell for dinner. Welcome to Nassau, Captain Randall."

Jack shook his hand but quickly pointed out, "I'd like to hear your report first thing, Mr. Willis – but indeed over dinner. Lead on, Officer Scott."

"Very well." Scott gleamed with pleasure and turned toward town. They immediately blended into the symphony of activity.

Hastening to catch up, Andrew spluttered, "Uh, Mr. Scott, are you quite sure? Perhaps Captain Randall would prefer to dine at the hotel, where he can settle in comfortably."

A dark eye slanted back over a massive shoulder. "What's wrong with The Salty Dog?"

"Well, nothing, I suppose, if you like the sort of place Blackbeard would have frequented."

Jack laughed out loud in delight. Scott paused and turned around to look at him and Lawrence. "Would you gentlemen prefer your hotel?" he asked in a measured tone.

"No, indeed," Jack assured him. "It's been a lifelong fantasy of mine to meet Edward Tench. Maybe we'll encounter his ghost."

Scott grinned, showing one golden tooth. "I thought you'd feel that way. The Salty Dog has been serving seafaring men for a century and none have left with complaints yet."

They followed the first officer down the nearest lane leading away from the harbor. On Bay Street, they turned aside. Jack admired the brightly colored buildings with French and Spanish architecture. Carriages and wagons rumbled past, and street vendors peddled their wares. Up ahead, a weathered sign depicting a sad-looking canine proclaimed the entrance to their destination. Andrew looked so dejectedly resigned – much like the tavern's mascot – that Jack smiled and clapped his back. The poor man would have been much happier if the adventures of war had never swept him from his comfortable routine in Savannah.

Inside, the few small windows did little to illumine the dim interior. Loud sailors shared their tales of the sea or hunkered over card games while downing tankards of ale at simple wooden tables. Andrew appeared slightly relieved when Scott led them to a back room. Here an oil lamp burned on a checkered tablecloth, creating a more welcoming atmosphere. Dean Howell rose from his meal to greet them with a hearty smile and handshake.

"Ye're right on time, I see," he remarked. "Have any trouble getting past the Yankees?"

"Luck was with us. She gave us a dark night, and we slipped right past them," Jack said.

The men all took a chair.

"Good for you," Howell declared.

A busty young woman in an apron appeared and asked, "Stew?"

Jack eyed Howell's fare and decided it looked quite appetizing. "Yes, please," he said. Lawrence echoed his reply. She went off with their orders.

Howell continued, "*Regale* came in bringing the medical supplies and cloth you ordered from England. My men are finishing the loading as we speak. Then we'll be ready to set sail for Charleston."

"I think that will be best," Jack said, "at least until we see what happens in Savannah. Should our home port remain too chancy, I'll take Willis with me to Charleston and set up an office there. I want the majority of the supplies to be taken down to Georgia, though. It is her people we serve."

"Of course, Sir. That should be no problem. I have friends on the railroad."

"Good. I was counting on that."

The stew arrived along with pewter cups of ale. It was not of the quality Jack would have chosen to imbibe, but he was even less trusting of the water in such a place.

"Are my lodgings in this part of town, too?" he asked Andrew with a grin.

"Oh, no, Sir! I've secured rooms for you at the finest hotel in Nassau, just opened – The Royal Victoria. It's but a short walk from here but in a very nice area, and surrounded by lush gardens. All the blockade runners are taking rooms there."

"So that's what we are, eh? 'The blockade runners'?"

"Yes, Sir, your own class of people," Andrew replied with a grin.

"I trust your quarters are adjoining so that we might conduct business."

"Yes, Sir. The office on the waterfront will do for some sorts of meetings and storage, but I wouldn't want to spend too much time there."

"Of course." Jack smiled, amused, but guessing he'd agree. "You've been a great help, Willis."

The young man's face lit up with pleasure.

As they were passing back through the main room minutes later, Howell and Scott bound for the waterfront and Jack, Lawrence and Andrew for the hotel, a silver-haired man in a black frock coat stood up and touched Jack's arm.

"Excuse me, Sir," he said in a pleasant low country drawl, "but are you the owner of that big side-wheel steamer that just drew into port?"

"The *Evangeline*, yes," Jack said.

"You're Jack Randall, then."

"I am, but I'm afraid you have me at a disadvantage."

"Robert Lawson of Importing and Exporting Company of South Carolina. I captain a ship for William Bee and Charles Mitchel."

"Oh, yes!" Jack shook the man's hand. "I've heard of the Bee sales in Charleston. Our operations in Savannah are very similar."

Lawson nodded and smiled. He glanced at Jack's employees and asked Jack, "May I have just a moment of your time?"

"Of course." Jack turned to the others. "Meet you outside?" he asked Andrew, and waved off Scott and Howell. Then he took a seat beside Mr. Lawson, who appeared to be alone with his drink. "How can I help you?" he asked.

"I think the question may be more how can I help *you*," Lawson stated. Though he said it gently, Jack was taken aback. "Please don't take offense," Lawson continued. "You're new here, and have yet to learn how things work. Only two flags are seen in these waters – the Union Jack and the Stars and Bars. There are those who murmur against any who fly other colors. Your choice of Georgia's banner without the Confederate standard will not ... has not ... gone unnoticed."

"It is Georgia I serve," Jack replied tersely, on his guard. He wondered whether this soft-spoken gentleman was friend or foe.

"Believe me, I understand. My feelings for my home state are equally strong. But we did join a Confederacy, did we not?"

Jack did not reply.

"This place is as thick with spies now as it once was with pirates," Lawson continued. "I am aware of your reputation as a prominent shipper – and your Northern background. I just don't want you to get off on the wrong foot. You know – suspicions, inquiries, detainments."

"Why do you care?" Jack asked bluntly.

"Four ships, when the South is clamoring for a Navy and for supplies for its citizens and soldiers. You need to ask? Here." Lawson slid a brown paper-wrapped parcel across the table to him. "Take this. Think about what I said."

"My firm is a private citizen chandlery," Jack pointed out stubbornly. "I have nothing to hide or defend."

"Just take it. You may find it saves your hide one day."

Jack didn't need to ask what was in the package. He sat staring at his companion for a full thirty seconds, judging the nuances of the aristocratic features. Then he reached out for the parcel and scooped it up as he stood.

"Maybe I'll save *your* hide one day," he said.

"That may well be. We're on the same side, you know."

Jack allowed a fleeting smile. He wasn't sure yet what he thought about Robert Lawson. But if what Andrew said about the Royal Victoria was true, that it housed all the blockade runners, he would probably run into the man again. It might serve well to pick Lawson's brain about Charleston harbor. But not now. He was faintly disgruntled by the man's assuming approach – and very tired. With a nod he turned and ducked through the door into the bright sunshine.

Saying nothing to his clerk or pilot about the exchange, Jack allowed himself to be led south into the city. They passed handsome public buildings constructed in British Colonial style some years before. Jack knew that in 1670 control of the Bahamas had been given to the six Lord Proprietors of the Carolinas. The reins had been taken back by the Mother Country in 1718, when Britain had recognized the islands as a colony. After the Revolutionary War, many American loyalists had journeyed to the area, establishing trade and plantations. But due to drought, insects, poor soil and tariffs, the Bahamas had remained impoverished.

But that was changing, Jack thought as he laid grateful eyes on the impressive Royal Victoria. Four-story twin wings with galleries extended from a pedimented frontage supported by seven slender columns. A cupola crowned the roof. The dark shutters and cool white porches beckoned from amid green palm trees.

"I asked Scott to see that your trunks are sent straight away to your lodging," Andrew told him.

"Very good." Jack made a mental note to be generous to the clerk when the time for raises rolled around.

A half hour later, Jack opened the French doors of his room and stepped out onto the veranda. He took in the rows of pastel buildings and palm trees marching down to the bright blue-green waters of the bay, where myriad masts reached to a cloudless sky. A gentle easterly trade wind caressed his face. It was truly beautiful here. It would be a pleasant place to remain, waiting out the war in comfort. But he couldn't do that, not while those he held dear faced struggles and deprivation.

As he turned back into his bedroom, Mahala's face – with eyes the color of the Bahamian waters – rose in his mind's eye. Now why did he always think of her?

He shook his head. She would surely love this place. He imagined the amazement with which she would take in everything. A girl that full of life deserved to see the world, not be stuck in one county all her years.

Thoughtfully Jack unwrapped the silk flag. He laid the bright colors of the Stars and Bars across his bed and stood looking at it for some time.

November 12, 1861
Clarkesville, Georgia

The lunch rush at The Franklin Hotel was over. Except for two guests lingering over coffee and pie near the crackling fireplace, the dining room was empty. Mahala piled dishes onto her tray and took them into the kitchen, where Maddie was elbow-deep in sudsy water at the sink.

"Your herbed roast hen was delicious," Mahala complimented her. "The Palace's French chef would have been scratching his head."

"Hmpf," Maddie replied disbelievingly. But she loved Mahala's flattery. A smile turned up the corners of her mouth as Mahala swung back out the door with a damp dish cloth in hand.

She scrubbed tables and chairs until her arm ached and tendrils of long dark hair escaped from her chignon. As she straightened to go back into the kitchen, her eyes fell upon a young woman standing in the foyer watching her. She must have been there for some time, for she wore a contemplative expression and gave no evidence of hurry. She was clad in a lavish ensemble of pink and chocolate stripes and solids, trimmed with fringe and tassels. Dark ringlets and a matching bonnet framed her fair face.

Mahala stepped toward the girl, asking, "May I help you?"

"You're Mahala Franklin."

"I am." Mahala patiently waited for the girl to reveal her own identity, though she thought something about her seemed faintly familiar. "Have we met?"

"No. I'm Sylvie Randall. Jack's sister."

Mahala's mouth opened and her eyes widened. "Oh!"

"You know him pretty well, don't you?"

"I – well, I suppose you might say that," Mahala replied. "I *have* heard of you," she admitted, extending her hand tentatively.

Sylvie smiled and took it, giving a tiny curtsy. Her curious, bright eyes never left Mahala's face. "You're part Indian, aren't you?" she asked.

Mahala nodded. "Half Cherokee."

"Fascinating. It makes sense now."

"What makes sense?"

"Oh, nothing. Do you live here?"

"Yes. You can access the family rooms through the foyer. I don't know why they never put on a front door. I guess they thought it would ruin the look of the hotel." Mahala paused, realizing she was running on foolishly. "Do you have news from Savannah? Your brother – is he …?"

"Not there. He's in Nassau by now."

"Oh! Would you like to come into the parlor and visit? I was just finishing up."

"Yes! I would," Sylvie said with apparent eagerness.

"Very well. Let me just take my cloth and apron to the kitchen, and I'll be right back."

Mahala hurried away, her heart beating fast with nervousness. What did Sylvie know about her? She had not known about her mixed ancestry, but she hadn't run out the door upon discovering it, either. She really wanted the younger woman to like her. And she realized getting to know Sylvie would provide a new view of Jack as well.

After fluffing her dress – wishing she was wearing something nicer – and smoothing her hair, Mahala hurried back out into the foyer. Her unexpected guest was patiently waiting, studying the art work in the hall.

"Here we are," Mahala said, opening the door to the family parlor. "Do please have a seat."

Sylvie did so, spreading her silk skirt on the sofa with an elegant swish.

"Would you care for tea?"

"Oh, no, thank you. I'm sure you'd like to rest. You looked ever so busy."

"It's all right. I'm quite used to it," Mahala admitted, taking a chair. There was no use in pretending she was a proper lady bred to the mansion.

"You and your grandmother run the inn?"

"With the help of two servants and my father's cousin, our manager. That is, my father – and my mother – are deceased."

"Ah," Sylvie said. "It must be exciting to be an independent woman."

Mahala shrugged. "Not really. Travel would be exciting, but there isn't the opportunity for that. But ... you said Jack – Mr. Randall – was in Nassau?"

Sylvie's eyes sparkled. "You can call him Jack. Apparently the two of you are on a first name basis."

"I – we have known each other for a good many years now."

"And yet he never mentioned you."

"He didn't?" Mahala fought to keep her face impassive.

"Not a word."

"Then how ...?"

"I saw your name and address on an envelope on his desk. I thought I'd come see his secret pen pal for myself." Sylvie chuckled as if it was all rather amusing. Then she continued pertly, "Yes, he's in Nassau. He made us come up here. Good thing, for I hear a big panic broke out after we left ... ladies and children mobbing the train stations, the banks sending out their gold and silver, and cotton and rice being shipped inland. Some of the planters are burning the cotton in their fields and sending their slaves from the coast. Jack asked us to warn my cousin Carolyn's family, the Rousseaus. Mr. Rousseau went down to take care of everything on their plantation."

"He did?" asked Mahala. "Mrs. Carolyn Rousseau is a good friend of mine."

"She is?" Sylvie seemed surprised. A sudden frown marred her delicate forehead. "It would seem there's plenty my big brother has not let me in on."

Mahala shifted uncomfortably. "You were saying ... about Savannah ..."

Sylvie nodded. "Anyway, the Yankees took Port Royal and Hilton Head. But then you probably don't realize how close that is to Savannah. It's within sight of Cockspur Island. Our men abandoned Tybee Island and have been mining the river with obstructions and some type of new Russian invention they call 'infernal machines.' I'm sure *I* don't understand it all. But I do know one thing. The Yankees might get onto Tybee, but with Pulaski and our flotilla, and General Lee there now to oversee our defenses, they'll never take Savannah. Still, Jack wanted us out of the way. He takes good care of us women, you know."

"Of course." Mahala blinked, folding her hands in her lap. "But does this mean he will be unable to return to Savannah?"

Sylvie seemed to measure her for a moment. Then she drew a deep sigh. "By water, I fear that will be true. But I never think for a moment that Jack will let the blockade stop him. I know he'll be back – somehow."

"Good thing he has a capable manager at his hotel," Mahala commented, half to herself.

"Oh, yes. I doubt *you'll* be seeing him much."

"I wouldn't expect so," Mahala replied softly.

"Well, I'd better go. I left Mother shopping. She thought I just went on to the next store." Sylvie giggled and stood up, looping her reticule around her wrist. "It was ever so lovely to meet you. I've always been curious about Jack's mountain friends. I'm discovering you're all just as colorful as I'd imagined."

Mahala's face turned red. Surely Jack's sister didn't intend the double meaning, did she? Mahala bit her tongue as a smart retort rose to her lips. In case Sylvie was just young and foolish, instead of purposefully cruel, she would give her the benefit of the doubt. She walked Sylvie into the foyer.

"Thank you for stopping by," she said stiffly.

The door to the street opened and a middle aged but still very attractive woman entered. Mahala recognized her instantly. Jack's stepmother obviously remembered her, too, for she paused but a moment while casting an indignant stare upon Mahala before hurrying to Sylvie's side.

"Whatever were you thinking, running off like that? It was only good luck that someone saw you come in here," she said to her daughter.

"Oh, it's all right, Mother. This is Jack's – and Carolyn's – friend, Miss Mahala Franklin. Miss Franklin, this is my mother, Mrs. Sunny Randall."

"Yes, I remember Miss Franklin," Sunny said tersely as Mahala curtsied. She put a hand on Sylvie's shoulder. "Come, let's go back for a rest and give Miss Franklin her peace."

"Goodbye, Miss Franklin," Sylvie said.

Mahala stepped around her to open the door. "Good day, Miss Randall. Mrs. Randall." She held herself erect as the two ladies sailed past. Then she slumped against the door as she closed it behind them.

Outside in the street she heard Sylvie say, "Wasn't she something, Mother? Quite pretty despite the olive skin. And really rather proper. I think she's quite taken with Jack. Her whole face lit up when I said his name."

"Oh, don't be ridiculous, Sylvie," Sunny retorted sharply. Their forms cast a shadow through the window as they moved away, the widow's voice trailing behind. "Jack would never have a serious thought about someone like that …"

CHAPTER SEVENTEEN

Late December, 1861
Clarkesville, Georgia

ahala walked to the post office with the letter to Jack in her mittened hand and a scarf 'round her neck. She thought about the contents of the correspondence and fought the urge to return home and rewrite it.

When she had received his postcard from the Royal Victoria Hotel, Nassau, Bahamas, she had hungrily read his descriptions of the tropical paradise, envying his opportunity for adventure. But she had been most interested in his mention of his family's visit to Clarkesville.

"You may see my sister and stepmother in town. I sent them inland against the threat of Yankees on the coast."

That was all. No "tell me what you thought of them" or "how did you get on if you met." As if a possible meeting between them was inconsequential. Maybe Sunny was right. Maybe Jack had no serious thoughts of her.

But then, she argued, why did he continue to write to her? No one made him and he certainly didn't have to. She couldn't bear the thought of severing that tie, though she did briefly consider it. She needed that link to Jack and through him to the outside world.

And so she had written her brief letter, allowing his manner to dictate hers, saying merely "Your sister did call upon me. She was just as you had described her, though she seemed rather surprised upon having learned of our acquaintance." She had permitted herself that much, that one pointed remark. She hoped it would jab his conscience. It was little enough, when inside she wanted to scream at him, "Why did you not tell them about me? Why did you act as though I'm a secret? Do I matter that little, or—"

Mahala stopped in her tracks. A wave of heat swept over her. She knew the answer to her own question. If Jack considered her merely a friend, he would not have been ashamed of her. One was not ashamed of casual acquaintances. He would only have been reticent to tell his family about her if he did care for her.

And that realization brought both joy and sorrow, for the only remaining question was which emotion would win out in the end – shame or love? It had taken years of acquaintance to get to this point – and really so little ground gained. And then another dilemma surfaced past her hurt: did she want a man who did not fully embrace all that she was?

Feet moving more slowly now, Mahala entered the little building. Mr. Erwin, over sixty now despite having had children late in life, greeted her. She called a hello and was forced to smile at the sight of George Blythe's cheerful countenance as the old man came to the counter. She knew that when the cold weather came Mr. Blythe ached with rheumatism. His hand was a crippled claw as he took the letter from her. But he never once complained. She could take a lesson from his positive outlook.

"Did you hear the news about our very own Mrs. Stanford?" George asked.

"No, what was that?" Mahala asked patiently. Mr. Blythe always had all the news. Cordelia Stanford was, of course, the wife of local lawyer John Stanford and the mother of four grown and near-grown girls. Mahala would always remember the first time she had seen the Stanford home, Pomona Hall, when Clay took her there on that ill-fated meat delivery route.

"Why, the *Richmond Enquirer's* done run a story on those fine woolen blanket shawls she's been making for our soldiers – because of her giving one to Jeff Davis himself. Seems we got a local celebrity."

"That's wonderful!" Mahala exclaimed. "I'm happy for her."

"You're one popular young lady, too," Mr. Blythe observed, fishing around behind the counter. "But then I always did expect a gal as pretty as you to have lotsa beaux. Here's another letter from Oklehomey Territory."

"Really?" Mahala stared in surprise at the letter the postmaster gave her. She had not expected to hear from Clay again so soon. The pressures of war must be causing him to value a confidant more than ever. She tucked the envelope in her pocket and added, "Thank you, Mr. Blythe. Good day, Mr. Erwin. Merry Christmas."

"Merry Christmas," they responded.

As George moved away, she smiled and slipped a box of chocolates on the counter. Whisking out the door, she caught a glimpse of his delighted face as he turned back around and beheld his surprise.

Mahala hurried home. She had unburdened herself of her coat, mittens, scarf and boots and had just pulled a chair up near the fire when Martha came in.

"Another letter?" she asked.

"From Clay."

"Does he never give up?" Martha sighed.

Mahala ignored her and started reading.

December 11, 1861
Fort Gibson, Oklahoma Territory

Dear Mahala,

Oh, if I thought it was a mess here before, how wrong I was! We had our official mustering in on November 5, with our one-year term beginning October 25. We were 1,214 men strong. We had intelligence that Opothleyahola was moving slowly north to remove from Confederate territory and meet with Federal officials. At the same time, we feared invasion by Kansas Jayhawkers. We were sent north to the border of our nation to cut off these raiders. 480 of us went up the Verdigris River Valley toward Coody's Bluff. Col. Cooper marched against Opothleyahola. We heard the Yankees were raiding our people's farms and settlements. We trailed the Jayhawkers into Kansas, but we didn't take enough to eat, and the cold set in. We had to turn back. Then we learned Opothleyahola had defeated Cooper at Round Mountain. At last we got supplies from Fort Gibson, and we rode to meet Cooper. Turns out we got there first – only a bit northeast of Opothleyahola's camp, and without our other forces.

That's when it all started. Or I guess I should say it started when Captain McDaniel and his company deserted to Opothleyahola's force. The night of December 7 some Keetoowahs were on picket duty. They met up with Captain McDaniel and made a plan. Of course I didn't know that then. When Opothleyahola sent over a message for Drew to send most of his officers to attend a peace negotiation, I thought it was legitimate. They went. While they were gone the Keetoowahs started telling everyone we were about to be attacked by a huge party of pro-Union Creeks and that Cooper was too far away to help. "Let's go join the other side and save ourselves," they said.

Men started agreeing and tying cornhusks in their hair, their special symbol. I argued that we had made an oath and we should not break it. But no one listened. They slipped over to the Union lines using Keetoowah passwords. By the time Drew noticed, it was too late. The peace officers returned, having been released only by insisting they had to secure women and children in our camp (of which there are none). Fearing we were surrounded, those of us remaining broke into small parties and made it to Cooper's camp. I think there were only about seventy of us still with Drew.

The next day they attacked our rear and we fought with Confederate Choctaws, Chickasaws and Texans trying to clear them from a big ravine on the east bank of Bird Creek. Most of them were grouped in a horseshoe of the river called Caving Banks. After four hours of see-sawing combat they withdrew.

We are now back at the fort. Drew is pleading for additional troops from Arkansas to stabilize the area. Oh, Mahala, I am so ashamed. What will the white men think of us? That we are untrustworthy and undisciplined. And what will happen to our fine hopes? Should the South win, they will not have to honor any agreements.

I wish I had never enlisted, but had made my way home to Georgia. I don't want to witness the further demolition of our people.

Yours, Clay

Mahala drew back from the paper, closing her eyes as she shared Clay's distress. For such a noble sort of man to be caught in such a debacle! It must be testing everything he had thought he believed in. How she wished he had someone to comfort him.

Well, the best she could do was write him back. Mahala rose to go to her room for pen and paper, but a knock at the door stopped her. She opened it to behold Carolyn, dressed in a fur cloak and wool bonnet.

"I know you weren't expecting me, but can I come in?" her friend asked.

"Of course! You're always welcome." Mahala held the door open.

Carolyn entered and divested of her wrappings, casting Mahala a concerned glance as Mahala hung up her things. "You look upset. Is something wrong?"

Mahala shook her head. "No – only that I just had a letter from Clay. Things are not going so well for him. A great number of Drew's Cherokees deserted to the Union."

"Oh, no!" Carolyn declared. "I take it your friend did not approve."

Mahala gestured for her to sit down. "He certainly did not. He's a man of his word, unlike many others." She could not resist adding the last wryly, thinking of Jack.

As usual, Carolyn followed her train of thought. "Don't put too much on the actions of Jack's stepmother and sister," she said. Having grown weary of the country, and with the Yankees apparently held at bay on the coast, the women had returned home last week – after taking great pains to avoid Mahala the whole month. "Jack does not seem to be the sort of man to be influenced by what others think."

"No?" Mahala raised a brow. "He's certainly made no declarations these past years. I think maybe I am a game to him – a novelty like I was to his sister."

Carolyn sighed. "I have to agree these men do test our patience to the limit," she said solemnly. "But what can we do but be true to our hearts?"

"At least you got Dev to the altar," Mahala pointed out.

"I might see him soon," Carolyn blurted. "That's what I came to tell you. Henrietta wants to rejoin Louis in Savannah. Dev has written that he hopes for a winter furlough, to come home recruiting."

"Oh, Carolyn. That's wonderful," Mahala said, leaning forward to pat Carolyn's hand. "But have the Yankees left?"

"Well – no. We hear Tattnall tried to engage them in late November, but after a brief skirmish the Yankees withdrew. They did leave for a time, but then they came back. They've sunk vessels across the river channel and put gunboats in Ossabaw and Warsaw sounds to prevent any of our ships going in or out."

"It doesn't sound safe."

"No, but things have quieted down. It just makes me mad to think what a stranglehold they have on us. But if there's any chance Dev might come … I want to be there."

"Of course," Mahala said. "When do you leave?"

"Tomorrow."

Mahala's face fell. "So soon?" She didn't think she could stand the long winter ahead without her friend.

Carolyn said, "Yes. I'm sorry. I'll miss you awfully. But I did bring a little something …" She hopped up and went to her cloak, drawing out a present wrapped with a red ribbon.

Mahala smiled. She took the parcel and unwrapped it to find a lovely stationery set. She burst into laughter.

"What's so funny?" Carolyn asked.

"Just a minute and you'll see." Mahala went to her room and returned with her gift to Carolyn – paper and envelopes. Carolyn also began to laugh. "I didn't have a chance to wrap it yet. I couldn't think what in the world you might need, except maybe some more writing paper."

"Which isn't exactly easy to come by these days," Carolyn agreed, happily taking her present. She embraced Mahala. "Thank you. Now we can both write each other often."

"Thank you." Mahala returned the embrace. "When will I see you again?"

"I don't know."

Unsatisfied but knowing it would do no good to press further, Mahala held the door open. "God go with you."

"And may He stay with you as well."

With a final smile over her shoulder, Carolyn walked out into the chilly December air. Mahala closed the door behind her and brushed away a tear. Would she ever be the one leaving, instead of always being left behind?

Early February, 1862
Savannah, Georgia

When Carolyn heard Jack Randall had returned to Savannah with a box-car-load of supplies from Charleston, she made haste to invite him, his sister and stepmother – her aunt and cousin – to dinner. Her motive was truly not merely to curry his favor – although the package of salt, spices and notions from the Caribbean Jack brought as a gift was not turned away – but in hopes of assisting her friend's standing with the Randalls. Over an elegant dinner of roast quail, Carolyn took the opportunity to sing Mahala's praises and to gauge the reactions of those gathered at table. Henrietta and Sunny looked annoyed and embarrassed. Jack would not meet her eyes, but he was listening intently to everything she said. Sylvie remarked with a combination of curiosity and wonder, "I find it surprising you would form an attachment to such a girl, Cousin Carolyn. Are her ways not quite different?"

"My thoughts exactly," Sunny put in. "I understand the Indian people, even the civilized Cherokee, still cling to many rustic – and sometimes alarming – practices."

Before Carolyn could answer, Jack cut in with barely restrained impatience. "Miss Franklin hardly lives out in the wilds. She lives in town with her very proper English grandmother, attends church, speaks French, dances a very elegant waltz, and has a better head for business than most men I know."

Sylvie tossed her curls. By Carolyn's estimation she was faintly irritated – perhaps even jealous. "You sound quite taken with her."

"I think highly of the lady. If you would have taken the time to get to know her while you were in Clarkesville, so would you." Jack abruptly speared a potato ball.

Carolyn bit her tongue but smiled to herself, immensely satisfied at the way Jack had rushed to Mahala's defense.

Sylvie effected a pout. "I wanted to, but Mother was quite adamant that I had better ways to spend my time. I *was* curious, though, especially since you seemed so secretive about the whole thing," she declared. Then a look from her brother silenced her.

Henrietta and Louis directed their attention to their dinners.

Carolyn decided it was time to sew up the discussion. "There is no secret," she proclaimed graciously, placing a hand gently on the table. "Miss Mahala Franklin is as refined as any lady to ever enter the drawing room of this house, and we are great friends … she, Jack and I. I hope it will always be so."

Jack looked up at her with a grateful smile. He nodded. "So do I, Mrs. Rousseau."

As he escorted her into the parlor after the meal, he asked her about Devereaux. A shadow crossed her face.

"I sent him a Christmas box of pies and candy and a new greatcoat," Carolyn answered. "He replied with a letter, and that was the last I have heard from him. The men were very grateful for the packages from home. Their spirits are low. Their lieutenant colonel was just thrown from his horse and died. And it's very cold there, rain and snow and the creeks freezing over."

"Do they have decent lodgings?" Jack asked.

Carolyn made a face. "There was some confusion as to who would build the winter quarters."

Henrietta heard her and chimed in, "The men had to do it themselves, of course. Out lumbering in the freezing cold. Six to eight log shanties per company. You think about that while you're in your silken sheets at the Royal Victoria Hotel."

"Mother!" Carolyn exclaimed, aghast at her mother-in-law's rudeness.

But Jack replied with surprising gravity. "Yes, Ma'am, I will."

Despite his composed response, Henrietta defended herself. "Well, that's sacrifice, is it not? That's what our boys in the field face."

Carolyn was well aware of the sentiment against civilian men, but she was humiliated that it would be exhibited here before a guest in their home. She felt the need to remind those present, "Blockade runners like Mr. Randall risk their lives and livelihood to bring us – and our soldiers – food, medicine, clothing and equipment. Without them, we could not survive."

"Quite right," Louis said, backing her up. "Without our blockade runners, where would we be? Now if President Davis can just get that one million Congress has fought so hard to keep from him and get that railroad constructed from Danville to Greensboro, it will help tremendously with moving supplies about. We're all on the same side here. Please overlook a mother's distress for her son," he added to the Randalls.

Jack shook his head and held up a hand. "Perfectly understood."

Sunny added, "I am equally proud of Jack and my two sons, who also serve in the military – here on the coast. We can be proud of *all* our young men."

Carolyn saw Sylvie glance at Henrietta, who was surreptitiously – guiltily – wiping her eyes in an embarrassing manner. The girl showed unexpected consideration by saying quickly, "You are so good at the piano, Cousin Carolyn. Will you play? I can sing. I do love the new military tunes. That should cheer us all up."

Carolyn smiled graciously, though she didn't really feel like playing – especially anything cheerful. But she said, "Of course," and moved to the piano to obligingly render "Dixie" and "Bonnie Blue Flag." In rustling silk trimmed with blue velvet bows, Sylvie trilled behind her. She had a lovely soprano and displayed it to its fullest with much hand-clasping and sighing.

Carolyn wondered how Jack felt about the tunes selected. He gave no indication of disfavor, watching them with a polite smile and even tapping a foot to the beat. She liked him even better. By the time she showed out the guests, she was fairly well pleased with the evening, despite its challenges. The most important thing was that she judged Jack to have serious feelings for Mahala, and she now believed him worthy of Mahala's affection as well.

Henrietta kissed her and said, "We're going up to bed, Carolyn. To be quite honest, dear, your choice of guests was rather taxing."

"I'm sorry," Carolyn replied. "I didn't think it would prove a problem, since you often used to invite the Randalls to Forests of Green."

Henrietta considered for a moment. "Things have changed since then. That Jack was always a handful, and now, with his choice of profession ..." She trailed off and sighed, then added, "But I do like little Sylvie. Maybe we should arrange for her to get to know Dylan, now that they're both grown."

Carolyn almost choked. There was no one she could imagine less as a pastor's wife – or Dylan's wife – than Sylvie Randall. From the way her alarmed gaze met Louis', she could tell he fully agreed. He even gave her a little wide-eyed head shake over the top of his wife's curls. Carolyn stifled a smile.

"He seems so lonely lately," Henrietta was continuing obliviously. "He could use someone to cheer him up. I wonder why he never comes to visit any more. Do you think there's someone in the country?"

"No, dear. Come. You're tired," Louis urged, taking his wife's elbow.

As they went up the stairs Carolyn heard her say, "I hope no one will think the worse of us for entertaining a blockade runner."

Carolyn smiled and shook her head. Socializing was still something of a strain on her. She needed time to wind down before bed. Perhaps, she thought, she could still play softly while her husband's parents got ready for bed.

In the parlor she tinkled out a few notes of "Juanita" before turning to "Lorena." The wistful love songs suited her far better tonight.

Truth be told, as much as she wanted to see Dev, she was afraid to. So much was riding on their time together. What if all her hopes were crushed again?

In a way, it was easier to not see him – to just go on hoping, held together by letters. But oh, letters were really not enough. She wanted so much more.

A cold draft swirled around her legs. She stopped and adjusted her skirts before rippling out another phrase. Then she became aware someone was watching her. Her eyes lifted to the parlor door. She merely sat there staring, certain what she saw must be a figment of her imagination, a product of her longing. But the vision moved. The man in the unfamiliar gray uniform standing just a few feet before her took off his hat, uncovering his dark hair. Then, heart-stoppingly, Devereaux smiled at her.

With a shaking hand Carolyn braced herself and rose. But her foot hung in the bottom rung of her hoop, her knees buckled, and with a little cry she very nearly went down in a wobbly heap.

In an instant Dev was there, pushing back the piano bench and helping her to straighten. Laughing gently, he said, "I was expecting that by now you might have gotten over this peculiar habit of falling down in my presence."

His voice was like the water of the creek branch at Forests of Green, rippling over the pebbles. She smiled. "Nope – still totally knock-kneed and tongue-tied."

"Ah, Carolyn." He caressed the side of her face, looking deep into her eyes. "I think that could be a good thing." Then he pulled on the elbow he still held, bringing her into his arms and lowering his lips to hers. His mouth was soft, but the stubble of a beard rasped against her smooth skin, awakening her to reality. She wasn't dreaming! Carolyn wrapped her arms around his neck. But she was hampered by the caped, thick wool greatcoat he wore.

He laughed and pulled back, shrugging out of it. "Rather like hugging a bear," he commented, running a hand over his jaw. "Sorry. Two days on a train."

"Oh, I don't care." Carolyn touched Dev's face, noticing its more angular look, his longer hair, and the captain's star on his collar. "I just can't believe it! I was hoping – but when we didn't hear from you …"

"I got the leave, and I came. I brought William Coombs, our only other married man. We got here as quick as we could. No time for a letter."

"Oh, Dev, I'm so glad."

"You look beautiful."

Carolyn smiled, meeting Devereaux's gaze. Was she wrong, or was there a new awareness humming between them? She was afraid to speak or move – do the wrong thing – afraid she might break it. And for the first time ever, did Dev actually seem tentative, too? Tentative meant he noticed. He cared.

She gradually became aware that they were both leaning, drawing in towards each other. Her heart beat fast. She could feel his breath on her face. His lips were mere inches away and she thought she might die with longing before they reached hers. And she heard footsteps on the stairs. Dev put a steadying hand on her arm, expelled a frustrated breath. They turned as Louis entered the room, necktie removed, in his suspenders and shirtsleeves, a look of astonishment on his face.

"Henrietta!" he yelled. "It's our boy! It's our boy!"

Devereaux was engulfed in his father's arms, then Henrietta came running, clad in her pink wrapper, and launched herself at him with tears and laughter. One of the servants came to see what all the commotion was about and received instructions to warm a plate of leftovers.

"For you must be hungry!" Henrietta exclaimed, placing her hands on either side of her son's face. "Look at you! So thin! Come, come to the dining room." She grabbed his arm and prepared to lead him away.

But Dev paused. Looking back at Carolyn, he offered her his other arm, which she took with a tender smile of thanks.

Little Joe met them in the hallway, running up with a broad smile and embracing his master.

"Massah Dev, it sure be good to see you!" he cried. Then he voiced the yet unasked question that was on all their minds. "How long you home for?"

"The leave is for two weeks," Dev said. "But of course a good portion of one of those is taken up in travel. And–" he glanced apologetically at the women – "I'll have to spend a good bit of time at the barracks and around town, recruiting."

"It's all right," Carolyn said with a smile.

Once Dev was seated at the table, a female servant came with coffee and bread.

"There's one man in particular I want to recruit," Dev added, taking a swallow of the hot liquid. He added to the passing servant, "Could you please draw a bath in the alcove off the kitchen? I feel like I could soak for days and still not be clean."

As the woman nodded, Henrietta asked, "Who? Whom do you want to recruit?"

"My brother."

"That's a wonderful idea," she replied. "We'll send a message to him that you're in town so he'll come in to see you."

Dev nodded. "That would be good. Boy, do the men need a chaplain."

"How are they faring, Son?" Louis asked.

"All right, I suppose. We're set up in the middle of a thick wood on Rocky Run near its junction with Bull Run Creek, about two miles from Centreville. We had a bunch of snow, then some rain, this past month. The mud was four to twelve inches deep!"

"Oh, dear," Henrietta moaned. "Are the houses adequate?"

The servant had returned with the plate from dinner, which Dev eyed ravenously. But he politely replied, "We officers have more room than the men. They're crammed into 15-foot square shanties only six feet high on the eaves – about seven per building. There were only enough shingles done to cover the roof of one cabin per regiment, so they drew lots. We put fireplaces in. They help some, but they're awfully smoky."

"Oh, Dev," Henrietta said, shaking her head and regretfully clicking her tongue against her teeth.

Dev took the moment to tear a piece of meat off the bird's carcass.

"You eat," his mother said, patting his arm. "Bless your heart."

With no apologies, Devereaux did just that. Carolyn had never seen him eat so fast. Her eyes met Henrietta's above his head.

"Sorry," he said then. "Didn't have time to cook up rations before we left. Hardtack isn't very filling."

"Of course, Son."

"Is there any chance of getting out to Pulaski to see the men there?" he asked them.

Carolyn shook her head sadly. "The Yankees have half a dozen gunboats in Tybee Creek. They were low on supplies out at the fort, so Tattnall went downriver just above a week ago with six months' worth of rations. He took five ships and ran past the Yankees without a shot being fired. Maybe they thought to take Savannah while Tattnall was at Pulaski. But the commodore left a guard boat at the dock and came back with *Savannah* and *Resolute*. There was a forty-minute battle – two of our ships against thirteen of theirs."

"Were they done in?" Dev asked with wide eyes.

Louis answered. "No. Only the *Sampson* was hit after unloading her cargo. They all made it back to the wharves. By that time we'd all heard the commotion, and a big crowd had gathered to cheer their return."

"What about my boys, the OLI boys we sent home?" Dev wanted to know. "Did they arrive safely and get a decent burial?"

"It was a touching burial, Dev," Henrietta said.

He wiped his mouth and gave her his full attention. "Tell me."

"We all went out to meet the funeral train at the depot on the first. Was it the first, Carolyn? Yes, that's right. An escort of militia stood at attention while they unloaded the coffins. They were taken to the Exchange, where they flew the flag at half mast. The next day they put all the coffins in one hearse with six white horses. After the service at Independent Presbyterian they tolled the bell as we all went to Laurel Grove. I think the families felt our sympathy deeply."

"They were duly honored," Carolyn added. Seeing that unexpected tears filled her husband's eyes, she placed her hand on his arm.

"I've got to go see them – the widows – the families. Tell them how brave the men were," he said.

"I'll go with you, if you like," Carolyn offered.

With a quick glance and nod, Dev blinked rapidly. "That would be good. Thanks."

Moved at the sight of this tender side of her husband, her heart started beating fast. It seemed everything in the room receded except for him and her. "I'll go on upstairs," she said softly. "See you in a bit?"

His eyes locked on hers. He nodded.

In her bedroom, Carolyn's fingers trembled as she unhooked her bodice and corset. She shimmied out of her petticoat, pantalets and chemise and pulled a nightgown over her head. She shoved the undergarments with an impatient gesture of her foot, hiding them behind the dressing screen. When she sat down to unwind her hair from its coil, precious pins flew from her clumsy grasp and scattered on the floor. She plucked them from the cracks and swept them up, depositing the bunch on her dressing table. She brushed her hair until it crackled and shone. Then she lay down on the bed and waited.

Fifteen minutes later the stranger who was her husband appeared in her doorway. His hair was wet and he now wore a clean shirt, with suspenders hung lazily from the buttons on his pants. His face glistened from a fresh shaving. She expected he would come right over in his old bold, assuming manner, but he just closed the door and stood there, looking at her. She sat up.

At last he spoke, saying with a faint smile, "Funny, but I feel like a bridegroom."

Carolyn nodded her understanding – though she was astonished that he shared her sentiments.

"It's been almost a year," he said with wonder.

She flipped back the covers on his side of the bed. "Enough time for a new beginning," she whispered.

He sat down beside her, smiled and reached for her.

Half an hour later, in marriage's most intimate embrace, he actually looked at her – into her eyes. As it happened, a brief expression of amazement crossed his features. Did he see a person, a soul, a love, looking back at him? Perhaps it was so, for instead of getting up and going to his adjoining room, he lay holding her, not speaking, stroking her long hair. She put her arms around him and clung to him, inhaling his scent, reveling in his warmth. For the first time she felt Dev needed her.

The next morning, he had risen, dressed, and gone downstairs before she awoke. When she joined the family for breakfast, he seemed hesitant to look at her. Not because he didn't notice her, for there was an unspoken magnetism between them, but as if he were afraid he might give something away. As if the awareness was an uncomfortable new sensation. She glanced at him. Ah, but the mere way his hair curled over his collar made her knees weak … still.

"I feel the first thing I should do is the most difficult," he said to his coffee cup. "God knows I dread the task, but I must go see Mrs. Charlotte Branch. John was our adjutant. It will be extra hard because Sanford will be there. Do you have the morning free?" Dev's eyes lit briefly upon hers.

"Of course," Carolyn murmured. "Should I change? Should I wear black?"

"No. A black armband will do. I don't want to see you in black." His reply was sharp.

Carolyn ducked her head and cut her sweet roll. She didn't want to contemplate the emotions behind Dev's words. Not when he was just now being so gloriously restored to her.

As Dev stepped out onto the stoop of 180 Broughton Street, he felt as if a chunk of his heart had been torn away. Witnessing the grief of the Branch family had been even more difficult than anticipated, bringing back the memories of slaughter and death, of familiar bodies laid in a common grave – and now respectfully interred in their home town.

Despite it all, Sanford, paroled in early December from Old Capitol Prison but as yet not officially exchanged, would return to the regiment as soon as his paperwork was filed.

Dev had been able to share reminisces of John, and provide an update on Hamilton. Mrs. Branch and her mother had seemed extremely grateful. Carolyn had been helpful, too, putting in a gentle word here and there as needed. He had watched her with wonder, looking for signs of the bumbling girl he remembered and finding only a graceful woman.

Putting on his hat, he looked at her now. She wore a soft brown paletot over a sage green visiting dress. Her bonnet was trimmed in matching flowers. He thought he had never seen a sight so fair – well, excepting last night, of course. She smiled at him and said, "You did well, Captain Rousseau."

He sighed and let his arms hang limp. "I don't like Sanford going back into the service," he said. "I hate to think of the risk that woman runs. There will be other times, Carolyn, when I again have to ask them all to charge into the mouth of hell."

"Dev," she murmured, touching his arm. "You do what you must, and so do they."

He met her eyes, and the pain she saw there made her raise her hand to his cheek. He captured her fingers and pressed a kiss onto them. "Come," he said, helping her into the waiting carriage. She had been so supportive, it occurred to him that he ought to spend a little time with her. "Where to now, Mrs. Rousseau?" he asked.

"Oh – I can't imagine you want to go anywhere else right now."

"Some place light hearted," he conceded. "Luncheon at the Marshall Hotel? We could practically walk, we're so close."

She scrunched up her nose. "It's a bit early for lunch. Shopping?"

He raised an eyebrow.

She hastened to explain. "Last night – before you got home – we had the Randalls to dinner. Mr. Randall was ever so gracious. He brought us a box of salt and spices – and the coffee you drank this morning." Carolyn paused, noticing Dev's now lowered brows. "He – mentioned he will be conducting one of his sales this afternoon at his warehouse. If – you wouldn't be too vexed to go, I could really use some green tea, and, well, some corset stays."

"Corset stays!" Dev thundered. "I won't have you buying corset stays from that Princeton jackanapes!"

"I can't find any about town," she answered meekly. "I can't imagine you want me going without them."

Dev rolled his eyes. He knocked on the roof, calling to the driver, "The Randall and Ellis warehouse on the wharf."

"Oh, thank you, Dev. He really has the best deals in town, you'll see."

Dev grunted. Though he could imagine no good coming from an encounter with Jack Randall, it might be enlightening to scope out what the man was up to.

When they arrived, he stared in surprise at the ridiculously long line that had formed before the as yet unopened doors of the low brick building. He had the driver pull up to one side. He was helping Carolyn down from the carriage when a smart buggy drawn by a sleek black horse pulled up beside them.

"Mrs. Rousseau! Why, Captain Rousseau!" a voice exclaimed. It was the jackanape himself. "What a pleasant surprise. Home on leave, I presume?"

"Yes," Dev said succinctly. He forced himself to smile at the man. Jack bowed over his wife's hand, then raked him with a penetrating gaze which Dev met head on. Apparently satisfied, Randall turned back to Carolyn.

"Is there something special you came for today?" he asked.

"Well, yes. Tea, any kind, but preferably green, and well …" She flushed a deep red.

Dev frowned.

"Say no more," Jack told her in a soothing manner. "Come right on in the side door with me."

"But – the line …"

"Not for friends." Jack smiled and offered his arm.

With a bemused but pleased glance at Dev, Carolyn took it. Devereaux followed behind them into the building, keeping his irritation to himself. He looked around at the piles of merchandise.

"You have quite a stock," he commented.

"My shipment from *Evangeline*, plus the cargo of *South Land II* just in from Nassau day before yesterday," Jack answered. "She unloaded south of the city from the Bona Venture River."

"I suppose you keep your armaments at a separate location."

Jack at least had the guts to meet his gaze when he replied, "So far I have dealt only in civilian cargoes. Mrs. Rousseau, the teas are along this wall, and the ladies' items you will find in that far corner. Also, if you see anything that you know to be needed in Clarkesville, just lay it aside – on me."

Carolyn gave Jack a beautiful smile. "Thank you, Mr. Randall. If I do, I will be certain to pass along your compliments."

As the doors to the warehouse opened and the people poured in, Dev stood back and watched. Despite what he considered to be outlandish prices, the shoppers scooped up the wares. Many actually paused to shake the hand of the man they were paying out of their precious hoard of gold, silver and Confederate bills. The handsomely attired blockade runner smiled and greeted his customers like a king at court. Dev's stomach soured. He thought of the widow whose home he had just left, she having given the life of her eldest son. He thought of the boys freezing back in Virginia, many succumbing to disease as his friend John Couper recently had. And Dev had to return to the coach.

"Are you ready?" he asked Carolyn abruptly.

"Well, I suppose, but look at these mother of pearl buttons," she replied. "They are half the price as at the millinery or the dry goods store!"

"That's because the milliner had to buy blockade run goods, too, at robber's prices!" Dev exploded.

"Dev, that's not fair. Jack really has the lowest prices of anyone. You just haven't looked around. And without people like Jack, we'd have nothing *to* buy!"

"Finish your shopping. I'll be in the carriage."

"But – who will walk me out?"

"I'm sure your good friend Jack will do the honors."

"Dev, wait!"

But he set his face and left the warehouse.

A few minutes later, Carolyn returned alone and quietly accepted his hand up into the carriage. He felt rather bad that the good feeling of the morning had gone, but his irritation that he was now prey to such unfamiliar guilty sensations overcame his remorse and kept him in a dark mood. He dropped

Carolyn off at the house and explained that he needed to spend what remained of the afternoon at the barracks.

When he returned home, rather than seek out his wife, he allowed Little Joe to bring him a warmed-up dinner and Madeira in the study. He told himself he needed time to go over paperwork necessary to open enlistment. But really he was still just grumpy. Tired, too, probably. And he didn't feel up to the complicated emotional vibes now passing between himself and his wife.

When he asked for a second glass of Madeira Little Joe questioned, "You outa sorts tonight, Massah Dev?"

"Why would you think that?" he asked.

"You usta stay away from de strong drink."

"I do. I – yes. I'm out of sorts. Shopping in Jack Randall's warehouse is entirely to blame."

"You doan like Mistah Randall?" Joe came over with the bottle.

"No. Do you?"

Joe shrugged. "Can't say, seein' as I don't known 'im much. But lotsa folks do. Lotsa black folk."

Dev paused and looked up. "Now why would black folks give a flying fig about Jack Randall?"

"You ain' heard de rumors?"

"That he's a Yankee sympathizer?"

"Well, dere be det, but what's more – det black folk in trouble kin go to him for help."

Dev turned over the other glass on the tray in front of him. "Sit down," he said. "Pour yourself a drink, and tell me everything you heard."

236

CHAPTER EIGHTEEN

ark had fallen by the time Jack locked the Bay Street office door, satisfied that both the *South Land II* and the *Evangeline* were almost ready to sail back to Nassau. The little packet was filled to the gills with cotton. More of that same crop would be taken to the railroad station in the morning, for transport to the Atlantic steamer waiting in Charleston.

He was so engrossed in his thoughts that he didn't notice the dark figure lurking under the shadow of the stairs until the man was upon him.

"Cap'n Randall?"

Jack jumped and dropped his keys on the bottom step. But he wasn't about to present this raggedy Negro man a bent back. The street was deserted. And the man, though middle-aged, was big and possessed a cruel-looking scar along one temple.

"Do I know you?" he snapped, irritated with himself for being caught unawares.

"No, Sir. My name's Nathaniel. But I know who you be. Ah'm stayin' with a bunch ob freedmen who tole me all about you." The man bent down and picked up Jack's keys, handing them to him.

"What can I do for you?"

"Ah'm tole you can help me leave de city."

Jack's left brow momentarily jerked down. "If you're a free man you don't need my help to do that."

"Naw, Sir, det's just it." The man glanced uneasily around, ascertaining that they were alone. "Ah run away from my master in de next county over. Come to stay wid de freedmen who took me in."

"Who was your master?" Jack asked, breaking his old rule. Something told him this was a "need to know" situation.

Nathaniel screwed up his face. "Aw, Sir … Ah'd rather not say."

"Then I'd rather not say anything further to *you*." Jack pocketed his keys and turned to leave.

"Wait, Cap'n Randall!"

When the black man put a hand on his sleeve, Jack paused, turning in surprise. All slaves knew not to touch a white man in such a manner. But

Nathaniel had an answer for him. "Harman Jones." However, as he spoke the name of a planter known to be harsh – in fact suspected by Jack to have owned the first runaway he had found on *Eastern Star* – Jack noticed the man did not meet his eyes, though he had upon introducing himself. Interesting. A finger of cold caution stole through his mind.

"Please," Nathaniel continued. "De law be on me soon – an' on de friends who be hidin' me. I gotta get away. Word is, you help slaves in a fix. Ah hear you boat leavin' soon down Wilmington Narrows. If you kin get me on it, my friends tell me Ah kin slip overboard off Tybee Island an' swim over to de Yankee men there."

"You've thought a lot about this," Jack said contemplatively. Most runaways had come to him scared witless and completely without a plan. He looked at the man a long moment, then added, "Let me see your back."

Without a protest, in fact almost eagerly, Nathaniel untucked his shirt, turned, and lifted the material. Jack beheld an array of grayish lash marks.

"These are old," Jack commented.

His companion turned and pulled down the bib of the shirt in front, silently displaying a swollen red branding mark on his breast.

Jack bit the inside of his lip. "Meet me here, same time, tomorrow night. I don't make any promises, but I'll see what I can do."

The next morning, February 13, Carolyn was dressing when she heard the boom of heavy guns in the distance. She paused to listen. Just under ten blasts. Then nothing more. Her heart raced, thinking it might be Jack's packet in trouble. But then she reminded herself the captain would never attempt a run in full daylight.

In any case, this would give her an excuse to seek out her husband and ask what trouble might be afoot. He had spent precious little time with her the night before, choosing to sleep in his own chamber. And this morning he had closeted himself in the study quite early.

She hurriedly finished hooking the front of her bodice. Slipping her shoes on, she descended the stairs. Standing in front of the study door, she was poised to knock when she heard an unfamiliar voice within.

"Nathaniel thinks he was convinced by the brand. He didn't exactly say anything incriminating, but we'll have our men in place. As soon as he moves to take Nathaniel to his ship, we'll bring him into custody."

Carolyn stood frozen as her husband answered, "Good. Then the Navy can confiscate his ships without any public protest and everyone will be well pleased."

"Indeed. Mr. Blinkwell has been looking for just such an opportunity ever since the day he asked the chief to keep an eye out – since the blackguard was so all-fired haughty to him."

"He's had this coming a long time," Dev agreed.

"He'll have plenty of time for regrets while he's sitting in prison," the other man responded. Then, with a chuckle: "And while his ships are gunning down the Yankees and bringing in arms for our boys, under their rightful banner."

"Thank you for coming by, Officer Blake."

Carolyn scrambled to hide herself in the parlor, hurrying over to a bookshelf in the corner. She was leisurely pulling a volume off the shelf when Dev showed a man in a police uniform to the door. As he closed it behind his guest, he caught sight of her. He walked into the room, showing no evidence of guilt or embarrassment, merely smiling gently.

"Good morning. Did you sleep well, my dear?"

Unwilling to hide her emotions, she turned to face him with a countenance that she knew was slack and white.

"You must be wondering why I had that gentleman over," Dev said, as if ready to offer an explanation.

Before he could proceed with a lie, Carolyn spoke. "No, I'm not wondering. I heard why he called. I heard – and Dev – I'm horrified beyond words. How could you? How *could* you?"

Devereaux's face paled, then reddened. To his credit, he did not feign ignorance. "How could *you* even ask me that? Jack Randall is a traitor. He should have gone up North when the war started. He thinks to refuse our men the supplies they need while profiting from our suffering women and children. Good heavens, Carolyn! Which side are you *on*?"

Dev had been cold, but he had never yelled at her before. Her lip wobbled. "I understand how you feel about the soldiers, Dev, but Jack is *not* wearing a Yankee uniform. He's not our enemy. He's one of us. Yet you'd so casually sentence him to prison and maybe even death. And what would become of his family, without his provision? I can't let that happen." Carolyn started past him, her head held high with resolve.

But Dev caught her arm. He snarled in her ear, "You won't leave this house. And neither will any of the servants, bearing your messages."

Carolyn's wide eyes sought his. He would really hold her prisoner? "Why do you hate him so much?" she asked breathlessly.

"Why do you love him?"

Her mouth dropped open. "I *don't* love him!" she exclaimed, pulling her arm free. "But my best friend does."

"Your best friend?"

"Mahala Franklin."

Dev squinted incredulously. "*What*? The Cherokee girl?"

"Yes, she loves him, and what do you think I'm going to say to her when *you* have him arrested? She would never be able to forgive me for letting that happen. And I couldn't stand that, Dev. While you've been gone – when I lost the baby – it was her friendship that pulled me through."

When his face changed to shock, Carolyn realized what she'd said and clamped a hand over her mouth – but too late. He stared at her in disbelief.

"Oh, Dev – I'm so sorry. I meant to tell you – I was going to tell – but I just couldn't in a letter, not when you were so burdened already. And then you came home, and it felt like we were starting anew, and then this business with Jack Randall came between us. Oh, I didn't want it to. But he *is* a good man, Dev, if torn in his loyalties, and now you see why I care so much about him. Not to mention the fact that his stepmother is my aunt. Think what this would do to my family. And then there's the fact that I guess if Mahala loves him half as much as I love you, don't they deserve half a chance?"

Carolyn's voice trailed off, and they stood there staring at each other. She saw tears form in Dev's eyes. Out of all she had said, his mind had fixated on one thing. He blinked and asked blankly, "When?"

Carolyn swallowed. "I didn't realize I was pregnant when you left. I miscarried right after Manassas. I was careful, I swear – very careful – but maybe I was too worried ..."

"Boy or girl?"

The memory of it made a sob rise in her throat. "Boy," she said brokenly.

The next minute Dev reached for her, his fingers biting into her forearms. Anger and sorrow contorted his handsome features, and he shook her. It wasn't hard enough to hurt her physically, but hot tears sprung to her own eyes.

"Why didn't you tell me?" he demanded through gritted teeth. "Why? How could you not tell me, Carolyn?"

"I'm so sorry, Dev," she kept whispering. And he kept shaking her. Finally, with a strangled sob, she attempted to wrench herself free. But he hauled her abruptly against himself. His roughened hand caught in her hair. With amazement, she realized he was weeping.

"I sh-should have told you, Dev," Carolyn whimpered, "but how could I put that in a letter? How could I explain how tiny and – p-perfect he was? How much he looked like you, even being so small?"

He groaned.

"When I lost him I felt like I lost my only tie to you. I … was so afraid. Can you forgive me?"

Keeping his head lowered, Devereaux smoothed a hand down her back. "I forgive you … for not telling me. I should have been the kind of husband you could trust enough to tell. What you must have been through alone!"

It was Carolyn's turn to weep with relief and regret, sobbing roughly onto the collar of his uniform. He held her and murmured the words of comfort she had longed for. She turned her face up to his, pressing her lips against his cheek and willing him to kiss her back, but suddenly he put her away from him. He stared at her like a man awakening on judgment day.

"This is my chance," he murmured aloud. "If I let this happen, you will never trust me again." Limply, Dev sat down on the chair behind him. His eyes swung up to her. "Go warn Randall."

Abruptly, Carolyn stilled the hand she'd been using to wipe tears from her face. "What?"

"You heard me. It's too late to call it off. Blinkwell and the police have scented their prey. But you can go to him. If you want him to escape their clutches, you'd better hurry."

Carolyn's eyes popped open wide. "I'm no longer under house arrest?"

"Go!"

Carolyn wanted to throw herself into his arms again and cover his face with kisses, but something in his manner held her off. That was all right. He couldn't change his feelings instantly, but he could control his actions. And he had chosen to act over his feelings – had chosen their marriage.

Before he could change his mind, she darted from the room, grabbing her cloak and calling for the carriage.

Dylan was waiting in the parlor when Carolyn came home.

It was roundly annoying, he thought, to no longer feel free to avail himself of his own bedroom. After the two-hour ride into Savannah, he'd allowed himself a quick wash-up in his old chamber, and he had looked longingly at the bed. He'd been up most of the night prior with an aged parishioner. The family had been certain that the ailing old gent would ascend into the heavenly realms before dawn, but he had surprised everyone by holding to this life more tenaciously than expected. Dylan had finally left his bedside, snatched a few hours rest, then set out immediately. He feared to be gone too long in case the situation should take a turn for the worse again. But of course he had to visit Devereaux while he was home.

Anyway, he hadn't wanted to startle Carolyn by appearing upstairs unexpected. So in the absence of his parents he'd settled back on the sofa and snoozed a bit. But when he heard the front door he came to and quickly lowered his feet to the floor.

And there she was, looking resplendent in a dove gray silk gown drawn up at the hem into rows of horizontal gathers held in place by buttoned, coordinating plaid tabs. The same plaid and buttons trimmed the bodice, he saw, as she swept off her cloak with a sigh. Her manner was discouraged, and, he thought, shaken. She turned and saw him and was instantly all surprise and pleasure.

"Oh, Dylan! You're here!" she cried.

She came toward him with hands extended, her sheer white undersleeves fluttering gracefully. He took her hands and very briefly kissed her upturned cheek in greeting.

"Carolyn, it's good to see you. But what's wrong? You're upset."

Again she looked surprised. "How observant you are! But then, you always were." She smiled sweetly. "I don't suppose there's any reason I can't tell you. Dev's not here?"

"No. No one."

"Oh." She paused as if uncertain – probably about being alone with him, despite their relation by marriage. Then she pulled the tapestry bell hanging. "I could use some hot tea, couldn't you?"

Dylan had a feeling the maid and the tea were both just diversions. But he said, "Most definitely."

Between the time the servant came and went, Carolyn told him of the events of the past two days concerning Jack Randall. He had a suspicion she left out a few details, but he found himself astonished to learn of his brother's unprecedented about-face.

"He just let you go warn him?" he asked blankly.

"He actually encouraged me to."

"Why would he do that?"

"I'd like to believe – I do believe – it was for me. For our marriage." She looked embarrassed.

"He felt he owed you, for arranging for him to go to Virginia," Dylan said, not quite willing to stomach Carolyn's explanation.

But she held firm in her defense of Dev's motives. "He's trying, Dylan," Carolyn said. "He really is. The war is changing him. And he really wants you to return to Virginia with him. It's a good opportunity, don't you see?"

Dylan looked unhappily at Carolyn's lovely, eager face. He had not expected pressure from this quarter. Turning the conversation back to its original course, he said, "But you looked disturbed when you came in. Were you not able to locate Jack?"

His tactic worked beautifully. The frown returned, accompanied by a heavy sigh. "No, I was not. I tried his office and his home. No one was to be found at either place. At the house the maid let me leave a note. I warned him to on no account have any dealings with the man named Nathaniel, or he would fall into a trap. But if he doesn't go home first ... if he goes straight to the meeting at his office ..."

"Perhaps someone could ride out there at the appointed hour," Dylan found himself saying.

"Oh, yes! Do you think you could? I actually thought about doing so myself, but I would be too conspicuous in the Rousseau carriage."

"And quite unsafe," Dylan snapped. He hadn't wanted to do this thing. But he could hardly let Carolyn go. Well, he did like Jack. He hardly deserved the fate his brother had arranged for him. Dylan said as much to Carolyn.

Carolyn smiled in a faint, regretful manner. "But he did choose rightly in the end, Dylan," she reminded him gently.

Dylan smiled back but felt slightly sick inside. He should be glad of what she said, but he wasn't. It meant Devereaux might actually be developing feelings for his wife – which was exactly as it should be. He told himself he should wish them both happy, if he claimed to care about them at all. And yet here inside his heart was something more selfish and cold than any behavior ever exhibited by his brother, and most alarming in a man of God: envy.

It only intensified when Dev came home, so confidently wearing his new gray uniform with its handsome gold braid, a new mane of authority and gravity hanging about him. Carolyn hurried out to him in the foyer, took his overcoat like a maid, and kissed his cheek almost shyly. It was as if Dev had never cost her a day of stress in her life, much less this day.

But then he asked her quietly, "Any luck?"

And she said "no" and gave a brief explanation, ending by telling him Dylan was here and would try tonight to intercept Randall on Bay Street.

Dev turned to him with what looked to be great joy. "Little brother!" he exclaimed.

Dylan came forward to welcome Dev home. Shortly thereafter, Louis and Henrietta arrived and they all went in to dinner.

Over the meal, Devereaux spoke of his men with pride and concern. Dylan could tell the company – and the regiment – had formed a close brotherhood, and Dev took his responsibility seriously. He expressed worry over the lack of a regular chaplain.

"That's why I hope you'll come down with me to the barracks in the morning," he told Dylan. "Sign up. Leave with me next week. There's no reason we can't have a soldier-chaplain from within the OLI."

"It could be just the thing you've been looking for, Dylan," Henrietta put in encouragingly.

"What makes you think I'm looking for anything?" he heard himself ask a bit shortly. He resented the implication that he was a searching lost soul when he was the father of a flock. Would they ever see him as anything but the little brother? He shook his head and attempted a calmer tone. "Look, I agree the men need a chaplain, but it's not me. I'm not the soldier type, remember? I'm doing what I've always been called to do. I have people depending on me. I can't just walk away."

"And yet men from all over the South are walking away from all manner of jobs," Louis pointed out. "And everyone understands. This would be the greatest ministry possible, Dylan, serving both your God and your country."

He felt pinned to the spot and he steamed, sensing the ever-lurking red color his face. They had all turned on him. He made the mistake of meeting Carolyn's eyes, and he saw pity there.

She spoke up. "Like Dylan said, not everyone is meant to be a soldier. That decision is really between him and God, isn't it? We should at least give him a little time to think about it."

Before Dylan could express or even feel gratitude, Devereaux looked at her appreciatively. "You're right," he said. "We *are* being too pushy. We can talk again tomorrow, Dylan."

"I have to go back tonight," he replied through stiff lips. "I have a parishioner at death's door. I only rode in for a brief visit to say hello."

"Oh, Dylan, not tonight!" Henrietta protested. "It's so dark out! What if something happens along the road?"

He wanted to remind her he was a grown man perfectly capable of taking care of himself, but he settled for saying, "I'll be fine, Mother."

"I'll be here until next Friday," Dev told him.

Dylan nodded curtly. "Thanks," he said, "for asking me."

"We need you, little brother."

That statement in itself was barely short of miraculous, if he was fair, thought Dylan. He couldn't remember the last time Dev had needed him for anything. He was moved. But another part of him pulled back.

If he looked at it logically, everything they were saying was true. Most young men his age were now in the army. To not be was to raise questions. He only escaped close scrutiny because he was hidden away in the country serving an elderly and peace-loving congregation. And it was also true that he could reach many more for the Lord in the army camp.

So why didn't he want to go?

It wasn't cowardice. Not really. Unless he considered a different kind of fear – the fear of again being in Dev's shadow, a private under his command, having to see and think about him every day. Every day being reminded that his brother had won the woman he loved.

He thought about it as he rode out to the waterfront, wondering why his feelings had surfaced again so strongly. He didn't like the answer.

When Dev and Carolyn had not gotten along, he had been able to comfort himself with the knowledge that he'd been right all along: Carolyn had been meant for him. He could pride himself that he still understood her best, would have made a far better husband.

When she had lost the baby, he had deeply regretted her pain, but there had been something else, too – something ugly. Relief. He hadn't wanted to see Dev's perfect son – their perfect son – every day for the rest of his life. The child would have served as just one more example that Dev had everything. And now, watching them make inroads to a real marriage was too much to ask of him. It was better for all of them if he just stayed away.

Dylan dismounted at a tavern some distance from the Randall and Ellis firm. He tethered his horse to the hitching post. A little black boy was sitting in front. Dylan called him over and paid half a promised fare to him for keeping an eye on the animal. Then he walked down the street until he found a building possessing a shadowy overhang with a distant diagonal view of the rendezvous point. He stood there feeling angry and impatient and very sleepy. He should be home by now. He was not here because he liked Jack Randall. He was here because he loved Carolyn. And he hated himself for it.

A few people came and went. At length a black man matching Nathaniel's description arrived. Aha. He skulked furtively into the shadows of the building. Dylan waited, tense, but the moments slowly passed with no sign of Jack Randall. Dylan sighed and popped open his pocket watch.

He jerked when a small flare of light appeared at his elbow. The same instant, a voice said, "He's not coming."

Dylan turned to behold a man that must be Dev's police officer, now puffing on a cigar. He remembered to act innocent. "Who?" he asked.

"Oh, come on. Your friend. Randall. Somebody must have beat you to the tip-off. That, or he made some discreet inquiries and discovered that my man over there's only an *ex*-slave who just owes us a big favor. In any case, he lit out. No sign of him at home or in the vicinity. He gave us the slip. Probably *en route* to Charleston as we speak."

"If that's the case, why do you have your man sitting over there? Not that I admit to having any idea what you're talking about."

"Ha, ha. Yeah, right. Just a precaution, in case he does double back. But half past ten? I don't think so." The burly officer blew a smoke ring into Dylan's face. Here, on the streets at night, a man was just a man. "You might as well go home and rest easy. But not Randall. No, Sir. We'll be watching him – like a hawk. And you can tell him so."

With that, the officer pushed himself away from the side of the building and sauntered off. Dylan waited another moment, glancing at the Randall firm. He kept watching until the man they called Nathaniel left, too, probably responding to some signal. Dylan's duty was discharged, very anti-climactically, except for a report to Carolyn. He went back to the tavern for his horse and rode to Oglethorpe Square. A light was burning in the parlor. Carolyn met him in the foyer, and he related the evening's events.

"Oh, thank God," she breathed. "Maybe he got my message."

"This might be a good time for him to rethink his ways," Dylan commented.

Carolyn made a face. "I get the impression Mr. Randall doesn't like to be *forced* to do anything."

"Most of us don't," Dylan agreed, rather pointedly.

Not noticing, she continued, "But I'll pass along what the policeman said. Mahala says Jack makes decisions based on what is best for his family and the firm. Maybe he *will* decide the time has come for greater compliance with the Confederacy."

"Indeed. Well, I've got to go."

"Oh, Dylan, surely it's too late to ride home. Just stay here tonight."

She caught his arm and he pulled away. Carolyn's eyes widened at his abruptness. He turned away from her so that she couldn't read his face. He could never tell her he'd rather sleep on the side of the road than pass the night across the hall from her nuptial chamber. "I'll be fine," he said.

The worried look lingered on her face. "Thank you, Dylan," she said softly, diplomatically. "I hope we see you next week."

"Yeah. Maybe." Dylan put his hat back on and opened the door. "Good night."

"Good night."

She stood there looking after him until he mounted his horse and rode away. Once he was out of sight, he pressed his heels into the horse's flesh and sped out of Savannah like the demons of hell were pursuing him.

Carolyn closed the door, sighing. *He's hurting,* she thought. When she turned back into the hall, Dev was emerging from the study. His cravat hung loose and his hair was tousled. He looked tired.

"You heard?" she asked.

He nodded. "I know you're pleased. I hope Jack Randall realizes what a debt he now owes you."

Carolyn merely smiled. "I am not concerned about that. Mahala would have done the same thing for me were your safety on the line. But I *am* worried about Dylan. He didn't seem himself."

"I noticed. And I think I know why," Devereaux said, coming to stand before her and studying her face in the candlelight. "I think we both know why. I robbed him of the thing he prized most."

"Oh, Dev, I can't think that."

"You don't want to, but in your heart, you must know it's true."

"You didn't *rob* anyone. I *chose* you."

"And would you still?"

"Yes. I still would, without a doubt, though it pains me greatly to see his suffering."

"And me." Dev kissed her forehead and caressed her hair and neck. Her skin prickled with awareness. "I took a lot for granted before the war," he murmured, "including everyone's feelings. Nothing much seemed to matter then, when I had everything and risked nothing. But now, with the threat of losing it all, I find I want it. I want our life together, Carolyn."

"I do, too, Dev."

"No more going backward, no more fighting. We don't have time for that."

She looked at him with wonder. Then she stepped into his arms. As much as her heart ached for Dylan, this was the man she had married. This was the man who stirred her beyond words. She swept her jaw along his, inhaling his scent, delighting in his nearness, but more than that, at his openness. Her dreams were all within reach.

His lips brushed hers tantalizingly. "I don't want to sleep in my own room anymore," he whispered.

"I never wanted you to."

The dimly lit foyer tilted suddenly as Dev reached around her and scooped her up into his arms. Then they made swift passage up the stairs.

Early April, 1862

Sautee Valley, Georgia

The letter was dirty and tattered by the time it reached Mahala in the Sautee Valley.

"All the way from Indian Territory," Nancy said wonderingly.

She was peeling potatoes near a simmering fire that chased away evening's chill. Outside, the branches were still mostly bare, except for the buds on the fruit trees. But the Cloth of Gold roses had bloomed, and Mahala had set a small bouquet on the dining room table.

"Yes. Hard to believe, isn't it?" Mahala commented, slitting the envelope and pulling out the paper. The writing was badly blotched by ink stains, which would make reading all the more challenging since the script was small.

"What's hard to believe is that he's still writing to you."

"I'm glad he is. Letters from Clay and Jack give me a personal, first-hand view of what's happening in other parts of the world."

"Too personal to share with your old mother?"

Mahala smiled. "Of course not. Let's see what he says."

She scanned the first paragraph silently, then read aloud:

> *March 12, 1862. Dwight Mission.*
> *Dear Mahala,*
> *How are you? Please tell me the war has not touched Georgia. For it rages ugly to your north and west. I wish I could paint a glorious picture of riding to great exploits with my Indian brethren, but in truth, I feel less and less like one of them. Some of my friends I enlisted with deserted long ago, and the reformed regiment of about 500 that was called to Arkansas at the beginning of this month was quite a different crew. We were to help chase the Yankees back to Missouri.*
> *You may have heard of the Battle of Pea Ridge in newspaper accounts, but if you did, you probably learned nothing of our part in it - unless you heard the worst. The worst was what occurred. I want to hide my face from the nation and from God, but to you I have to write the truth.*
> *The Yankees were entrenched on a bluff of the creek. We were to circle them and attack their rear, cutting off their supply line. Pike's Indian Brigade was to attack through the small village of Leetown.*
> *When the regiment heard the plan, they took charcoal to paint their faces - our faces, for I had hopes of shared glory. We used*

black instead of red war paint because we hadn't eaten in days. The men were excited and rode to position yelling war whoops and wearing tomahawks and turkey feathers. That was about midnight.

It took so long to cross the creek on the tiny bridge and then to march around that I think the Yankees discovered we were coming and shifted troops to meet us. As we rode through some woods we heard sounds of battle, and then, about 300 yards away on the prairie there was a three-gun Yankee battery. We Cherokee, Watie's and Drew's, with some Texans, charged them. We overpowered them in seconds. One of the enemy not running away hit me with his rifle butt and I went out cold.

I came to moments later to an awful racket – our men victoriously whooping and running in circles around the captured guns. But around me I saw the Union dead – some mutilated and scalped.

Mahala stopped, a hand to her throat. "Oh, Mama!" she exclaimed. "It can't be!"

"Heaven above. Keep reading, Mahala."

She went on:

No words can describe my horror. I don't know who did it. Later our men blamed Watie's, their men blamed ours, and we heard later a Yankee told someone, maybe a reporter, that they saw the Texans do it. But I fear it will haunt us forever. A great furor has arisen, between the commanders and in the newspapers.

After the incident, our men were so disorganized that two new Union batteries moved up and started shelling. We all retreated to the woods with our horses. Some of Watie's soldiers finally got two of the captured guns into the woods, but Pike ended up having the carriages burned for lack of caissons to haul them off.

As dark fell some of the troops got the order to join the main body at Elkhorn Tavern, but our regiment did not hear and were left facing the enemy alone. We made our way back to Bentonville and guarded the wagon train until it was called home the next day.

I can't begin to tell of my chagrin. This is not what I signed up for. Watie's men have at least garnered a bit of respect in the past, but this latest event taints us all. We will be the everlasting shame of the Confederate Army. Yet honor will not let me go.

> *Can you still bear to call me friend?*
> *I wish now I had done many things differently.*
> *Yours, Clay*

Mahala folded the paper and sat over it with bent head.

"Oh," said Nancy sadly. "Oh, poor boy. It's not his fault."

"Of course it isn't," Mahala agreed. "He deserves better."

"Human nature," Nancy commented. "It's the same in all of us. The wildness of war brings out our weakness."

"I'll have to write him back soon, once I've thought of what to say. He sounds sore in need of comfort."

"Just be sure you want to be the one to provide it," Nancy said.

Rather than respond to that – for how could she not write Clay back? – Mahala said, "I can't tell *Ududu* of this. And he does so love Clay's letters. He makes me read them again and again."

"No, you'd best not. Was he any better your last visit?"

Mahala shook her head. "He was alert and responsive, but Jacob says he no longer has any strength. He sits most days whittling wood."

Nancy clicked her tongue on her teeth.

"I think I'd best go over there again tomorrow morning," Mahala told her. Then she added, "I feel bad, Mama. I never meant for Jacob to be saddled with the care of an aging man not even his relation."

"Your brother isn't put upon. He does things of his own free will. He has a nice bit of land to farm and a companion to help him pass the lonely hours. The two enjoy each other. They've become very fond of one another."

"Just the same, I think I ought to offer to bring Grandfather back to town with me next month."

"To town? Oh, no, Mahala. Henry has the right to die on his family lands in this peaceful valley. He has no place in Clarkesville. He'd be a lonely oddity."

"To die? Mama, how can you talk like that?" Mahala cried. The thought of Henry's mortality filled her with fear. She stood up, her face angry. "I'm going out to plant the tiger lilies," she announced.

Before Nancy could call her back, she abruptly left the house. In the barn she found the bulbs she had brought from town, a hand spade and a wheelbarrow. Mahala shoveled some fresh manure into the cart. Then she took her supplies to the side of the house near Nancy's daylily patch, found a spot and started digging. She dug hard and fast. The exertion felt good.

Mahala tenderly unwrapped the bulbs and set them out, one by one. She scooped fertilizer in around them and scorned the shovel for using her hands in the black dirt and red clay. She patted and smoothed until she was content. Then she sat back on her heels. She closed her eyes and felt the sun on her face. The smell of fresh earth filled her nostrils, and birds tweetered in the trees. Her spirits lifted slightly. Spring was coming. Like the spring, her life couldn't be sadness, loneliness and death forever, could it? At some point joy had to come along. She recalled a Scripture, heavily underlined in her Bible. Joy came in the morning after the night of sorrows. Was her night of sorrows over? Even if it wasn't, she told herself, she just had to hold on long enough for joy to catch up with her. It was coming. One day soon.

End of Book Two

Coming Spring 2014—

The Crimson Bloom:
Book Three of the Georgia Gold Series.

Four families are put to the test as relationships,
a mystery from the past and national events come to full flower.

ith her husband Devereaux Rousseau now a captain commanding Savannah's elite Oglethorpe Light Infantry on the Civil War battlefields of Virginia, Carolyn Calhoun Rousseau must prove her own backbone as she operates the family's last functioning farm in the hills of Habersham County. She draws on the support of her best friend, Mahala Franklin, half-Cherokee granddaughter of a local inn owner. Mahala battles her own frustrations with Jack Randall, competing hotel owner and coastal shipping magnate. Jack's continued reticence to commit threatens to drive Mahala into the arms of her Cherokee childhood sweetheart, Clay Fraser.

Then, tragedy brings Mahala and Carolyn to Savannah just as Sherman advances on the city -- and forces everyone to confront their true feelings. Will Jack abandon his ship and its profits to the Yankees in Wilmington Harbor in order to guide them on a perilous wagon journey across Georgia, or will he abandon the woman he claims to love, but whom he now knows also has feelings for another? And even if Mahala reaches safety, could her discovery about her father's long-ago murder and missing gold prove far more dangerous than the war?

Join Jack, Mahala, Clay, Carolyn, Dylan and Dev as their adventure heightens and romance blossoms in The Crimson Bloom.